The Cornish Bride

THE CORNISH LADIES
BOOK TWO

FIL REID

DRAGONBLADE PUBLISHING, INC.

ARE YOU SIGNED UP FOR DRAGONBLADE'S BLOG?

You'll get the latest news and information on exclusive giveaways, exclusive excerpts, coming releases, sales, free books, cover reveals and more.

Check out our complete list of authors, too!

No spam, no junk. That's a promise!

Sign Up Here

www.dragonbladepublishing.com

Dearest Reader;

Thank you for your support of a small press. At Dragonblade Publishing, we strive to bring you the highest quality Historical Romance from some of the best authors in the business. Without your support, there is no 'us', so we sincerely hope you adore these stories and find some new favorite authors along the way.

Happy Reading!

CEO, Dragonblade Publishing

ADDITIONAL DRAGONBLADE BOOKS BY AUTHOR FIL REID

The Cornish Ladies Series
The Cornish Mermaid (Book 1)
The Cornish Bride (Book 2)

Guinevere Series
The Dragon Ring (Book 1)
The Bear's Heart (Book 2)
The Sword (Book 3)
Warrior Queen (Book 4)
The Quest for Excalibur (Book 5)
The Road to Avalon (Book 6)

Chapter One

THE HONORABLE YSELLA Carlyon, youngest sister of Viscount Ormonde, stepped with dainty care out of the carriage that had transported her and her mother, the elegant dowager viscountess, to the Duke of Denby's London house. The stuccoed façade of the enormous house glittered in the glow of many oil lamps and the steps up to the imposing front doors were lit as brightly as if it were daylight still.

Ysella paused on the wide pavement for a moment, drawing in a steadying breath. This was to be her first large ball after her presentation at court, and her heart was beating in a frantic rhythm of excitement within the tight restriction of her stays. Of course, she couldn't count the few dances and routs she'd attended up until now, as they had been small by comparison. Nor those she'd been to in the country, while she and Mama were residing at Ormonde Abbey, her brother Kit's country seat. And anyway, she'd been just a girl then. Now, with her presentation behind her, she felt she'd become a young woman at last.

"Come along, Ysella," Mama, a veteran of two much older daughters she'd brought out and seen safely married off, said with a sigh. "Let us go inside before you catch a chill."

The possibility of this was real, as the night was cold and Ysella was wearing a gown of the finest silk and chiffon, with no sleeves and only her long silk gloves and a light, gauzy shawl to keep her warm. She followed her mother up the steps, past the waiting, liveried footmen, and into the enormous hallway of the house.

Not as big as the one at Denby Castle, which Ysella knew well. She'd been there many times over the years, as Denby lay only ten miles from Ormonde Abbey, so she wasn't about to be overly impressed by the magnificence of the old duke's townhouse. Not that he'd be here. Last year he'd suffered another of his turns and was now confined to his room at the castle, with, according to Ysella's maid Martha who knew everything, not long to live. No. Tonight was to be hosted by his only son and heir, Jasper, Marquess of Flint.

And there he was, waiting near the foot of the stairs to greet his guests. A corpulent man in his early fifties, Jasper might once have been handsome, but the years had not been kind to him and Ysella had no memories of him as anything other than the rather roly-poly gentleman now taking her mother's hand and kissing it.

"Elestren!" He beamed at Mama. "Lovelier than ever, I declare. And you've brought Ysella with you. Delightful." He turned slightly to the young woman standing by his side. "Allow me to introduce you both to my wife, the new Marchioness of Flint, Charlotte." His smug glance at his wife betrayed a certain amount of pride. "Lady Ormonde, my dear, and Miss Carlyon, her youngest daughter."

Ysella regarded Jasper's new wife with interest, as she'd once had a fleeting fancy to pair him off with her best friend, Morvoren. Luckily for Morvoren, who now happened to be happily married to Ysella's brother, the viscount, this hadn't succeeded. The cut of the new young marchioness's gown fought a losing battle to disguise the swell of her stomach. She must be in the same delicate condition as Morvoren, although perhaps not so far along. Morvoren's state accounted for the fact that only Mama had brought Ysella to London. Kit had remained at Ormonde Abbey with his wife, sending almost daily reports to Mama and Ysella. A nervous father, Mama had said only this morning when the latest missive arrived, her smile knowing and indulgent.

Apart from her delicate condition, the marchioness had nothing of particular notice about her and for a moment Ysella, never averse to speaking her mind, wondered why Jasper had chosen her out of all the available young ladies of the ton. Luckily, she didn't voice this doubt out loud. Mama had cautioned her extensively about not speaking her mind.

The marchioness possessed mousy brown hair piled on top of her head in prettily arranged curls, and her gown was of the most beautiful brocade and silk, but nothing could disguise her plain face. However, she did have a look of robust and sturdy health about her. Mama would say, and indeed had said on several occasions, that Jasper had gone for stamina this time, not a fortune such as his late first wife had brought him. Along with six daughters. He must be hoping fervently that his new wife would present him with the son and heir he needed this time. How funny would it be if it were to be another girl, though.

The marchioness executed a creditable curtsey for someone so unbalanced by her stomach. "Delighted to meet you, Lady Ormonde. Miss Carlyon."

Mama spoke a few polite words to the marchioness, complimenting her on her healthy color, while Ysella's eyes roamed the gaudily clad crowd. She managed to remember to bob an elegant curtsey herself, and she and Mama moved on into the ballroom.

Ysella caught her breath. The candles on the many chandeliers suspended from the ornate ceiling spread an almost ethereal light over the gathered company, making the ladies look like glowing fairy sprites in their shimmering gowns. Most of the men had chosen more muted colors for their immaculately cut coats, but amongst the crowd sparkled the scarlet of regimentals, like bright berries on a holly bush in winter. Soldiers back from the continent on furlough, no doubt, or perhaps officers of the local London militia.

Ysella followed Mama around the crowded perimeter of the room, gazing in fascination at the little groups of ladies wielding their fans, their headdresses bobbing. The eyes of these young women strayed sideways in flirtatious glances as they chattered, towards young men gathered in similar groups almost as though both groups were wary of each other. Just as they'd been at the ball Kit had held at Ormonde, and the one she'd attended with Morvoren last year at Denby Castle. Only everything here was bigger, more splendid, more exciting.

Mama spotted someone she knew and sped up, and Ysella, nervous at being lost within this crush of people she didn't know, hastened in her wake. Who had Mama seen?

Cousin Marianne, darling Fitz's older sister, but nothing like him to look at. Whereas Fitz had inherited all the Carlyon good looks from his ne'er-do-well, late and unlamented father, Papa's younger brother, Marianne took after her mother's side of the family. Not that Aunt Elizabeth hadn't been a beauty in her time. She had. But sadly, her looks had come from her own mother and Marianne's all came from the Denby side. Every bit as tall as her brother, she possessed unbecomingly broad shoulders and a waist that had never been small even with the aid of stays when she was young. Heavy brows, a square chin and small, too-close-together eyes did nothing to enhance her looks, even with her squeezed into a dress that could have been called the height of fashion.

Mama greeted her like a long-lost friend, even though they scarcely ever met. "Marianne, my dear, how lovely your gown is. It's such a long time since I saw you." Well, Mama could hardly say Marianne herself was lovely, now could she? Not with her looking like a well-built man in a dress. Ysella stifled the smile that wanted to escape—how shocked Mama would be if she could read her thoughts. Ysella was beginning to learn to keep her irreverent thoughts to herself. At last.

Beside Cousin Marianne, Mama, who Ysella guessed to be a good fifteen years her senior, had the appearance of a dainty and dazzling flower. Her dark hair had been arranged by her maid in a style befitting a matron, but at the same time emphasizing her exquisite features. Features Ysella had been lucky enough to inherit, along with the dark hair, of which she was not quite so fond. She nurtured a secret longing to be a blonde, like dear Morvoren.

"Elestren!" Marianne gushed, perhaps genuinely pleased to see her relation, although it was always hard to tell with her. "And you have dear little Ysella with you." She beamed. "What a coincidence that you should be presenting Ysella in the same year I'm presenting Charlotte."

For the first time, Ysella's attention, that had been wandering around the crowds in the ornately decorated room, focused on the girl standing beside her cousin.

Charlotte made an elegant curtsey and rose, her muddy brown eyes meeting Ysella's in something that might have been a challenge.

"I believe you girls know each other already," Marianne said with a wide smile. "I'm sure Charlotte has mentioned to me that you were at school together in Bath."

School? That had been a thankfully short-lived experiment in Ysella's life, but she remembered Charlotte very well. The girl with glasses who'd always had her nose in a book. Such a boring bluestocking. Well, no glasses now, so maybe she'd changed. Ysella dredged up a polite smile and bobbed a return curtsey. "Charlotte. Of course I remember you."

Charlotte, whose hair had been confined in a rather austere bun on the back of her head with just a few tendrils of hair framing her face, didn't smile back. "And I remember you," she said, the edge to her tone hinting that the memory wasn't a good one.

A wave of heat washed up Ysella's neck to her cheeks. Of course. She and some of the other girls had teased Charlotte dreadfully for her studious ways, taking and hiding her books, hanging her shoes on a tree Ysella had climbed, putting a frog in her bed. The list was endless, or it might have been had the headmistress of the school not decided Ysella, despite being the sister of a viscount, was too much trouble to keep. She had packed her off home to finish her education with a governess. Something Ysella had been very proud of. Not so her brother and mother, who had added this shame to the list of her other perceived misdemeanors to chide her with. Regularly.

"Shall we go through and take a glass of lemonade?" Marianne asked Mama. "Charlotte and I have been here a full half hour already, and all the talking I've been doing with my friends and acquaintances has made me quite thirsty. Walk with me and our girls can accompany one another." From her tone, it seemed likely she didn't know what Ysella had done to Charlotte at school. Thank goodness.

They set off through the throng towards the refreshment room. At the far end of the ballroom a small orchestra was playing, but the noise of chatter almost drowned out their music. Some couples had taken to the dance floor already, and others promenaded around the edge of the room, young ladies in dazzling gowns with flowers or jewels in their hair simpering on the arms of immaculate young men. The scent of perfume filled the air—from both the ladies and the gentlemen present, and a slight breeze blew in from a pair of open French doors. No doubt someone had thought the room already far too hot.

"I didn't see you at court," Ysella said, having scraped around to find something to say to Charlotte. "When I was presented."

Charlotte turned her head and narrowed her eyes. "I saw you though."

Oh. Somehow that didn't come over in a nice way. "Did you enjoy it?" Ysella tried. Mama had instilled in her, more than once or twice, that the most important thing at a ball was to be polite. To everyone. Even if you thought them a crashing bore. Which was how she still viewed Charlotte.

Charlotte shook her head. "Not at all. A complete waste of time and Papa's money, as I have no intention of marrying. I did tell Mama, but she insisted I'd change my mind."

Goodness, how outspoken Charlotte had become. She hadn't

been like that at school, which was what had made her such a good target for teasing. "And have you?"

Charlotte's rather thick, dark eyebrows creased in a frown. "What a silly question. But then, you always were a little on the silly side, weren't you?"

Ysella's mouth fell open. Kit sometimes called her silly, but for someone she didn't know all that well, and indeed hadn't seen for years, to do so felt downright rude. Hadn't Cousin Marianne given her daughter the "you must be polite at all costs" lecture Mama had given Ysella? Not a girl to take being insulted lying down, and forgetting Mama's well-intentioned advice, Ysella was ready with a retort. "And you weren't as rude as you are now."

Charlotte pursed her lips. Luckily for her she hadn't inherited her mother's facial shape and her lips were not as thin as Marianne's. "On the contrary. I was obeying rules when I was at school, and one of the rules was to think before you speak. I was merely holding my tongue for fear of being found guilty of infringing upon those rules. Unlike you, who thought bullying your main raison d'être and quite forgot the rule to be kind to everyone."

Ysella's mouth worked as for a moment words escaped her. "My what?"

Charlotte gave her a smug smile. "Reason for being. If you hadn't been expelled, you might have learnt some French while you were there so you would know what that means."

How unfair was this? Ysella's own brow lowered in a scowl. "I was *not* a bully," she managed. "I was just bored and having fun."

Charlotte halted, facing Ysella. Their respective mothers didn't seem to have noticed and had vanished into the crush in search of lemonade. "It may not have felt to you like you were bullying me, but you were. You picked on me because I was an easy target, not being like the other girls. You made me very unhappy, and you didn't care."

Ysella sucked in her lips, a wave of guilt washing over her. "I-I didn't know you were unhappy."

Charlotte narrowed her eyes again. "Well, I was. And I was really pleased when you were expelled. The other girls left me alone after you left. And I could get on with doing what I was there to do—learning. Reading my books. In peace."

Heat rose to Ysella's cheeks. She'd indulged in the teasing Charlotte had seen as bullying because she'd been bored and annoyed with Kit and Mama for sending her away to school. "I-I'm sorry, Charlotte. I thought you'd think it was funny too. I didn't think." She put a hand on Charlotte's arm, genuinely contrite and regretting her previous thought that Cousin Marianne looked like a man, as though all her sins needed atoning for. "Can you forgive me?"

For a moment, Charlotte regarded her out of unblinking eyes. "Do you mean that?"

Ysella nodded. "I do. Let me make it up to you. I promise never to tease you about your books again. That is, if you still read them." She paused. Was that even possible? "Well, I'll try not to." She gave a hesitant smile.

A smile crept across Charlotte's sober face, crinkling the corners of her mouth and eyes and bestowing on her a beauty Ysella hadn't expected. She gave a little gasp. "Why, you are quite pretty when you smile."

Charlotte frowned again. "That counts as teasing. The very words you speak imply that I am *not* pretty when I am not smiling."

Ysella giggled. "That was not what I meant. Here." She tucked her hand through Charlotte's arm. "Let us catch up with our illustrious mothers or we shall be in trouble."

She turned to look for the entrance to the refreshment room, and as she did so two young gentlemen stepped into her path.

"Fitz!" Ysella exclaimed in delight. Her eyes flicked over the second young man, taking in his extravagant good looks and the smoldering fire in his eyes. Her heart did a little jolt but she forced her attention back to her cousin.

Captain Fitzwilliam Carlyon, Charlotte's uncle and Marianne's much younger brother, handsome in his dashing regimentals, swept the two girls an extravagant bow. "Cousin Ysella, Harry, what luck to meet you both here." He took Ysella's gloved hand and kissed it, raising his eyes to meet hers, an impudent gleam in them.

Ysella smiled back. How could she not at her handsome cousin, even though everyone knew he was such a terrible rake and had such a bad reputation. He was family, after all, and so dashing. How could a girl not have a soft spot for a man like him? Her eyes slid over his shoulder for a moment, meeting those of his friend. The stranger held her gaze for a moment that stretched into an eternity before she could drag her attention back to Charlotte and Fitz.

Charlotte held out her gloved hand to her uncle. "Please don't call me Harry, Uncle Fitz. You know very well how it vexes me."

He brushed his lips over her fingers in a perfunctory gesture. "So, little Harry—sorry, Charlotte, is finally out in society? I thought I'd never see the day. And you, too, Ysella."

Charlotte gave him a decided glare. "Neither did I. And nor do I see the point of it."

Fitz grinned. "You'll soon change your mind when you meet some handsome beau." He gestured to his companion, a man who fitted that description to perfection, who stepped forward and swept a bow. "Allow me to introduce you both to my dear friend, Captain Oliver Featherstone. He was dashed anxious for me to make an introduction so he could procure a dance with you, Cuz."

This last was addressed to Ysella, who was staring at Captain Featherstone out of wide eyes, unable now to drag her gaze away. Of a height with Fitz, who was considered tall, Captain Featherstone had to be quite the most handsome man Ysella had ever seen. Regimentals had the habit of making men appear more handsome than they were, of course, but nevertheless, he was every bit the paragon she'd taken him for at first glance.

Rich, chestnut hair had been artfully combed into something resembling a Grecian statue, and his features matched that in perfection. Wide brown eyes, a straight nose and lips that had an inviting curve to them, all added to the air he carried of being a fugitive from Mount Olympus.

"Miss Carlyon," he said in a deep, melodious voice, his dark eyes twinkling at her with something more than ordinary friendliness. "Might I beg the favor of a dance with you?"

Ysella had to close her mouth and swallow before she could reply. Her voice came out a little hoarse. "Captain Featherstone. I should be very happy to take a turn around the dance floor with you." She groped for her dance card and pencil where they were hanging from her wrist. Nothing was as yet written in it. "Which dance would you like?"

Those eyes. Heat rose up through her entire body as his gaze lingered on her. Almost, her knees buckled, which would have been mortifying, but with a Herculean effort she managed to remain upright. What would it be like to dance with him? The thought that she'd like to be able to dance the forbidden waltz with him surfaced and her cheeks flamed even more. Oh, to be held in those strong, scarlet-clad arms. Oh, to be whisked out onto the terrace into a shadowy corner and have him press those perfect lips against hers. Her rather too romantic heart soared.

He stepped closer, ostensibly to peer at her dance card, the scent of his perfume strong.

How tall he was. Taller than Fitz, even, now he was close up. Her breath came unevenly as awareness of his proximity drenched her. She held out her dance card with fingers that trembled.

He looked down at her and smiled, and her heart did an un-accustomed somersault. How could smiling make him even more handsome?

"If you don't mind," he said, his voice deep and resonant. "I'd like this next dance."

Chapter Two

CAPTAIN FEATHERSTONE HELD out a gloved hand to Ysella, and she slipped her own into it, feeling the warmth of his body through the two thin layers of fabric. Her gut twisted as the idea of touching skin to skin came to her, and the hot color in her cheeks did nothing to dissipate. "Thank you, Captain Featherstone," she managed to articulate, as he led her out onto the dance floor.

A good score of couples were already out there, ready for the next dance, but plenty of room remained. As the musicians struck up their lively music again, Captain Featherstone led her to join a group of three other couples, two of whose number he appeared to know—both young gentlemen in similar regimentals to his who seemed pleased to see him.

"Featherstone, damn me if you haven't cornered the prettiest girl in the room again."

"Why do you have all the luck?"

Were they talking about her? Ysella kept her eyes down, overcome by unaccustomed shyness. Not at all like her.

She and the captain took their places as the third couple making the square for the cotillion, with the captain to Ysella's left. The first bars of the change were played and all eight dancers joined hands and started to skip to the right. Ysella found herself holding hands with the captain, a fact unlikely to aid her equilibrium. Soon the couples were dancing the figures, their feet performing the elegant skipping steps Ysella had learned as a young girl and so recently taught to Morvoren. No time to exchange conversation with the captain, even if she could think of anything to say.

However, she forgot about the disturbing touch of the captain's warm hands as she settled into enjoying the dance, until, that was, the next figure involved him putting his arm across her back and holding her disquietingly close. More heat flushed through her body and she quite forgot her steps, stumbling like a beginner. His hold on her tightened and, so close were they, she felt the chuckle that ran through his body against her own. What a delightful but disturbing sensation. She was going to need her fan.

"Miss Carlyon, you need not worry for I have you safe." The first words he'd spoken since they took to the floor.

"I'm sorry," Ysella managed, flustered by the touch of his silk coat along the exposed skin of her shoulders. "I'm not usually so flat-footed. Only this is the first proper ball I've been to since I came out." She peeped up at him. "I've been to a few smaller dances, and to soirées and routs, but not to a ball as big as this one."

He smiled down at her. "I do seem to have this effect upon young ladies, although I can't for the life of me see why. I find myself quite unnerved to be dancing with the most beautiful girl in the room, just as Fotheringay said."

More confident now, and emboldened by his display of fellow feeling and flattery, to which, of course, she was susceptible, Ysella dimpled up at him. "Really? Why, Captain Featherstone, I believe you are being too modest." Best to ignore the flattery, as what was she supposed to say to that? She didn't want to be like those awful simpering girls she'd seen when she came in. Perish the thought that she should simper, something she'd always scorned. Or hide behind a fan.

His laugh rumbled again, and they separated while the other

pair of couples danced. When they came back together again, he pulled her in yet a little tighter. "You must be aware of the effect you yourself have on a gentleman's heart? *This* gentleman's heart in particular. I find you mesmerizing."

This was just like one of the books she'd read and that Mama would have confiscated had she known. A fairytale story of a handsome young man smitten at first sight by his lady love. Did fairy stories really come true like this? The sensation of having gone one up on dowdy Charlotte assailed Ysella, and she had the grace to feel a hint of guilt, due, no doubt, to their newfound truce.

It was their turn to dance again. Ysella remembered to skip correctly this time. How awful would it be if she were to trample on his foot as she'd done so many times when practicing with Sam, back home at Ormonde? She'd never forgive herself. Sam had always claimed not to have minded, and Ysella had on occasion done it on purpose to see how far she could goad him. It had been impossible, and Sam had merely smiled and bowed to her, the epitome of politesse, even though he was only the land agent.

Over by the open French doors, Charlotte was standing, watching her beside Mama and Cousin Marianne, who both held small glass cups of lemonade. For some reason all three of them had forbidding expressions on their faces.

"I've danced with so few young men," Ysella said, determined to ignore her parent's apparent approbation, secure in the knowledge that her mother could hardly step onto the dance floor and prise her from the captain's grip. "I have no way of knowing what effect I might be having."

The captain swung her around as required by the dance, twirling her so her skirts, of creamy damask, spun out around her. "Then I shall tell you." He twirled her again, then caught her as they skipped in time with the other couples. "From the moment I spied you across the ballroom, you set my heart pounding with your beauty. And when I learned you were my dear friend Fitz's cousin, I had to secure an introduction and a dance with you." He smiled a seductive smile, his eyes full of something Ysella had never seen before and which she suspected might be improper. "You are the belle of the ball, Miss Carlyon, if not of the season."

A warm glow encompassed Ysella's heart, thoughts of his impropriety flown. He thought her beautiful. Not that she didn't already know she was pretty, for she closely resembled Mama and everyone called her a beauty. But... to have the most handsome man at the ball, who must be desired by all the young ladies present, declare her to be the belle of the ball, made her almost giddy with delight. She gazed up into his chocolate brown eyes and was lost.

The dance came to an end all too soon, but the captain didn't return her to her mother, whom he must have seen as well as she had. Instead, he pulled her hand through the crook of his arm and promenaded the perimeter of the dance floor, nodding to and greeting people he knew. The two young officers who'd danced the cotillion with them approached, minus their partners, eager looks on their young faces.

The captain halted, if with a touch of reluctance, but manners dictated that you couldn't ignore the approach of acquaintances. Ysella bestowed a smile upon the two young men.

"I say, Featherstone," the first young man, who could only have been a year or two older than Ysella herself, began. "Introduce us to your lovely companion, if you dare, so we too can mark her card."

The second man, who must have been all of thirty, so really old, like Kit and Sam, made a smart bow to Ysella. "I believe I'm acquainted with your brother, Viscount Ormonde, Miss Carlyon."

Ysella unhooked her hand from the captain's arm and deployed her fan, not to peek from behind but because she had an inkling her face might be quite flushed. And not just from the dance. "It's Major Hamilton, isn't it?"

The major nodded, smiling, his gaze fixed on her face. "I'm

surprised you remember me. Last time I was at Ormonde, you were still a chit in the schoolroom."

Recovering her composure a little now she wasn't quite so close to Captain Featherstone, Ysella dimpled at him. "Of course I remember you. You may yourself have left the schoolroom well behind, Major, but rest assured that whatever goes on in a house is known within its confines almost the moment it happens. Only I think when you called before you were only a lowly lieutenant, were you not?"

"I say, you two," put in the younger man. "You rather have the advantage of me, and I'd like a proper introduction if you don't mind."

Captain Featherstone sighed and turned to Ysella again. "Allow me to introduce you, Miss Carlyon, to Lieutenant Roderick Chatham."

Lieutenant Chatham made a smart bow to Ysella. "Delighted to make your acquaintance, Miss Carlyon. Might I trouble you to put my name on your dance card? I couldn't help but admire the grace with which you were dancing with Featherstone."

Ysella suppressed a giggle. What a flatterer. She had not been dancing well, what with the distraction of the captain's touch, but nevertheless, she wasn't about to argue with the young man. She brought out her dance card and pencil and smiled. "You may indeed."

The major looked miffed. "Damn you, Chatham, pushing in. I was here first."

Ysella ignored the spat and wrote down Chatham's name on her dance card, and with a smile for the venerable major, added his name as well. Whereupon she became aware of a growing crowd of young men surrounding them, all of them clamoring for an introduction and to be included for a dance. This was better than the ball last year at Denby Castle. Not only were the young men eager for her attentions slightly older and more sophisticated than the sons of the Wiltshire gentry, but they were also better looking.

She was just adding yet another name to her card when her mother hove into view with Cousin Marianne and Charlotte in tow. They rather had to shoulder their way through the throng to reach Ysella.

"Ysella, there you are," Mama said, bestowing her most withering frown on the gathering of beaux, but most particularly on the captain. "You should not have left poor Charlotte alone like that. You must think before you act, my dear."

Captain Featherstone stepped forward and made a bow. "Lady Ormonde." He smiled at her as he rose. "I would know you anywhere for your lovely daughter is cast in your image. Had I not known better, I'd have taken you for Miss Carlyon's older sister." He smiled. "Allow me to introduce myself. Captain Oliver Featherstone of the West London Militia, at your service."

Mama didn't alter her expression of disapproval by one iota. Not a woman to be swayed by casual flattery. Ysella wanted to giggle but suppressed the urge.

Captain Featherstone seemed unfazed by Mama's matronly disapproval though. "Might I call upon you tomorrow at Ormonde House?"

Mama wanted to say no. Ysella could feel it in every pore of her body. But manners dictated that she should say yes. With no hint of welcome on her face, Mama bowed her head in acquiescence. "That would be most pleasant, but not before one, please, Captain Featherstone."

Ysella glanced at Charlotte, who'd pulled her muslin shawl about her body as though in an effort to protect herself from the gaze of the crowd of eager young men. Not that any of them were looking at her. They only seemed to have eyes for Ysella. Inspired by her promise to be nice to Charlotte, and still guilty after her discovery that her teasing had been viewed as bullying, the conviction that she could do something helpful for her cousin came over Ysella. "This is my dear cousin, Miss Fortescue," she announced with a cheery smile for the assembled crowd of young men. "I'm sure all you young gentlemen would love to dance with her as well as with me."

Charlotte's face took on a mulish expression and the shawl tightened as some of the more polite young men turned their attention to her.

Mama's face became even more disapproving.

Ysella frowned. What had she done now? Surely helping to fill Charlotte's dance card was to be smiled upon?

Lieutenant Chatham made Cousin Charlotte a smart bow. "Miss Fortescue, might I trouble you to put my name on your dance card?"

Charlotte shot a pleading glance at her mother, who moved in for the kill. "Of course you may, young man. Charlotte. Get out your card and pencil."

The next glance that came from Charlotte was for Ysella, and it was *not* a pleading one. With her brows set in a heavy scowl, she consented, under her mother's strict supervision, to writing down the names of half a dozen young men on her card, all the while shooting death stares at Ysella.

The music for the next dance began, and Ysella, with a cheery smile for Mama and Cousin Marianne and not even a glance for Charlotte, twirled off onto the dance floor with the lieutenant.

A determination to discover more about Oliver Featherstone seized her. And, as the lieutenant knew him, this gave her the perfect opportunity to employ her interrogation skills.

"How long have you known Captain Featherstone?" she asked, deciding not to beat about the bush, as she and the lieutenant came together and danced a figure.

The young man seemed somewhat put out that she wanted to talk about his friend. "Wouldn't you rather tell me about yourself?" he asked, setting a hot hand in hers.

Determined not to be distracted, Ysella shook her head. "I am so boring. All I've ever done is live in the country with my mother and brother. Whereas you brave soldiers must have many exciting stories to tell. And although you are scarcely older than I am, the captain looks as though he has some years of service you could tell me about."

The lieutenant frowned as they parted, and when they came together again, he heaved a deep sigh. "It's only the London Militia, you know. Not one of Wellington's crack regiments."

Ysella smiled her sweetest smile. "On the contrary. You have a vitally important role to play. My brother has told me so concerning our Wiltshire Militia. It is beholden upon you brave men to defend the country and our lives while the main force of our armies is on the continent with Wellington himself." She dimpled. "Just in case the French turn up on our doorsteps."

The young man colored at the lavish praise, even though she'd been aiming it at Featherstone and not him. He probably didn't realize that. "I've only known Featherstone a year, since I took up my commission."

"My mama would want to know what sort of a family he comes from," Ysella said, deciding her wisest move was to discover everything Mama would want to know, lest a disagreement might arrive in the near future. She might need ammunition to hurl back.

"And you wish to know that too?"

Ysella nodded. "And why not? Does he have what my brother would call *prospects*?"

Chatham laughed. "I daresay. I believe his father is a bishop. I doubt you can get much more respectable than that."

A bishop. The thought of the captain having been brought up in a religious household surprised Ysella, but would no doubt mollify Mama and Kit somewhat. He had such an air of… what? Of nothing mattering to him. Not religion or politics or what a girl's mother thought of him. That warm feeling around her heart descended into her stomach and made it give a little flip. No son of a bishop should possess the air of latent excitement she'd sensed in the captain. With unusual perspicacity, she concluded he could only be a disappointment to his father. And a delight for a young girl with a romantic heart.

Major Hamilton, when it was his turn to escort her onto the

dance floor, proved a little more helpful. "His father is the Bishop of Bath and Wells," he told Ysella during the moments the dance brought them together. "I believe his mother is dead and he has one sister, younger than him. He's a damned good soldier."

"Does he have… is he attached to a particular young lady?" Ysella asked, coloring as the words came out, not at all sure how to couch such an enquiry.

Major Hamilton laughed, but with restraint. "Not as yet. He's in no position to offer for a girl, if that's what you mean. Being the son of a cleric doesn't exactly leave a young man with much in the way of funds." He twirled her round. "I should know. My own father is a sight lower in the clergy than Featherstone's father, and I doubt I'll ever be in a position to make an offer for anyone."

"Oh." Ysella digested all this information and stored it away for future reference. After all, she was a girl with a sizeable dowry endowed upon her as a child when her dear papa died. He'd made sure all his girls were well provided for without encumbering the estate Kit had inherited. She had no need to marry well, as Mama would have put it. Indeed, her sister Meliora had made a love match with a lowly lawyer who had to work for his living, and no one had protested at that. So the impecunity of Captain Featherstone, who she was already seeing in the light of a suitor, need not matter a jot.

To her delight, the dashing captain sought her out after midnight when they all went in to supper, tucking her small hand into the crook of his arm and smiling down at her as though she were the only girl at the ball. "How could I not choose you to lead in to supper?" he said, his dark eyes smoldering with promise. But of exactly what, Ysella couldn't guess.

She took her place at the long supper table, glowing with pride, but she could only pick at the food he put on her plate and sip the wine a liveried servant poured for her.

If only etiquette didn't dictate that she could only dance once with a young man. She still had one or two gaps on her dance card and longed to be able to write the captain's name in one of them. How silly were the rules of polite society, and how very annoying. Her dear friend and sister-in-law, Morvoren, would rail against them as much as she was, if she were here instead of stuck down in Wiltshire "as big as a house." Morvoren's own words in a letter she'd sent, not Ysella's own. Having to produce an heir was one of the downsides of courtship and marriage, in Ysella's opinion, although last time she'd seen Morvoren, her sister-in-law had seemed quite content, if not ecstatic, about the state she was in.

"Tell me," the captain said, dabbing his mouth with his napkin. "Have you been to the Lyceum yet to see Mrs. Dickens in *Devil's Bridge*? I hear it's very good."

Ysella shook her head, refraining from telling her beau that she'd never yet been to the theater. Best not to look too much like a country bumpkin in front of a young man for whom London and all its refinements was home.

Undeterred, he went on. "Or there's Quadrapeds at Covent Garden. And I do believe I heard they had an elephant on the stage at one point, although I couldn't be certain if this tale is true, elephants being so very large."

"An elephant?" Ysella had but the vaguest notion of what an elephant looked like, her schooling having been somewhat deficient about natural history. Somewhat deficient, in fact, in most subjects, once she'd been expelled from school.

The captain nodded. "If you've never seen one, perhaps you could be persuaded to accompany me to the Royal Menagerie at the Exeter 'Change? I hear they have a fine selection of beasts there—definitely an elephant, but also a hippopotamus, that is a water horse, although it looks nothing like a horse to me, and a rhinoceros. Huge animals you can't see anywhere else. You would be amazed at the variety of beasts other countries abound with. We're very lucky to be able to go and see them here in London."

Ysella's curiosity was aroused. Of course she would like to go to the Exeter 'Change and see these strange and exotic animals, but would Mama allow her to go with the captain? This would need careful handling, but at least Kit wasn't here to stop her. There was that.

Chapter Three

A DISCREET COUGH woke Ysella from sleep. She rolled over in bed, blinking in the bright daylight streaming in through her bedroom window, to see Martha, her maid, just stepping back from where she'd drawn aside the thick curtains.

"Good morning, Miss Ysella." Martha, a young woman perhaps five years older than Ysella, picked up a tray from the table near the window and approached the bed. "Your Mama asked me to make sure you was awake and to bring you breakfast."

Ysella sat up in bed, wondering why her stomach felt so unsettled. "Good morning, Martha." She rubbed the sleep out of her eyes. "I'm not at all sure I can bring myself to eat anything. Just a cup of tea, perhaps."

Martha set the tray on its little legs across her mistress's knees. "I brought hot chocolate, Miss," she coaxed. "Your favorite."

Ysella eyed the contents of the tray—a silver cloche hid a plate that might contain scrambled eggs, another of her favorites, and several slices of toast occupied a toast rack. She had to eat something, or Mama would wonder what was wrong with her. Maybe just a small slice of toast.

Martha observed her nibbling the toast for a few moments and with a sigh, set her hands on her ample hips. "Are you sickening for something, Miss Ysella? Should I be telling your mother?"

Ysella set down the toast after only one bite and frowned up at her. Martha had been her maid for the last seven years, and knew her all too well. "If I tell you," she said, leaning forward across the breakfast tray. "You have to promise not to breathe a word of it to Mama. I want to wait a little before I mention anything to her. Until I properly *know* things. Until I'm *certain*."

Martha leant forward a little as well. "If 'tis something bad, I might have to tell her. You know I might."

Ysella licked her lips. "It's not bad at all, so you don't need to worry. It's just private, and I want to share it with someone, just not Mama. Not yet." She frowned. "If Morvoren… I mean Lady Ormonde… were here, I'd tell her. But she's not. She's miles away at Ormonde and in a delicate condition so can't be told things that might excite her. So, I thought I could tell you, as you are quite the friend to me." She paused after that bit of flattery, biting her lip. "And I *will* tell Mama, I promise. Just not yet. For a while I'd like it to remain *our* secret. What do you say?"

Martha also frowned as though digesting this rather garbled announcement might have been difficult, but she was probably used to Ysella's tumbling thoughts and, after a moment's pause, she nodded, her expression grave but curious. "I promise, then."

Ysella, ignoring Martha's less than enthusiastic agreement, fought to suppress the smile that threatened to widen her mouth. "I think I'm in love."

Martha's expression gave nothing away. She regarded her mistress out of solemn gray eyes as though Ysella had just told her which gown she wanted to wear today. Most unsatisfying as reactions went. If only Morvoren were here. *She*'d have reacted properly. Wouldn't she?

"Well?" Ysella almost snapped. "Don't you want to know who with? All the details?" Telling Morvoren about Captain Featherstone would be much more satisfying. What a letdown Martha was.

Martha sucked in her lips. "Will I know the gentleman?"

"Well, no," Ysella conceded, disappointed. Had Morvoren been with her last night at the Denby House ball, then she would have seen what a paragon the captain was and been suitably impressed at his interest in Ysella, and perhaps a teeny bit jealous at his good looks. Although maybe not that last bit—Morvoren was of the opinion Ysella's older brother Kit was the epitome of handsomeness and had told Ysella this on several occasions recently. Even though he was just ordinary Kit.

"Did you meet him last night, then?" Martha asked, her voice still sadly lacking the required response to Ysella's announcement. "At the ball?"

Ysella nodded, determined not to be discouraged. "The most handsome man there," she declared, clasping her hands against her chest. "An officer in the militia. A captain, no less. All the other young ladies clamored to dance with him, but he chose me first of all of them."

Martha, who must have been well aware of the etiquette required at society gatherings, wrinkled her nose. "I hope you didn't forget yourself, Miss, and dance more than once with him."

Ysella shook her head. "I'm not a ninny, Martha."

Martha's expression implied she hadn't believed her mistress, either about not dancing more than once with someone, or not being a ninny, but she held her tongue.

Ignoring this, Ysella sailed on. "Out of all the young ladies present, it was me he took into supper. I couldn't eat a thing. All the girls were watching me, jealous of his attentions, I'm sure."

Martha raised a sardonic eyebrow. "Are you sure you aren't so pleased with yourself because you think you got one over on the other young ladies? And confusing it with love?"

Ysella shook her head with vehemence. "Of course not. I know quite well that I'm in love. Why else would my heart be pounding in my chest all last night and still be doing it right now?" She pressed her hands against the pattering. "And I'm unable to eat. I know all the signs." She beamed. "I've read about them in books."

Martha snorted. "Books?" The word came out as though she had to force herself to spit it forth, as though a book were the worst possible thing in the world. A misleading, lying, downright dangerous object never to be consulted for advice.

"Yes, books," Ysella retorted with asperity. "You know I read a lot of books."

Martha nodded, her gaze sliding sideways to where Ysella's latest tome lay on the chaise longue by the window. Her fingers twitched as though she might be itching to tidy it.

"Leave it there, please," Ysella snapped, picking up the tray and holding it out to her maid. "I'm getting up. The captain is coming to call on me this morning so I need to be up and ready to receive him." She smiled. "In fact, I believe quite a few young gentlemen might be calling. Do you know what time it is?"

"Gone eleven, Miss." Martha took the tray and dumped it with a definite annoyed bang back onto the table, as Ysella swung her legs out of bed and stood up.

Ysella stretched. "With young gentlemen coming to call, I need to look my best. I think the gold day dress with the little puffed sleeves."

Martha went to the wardrobe and flung it open. Everything she was doing this morning seemed to be requiring loud noise. Maybe she didn't like being asked to keep a secret. Maybe she disapproved of Ysella's choice of beau even though she'd never set eyes on him.

Preparing for visitations by young admirers, something Ysella had never had to do before, took longer than her normal morning ablutions. Once she was dressed in her muslin petticoats, and the gorgeous gold dress Kit had commissioned for her from the Misses Sedgewick dressmakers shop in Marlborough, was hanging on the wardrobe door, Martha had to do Ysella's hair and makeup. The hair took the longest, as not only was Martha new to the style Ysella demanded, but Ysella had determined to be picky this morning.

"I don't think you quite have it right," she complained after

Martha's third effort to get her curls arranged to her mistress's liking. "Look at the picture again." She wafted the ladies' fashion paper in front of her maid for the umpteenth time.

Martha huffed. "I'm doin' my best, Miss Ysella, workin' from just a drawing. 'Tisn't that easy to see how to get the effect you want." She unpinned Ysella's curls again. "One more try and that'll be my last. I'm a maid, not a miracle worker."

From anyone else Ysella would not have tolerated such a remark, but she and Martha understood one another tolerably well, and Ysella was fond of her. When at last, the fourth attempt had been completed and Ysella, pulling a face of slight dissatisfaction, agreed with Martha that nothing more could be achieved, Martha helped her on with her gown.

Ysella admired herself from all angles in the cheval mirror in the corner. Here and there, rich chestnut curls escaped in artful disarray to her shoulders and clustered around her brow. A sash of the same gold fabric as her gown held the curls in mock control, and the gown itself hung in perfect lines almost to the ground, allowing her gold slippers to peek out. The swell of Ysella's small breasts, pushed up and enhanced by her stays, emerged daringly at the low neckline of the gown.

Martha handed her a lace fichu. "'Tis morning, still, Miss Ysella. Best cover up a little."

With a frown, Ysella took the fichu and tucked it around her neckline to cover up her cleavage. Once Mama and Martha were not looking, that could go. Young men liked a girl's assets to be on display, and with a young man as handsome and popular as the captain, she was going to have to work hard to hold his attention.

She bit her lip. Supposing he didn't come? He'd been so attentive last night, so full of flattering words that had made her blush, but perhaps he did that with a different pretty young lady at every ball he went to. Perhaps she was no different than countless other young ladies he'd flattered. Perhaps he told each of them they were the belle of the ball and of the season. She crossed her fingers where Martha couldn't see them as her confidence in his arrival diminished. Last night had been like a fairytale dream, and with daylight, had been swept away.

By the time Ysella's toilette had been completed, and she descended the wide staircase to the drawing room, the tall clock in the hallway was striking the half hour after midday, and she was more than three quarters sure he wouldn't come and was off at this very moment trifling with some other young lady.

She found Mama seated on one of the brocade sofas in the drawing room, her sewing in her hands. "Ysella, my dear, you look particularly beautiful this morning. I trust you slept well after last night's excesses."

Ysella's polite curtsey provoked a raised eyebrow. The Dowager Lady Ormonde was probably not at all used to her daughter behaving so decorously. "Perfectly well, thank you, Mama." Which wasn't true at all, as she'd lain awake half the night thinking about the captain's handsome face and his warm touch on her hands and waist. The thought of it now brought heat to her cheeks, so she hastened across the room and looked out of the window while she fought for self-control. Mama mustn't guess how she felt. Not yet, at any rate.

The drawing room window looked out across the street at the little park opposite the house. Right now, in the middle of the day, the park was full of people taking advantage of the weather for an airing. A few tradesmen and hawkers hung about, and several carriages rattled along the cobbles.

Better not stay here too long, in case the captain arrived and thought she was watching out for him. Which of course she was. She mustn't look too keen—that would be awful. Her Wiltshire friend, Caroline Fairfield, had counselled her to maintain a discreet distance between herself and any possible suitor for fear of frightening them away. "It's bad enough having one's mama at one's shoulder the whole time," she'd said, when she visited Ormonde just before Ysella and Mama left for Town. "Indeed, it's a wonder young men attend any balls at all with the way all the mamas hang about like vultures waiting for their prey."

This had made Ysella laugh and Caro confide that she was heartily glad that at five and twenty she was no longer expected to parade herself in the marriage mart. "I think I shall much prefer to become an interesting maiden aunt to my four little nephews."

Ysella took a seat beside Mama, folding her hands in her lap.

An urge to confide all swept over her for a wild moment, and she struggled to keep her mouth closed. Instinct, and Mama's disapproving expression as she'd watched Ysella dance with the captain, warned her not to reveal the way she felt, despite the temptation. Mama had about her the air of someone who would not approve of a mere militia captain, son of a bishop or not, for her youngest daughter, especially not one as rakishly attractive as the captain.

They sat in silence for a long minute before inspiration seized Ysella. "Shall I play the piano for you?" Anything was better than having to get her own sewing out.

Mama brightened. "That would be lovely. Thank you, Ysella." She smiled. "I do miss having dear Morvoren read aloud to us. I've never heard anyone read with such vigor and expression. But some music would be delightful."

Ysella took the stool at the grand piano, lifted the lid and set her fingers to the keys. She was not a gifted musician, merely a capable one, so she stuck to the pieces she was best at, her fingers dancing across the ivory.

It was thus occupied that Captain Featherstone found her, when Forbes the butler showed him into the parlor twenty-five minutes later.

Ysella's fingers stopped mid-bar and color rushed to her cheeks. He'd come! Her heart leapt into her mouth and she rose from the piano stool, her legs suddenly weak at the knees. He was every bit as handsome as she remembered.

"Lady Ormonde," Featherstone said, taking Mama's hand and bowing over it as he brought it to his lips. "I must thank you for allowing me to call on you this morning."

Mama's eyes narrowed, but her reaction would have been imperceptible to anyone but Ysella, who knew her all too well. That was disapproval in them, for certain. However, Captain Featherstone was here, so it was already a fait accompli and Ysella was determined nothing would spoil his visit.

He turned towards her, a smile curving those eminently kissable lips, just as the heroes in all her books looked, which brought an even warmer glow to Ysella's cheeks. "Pray don't desist. I should love to hear you play."

Ysella wanted to frown, but resisted the impulse. This was *not* what she wanted to do. She wanted to sit and talk to him, but now she was caught and would have to waste his visit playing the silly piano. And if other young men came to call as well, as she was sure she'd invited them last night, she wouldn't have him to herself at all. Fingering her music, she scraped for excuses not to have to play.

Mama looked a touch smug. "Of course she'll play for you. Do sit down, Ysella, you look a little silly just standing there."

Ysella sat down with a thud on the piano stool. Thwarted. *Bugger it.* For a gently brought up young lady, she had an interesting vocabulary learnt in the stables at Ormonde Abbey. She'd never have said this forbidden phrase out loud in front of her mother, but inside her head she was wont to use it with alarming frequency. One day she was going to make a mistake and it would come popping out and shock everyone.

She began to play. But this time the proximity of the man who'd come specially to see her made her fingers clumsy and slow, and the music emanating from the piano grew steadily worse.

"Good heavens," Mama said at last, as Ysella paused to turn the page in her music after having had to restart a piece three times. "I believe you get worse with practice, child. Come and sit down instead, before Captain Featherstone runs away thanks to the assault on his ears."

Well, at least she'd got what she wanted. She needed to remember that trick.

Ysella took the seat closest to Featherstone and folded her hands demurely in her lap. Now all she had to do was get rid of Mama.

But luck didn't favor her today. The door opened and Forbes announced another of the young men she'd danced with last night. He seemed a little annoyed to find Featherstone already in residence, but settled with satisfaction onto one of the brocade chairs.

Shortly after this arrival, a second young man arrived, and then a third. Then Lieutenant Chatham turned up with Major Hamilton. Had Ysella truly invited all these young men to call on her today? What had she been thinking? Or had they just taken it upon themselves to call without invitation? Mama's smug expression grew more noticeable. No doubt she considered the number of young men arriving a reflection of Ysella's success at her first ball.

Within a short space of time eight young men occupied the drawing room and Mama, probably seeing safety in numbers, withdrew. Forbes brought in light refreshment and the young gentlemen appeared settled in for the foreseeable future.

A cough sounded at Ysella's right shoulder. She turned her head and almost bumped noses with Featherstone. "Miss Carlyon," he said, keeping his voice low. "Might I trouble you to take a turn around the garden?" He smiled. "It would be quite respectable, as I see your garden is probably visible at all times from the house."

Ysella's eyes widened. She glanced back at her erstwhile suitors who were engaged in a discussion of the merits of various racehorses, a subject they seemed to think would be fascinating for her to listen to. What would Mama say? The thought that she might greatly disapprove surfaced and even excited her, a hint of the forbidden proving more than attractive. But Mama was not here. And, as he said, it was quite a respectable thing to do. Surely it could do no harm.

She rose to her feet. "I would love to, Captain Featherstone."

Drawing her hand into the crook of his arm, he pushed open the double doors on to the terrace and led her out of the drawing room. The clamor of voices insisting their own particular horse was the best died away.

The garden at Ormonde House, which was not overly large, had been laid out by Ysella's grandfather over sixty years ago, and was a maze of graveled pathways in between neat flowerbeds. Perfect for a promenade with all decorum, although the knowledge that the summerhouse would bestow some privacy rested at the forefront of Ysella's racing mind. Could she but hope that the captain had suggested this walk because he desired a moment's privacy with her? Should she even be entertaining such a thought? Mama would not approve, which made Ysella all the keener to accomplish what had fast become her dearest wish.

Captain Featherstone heaved a deep sigh as they walked down the central path towards the end of the garden, where, of course, the summerhouse lurked. "I've been wanting to get you to myself ever since I arrived," he said, his voice low and husky.

Aha. She'd been right in her surmise.

Ysella's heart skipped several beats, or so it seemed to her. "You have?" To her embarrassment, her voice came out squeaky and high, but he seemed not to have noticed.

He nodded, and his free hand patted the hand she had tucked in his arm. "All I've been able to think about since last night is you."

A starburst went off in Ysella's head. "You-you have?" Could she believe her ears? Did he feel the same way about her as she did about him? Could it be love at first sight, just as in one of her books?

"How could I not have done? You're the most beautiful girl I've ever seen and I have to have you."

Was this a proposal? She'd never had one, unless she counted Archibald Hatherleigh's and she shouldn't really as she'd only been twelve and he'd been fourteen and home from Eton for the summer holidays. Not really a proposal to be taken seriously—she'd laughed in his face and told him she was never getting married because she preferred horses to boys.

Ysella stopped walking and stared up at her handsome beau. A last vestige of common sense remained to her. "But, we've only just mct…"

"Don't you believe in love at first sight? The lightning strike of cupid's arrow in the heart?"

She swallowed. Surely his very soul must be in sympathy with hers. Having read rather too many romantic novels, of course she'd more than once dreamed of love striking like the proverbial lightning bolt, usually just after she'd finished the latest book and taken a passing fancy to its handsome hero. Last night she'd experienced a strong attraction for a man such as she'd never felt before, and today, all she'd dared to hope was that he'd be able to pay her a visit. But for him to say *this* to her? Weren't men renowned for not divulging what they felt? Especially not straightaway like this. Or so Morvoren had warned her. A tiny alarm bell of caution went off in her head, but she ignored it. Instead, she nodded. "I-I do."

"Then you'll understand. Tell me you feel the same way about me as I do about you, and I shall be content."

She glanced back at the blank windows of the house. Were the other young men still comparing notes on horses, or watching them, unseen? Or worse still, was Mama?

He smiled, that devastatingly charming smile.

She bit her bottom lip, reeling a little in shock. "I-I don't know what to say."

He gazed down into her eyes. "Tell me you don't love me, and I'll go and leave you in peace."

Was she being an idiot? She should tell him how she felt or she might lose him. A man as handsome as he was could have his pick of any society young lady. She swallowed. She certainly didn't want him to leave, which he well might if she wasn't careful with her reply. She licked her lips. "Captain Featherstone.

I-I believe I do have feelings for you. Please don't go."

He caught her hands in his. In full view of the house. "Please call me Oliver. And may I call you Ysella? Such a lovely name. Like music on my lips."

Bearing in mind that he'd not objected to her execrable piano playing, this praise might not mean that much. The possibility that he might be tone deaf popped into Ysella's head.

However, she had more important things to deal with. She nodded, enthralled by the sound of her name. "You may. And I will." She paused. "Oliver."

At the top of the steps leading down from the terrace into the garden, Mama appeared, a determined air to her walk as she headed in their direction.

Casting a glance towards Mama, Oliver tightened his hold on her hands. "When can I see you again? Tell me I can, or I shall die."

Ysella had to think quickly. "Tomorrow. I shall go for a walk in the park at about this very time. I'll only have my maid with me, I hope."

Oliver released her hands and turned towards Mama. "Lady Ormonde. I've been admiring your splendid garden and was just about to take my leave, I'm afraid."

Mama fixed him with a gimlet stare as though, perish the thought, she could see right through his dissembling.

He swept Mama a flamboyant bow and then a smaller one to Ysella. "Miss Carlyon. Thank you so much for showing me the roses. It saddens me to have to bid you farewell."

He walked away, with a slight swagger to his step, as Mama docked beside Ysella with a harrumph. "I'm not sure I like the cut of that young man."

Ysella assumed her most innocent expression. "He seems perfectly pleasant to me." Hopefully, Mama wouldn't notice her warm cheeks and how flustered she was.

Chapter Four

GOING FOR A walk in the park without Mama proved a difficult undertaking. Ysella could not shake her off. "Just what I need to blow the cobwebs away," Mama said, after she caught Ysella putting on her warm pelisse in the hall, with Martha hovering in attendance. "I've been cooped up indoors for far too long, bent over my sewing. A stroll with you in the park will be a tonic."

Ysella groped for something to put her mother off. "Don't you think you need to finish that baby gown for Morvoren? Surely she's going to need it quite soon?"

"Nonsense," Mama retorted. "It's nearly finished already and, in her last letter, she told me she's sure the baby isn't due for another few weeks." She paused, her brow furrowing. "She seems to know such a lot about her condition. Much more than I did before your sister Derwa came along."

Ysella glanced sideways at Martha, who wore an expression of what could be called smug disapproval. She'd had to be taken into Ysella's confidence about the reason for the walk.

"There's quite a cold wind blowing," Ysella tried. "You might catch a chill after being indoors for so long. At your age."

Uh oh. The wrong thing to have said. Mama fixed her with a steely and somewhat frosty gaze. "I am not yet in my dotage, Ysella. And I'm quite capable of withstanding a light breeze in the park. Anyone would think you didn't want me to accompany you."

Ysella chided herself in silence. "Of *course*, I want you to come," she lied. "I just worry about you, Mama. After what happened to dear Papa."

As Papa had died from an apoplexy which had not been caused by a walk in the park, this too was a lie, but it had the desired effect, or at least partly so.

"You sweet girl," Mama said. "To be concerned for your Mama like this. But don't worry. We Tremaines are made of sterner stuff than the Carlyons. Martha, can you fetch me my pelisse please. And my bonnet and gloves."

Martha hurried to do as she was bid, and Ysella schooled her features into some semblance of calm. How was she going to meet up with Oliver if Mama insisted on coming? Well, they could still meet, but it would be under Mama's disapproving stare as well as Martha's. They wouldn't be able to talk privately at all with no less than two chaperones in tow. So frustrating.

Martha returned with the requested garments and helped Mama into the pelisse, which had a warm fur collar. Mama fussed about her gloves and reticule, making Ysella struggle not to hop from foot to foot in impatience. But at last, Forbes opened the front door, and Ysella stepped out into the porticoed porch. Just as a liveried messenger boy scurried up them bearing a letter.

"Lady Ormonde?" He looked from Ysella to Mama, uncertain as to whom he should be addressing. Mama held out her hand for the letter.

Ysella paused, irritated by this further delay, watching Mama break the seal and unfold her missive. She read for a moment or two, then raised disquieted eyes to meet Ysella's. "It seems I was quite wrong. Our dear Morvoren has already obliged and been brought to bed of an heir for Ormonde, but she's been taken ill with a fever. Your brother asks for me to come down immediately to help take care of her and my new grandson."

Momentarily distracted from her own perceived problem,

Ysella clapped her gloved hands together. "A boy! An heir for Ormonde! What wonderful news."

Her mother's face had gone a shade paler and lines of worry had etched themselves into her brow. "Good news indeed, but I'm worried about Morvoren if she's unwell. There are far too many things that can go wrong after a lying in."

Ysella's euphoria blew away. Mama should know about things like this—she'd had four surviving children of her own, after all. Derwa, twelve years older than Ysella, had once implied that there should have been more children but something unspecified had happened to them. A mystery Ysella had never yet solved. And of course, the Marquess of Flint, their neighbor down in Wiltshire, had lost his first wife in childbirth. Not that Ysella was supposed to know that. Surely nothing could happen to Kit and Morvoren's firstborn? She clasped her hands under her chin in a short and fervent prayer.

"I'm sorry, Ysella," Mama said, "but we shall have to cut short your season for a while. I can't leave you here on your own—it wouldn't be at all proper. I shall prepare immediately for us to travel down to Ormonde." She peered up at the gray, afternoon sky. "It will have to be tomorrow, now, but we'll set off straight after breakfast." She turned back to the door where Forbes was still hovering. "I can only hope it's nothing too serious and that by the time I reach the Abbey she'll be improving."

Ysella's vacillating brain returned to today with a thump. Tomorrow. They had to travel tomorrow. Which meant she could still go for her walk and meet up with Oliver. At least Mama wouldn't be coming with her. Guilt at turning such a worrying happening as Morvoren being ill to her own gain tightened her stomach. Was she being a tiny bit selfish? But this might be her only opportunity to see Oliver. If she had to be away for long he might forget all about her. Might find some other pretty girl to pay court to. Morvoren wouldn't want her to miss this opportunity on her account, and besides, what could she do if she were to stay behind with Mama?

She bit her lip. "If you don't mind, Mama, I'll have Martha do my packing when I've taken some air. If we're to travel tomorrow, then I need to take some exercise today. It's so cramped in the carriage."

Mama's mind had flown miles away, though, down to Wiltshire to Kit and Morvoren and their child. "Yes, yes. You enjoy your walk while you can. I must organize the house if we're to leave in the morning. Off you go, but try not to be long. There's so much to do."

And with that she re-entered the house and Forbes closed the door behind her.

"Well," Ysella said to Martha, refusing to acknowledge the guilt. "I'm sure Morvoren and the baby will be quite all right." She crossed her fingers behind her back, far less confident than she sounded. "At any rate, there's nothing I can do at the moment, so we'd best make hay while the sun shines, as Sam says, if I'm to be stuck in Wiltshire for the rest of the season, or at least some of it. Come along."

Martha's expression conveyed deep disapproval, but Ysella ignored it.

The park, barely more than ten minutes' walk from Ormonde House, was an expanse of carefully manicured greenery with tastefully planted trees and tan roads laid out for the gentry to promenade either in their carriages, on horseback or on foot. In the middle of the afternoon, with the weather fine for once, a fair number of people were already letting themselves be seen and meeting with friends and acquaintances.

Ysella paused at the wrought-iron gates, surveying the park and considering the age-old adage of finding a needle in a haystack. How was she to find Oliver or Oliver to find her? Best to start walking and hope he'd spot her.

"Keep an eye out for him too, Martha," she whispered as her maid followed half a step behind her, chin up and proud of her exalted role as a lady's maid.

"I'm not sure I can recognize him from only having seen the

top of his head." Martha had taken a peek at Oliver by peering over the banisters from upstairs when he arrived yesterday, something she'd confided to Ysella that morning.

"He has such wonderful hair," Ysella said, thinking how lovely it would be to run her fingers through it. "You should be able to recognize that. Quite the best hair at the ball—on a gentleman. So I'd say he most likely possesses the best hair in London."

Martha's snort told her perhaps not.

Ysella's luck was in, though. She and Martha hadn't walked far along the main thoroughfare of the park, past other ladies promenading with either their snooty maids or on a gentleman's arm, when Oliver approached from a side path.

"Is that him?" Martha asked, nodding in his direction.

Ysella, who'd been searching in quite the opposite direction, swung her head around in time to see him nod to a gentleman he knew and take a sort of hop and skip over the edge of the path. Her heart did a leap that was becoming all too familiar at the sight of his handsome face. Today, he was no longer sporting his regimentals, but an immaculately cut tailcoat and breeches over shiny top boots. With the points of his collar almost up to his cheeks, and his artfully dressed hair, he looked quite the man about town. Like a picture out of one of Ysella's fashion papers. Like a hero out of one her novels.

"Ysella!" He kept his voice down low, but Martha couldn't have avoided hearing the familiarity with which he spoke.

"Oliver! I didn't know how we were to find each other in such a crowd of people taking the air." Ysella slipped her hand into the crook of his arm, and sent a quick frown at Martha, intended to banish her to a good ten steps back. Martha took up sentry duty only three steps back, her face set like a pugnacious guard dog.

Unable to reprimand her maid without appearing too obvious, Ysella turned back to Oliver and gazed up into his face, drinking it in. She'd just have to ignore Martha and deal with her later. In private.

He smiled down at her. "I scarcely dared hope you would come."

"I nearly didn't. I thought Mama would insist on accompanying me, but then she had a letter from my brother." No need to tell him the details, but he would need to know she was going to have to leave London. A nugget of resentment surfaced in Ysella's heart that Morvoren should need Mama right now. She loved Morvoren deeply, and was worried about her health of course, but why couldn't she have waited a few more weeks before producing the son and heir they'd all been waiting for?

Oliver patted her captive hand. "I have to say, I'm glad your mother isn't with us."

Ysella shot a brief frown back at Martha. "I'm afraid we do have Martha, though."

Oliver chuckled. "My intentions are nothing but honorable, Ysella, so you need not regret having to be chaperoned by your maid."

The idea of his intentions being dishonorable was not as disturbing as it ought to have been. Ysella's smile widened. However, there was nowhere in the park where dishonorable intentions could have been carried out. At least, nowhere she knew of. It was a place to see and be seen, and to be remarked upon by others less fortunate than oneself. And Ysella was feeling very fortunate indeed to be on the arm of the most handsome man in London.

"I was wondering," Oliver said as they strolled towards the lake in the center, "if you would care to accompany me to the Exeter 'Change tomorrow? As you showed some interest in seeing an elephant for yourself. Perhaps your mother might allow me to escort you there?" He, too, shot a glance at Martha. "We could take your maid for propriety's sake. Of course."

Ysella sighed. She would very much like to see a real elephant, although the attraction of this outing would be the company of her handsome captain. However, she had to impart her unhappy news to him some time, and now seemed like the opportune moment. "I'm afraid I shan't be able to."

The grip his arm had on her hand tightened a little and a frown creased his brow. "You won't?"

Ysella shook her head. "Through no fault of my own. We had news today from Ormonde." She paused, uncertain how to broach the subject of her sister-in-law's condition to a gentleman. It was not a subject she was conversant with herself.

Oliver nodded. "You did?"

"Um, yes." Ysella caught her bottom lip with her teeth searching desperately for a polite way of saying this. Inspiration dawned. "My brother's wife, who is my dearest friend as well, has been taken ill. Mama is needed to care for her, and I must accompany her."

Oliver's small frown deepened. "Do you want to go?"

Ysella bit her bottom lip again, torn. Of course she wanted to help Morvoren if she could. Of course she wanted to see the new heir who was bound to be the sweetest baby ever. And of course she knew, just as Mama did, that danger could threaten in the days after a lying-in, for mother and baby alike. But a huge part of her ached at the thought of being parted from Oliver, even though she'd only known him a few short days.

"It's not a question of do I want to go," she said, at last. "I have to go, because Mama can't leave me here unchaperoned. I must go with her." She frowned, the guilt returning because the larger part of her wanted to stay here and keep going to balls and meeting up with Oliver. "But I do love Morvoren very much, so I'm worried about her."

Oliver halted and half turned towards her, taking both her hands in his.

Out of the corner of her eye, Ysella spotted the mutinous expression on Martha's face. Any minute now she was going to interpose herself between them.

"What am I to do without you?" Oliver asked, his gaze holding hers. "I won't be able to sleep or eat if I can't see you."

Good heavens. This was more than ever like one of the romantic novels she liked to read. Wonderful. He was one of the manly heroes and she the damsel-in-distress heroine, waiting for him to sweep her off her feet. The idea of being swept off her feet was very appealing.

Ysella swallowed. That a man, a real man and not just a storybook man, might declare himself like this to her was beyond her wildest dreams. "And I shall be the same," she managed to stutter.

Martha coughed loudly.

Oliver shot Martha a dark glance and repositioned Ysella's hand tucked into his arm so they could continue walking. Probably he was annoyed that Martha considered herself such an arbiter of good behavior. But then, they *were* out in public and already a few heads had turned in their direction. Not wishing to be the subject of gossip and speculation, Ysella resolutely kept her gaze forwards, ignoring Martha's presence.

Ahead of them, two officers in regimentals approached down the long walk, chattering together in an animated fashion. As they drew nearer, Ysella recognized Cousin Fitz and young Lieutenant Chatham from the Denby House ball.

Fitz hailed Oliver in a cheery fashion. "What, ho, Featherstone! Fancy meeting you here." His penetrating gaze ran over Ysella and flicked for a moment to Martha and her heavy scowl. "Out with my coz, are you? Without her brother here I feel myself a little responsible for her. I hope your intentions are of the best?" He said this with such a mocking tone, Ysella couldn't quite be sure if he meant it or not. One never could be quite sure of anything Fitz said.

Oliver seemed unfazed by it though. "All above board, I hasten to say. You can see we have her maid in attendance. I'm not about to run off with her just yet."

Just yet? A delicious coil of excitement tightened in Ysella's stomach. Did he mean that? Might he want to run off with her to marry her? At only nineteen, she needed her brother Kit's permission to marry, and a tiny nagging doubt persisted suggesting that Kit might not approve of the dashing captain. No. Not at all. Which only served to make him all the more attractive.

"I should hope not or I might have to call you out," Fitz laughed. Behind him the young lieutenant's face blushed crimson—perhaps at the thought of running off with any young lady. Ysella had a fair idea of what marriage entailed and it was certainly blush inducing. Morvoren had explained it to her some time ago, expressing shock that her young sister-in-law should be that ignorant. She'd also told her how babies were made in some biological detail.

Ysella in her turn had been quite shocked that Morvoren knew all this, especially the details of how babies were made. The thought that it might not have been true persisted. One of her friends, during her short sojourn at school, had told her a man gave you a baby by kissing you with his tongue. Another thing that had shocked her.

Fitz's eyes wandered back to Ysella again, something in his expression unreadable. A wariness? What might that be for? Ysella tightened her fingers on Oliver's arm and let her own face slip into a frown of admonition, willing him to go away and leave her with Oliver.

It must have worked. Fitz grinned. "I see we are but spare parts here, Chatham. We'd best be off." He tipped his hat to Ysella. "I expect I'll see you at the next ball, Coz. M'sister insists I should take her and Charlotte about town because that bore of a husband of hers is too busy." He laughed. "Not that poor Harry wants to be primped and paraded on the marriage mart. By God, she'd have been better born a boy then she could have got away with her academic fancies. Squiring her about is a total waste of her time and mine—she frightens off the gentlemen with her ferocious nature."

Ysella giggled. A good summing up of Cousin Charlotte. Then she remembered her promise not to be mean to her and regretted the giggle.

Fitz and Lieutenant Chatham departed, still gossiping together and nodding and bowing at their acquaintances as they passed. A large part of whom seemed to be ladies.

Martha coughed, not at all discretely.

Time was getting on. If Ysella wasn't careful, Mama would send out a footman to find her. "Perhaps we should walk back towards the gates," Ysella said, her tone tinged with regret.

Oliver steered her around and they headed back in the required direction, Ysella searching for something to say. There was so much she'd like to be able to say, but most of it was quite unsuitable for a chaperoned stroll in the park. At last, she had an idea, faint though it might be. "Might you like to pay us a visit at Ormonde Abbey? As I have to be down there for the next few weeks?" Inspiration seized her. "The hunting is very good, and there must still be a few weeks left in the season. I'm sure my brother Kit would horse you." She dimpled. "I do so love to ride to hounds."

Oliver's face, that had still been hosting a frown, broke into a wide smile. "Why, that's a capital idea, Ysella. I should love to take a country break from the rigors of city life, and to see you at the same time would be perfection." He drew her closer, eliciting another cough from Martha. "I'll give you a day or two then follow you down and take a room at The Castle in Marlborough. I hear it's a tolerable good place to stay. I can ride out to call on you from there with ease."

Ysella beamed back up at him in delight. Her first ever invite to Ormonde now issued, and to the man of her dreams, she could sleep contented tonight and endure the long carriage journey down to Wiltshire in the morning. Wonderful. It didn't occur to her to wonder how he was so familiar with where Ormonde was, nor the name and reputation of the local hostelry.

Chapter Five

SAMUEL BEAUCHAMP, LAND agent and estate manager for Ysella's brother, Christopher, Viscount Ormonde, closed the accounts ledger on his desk and leaned back to stretch his aching back, rolling his shoulders to loosen his cramped muscles. Finished. After a long day spent poring over the books, everything added up with no mysterious amounts left unaccounted for. Kit would be pleased. One less thing to worry about with young Lady Ormonde so ill.

Sam's office lay towards the rear of Ormonde Abbey, a rambling pile of a house that was more like a rabbit warren than a stately home. As suggested by its name, it had spent its first four hundred years as a Catholic abbey but lost that status during Henry VIII's acquisitive Reformation. An ancestor of Kit's had been awarded the estate by good old Queen Elizabeth, Henry's daughter, for unspecified services to the crown that might well have included some privateering. Since then, each incumbent had added their own bit onto the house as and when they felt like it.

Sam rose to his feet and took the ledger to join its companions on the rack of shelves that occupied the whole of one side of his office. Records that went back to that initial gift of the estate and even encompassed a few records concerning its time as the foremost religious house in Wiltshire. The rows of books were dusty. He'd have to ask Mrs. Felton, the Abbey's housekeeper, to make sure the maids were more rigorous with their dusters. If they could avoid it, the lazy girls missed out this part of the house altogether.

He unhooked his topcoat from where he'd hung it earlier in the day, slung it over his arm, and picked up his beaver hat. Then, once through the heavy oak door, he closed and locked it behind himself. He kept a certain amount of ready cash in there and it wouldn't do to leave temptation in the way of any of the servants. They all seemed trustworthy, but you never knew.

The spartan, stone-flagged corridor that led to the servants' hall and kitchens lay empty, and Sam's booted footsteps echoed as he headed for the main part of the house where he hoped to find Kit. It had been three days now since the new young Lady Ormonde had given birth to her child, and Sam was as anxious as everyone else on the estate about her condition.

He found Kit in the oak-paneled library, standing by the blazing fire with a glass of whisky in his hand. Two liver and white spaniels and a black labrador sprawled on the rug at his feet, oblivious to the world. The two young men could not have been more different. Whereas Kit was tall, lean and dark, Sam, although equally tall, was more sturdily built with a mop of unruly sandy hair, a surfeit of freckles and candid gray eyes. Eyes that at this moment brimmed with concern for his friend and employer.

"Sam," Kit called, abandoning the fire and going to the table where the whisky decanter stood. "Did you manage to get it done?"

Sam nodded, accepting a half-full glass. "All done. But that's of no importance. What matters is her ladyship. I saw the doctor had been again. How is she now?"

Kit sucked in his lips. "Sleeping, at least. The doctor's coming back tomorrow. He hopes her fever will have broken by then. But she's very weak."

Sam downed half the whisky, the liquid leaving a trail of fire down his throat. "I'm sure he's right. She's a strong woman."

Kit nodded, brows meeting in a heavy frown. "I can only hope the doctor knows what he's doing. He leeched her again today, and afterwards she seemed so frail. She didn't want him to, but he insisted." He frowned further, shaking his head. "Perhaps I should have refused my permission."

Sam stayed silent. He knew as well as Kit did that an infection picked up during childbirth could be fatal. His own mother had died in just such circumstances. But that had been thirty years ago. Surely times had changed by now.

Kit paced to where one of the long, rain-spattered windows looked out over the formal gardens. "I sent for my mother when it became obvious how ill Morvoren is." He stared out at the wet garden. "She'll come as soon as she gets the message. She should be here tomorrow, I hope."

If she's in time. This thought hung unsaid between the two young men, neither of them wanting to put their doubts into words.

"And the child?" Sam asked, hardly daring to. The new heir had been born several weeks early and even a single man like him knew what that meant. Babies born early rarely survived, especially not when their mothers were taken ill.

Kit's mouth set. "Luckily for us, a woman on the estate gave birth on the same day as my wife. She's a strong young woman and it's her first child. She has plenty of milk for two. I've installed her in the nursery with both babies to feed. The child is thriving, so she tells me."

Sam heaved a silent sigh of relief. One thing to be grateful for, at least. "Would you like me to stay a while?"

Kit shook his head. "No. You go home and eat and rest. One of us needs to keep on top of things regarding the estate. I shan't be staying down here in the library. I'll go back up to Morvoren's room and sit with her for the night." He managed a drawn smile. "I only wanted to take my mind off everything for a while by making sure the accounts were tallied properly. I don't relish being left with time to think."

Sam nodded. "Don't concern yourself with the estate. You know I'll make sure that's running smoothly. You concentrate on Morvoren." He set his empty whisky glass down and going to the window, patted Kit's back with a touch of awkwardness. "Try not to worry too much."

Kit glanced sideways at him. "Impossible not to."

Leaving Kit in the library, Sam let himself out and departed via the back door of the house. One of the many back doors, as there seemed always to be a door to the outside wherever you went. Not exactly secure, which was why Sam always locked his office. Anyone could get in here really, if they wanted to.

Shouldering on his heavy topcoat, and putting on his beaver against the mizzling rain, he set off down the lane at the back of the house that led to the cluster of estate houses where his home lay. His was the largest, set within a stone walled garden and a little back from the laneway. He pushed open the gate and strode up the path towards the ivy-hung porch.

Mrs. Higgins, whose bat-like ears must have heard the front door open and close, called out from the kitchen. "Is that you, Mr. Beauchamp?"

Sam smiled to himself as he hung up his wet topcoat and hooked his hat onto its peg. "Who else would it be, Mrs. Higgins?" Wiping his muddy boots on the mat, he walked down the hall and into the enveloping warmth and delicious aromas of the kitchen. As spring had still not fully established itself this year, he'd been taking all his meals in there with his housekeeper.

Mrs. Higgins, in a floury apron and with all but a few strands of her graying hair caught up in a white mob cap, bent over the range to give the coals a rousting. "Not burnin' at all well today," she grumbled. "It's a wonder I managed to get the bread baked and the beef roasted." She swung to one side the large joint that had been hanging before the fire on a clockwork roasting jack and deftly unhooked it from the jack.

"Have I time to get more comfortable?" Sam asked, easing himself out of his navy tailcoat as he spoke. The heat in the kitchen was enough to make sweat spring out on his brow.

She nodded. "I needs a minute or two to get it all on the table." She went to the door that led into the scullery. "Jack! Come here, can't you? Drat it, where is that boy when you need him? Jack?"

Sam smiled to himself. He'd taken young Jack Deacon on as a favor to Kit, so the boy could bring some money in for his widowed mother and help with the upkeep of the rest of her children. The boy's father had died last autumn of what might only have been a chest infection, or could just as well have been consumption. Jack had begun work for Sam in the new year and was proving himself adept at performing vanishing acts just when he was needed. Much as his ne'er-do-well father had done when the rent on their cottage was due.

"I'll box your ears for you if you don't hurry up," Mrs. Higgins, who had no children of her own and secretly doted on Jack, shouted into the gloom of the scullery.

A rattling as of something falling sounded, and the boy emerged, a little tousle headed as though just roused from sleep. Sam suppressed a snort of laughter. He mustn't give the boy any hint that he found his behavior amusing.

"I was just in the glass house, a-weedin'," Jack said, rubbing a hand through his hair and making it stand up more than ever. Small and skinny for his age, which Sam knew to be fourteen, Jack had the look of a boy of eleven or twelve, with not a sign yet of whiskers on his chin or acne on his face. Wide and innocent brown eyes gave his face the look of a Botticelli cherub, which he most certainly was not. His appearance only served to conceal the amount of mischief he could get up to. His mother must be very glad he was off her hands now, as well as for the money Sam paid her for her son's services.

"Pull the master's boots off and make it quick," Mrs. Higgins said, adding her own large hand to his hair and giving it a second ruffling instead of the blow she'd threatened. "Dinner'll be on the table in a minute and he needs his old shoes to put on. Get a move on, now."

Jack moved crabwise across the kitchen flagstones to the table, via the stove where the old shoes Sam wore around the house had been put that morning to keep warm. Sam sat down in his highbacked chair in the corner and with a cheeky wink at his employer, Jack went down on one knee and proceeded to heave Sam's boots off.

"Put 'em where you won't forget to polish 'em after dinner," Mrs. Higgins scolded the boy as Sam slipped his stockinged feet into his comfortably worn old shoes. Lovely and warm. That was better.

Mrs. Higgins set the roast beef on the table and dinner began.

After a meal punctuated by Mrs. Higgins rebuking Jack's table manners, something she'd determined to take in hand with her usual zealousness, Sam retired with his port into his study, the only other room in his house where a fire was kept burning all day. But he had no work to do this evening, and instead, pulled his wing chair up to the fire and settled his feet, minus his old shoes, on the ornate fire surround. Just far enough away from the blaze not to burn his stockings.

He picked up his glass of port, took a sip, and stared into the flames.

Tomorrow would bring the dowager to their aid. Not that she'd be able to do anything, but her presence would provide support for Kit. Much needed support, especially if the worst, God forbid, happened. Sam had done his best for his old friend and employer, but a mother's help would be better.

He frowned into the flames as he considered what the dowager's return signaled for him.

Because with the dowager would come Ysella. She'd been gone from Ormonde Abbey now for two months, and Sam had only just been managing to stop thinking about her every five minutes. Part of him had been hoping she'd meet some lord in London and be married there, meaning he'd never have to see her again. But that was only the smallest, most sensible part of him. The rest of him longed to see her lovely face again, to hear her running footsteps and laughter in Ormonde's corridors, and perhaps ride out with her and Kit around the estate. This part of him couldn't stop thinking about her. It had been bad enough when she'd been in residence, but now she was gone, his mind refused to abandon the pictures that kept flashing into his head of what she might be doing now. Who she might be meeting, who would be dancing with her, who might be kissing her hand, or even her lips.

And now she would be home again, unmarried, as beautiful and naively charming as ever, only partway through her season. That small sensible part of him boiled with fury, but the rest of him, including his sore heart, soared with anticipation of her arrival.

He'd been half in love with Ysella now for several years. How could anyone who met her fail to be charmed by her? But it had been over the past year, since Morvoren had arrived at Ormonde, that his love had blossomed into hopeless obsession. Not that he could ever do anything about it. He was just the land agent, son of the last land agent whose father had been a simple tenant farmer. Nothing he could do would ever put him on par with his beloved Ysella. All he could do was admire her careless beauty from afar.

She was always kind to him, using him on occasion when she required help with something, such as the time she'd involved him in teaching Morvoren to dance. Kit had partnered Morvoren, and he, Sam, had partnered Ysella. Every moment of those dance sessions had imprinted on Sam's mind indelibly. The touch of Ysella's hand in his, the scent of her perfume, the joyful sound of her infectious laughter as Morvoren struggled with the steps. A memory to hold close to his heart and treasure during the long cold nights, of which there had been many. He could but dream.

He refilled his glass and sipped it slowly as the flames of the fire began to die down. He should call Jack to bring in more logs, but why bother? Tiredness crept over him. Tomorrow would bring Ysella, and he should get to bed. Heaving a deep sigh, he pushed himself out of his seat and set down his empty glass. Who knew what the future would bring?

Chapter Six

THE DOWAGER'S CARRIAGE arrived at Ormonde Abbey late on the following afternoon, having broken the journey in Reading at the commodious and well-renowned George inn. As they rattled up the graveled drive, Ysella peered out of the carriage window at the watery vista of Ormonde's parklands, the cedars of Lebanon dark and forbidding. Much as she loved Ormonde, she couldn't help the feeling of depression that had lodged in her heart as though never wanting to leave.

The coachman swung the carriage around in the wide fore-court so its doors faced the steps up to the double oak front door. One half of this door opened, and two liveried footmen hurried out. A moment later, Kit emerged, his cravat missing, hair awry and at least a day's growth of stubble on his chin. He almost ran up to the carriage doors and flung them open without waiting for the footmen to do so.

Ysella tumbled out into his arms, forgetting her own misfortune for a moment. "Kitto, dear Kitto. Tell me she is better. Please."

Kit disentangled himself from her embrace and handed his mother down.

She gripped his hand and stared into his eyes. "*Is* she any better?"

Somber-eyed, Kit shook his head. "The fever still rages."

Ysella bit her lip. She'd never seen her brother like this. Beneath his eyes, dark shadows betrayed the fact that he had probably had little or no sleep since his wife fell ill, and the whites were bloodshot. The cuffs of his shirt were stained. Had he not even changed his linen? She would have to take him in hand. Morvoren should not see him like this on her recovery.

Mama tucked her arm into Kit's in a comforting manner. "Take me to her straightaway. I need to see her condition for myself. Which doctor have you had for her?"

Ysella followed them into the house as her mother swept past the waiting servants and up the stairs to their private bedchambers. A frightening quiet she'd never noticed before clung to the house. A quiet that made Ysella's blood run cold.

They reached the corridor that ran down the west side of the house. The wooden shutters remained closed on some of the long windows bestowing a dreadful gloom on the corridor, but that was the custom when someone was ill. The same thing had happened six years ago, when Ysella's father, the old viscount, had fallen ill. And that had not ended well.

Opposite the windows, solid oak doors marked the family's bedrooms, but Kit's and Morvoren's rooms were at the far end, being the biggest and most stately of them all. Was that the sound of a baby crying, somewhere far off in the house? The little heir, or the child whose milk he was sharing? Was Morvoren aware of her baby crying for her?

Kit pushed open his bedroom door, the door to the splendid rooms that until recently had belonged to Mama. She'd insisted on giving them up to Kit once he and Morvoren had married, waving away his protests. "Nonsense. These are the rooms of the master and mistress of Ormonde. I am no longer the mistress, Morvoren is."

The bedroom, like the corridor, lay in gloomy darkness. A fire burned with sluggish lack of conviction in the grate, and an almost suffocating warmth filled the air. The unmistakable tang of sickness caught in Ysella's throat.

Morvoren lay propped on her pillows, her beautiful blonde hair spread out around her, made lank and dull by her illness. Her haggard, pale face glistened with sweat, and her breathing in the silence of the room seemed shallow. Ysella caught her breath. The only sick person she'd ever seen had been Papa, and that only briefly.

Loveday, Morvoren's Cornish maid, sat on a stool beside the bed, a damp cloth in her hand, dabbing at her mistress's hot brow. She looked up as they entered.

Ysella hung back, something about this scene laid out before her too frightening to face. She'd thought Morvoren would be just a little bit ill, not like this. Not looking so nearly dead. She swallowed in fear, her hands clenching by her sides into fists, fighting to control the impulse to turn and run.

She had so little experience herself of illness. She'd been only thirteen when Papa died, and remembered little of it bar the shuttered windows. She'd been allowed in only once to see him and had wiped that disturbing memory from her mind. Now, it came rushing back. From what she recalled of that glimpse of Papa, Morvoren's countenance closely resembled his for pallor. Apart from the red spots of heat that burned on her cheeks.

Might this be the last time she saw Morvoren alive?

Mama went to the bed and Loveday rose to her feet to give up the stool, stepping back respectfully, her normally cheery countenance pale with worry. Mama sank down into the vacated seat and took Morvoren's limp hand in hers. "My dear, I am here. You will be better soon, I promise."

Morvoren, her eyelids like two bruises and her lashes dark against her pale skin, didn't stir.

Mama looked over her shoulder at the stricken face of Kit. "When will the doctor be here?"

Kit didn't move from his position by the door. His hands, like Ysella's, had bunched into fists, perhaps in an effort to hold his tears at bay. "Doctor Nash has other patients to visit. He said he would be back by this evening."

Ysella suppressed an urge to take him in her arms and hug away his fears, as he'd done for her when she'd been a little girl.

Mama inhaled deeply, her chest rising and her eyes flashing. "Doctor Nash? You called him? And he's too busy to stay by her side? That's not good enough. Send for Doctor Busick at once. A second opinion is required here. Has Nash been bleeding her?"

Kit nodded.

"What nonsense," Mama spat, into full flow now. "The girl needs her blood to fight this infection."

"He said her blood was stagnating and needed reducing."

Mama shook her head with vehemence. "All he's done is weaken her. I am a proponent of William Harvey's declaration that bloodletting is not useful in fevers, as is Doctor Busick. If you don't send for him, Kit, then I will. He attended you children in all your childhood ailments and never once bled any of you. You all survived. I don't know why you've let Nash with his old-fashioned ideas anywhere near her."

Kit's expression darkened at her words, as though, perhaps, he felt the accusation was aimed at him. "Nash was the only one available when she fell ill. Busick was away from home at a distant farm. We had to take what we could get."

At the stricken expression on her brother's face, Ysella laid a nervous hand on his arm. "You weren't to know. *I* didn't know this." Morvoren would have done though, only she'd been too sick to protest.

Kit shook her hand off. "I'll send for Busick." He hurried from the room.

Mama's gaze slid to Ysella. "You had better leave us, as well. The sick room is no place for a girl your age. I shall remain to help Loveday with Morvoren."

Ysella slid out of the room behind Kit, but the corridor was already empty with not even the echo of his footsteps. Relief that she wasn't expected to stay flooded over her, side-by-side with guilt that she hadn't protested and begged to stay. That was her dearest friend lying there. Something she was having trouble assimilating. The last time she'd seen Morvoren, more than two months before, she'd been so full of joy at the thought of her coming child. And now its birth had reduced her to this.

A cold hand clawed at Ysella's insides. If she and Oliver were to marry, and of course, she'd considered doing just that if he were to ask for her hand, then might this very thing happen to her if she were to give him a child? Did she want to marry at all, in that case? Would it not be just too frightening and risky? But Mama had given birth to four children and was still living. Only, there were those mysterious other children Derwa had hinted at to account for. They had not lived, even if Mama had, so Mama had been lying when she'd claimed all her children had lived thanks to Doctor Busick.

Ysella, intent on something to take her mind off her dearest friend's predicament, descended on determined feet to the library. None of the servants were about, so she hastened to the shelf where the family Bible was kept. A huge tome, it took both hands to lift it down and place it on Kit's desk. A sluggish fire burned in the wide hearth, doing nothing to alleviate the chill. The whole house, bar Morvoren's room, felt icy cold, as though it were as ill as its mistress. A shiver ran down Ysella's spine.

She opened the front page of the book, where their family tree was drawn. It was something she'd always known existed but had never thought to consult before. Spidery handwriting from yesteryear crawled across the page, faded and difficult to decipher. Ah, there was Papa's name, beside those of his two brothers. Uncle Robert, Papa's twin but the younger by just minutes, the father of Cousin Marianne and Fitz. And the mysterious Uncle William who'd gone off years ago to America or somewhere like that and never come back. Beside the year 1790 for his death, someone had penciled in a question mark, as though this was in dispute.

Mama's name, Elestren Tremaine, had been written in beside Papa's with the year 1780 for their marriage, and, beneath this, lines ran off for their children. There was Derwa, now Lady

Monckton, and her children, little Thomas and Amelia. Beside her was Meliora, the most irritating of Ysella's siblings, now Mrs. Reginald Griffiths, and their baby Leonora born last year. And Kit and Morvoren, with a space beneath them for where their baby's name would go.

Then there was a big gap to Ysella's name—for she was nine years younger than Kit. And in that gap, someone had written a string of names in pencil, pale and difficult to read, as though the owners of those names had not been quite important enough for ink. Five names. Five children younger than Kit but older than herself, all of whom she'd never known existed. Children who hadn't survived. Five in a row. No hint as to how long they'd lived, but all had been given names—Corentyn, Gryffyn, Elowen, Melyonen, Peran. Good Cornish names as befitted a Carlyon. She might have had sisters nearer to her in age than Derwa and Meliora. Sisters to play with. But none of these children had lived.

Mama hadn't died with them though. She'd gone on and produced a healthy baby in Ysella only a year after Peran's birth—and maybe his death. Or had he been there to admire a baby sister he'd never seen grow up? She tried to picture these lost children, but failed.

A small resolve emerged in Ysella's heart to one day ask her mother about these children. But only if Morvoren's fever broke. She made a little promise to herself, and perhaps to God. *If you spare Morvoren, I'll bring my lost brothers and sisters back to life by speaking their names to Mama and finding out what happened to them.* Perhaps most of all little Peran who would have been only a year older than her. A lost playmate.

She closed the family Bible and hefted it back into its place on the shelf. Better go upstairs and see if Martha had unpacked her clothes. She needed to change out of her traveling gown and boots into something more suitable for evening wear.

She emerged from the library into the rather grand hall, where family portraits and crossed weapons covered the walls. The huge fire burning in the massive stone fireplace shed no more heat into the room than the one in the library had.

At that same moment Sam Beauchamp walked into the hall, his coat over one arm and his hat in his hand. He stopped on the threshold, staring at her.

Dear Sam. What a delight it was to see his familiar face, his reassuring solidity, soft sandy hair and gentle gray eyes. How comforting his normality seemed. "Sam," she exclaimed, and ran the few steps that separated them, taking his free hand in hers.

His face, that had been rosy-cheeked before, seemed to bloom with color. He must have just come in from the cold.

"Miss Ysella," his voice came out a little hoarse, but he managed a welcoming smile.

He too must be as concerned about Morvoren as the rest of them were. Here was someone, though, who could fill her in on everything that had been happening without getting too upset. She couldn't possibly have asked Kit, nor even Loveday, even if either of them had the time to talk. But Sam—he would have time to tell her everything he knew. "Might we go to your office?"

"Um," Sam said, sounding flustered, presumably at this disruption to his evening routine. "Of-of course we can."

Ysella slid her hand around his arm and set off with determination in her stride towards the rear of the house, conscious of his hurried footsteps beside hers. He must have been on his way home when she caught him. Poor Sam, here she was about to interrogate him and all he probably wanted was his dinner. Well, Mrs. Higgins would have to wait.

At the office door, he fumbled in his pockets until he found his keys, failed the first time to get the right key in the lock, but at last swung the door open to allow Ysella entrance.

She swept into the room and sat down in the chair opposite his desk.

Sam took his customary chair behind his desk, a look of what might have been relief on his face.

He was such a stickler for etiquette. Once, nearly a year ago, he'd allowed etiquette to evaporate, when they'd raced across the southwest of England with Morvoren on a mission to save Kit. He'd called her Ysella then, and held her hand more than a few times in comfort and encouragement. Now they were back to being the daughter of the house and her brother's employee, Ysella couldn't help but feel a little sadness. After all, Sam was a close friend of Kit's, on first name terms with him, and had been the boy used as a partner to teach both of Ysella's older sisters and herself how to dance. Which had made him an accomplished dancer himself. However, the barrier that had risen between them since that hell-for-leather ride seemed higher now than it had ever been.

"What can I do for you, Miss Ysella?" Sam asked, steepling his fingers as he leaned on his desk, as though she were a business associate of some kind.

"Tell me everything," Ysella replied, leaning forward to match. "I can't ask Kit. He's in no condition to talk. You must know the details."

Sam sucked in his lips as though he thought such details were not fit for Ysella's delicate ears. "I'm not sure I should."

Ysella favored him with a heavy scowl. "*I* think you should, if you want to remain in my esteem." She pursed her lips. "You have no need to worry you might offend me. I have a good working knowledge of childbirth thanks to Morvoren."

Sam's eyes widened. A 'good working knowledge of childbirth' was not something other girls possessed, and Ysella knew this. Having Morvoren as a sister-in-law came in very handy as she was like a walking encyclopedia. Not that Ysella herself would ever have stooped to consult one, even if she hadn't had Morvoren to ask questions of. Far too much trouble. She stopped scowling and gave Sam her sweetest smile. "Tell me."

Sam, who clearly did not possess the same working knowledge as Ysella, recounted the story with obvious reluctance and embarrassment concerning his subject. Morvoren had slipped on the stairs a week ago, fallen, and within a few hours had declared the child was about to arrive.

Poor Sam. He did *not* want to be telling such feminine secrets to a girl. If Ysella had not been so worried, she might have chuckled at his discomfiture.

However, he soldiered on. The child had been born with the attendance of Doctor Nash, and Morvoren had seemed to recover quite well. Until the third day, when a fever had come upon her. Sam stopped here, chewing his bottom lip. "They say it is the puerperal fever."

Ysella had not heard of this, but from the look on Sam's face, she divined it to be most dangerous.

She was right.

"It took my own mother a week after I was born," Sam said.

Oh. How was it she'd never known Sam's mother had died like this? She'd known him all her life, and yet she had no idea of his family life, and now it appeared he might not have had one. But the worry of this happening to Morvoren reared its ugly head, shoving aside her concerns for Sam. "Is it possible to survive it?"

This was a blunt question and Sam's expression told her, without him having to say so, that he didn't know. "I believe it is dangerous, even now."

Ysella sucked in her lips and frowned. "Mama has sent for Doctor Busick who she declares is better than Doctor Nash. Let us hope he will be of use."

Sam nodded. "All we can do is pray, I fear."

Chapter Seven

SAFE BEHIND THE comforting shelter of his desk, Sam regarded Ysella with a distinct lack of equanimity. His heart beat a painful tattoo, and he'd steepled his hands to keep them from fidgeting. He had to keep telling himself this was just an infatuation. She would be married off soon, and go to live in the house of her new husband, whoever the lucky devil might be. A burning desire to plant a facer on whatever young gentleman she ended up with curdled his stomach. The thought of any man laying a hand on his beloved Ysella—in lust—made his blood run cold.

That he himself was capable of lust, and indeed was feeling it right now, made his cheeks flush more warmly than ever. Thank goodness she appeared not to have noticed. For want of anything else to say, he tried, "If Doctor Busick is coming, I think I shall remain here for a while rather than return to my house. Perhaps he'll have some new treatment that will help Lady Ormonde."

What a formal idiot he sounded. As if there was any new treatment available or he would be of any help if he remained here. Even Ysella must know the likelihood of either of these things was remote. The only thing he'd achieve by staying would be to annoy Mrs. Higgins by not turning up for his evening meal. And yet Ysella's presence drew him like a magnet and he couldn't bring himself to leave.

Ysella rose to her feet. "I need to change out of my traveling clothes. Are we taking dinner as normal in the dining room, do you know?"

Sam hesitated. "I couldn't say. Perhaps your mother would like to take her dinner on a tray in the sickroom, like Kit?" Kit had been taking his meals by his wife's bedside for days now, not that he'd been eating much. Sam had seen the trays come downstairs with the food barely touched, and Cook kept fussing over trying to find something to tempt her master to eat, muttering under her breath about keeping his strength up to help her ladyship.

Ysella nodded. "A good idea. I'm sure she'll want to keep Kit company. Perhaps you could tell Cook to organize this. But as for me, *I* would like it if you would dine with me, if that is agreeable. Otherwise, I'll be quite alone, and I don't want to be. Not tonight. Perhaps we should order it brought to the library. It might be just a tiny bit warmer in there than it is in here. You could tell Cook that as well. I can't see the point in opening up the dining room and lighting its fire just for us two. You can tell her just a light repast will do me."

Cook, who had been preparing food all day for the return of the dowager and Ysella, would not be pleased to hear *this* news. But Sam nodded, rising to his feet and abandoning the security of his desk. "I'll do that straightaway, Miss Ysella."

She shot him an unreadable look through her thick eyelashes, but said nothing and moved over to the door. He opened it for her, and she went out into the corridor. Without glancing back, she disappeared towards the main part of the house, her skirts swishing behind her. Gone, leaving only the scent of her perfume hanging in the chill air.

Sam stood for a moment staring down the empty corridor. He hadn't planned on eating with Ysella when he'd suggested he might stay. But what had he wanted? To know he was near her, perhaps, but nothing more. Her proximity brought out the worst in him, turning him into a tongue-tied idiot, blushing at the smallest thing. Should he be upset that she didn't even seem to have noticed his awkwardness, or glad?

He gave himself a shake, rather like a dog after a bath. Remembering to lock the office door again, he turned towards the kitchens.

Cook was pleased to see him. "I hear the dowager's arrived," she said, the moment he walked through the door. "She'll be wanting dinner in the dining room?"

He'd best get this over with.

Five minutes later, a little the worse for wear after Cook's righteous indignation that no one wanted the six-course meal in the dining room she'd been preparing them, he left the kitchens and headed back into the main part of the house. The kitchen boy had been dispatched to inform Mrs. Higgins that he would be dining at the Abbey, and Sam had distracted Cook with the suggestion she should concoct a tempting menu for Kit and his mother, both of whom might be lacking in appetite.

He went into the library and added some logs to the dying embers in the hearth. A maid's job, but he didn't feel like sending for one. Not that even the most blazing of fires would warm the large room up in so short a time. He needed to have a word with the maids about keeping the fires going. They'd become slack since Morvoren was taken ill, and it wasn't as if they didn't have plenty of firewood stored.

Taking a book at random from one of the shelves, he drew a wing back chair up to the fire and sat down in it.

But he couldn't settle. After a while, the realization dawned on him that he'd read the first page of a stodgy book on Roman history a good half-dozen times without taking any of it in. The fire was now going well, the flames leaping up the chimney, but the heat only reached a few short feet from the fireplace. There was a lot to be said for the smaller, cozier rooms in his own house. He'd be glad when summer came.

Ysella would be cold in here. Perhaps he should get a blanket for her. For himself as well. Putting the book down, he went over to the window seat nearest the fire and lifted the upholstered lid. Hidden beneath the brocade cushions lurked a useful storage box filled with blankets. A house this size deep in the country would never be the warmest of habitations and there were similar blanket boxes stowed in most of the rooms. High ceilings did little to help, and without the fires kept in every day, the house quickly became glacial.

He put a thick plaid blanket on the second wing chair, ready for Ysella, and settled back into his seat. This time he didn't pick the book up, as his mind wandered to the uncomfortable subject of Ysella again. Was she going to be here for long? Surely her mother wouldn't want her to miss too much of her first season? Although what happened next depended on the outcome for Morvoren, and for Kit. If the family went into mourning, Ysella could not expect to attend any social functions at all. She'd be wearing black for months.

It occurred to Sam that from his point of view this might be a good thing. She'd remain here, in mourning, with no danger of suitors carrying her off. But he dismissed this thought immediately, and with horror. It would mean Morvoren had died and he couldn't bear that thought.

Doctor Busick arrived at last, the noise of his arrival carrying to Sam in the library. He got up and went to the door, peering through a crack as Bannerman, the butler, ushered the doctor in. "No need to show me," the newcomer said. "I know the way very well." Carrying his leather bag, he hurried up the stairs to the upper floors, vanishing from sight. Sam went back to his seat with his shoulders slumped. If only a new doctor could be relied upon to effect some sort of cure.

He didn't remember his own mother, of course, but he'd grown up with a father perpetually with one foot in the past, grieving his lost wife until the day he died, only a few short years ago. He'd given Sam the distinct impression death had come as a welcome friend.

He was still ruminating on his father when the library door opened and Ysella came in, followed by Kit's three dogs, their claws clattering on the wooden floor. She'd changed into a rather somber cream gown and thrown a suitably thick shawl about her shoulders. Sam stood up. Perhaps tact, something he had to acknowledge she'd shown remarkably little of in the past, had finally settled on her.

She hastened over to the fire to stand a little too close to it for comfort, holding out her hands to the flames. "It was quite chilly in my room even though the fire was lit. I suspect the maids have been careless of keeping anywhere but the sickroom warm."

The tip of Ysella's nose glowed a little pink, as if from the cold.

"Doctor Busick went upstairs a little while ago," Sam said as they both sat down. A longing to tuck the blanket around Ysella himself washed over him, but he resisted. Not his place.

Ysella nodded as she arranged her blanket over her knees and the dogs ranged themselves as close to the fire as they could get. "Mama came to tell me. She says he thinks the bloodletting has not helped, but that Morvoren's fever might well break tonight, if we are lucky." She paused. "But she also said that if it does not, we must prepare ourselves for the worst." She shivered. "An honest doctor is not always a comfort, is he?"

Sam leaned forward and added another log. "I happen to know it was old Doctor Nash who attended my own mother to no avail. Doctor Busick, who was not around then, is younger and more modern in his outlook, and a man your mother trusts. If there is something that can be done, we can rely on Busick to do it."

Ysella, who'd been gazing into the heart of the fire, turned her head. "I'm sorry, Sam, that I didn't know you'd lost your mother like that. I feel it is something I should have known, as you are my friend."

Sam, glowing internally at being classed as her friend, shook his head. "It doesn't matter. I didn't know her, so I don't miss her, I suppose."

Ysella inclined her lovely head, her chestnut curls bobbing against her alabaster neck. A finger of electricity coursed down

Sam's spine making his knees weak, even though he was sitting. He had to fight to still the shake in them.

"Every child needs their mother," she said, stretching out a hand and resting it on Sam's knee. Could she feel the tremor in it? He willed it to be still. She regarded him out of candid dark eyes. "I would have been such a sad specimen had I not had my own dear Mama throughout my childhood."

Sam couldn't drag his own eyes away, much as he longed to. She had him snared.

Heat radiated from her touch, across his legs, down to the tips of his toes and up to his... stomach, making him want to twist with discomfort and shake her hand off even though at the same time he never wanted her to remove it.

"I can't bear to think of that dear little mite up there having to grow up without his mother," she went on, oblivious to what her touch was doing to him, still holding his gaze. "I went into the nursery to see him, and he is the most delightful creature. No name, as yet, his wetnurse told me. Her own child is a girl, so there's no fear of mixing them up. She told me that, too, and laughed a little as she said it. I daresay at some point in history a wetnurse's child must have been confused with the true heir, if both were boys, and a peasant brat has grown up to be a lord. But she's very sad for poor Morvoren."

Sam got to his feet and made an elaborate show of fetching another couple of logs for the fire, watched with approval by the spaniels, Dash and Duster, although Hector the labrador didn't even cock an ear. When he sat down, to his relief, Ysella kept her hands to herself.

"We shall just have to keep praying that Doctor Busick is right and her fever will break tonight," he said, feeling this to be a lame statement. Being this close to Ysella had rendered his brain in some kind of soupy fog and, try as he might, he couldn't find anything sensible to say. She'd be thinking him an addlepate. Which he was where she was concerned. So much easier to talk to Kit than his sister, but then, he wasn't nurturing disturbing feelings of love for Kit.

The library door, as if in answer to his prayers for a distraction, opened yet again, and two of the footmen carried in a tray each, the plates covered by the silver domes of cloches. Bannerman accompanied them bearing a tray with a decanter and glasses. These he set down on the round table between the two wingback chairs. "Cook rather thought you would like your dinner on trays, like his lordship and the dowager."

Sam jumped to his feet, his blanket falling to the ground, but Ysella remained seated. The first footman lowered his tray onto her lap and stood back, hands behind his back, chin up.

"This is perfect," she said with satisfaction. "Like a picnic. Bannerman, we'll be fine without you and Albert and Joseph. You can all return to the servants' hall for your own supper. Mr. Beauchamp will serve the wine. No need at all to stand on ceremony when the house is upside down like this."

Sam sat down, the feeling of awkwardness increasing, and Albert handed him his tray. Both the cloches having been removed, the servants departed on silent feet. Cook had provided a light chicken dish with small whole potatoes and a few vegetables. Sam wasn't sure he had the appetite for any of it. Not with Ysella this close.

It appeared she didn't either, for she only picked at the food with a noticeable lack of enthusiasm. But that was probably from worry about Morvoren. Cook would not be amused.

After a bit, she raised her eyes to meet his. "It's no use. Worrying about Morvoren has taken my appetite away entirely. Even though I've hardly eaten today. And Cook has made such an effort." She put the tray on the floor beside the fireplace, and all three dogs, who must have been feigning sleep, leapt up to clear the plate in an instant. Sam had to smile. Cook was going to think Ysella had licked her plate clean herself.

She smoothed down her blanket. "But I am feeling a little warmer. I think I'll take a glass of that claret. I feel my spine needs some fortifying for this night."

Sam, glad to set down his own tray, for which the dogs re-peated their efficient clean, filled two glasses and handed one to Ysella. "Best not drink too much on an almost empty stomach."

She shook her head. "On the contrary. I feel it would be a good idea to lose myself in the claret. Otherwise, I shall never sleep this evening but lie awake worrying, even though there seems nothing I can do. Mama and Kit and Loveday have the sickroom all sorted, and I'm nothing more than a spare part. I feel quite useless."

Sam drained half his glass. Maybe he too needed to find sol-ace in the wine. It might numb the overwhelming feelings for Ysella he was fighting to control. Her two months away had proved the truth in the old adage that absence makes the heart grow fonder.

She did the same with her wine, bestowing a wan smile on him over the rim. "In fact, I'm very tired now after our precipitate journey, and I think I might retire to bed myself." She drained the glass and held it out. "Another one, before I go."

Sam shook his head. "Unwise, Miss Ysella. You might be called upon to help during the night, and you wouldn't like to be found the worse for drink."

She squinted up at him, a slight frown furrowing her brow. "Perhaps you are right. But the temptation is enormous." She rose to her feet and put the blanket to one side. "I shall retire now, before that temptation overcomes me." She settled her shawl more firmly about her shoulders, drawing it close at the front. "And it is still very chilly in here. I've had Martha put a hot brick in my bed for me so that at least should be comfortable. I bid you goodnight, Sam, and a safe walk home."

Sam, who had risen to his feet as well, went to open the door for her. With only a fleeting backward glance, she hurried across the cold hall to the staircase and, with her gown swishing on the treads, disappeared from sight.

Sam sighed. Maybe he wouldn't go home tonight, not with the crisis looming for Morvoren. Maybe he'd try and sleep here in front of the library fire so he could be on hand if Kit were to need him. He went back to the fire and gathered up the two blankets. The wing back chair was comfortable enough. Having stoked the fire again, he dragged the second chair close enough to put his feet on and settled back under the blankets. This was going to be a long night.

Chapter Eight

YSELLA AWOKE THE next morning to the sound of cheerful humming. Martha was drawing the curtains to let bright sunlight spill into the room and a fire already blazed in the grate. "Good morning, Miss."

Ysella sat up and Martha brought her the warm shawl she'd discarded the night before. Glad of the thick fabric, Ysella drew it close around her shoulders to keep the warmth in. Fire or no fire, her bedroom did not feel cozy.

A moment passed before it dawned upon her that the humming she'd heard indicated good spirits. And good spirits could mean nothing else. "Martha!" she called out as the maid bustled about the room, tidying what didn't need tidying. "Morvoren—how is she?"

Martha turned her round face towards her mistress, a smile splitting it almost from side to side and revealing a few gaps in her dentition. "The fever's broken, Miss Ysella! Doctor Busick's been here all night with her ladyship, and he says the crisis is past. Her ladyship's over the worst."

Forgetful of the chill, Ysella bounced out of bed, the shawl dropping to the floor. "Good heavens. That's wonderful news. Might I go and see her today, do you think? I need to get dressed. Whatever is the time? Where are my clothes?"

"The dowager said I was to let you sleep in. She said you

were right tired after the journey and all the gallivanting you've been doing in Town. So I did. But then his lordship told me to get you up because he wants to celebrate and he needs you to help him. It's gone eleven, Miss."

"Gone eleven! Then I'll have missed breakfast and I am *starving!*" Ysella's stomach rumbled as if in agreement, and she giggled. "Quick, where are my clothes? Not that dress. This house is like an ice box. I'll have the brown one with the long sleeves. Not the prettiest of gowns, but by far the warmest."

Within a very short space of time, Ysella was skipping along the corridor to her brother's rooms, her heart suddenly as light as air. Morvoren had turned the corner. Her poor little baby boy was not going to grow up without his mother like Sam had. All was right in the world.

Kit must have heard her coming. He stepped out of the bedroom and closed the door behind him with a soft click.

Ysella threw her arms around him, holding him tight. "Oh, Kitto! I'm so happy for you. Can I see her? Just for a moment?"

He held her close, his face against her hair, his heart beating against hers. His body shook. With gentle care, Ysella extricated herself from his hold. He was crying.

"Oh, Kitto, don't. I can't bear it if you cry." She took his face in her hands, the stubble rough under her touch. "She's going to get better now. You don't need to cry."

He shook his head, the tears streaming down his face. "I can't help it. When she was so ill, I forced myself not to give in to tears. I thought if I cried, then she'd surely die. It would seal her fate, because I'd be accepting what was going to happen to her." He managed a feeble laugh. "Make no mistake. These are tears of joy, not sorrow. And now I don't seem to be able to stop them." He wiped the back of his hand across his cheeks. "It's ridiculous, I know. But if I'd lost her... well, then I'd have been lost too. I couldn't have borne it."

Ysella hugged him again, his head on her shoulder. "You can cry with me if you need to." This seemed to be the thing to do, because he hung onto her like a drowning man for several minutes. Indeed, until Mama emerged from the sick room.

Ysella and Kit separated, and Mama put a gentle hand on his back. "Do you want to come in and see Morvoren?" she asked Ysella. "Just for a minute or two, as she's so very tired. But she asked for you as soon as she heard you were here." She smiled at Kit. "And you, my darling boy, can go and eat something, then try and get some sleep. Loveday and I will attend to anything Morvoren needs this morning. You've done more than enough. Time to look after yourself."

With a rueful grin, as of a man put upon by his womenfolk, Kit departed, and Ysella followed Mama into the bedroom. The curtains had been drawn back to let in the sunlight of a spring day at last without rain, and the room was no longer as stifling hot as it had been just a few short hours ago. Morvoren lay propped up on at least half a dozen pillows, as pale and wan as before, but at least now without the sheen of sweat on her skin.

Ysella ran to the bed and plumped herself down on Loveday's low stool. Reaching out with both hands, she took one of Morvoren's in hers and clung onto it. How thin it felt in her own strong grip. So unlike the Morvoren she knew and loved.

Morvoren's dry, cracked lips curved into a smile. "Ysella. I can't tell you how pleased I am to see you." Her words emerged as croaky as a frog. "I'm so sorry I've spoiled your season."

Ysella shook her head. "Nonsense. That doesn't matter a fig." Only that wasn't quite true, was it? An image of Oliver in his scarlet regimentals leapt into her head, only to be pushed away. The image didn't want to go.

Morvoren licked her lips. "Have you been having fun?"

The urge to be honest and disclose to Morvoren that she'd fallen in love with someone burgeoned, but Ysella held her tongue. No heart-to-hearts with Mama and Loveday so close. Maybe tomorrow? She yearned to share her excitement with someone, and Morvoren would be by far the best person. She understood all about love.

"It's been wonderful," Ysella said, choosing her words with care. "After I was presented, I had so many invitations to soirées and picnics and dances and routs. And Lord Flint organized an enormous ball to honor the new Lady Flint—and guess what, she's as big as a house, just as you said you were. Who'd have thought it? He's hoping for a boy this time, of course, but I'll wager it'll be another girl. How cross that will make him. I shall laugh, and I daresay others will too. Mama took me to the ball, and I danced with so many handsome young gentlemen. Such a press. The whole world had come, it seemed."

Morvoren was looking at her as though she suspected there might be more to her experiences in London than she was letting on.

Ysella chided herself. Maybe she was prattling on just a little too fast. Despite Morvoren's weakened condition, it seemed her astute nature had not vanished.

Ysella gave her sister-in-law the sweetest of smiles.

"That's enough for now, Ysella," Mama said, her voice stern. "Morvoren needs to sleep a while before taking some beef broth to build her strength. You need to let her have some peace from your chatter. You can visit again tomorrow."

Morvoren squeezed Ysella's hand. "Perhaps you might visit the nursery and see how my son is? Before tomorrow? And let me know? Your mama says I'm still too weak to see him."

Mama harrumphed in a way that was remarkably similar to the way Martha harrumphed when displeased.

Ysella squeezed Morvoren's hand in return. "I saw him yesterday, and he is thriving. But I shall go again today and then again tomorrow morning before coming to see you. I promise."

She bent and planted a kiss on Morvoren's thin cheek. "Until tomorrow, Sister."

Back out in the corridor, Ysella skipped her way down to the nursery on feet as light as air. Morvoren was getting better, and the sun was at last shining through windows where the shutters had been drawn back. Everything was fine in the world. The right way up again at last. She would confide in Morvoren about Oliver tomorrow, if Loveday and Mama could be got rid of. The thought left a warm coil in her stomach. Nothing would be better than telling Morvoren how handsome Oliver was and how he'd declared his passion for her and how she cherished the hope that he would soon ask for her hand in marriage. She could even dismiss the nagging doubt that he wouldn't come down to Marlborough as he'd promised, and that right now he was still enjoying the season by dancing attendance on some other young lady. No, that could not happen.

But what to do now? Mama was busy with Morvoren, Kit had retired to his old room to take some much-needed sleep, and no one else was about. Her whole body itched for action. What about a ride? With the sun shining down on the damp world, she was in the mood for a helter-skelter gallop.

She repaired to her own room and summoned Martha.

Half an hour later, she emerged from the servants' hall corridor into the stableyard in her dark-green riding habit. All was quiet. The stable staff must be eating their midday meal. Good. Since she'd first learned from Morvoren, she'd become adept at saddling her own horse, Lochinvar. And she fancied a ride out all by herself, not with some groom trailing after her. She wasn't planning on leaving the estate, after all, so what harm could there be?

She went into the large tack room, the aroma of well-cared for leather and horse assaulting her nostrils. A smell she'd liked from being the smallest of girls with the first tiny pony Papa had presented her with. She inhaled deeply—what a heady perfume. With a longing glance at the regular saddles used for riding astride, she lifted down her own side-saddle with some difficulty as it was heavy, and Lochinvar's bridle, then took the side door into the stable building.

Bypassing the first looseboxes, she headed for Lochinvar's stable, and, seeing her coming, he let out a low whicker. Setting down her load, she put her finger to her lips. "Sshh! I don't want them hearing us."

It took her only a moment to slip a headstall on and tie him up. His gleaming chestnut coat required no grooming, but she picked the loose straw out of his long tail. Not being a tall girl, she had to fetch a bucket to stand on for saddling up, but he stood patiently while she worked. With a heave, she managed to get the side-saddle onto his back, then fastened his girth. The bridle went on more easily, because he'd been trained from colthood to lower his head for the bit. She tightened the girth a second time, something Morvoren had taught her, and led him out into the yard, his shod hooves making far too much noise on the cobbles. Ysella sent a wary glance towards the servants' door, but no one came.

Luckily, a high mounting block stood to one side, otherwise she would have found mounting up impossible. Positioning Lochinvar with care, she climbed up the steps and slipped onto the saddle. Her right leg hooked around the pommel, and her left foot slid into her one stirrup. She gathered up her reins and with a click of her tongue, trotted Lochinvar out of the courtyard, certain no one had seen her go, or a groom would have been dispatched to accompany her.

As Lochinvar had been standing idle in his loose box, what she should have done, and what had been hammered home to her by Mama from her earliest childhood, was walk to begin with. But that would have involved staying within sight of the Abbey's many windows for far too long. So, instead, she urged her eager horse into a canter until she reached the track that ran through the woods, where she let him slow to a walk. "Sorry, Lochy," she muttered, almost to herself.

The Ormonde Abbey estate covered over five thousand acres in a shape a little like a crescent moon, but the majority of those acres were farms let out to tenants. Some large, some small. The estate woodland, used for pheasant rearing and shooting, wasn't in a block, but stretched out between the farms with tracks through it linking them together. A few handy jumps littered the woods, built by the gardeners at Kit's request. A request that had ultimately come from Ysella, who loved to hunt and therefore to jump.

The amount of pocking in the mud around the jumps suggested to Ysella that Kit had been out here jumping them himself not too long ago, but it didn't deter her from popping over them with Lochinvar. He loved to jump as well, and, as they landed, snatched at his bit in an effort to get his head. Ysella reined him in. Too many low branches in the woods for a flat-out gallop, which was what both she and her horse were longing for. But, if she rode down towards the village, an inviting long track ran back towards home. It curved around to the west with an uphill incline that would be perfect for a gallop. She set off through the woods in that direction.

The thatched rooftops of the village came into view down in the hollow, woodsmoke curling up from their chimneys to hang in the air, the smell of it a sharp tang on the breeze. As she drew closer, she spotted the bent figures of some of the women at work in their stone-walled gardens. They must be digging their vegetable patches ready for planting. Ysella, who knew next to nothing about vegetable gardening, tipped her hat to them in greeting. They straightened up, most of them bobbing wobbly curtsies.

One of the oldest, who Ysella recognized as the Widow Elkins, set her hands on her hips and called out. "The young Lady Ormonde. Be she all righty, Miss Ysella?"

So even down here they'd heard. Ysella drew rein in front of her, and the other women approached, wiping dirty hands on aprons, all agog to hear the news. "The fever has broken," Ysella announced, proud of being able to bring them good news about Morvoren. "Doctor Busick expects her to recover."

The Widow Elkins' lined face creased even further in a toothless smile. "Mind'n tell her we was askin' after her, if'n you don't mind, Miss Ysella." The other women nodded, echoing her words in a muttered chorus. "Tell her she been missed."

A little cheer went up, and, with a nod and a smile, Morvoren turned Lochinvar between the houses towards the entrance to the long track home. The sound of trotting hooves interrupted her. She turned her head. A handsome bay was approaching down the dirt road, astride it a gentleman, whose identity, even though no longer clad in scarlet regimentals, she could not mistake.

"Oliver!" She tightened her hold on Lochinvar who had been anticipating his gallop as much as she had, and Oliver brought his sweating horse up beside her, his face wreathed in smiles.

"Ysella! I could hardly dare to hope that if I rode this way I might find you also out on a horse. This is wonderful. Meant. Fate must be smiling on us."

She gazed at him in awe. Even without his regimentals and with his wavy hair concealed by a dashing top hat, he was a vision to behold. Even more handsome than her memory had allowed her to recall. And he'd kept his promise. Her doubts had been unfounded. He'd followed her down from London to Wiltshire and come looking for her. Her stomach did a delightful leap, and her cheeks flushed with heat.

"I'm so pleased to see you, and I have good news. My sister-in-law is recovering and is on the mend. I only found out this morning. It felt as though a great load had been lifted from my soul, so I decided that what I needed was a gallop in the fresh air. So here I am. And the sun is smiling on me."

Oliver peered up the track, which was narrow and ran between two thorny hedges. "Is that your intended galloping track?"

She nodded. "Absolutely." Her lips curved into a smile she couldn't hold in. "Do you fancy a gallop as well?"

Oliver's eyes twinkled in a way that set Ysella's heart to pounding. "A race," he said, grinning. "But a race is nothing without a wager."

He was going to have a hard job beating Lochinvar, so why not? Mama would be horrified at her making a wager like this with a gentleman, but then, Mama would be horrified that she was out without a groom, as well. And that she was all alone with said gentleman. But what Mama couldn't see, Mama couldn't rail at, and besides, she was probably far too busy with Morvoren to notice anything Ysella got up to. She nodded, lifting her chin, her dander up. "A wager indeed, then. What are the stakes?"

Oliver's eyes smoldered. "A kiss."

More heat rushed to Ysella's cheeks. Far more than she would have liked. How forward of any young man to demand a kiss in return for a race victory. Well, how forward of him to suggest the race in the first place. Oliver seemed intent on proving himself an altogether *very* forward young man indeed. But wasn't that rather nice? At least she had an idea what he wanted, and if it happened to coincide with something she wanted... like a kiss... which of course she *did* want. Although, of course, he'd not yet mentioned marriage even once, only, rather deliciously, that he had to have her. But that didn't matter. Wasn't marriage what all young admirers came to in the end?

"Very well," she said, heart hammering at her own daring. She'd raced Kit and Morvoren countless times, and usually won as she had Lochinvar, but this was different. "For a kiss." She narrowed her eyes. "If you win, you may steal your kiss. If I win, you will go away empty-handed."

He nodded. "May the best man win."

"Woman," Ysella retorted, and leaning forward on Lochinvar, set her heel and whip to his sides. He leapt forward like a coiled spring unleashed, and by her side Oliver applied heels and whip to his own bay's flanks. The horses thundered up the narrow track, Lochinvar just in front of the bay, his neck stretched out, just like one of the hunting pictures in the hall at Ormonde.

Crouched as far forward as she could go, Ysella glanced to her right, where Oliver was lashing the bay with his whip. Did she want to win that badly? Or did she want him to kiss her? Part of her, the competitive side of her that never liked to lose, fought against the side of her that longed for the touch of Oliver's lips on hers.

Lochinvar began to slow. The going was heavy after all the rain, and all uphill. Perhaps the bay was a fitter mount. After all, Ysella had been in London for two months, so perhaps all he'd been having was a gentle hack with one of the grooms. At this rate she was going to lose without even trying.

The bay surged ahead, the end of the track in sight. Oliver pulled his horse up and Ysella brought Lochinvar to a halt beside him, his chestnut flanks heaving and flecked with foam.

"I think I win," Oliver said, his eyes hot with… what? Triumph? Desire? Were her own eyes as hot? Because she *did* want him to kiss her. Oh yes, she did. Without a doubt. Definitely. It would be her first ever kiss with a real man. Her heart, that had raced with the effort of the contest, showed no sign of slowing.

Oliver pushed the bay so close that his leg rubbed against Lochinvar's sweaty side, his eyes locked on hers. He leaned towards her, his face only a foot or so from hers. "Are you ready to surrender my prize?" His voice had taken on a husky depth. The tip of his tongue slid around his lips, as though hungry to taste hers, and a shiver ran through her from head to toe.

Her heart thundered faster still, her stomach did a convoluted back flip, and her breath came fast and urgently. She was really going to be kissed. At last. The chaste one Archibald Hatherleigh had stolen when she was twelve didn't count. This was the real thing. A kiss from a handsome man. A kiss from the man she loved. The man who loved her. Didn't he?

She leaned towards Oliver as though drawn by a magnet. His face moved towards hers. So close she could feel his warm breath on her cheek. She closed her eyes. Her fingers tightened on the reins as his lips touched hers. How cool and dry they felt at first. He pressed his closed mouth against hers for a couple of seconds that seemed to last forever. Was this how being kissed should feel? Memories of much the same kind of kiss from Archibald rose to her mind. Was *this* what all the fuss was about?

Then something wet slid between her lips, forcing them

apart. Something moist and demanding. His tongue. She started with shock, but his hand came up behind her head and stopped her retreat. Her lips opened under his pressure, her teeth parted, his tongue invaded her mouth. Did this mean he was giving her a baby? Not if Morvoren was right. She'd just have to hope she was.

But… was *this* kissing? Was this what Kit and Morvoren did? What every couple did? Probably, if Morvoren was to be believed. This quite delicious and daring entry of a part of another person's body into one's own. This invasion of her mouth. A glorious shiver of ecstasy trickled down her back to her stomach, and then lower. Good heavens! What *was* that delicious feeling? Her own tongue met Oliver's, unbidden, as though two wrestlers sparred, and his mouth pressed ever harder, demanding more. His other hand—was he no longer holding his bay's reins?— moved to her breast.

This time she did start back so hard he couldn't hold her. His roaming hand fell to his horse's neck and he laughed. Was that an even greater look of triumph in his eyes?

She gave a little nervous laugh in return, frightened by how much she'd liked what he'd been doing, even when he'd touched her breast. She felt very grownup, but at the same time flustered and confused.

He gathered up his reins. "I'd best be getting back to my hostelry. As I said I would, I'm staying at the Castle in Marlborough. It turns out to be a very fine establishment. Perhaps I can call at Ormonde Abbey tomorrow? If you'd like that?"

Like that? Of course she would. Common sense prevented this reply though. Instead, she gathered up her own reins and inclined her head towards him. The man who had just put his tongue down her throat in that wicked fashion and provoked a reaction she didn't understand. "That would be most pleasant, Oliver. I'm sure my brother the Viscount will be pleased to meet you." They sounded like two casual acquaintances, not two people who'd just shared the most intimate of moments. Should she be disappointed?

With a knowing smile, he turned the bay away from her, and set off back down the track in a steady trot. Ysella watched him go, until at last a bend in the track concealed him. She'd better return home herself, before someone noticed her absence and reported it to Mama.

Chapter Nine

YSELLA DID AS she had promised Morvoren and, the next morning, after breakfast, hastened upstairs and along the corridor to the nursery wing. Although the Abbey could not be truly said to have separate wings, being such a hodge-podge of additions, everyone always referred to different parts of it as being wings, out of habit. Hence the east and west wing, and the nursery wing, where she and Kit and their two older sisters had grown up.

Mrs. Jessie Jenkins, the wetnurse, was feeding a baby when Ysella breezed in, although which baby, it would have been hard to say, wrapped up as each one was in identical shawls. Nanny Boyle, who Kit had informed Ysella had stepped out of retirement and into the breach at very short notice, stood with the other baby over her shoulder, patting its back for some reason. The little nursery maid was stacking piles of clean napkins. Two babies must be getting through a lot of those.

"Good morning, Nanny," Ysella said, beaming at her old nurse and looking with raised eyebrows from one baby to the other. "I've come to see my little nephew again, but I have no idea which he is."

The baby Nanny was shouldering gave a loud burp, making his carer smile with satisfaction, her face puckering into even more wrinkles. She must be very old, as she'd been nanny for all of Ysella's siblings, and Derwa was over thirty now. Which made her quite old in Ysella's mind.

"This one is young master George," Nanny said, transferring the baby with an adroit movement born of years of practice, and cradling him in her arms. "He has a name at last. His lordship informed me this morning. All nicely fed and changed and ready for his nap. Jessie's just seeing to her own baby now." She nodded to an armchair by the blazing nursery fire. "If you sit yourself down, I'll put him in your lap for a moment."

Ysella had never held a baby before, not even any of her sisters' children, but she didn't dare argue with Nanny. Years of automatically obeying her came into operation and she sat down in the chair with a thump. She held out her arms, willing the tremble in them to stop, and unsure whether it was to do with holding so precious a bundle as little George, or how she felt about Oliver, whose perfect visage she couldn't oust from her head.

Nanny laid the tiny, swaddled bundle in her lap, his downy head held in the crook of Ysella's arm. His rosebud mouth stretched into a wide, toothless yawn, and his eyes closed.

Nanny chuckled. "You have the knack, Miss Ysella. He's off to sleep now, like a good boy, with his belly full of good milk." She laid a gentle hand on Ysella's shoulder. "You can tell Lady Ormonde he's in good hands when you see her."

"He's so tiny," Ysella whispered. "Look at his little face. Look at his eyelashes." A tide of love swept over her, quite different to the love she felt for Oliver. Might she one day be holding a little creature like this in her arms with the features of Oliver stamped across him? The thought sent a current of excitement through her from her toes to the top of her head and back down again. She glanced at Nanny, sure she'd have noticed, but the old lady's expression hadn't changed.

"Best to put him in his cradle now," Nanny said. "So he can have a peaceful sleep and learn that's the place to do it, not the arms of his aunt or mother. Babies have to learn their place in the world." She scooped baby George up with ease and transferred him to the old cradle in the corner that had once been Ysella's, and before that Kit's and Derwa's and Meliora's.

Ysella rose to her feet. "I shall go now and report on him to his mama." She glanced back at Jessie Jenkins, but her dark head was still bent over her own child. "And Jessie?" The woman looked up, and Ysella saw with a start that she must be younger than she was. Just a girl. "I will tell her ladyship how well you are providing for her son."

Jessie's honest face broke into a contented smile. "Thank you, milady."

Ysella laughed. "I am not a milady, Jessie, any more than you are. You may simply call me Miss Ysella, as Nanny does." She put out a hand and stroked Jessie's baby's head—the hair thinner and fairer than George's dark fuzz. "Your own baby is very beautiful, and very lucky to have so kind a mother as you."

A quick trip along the corridor and Ysella was at Morvoren's door, tapping on it gently with her knuckles. Loveday came to open it.

Morvoren was sitting up in bed with a breakfast tray across her lap, the curtains had been flung back, and the morning sunlight was streaming in. Her cheeks had gained some color, and someone had confined her hair in a braid, the whole making her look tidier and healthier than she had the day before.

"Ysella!" she exclaimed with delight. "You came. Have you been in to see my son?"

Loveday pulled a chair up beside the bed for Ysella. "I'll just be off now to see to her ladyship's laundry, as you're here, Miss. Your mama did say as you could stay half an hour but not to tire her Ladyship out."

Ysella sat down on the chair. "Of course I won't. I'll look after her while you're busy, have no fear. Off you go." Just what she wanted. Time on her own with her best friend.

Carrying a wicker basket of laundry, Loveday departed, the door closing with a satisfying clunk behind her.

"My son?" Morvoren repeated. "How is he? They won't let me see him yet. They say I have to wait another day or two. They think I'm too weak, but seeing him would be such a tonic, Ysella. Tell me he is well."

Ysella, not usually known for her tact, forbore from telling Morvoren she'd held baby George in her arms. "He's thriving. Mrs. Jenkins the wetnurse is younger than me and both babies are doing well. Nanny Boyle is in charge…"

Morvoren nodded. "I know. Kit put her on standby when we found we were to be parents." She wrinkled her nose. "She seems a bit of a dragon, and I'm still not used to the idea of letting someone else care for my child, but I daresay she will look after George with great care. At least until I'm fully recovered."

Ysella nodded. "You only have to look at Kit and me to tell she's a good nanny. George is in good hands. You needn't worry about him."

Morvoren glanced across at the long window. "If only I could get outside in the fresh air, I know I'd feel better quicker. But I suppose they're right. I'm weak as a daisy." She gave the breakfast tray a push. The remains of scrambled eggs and toast lay on her plate. "Can you take this away. And then, because I'm fed up with talking about being ill, you must tell me all about the season. Your letters have been sadly lacking in detail and, I have to say, very badly spelled."

This was more like it. Ysella put the breakfast tray on the table by the window and sat back down again. With the half hour limit set on her visit, no beating about the bush was required. She needed to get straight to the point.

"Oh, Morvoren," she half whispered, as though there might be an ear pressed to the keyhole. You never knew in a house this size with the number of servants they had, and she didn't want gossip reaching Mama's ears. "I've *met* someone."

Morvoren's eyebrows rose. "Do tell me all about him before Loveday gets back then." She must be as aware as Ysella of how gossip could run rife in a servants' hall.

Ysella leaned forwards and seized Morvoren's hand. "He's the most handsome man in the whole of London, I swear! And he loves me too. I can't believe I've been so lucky."

Morvoren gripped her hand, her eyes alight with pleasure. "He loves you? How wonderful for you. I take it you love him, as well? Where did you meet him and what is his name? Does he have a title?"

This was a pleasing reaction. "Oliver Featherstone. He's a friend of Fitz's and a captain in the militia. The West London Militia. He looks *so* dashing in his regimentals, Morvoren! But of course, being in the militia, it's not quite full time, so when he met me in the park, he wasn't in uniform. But he strikes a fine figure in his tailcoat—quite the dandy."

Morvoren's brow puckered in a small frown. "He's a friend of your cousin Fitz?"

Ysella nodded, the worry that this was not a fact that would endear her beau to either Morvoren or Kit leaping to the forefront of her mind. "He introduced us. At the Denby House ball. I told you already how Lord Flint, Fitz's uncle, was showing off his new young wife. So unseemly, really. I had to feel sorry for her, being paraded like a prize heifer. But you know Flint. Not an ounce of consideration for common decency. But he does throw a wonderful ball. Even better than the one at Denby Castle last year. Fitz was in his regimentals, as was Captain Featherstone."

Morvoren nodded and her frown deepened.

Ysella bit her lip. Was it the mention of Fitz or his uncle that had brought that expression to Morvoren's face? Why mention of either of them should do that, Ysella had no idea. She herself was fond of Fitz, who could be such fun in a rather wicked way, and she'd once thought to pair Morvoren off with Lord Flint, who'd shown great interest in her at the Denby Castle ball.

With a little internal shake, Ysella ploughed on. "And you'll never guess what."

Morvoren's brows rose. "You're right. I won't. What?"

"Oliver, I mean Captain Featherstone," Ysella blushed at her mistake. "He's here in Wiltshire. At the Castle Inn in Marlborough."

More frowning. "He is? How on earth do you know that?"

Ysella shifted in discomfort. This conversation wasn't turning out quite in the way she'd planned. Morvoren was supposed to be pleased for her—over the moon if possible. And yet, her expression, since the mention of Fitz, seemed to betray suspicion and disquiet. Not that Ysella was gifted in reading people's expressions, but this one was difficult to ignore. "I, er, I went out for a ride yesterday morning, after I heard you were on the mend, and I, um, I happened to meet him." Probably best not to divulge that she'd invited him to come down here in order to call on her.

Morvoren's eyes narrowed.

Ysella shifted again, acutely aware that her sister-in-law knew her all too well.

"And did you take a groom with you?" *Much* too well. No one else would have assumed Ysella had escaped unchaperoned onto the estate. Well, Kit might have, but he was otherwise engaged.

"Um… no…"

Morvoren sighed, but amusement twinkled in her blue eyes. "Ysella, you are just what Kit calls you—a minx. Did you know Captain Featherstone was going to be out riding yesterday morning? Did you know he'd be staying at the Castle?"

Ysella made a moue, something that had frequently extricated her from tight spots with Kit in the past. It didn't work on Morvoren.

"Ysella, did you *invite* him down?"

Ysella bit her lip and scowled. "Well, perhaps I might just have *hinted*," she admitted, in a feeble attempt to remain evasive but not tell an outright lie.

Morvoren giggled. "Oh Ysella, no wonder Kit despairs of you. You are quite incorrigible. Does nothing sway you? Not even the fact that you might have been inviting him to pay a visit on a household in mourning?"

Ysella had the grace to blush. Hotly. "Oh," she mumbled. "I

was sure it wouldn't be a house in mourning. I didn't for a moment believe you would die."

"All the same," Morvoren rejoined, some of her old asperity back in her voice, "you took an enormous risk. And then you rode out by yourself, without a groom, and had a secret rendez-vous—with a man!"

"I didn't *arrange* the rendezvous," Ysella protested. "It just sort of happened. A lucky coincidence that Oliver—Captain Featherstone that is—should be out riding in exactly the same spot. We met in the village. I'd ridden down there so I could give Lochinvar a gallop up the long track. You know. Where you and I used to gallop before you began to increase and Kit so meanly stopped you riding."

Morvoren scratched her head. "What will we do with you? Despite everything, you manage to behave like a hoyden at every turn." This was strong approbation, but the amusement in Morvoren's voice, mixed with exasperation, softened it.

Inspired by this apparent softening to more confidences, Ysella continued. "We had a race. He had a rangy bay, and of course I was on Lochinvar who is the fastest in our stables and out to hounds. But those lazy grooms haven't been exercising him properly while I've been in London, and Oliver won the race. Poor Lochinvar just wasn't fit enough. I shall be working on *that* while I'm down here."

Morvoren pursed her lips. "A race? Well, at least he didn't come across you in your boy's clothes. There's a blessing in that."

Ysella chuckled. When Morvoren had first come to Or-monde, Ysella had prevailed upon her to teach her to ride astride, for which both of them had purloined some of Kit's old clothes. He'd discovered this, of course, but been persuaded to allow them to continue once a week, in his company, until Morvoren's condition had prevented this. "I very nearly wore them," she admitted with a grin. "It was just luck that I didn't."

Morvoren shot her a frown of recrimination, and her eyes narrowed again as though a thought had suddenly occurred to her. "And was there a *wager* on this race? If I know you, there was."

Ysella dimpled at the memory, heat surging up her throat to her cheeks. "Just a *small* one."

Morvoren regarded her in silence for a moment. What was going through her head? Had she divined the nature of the wager? Did she possess mind-reading powers? Or was giveaway guilt written over Ysella's face? Her cheeks grew warmer by the moment.

"I think I'd rather not know the nature of your wager," Morvoren said, at last. "If I don't know, then I won't have to decide whether to tell Kit."

A good plan. Ysella smiled, and dropped her bombshell. "I invited Captain Featherstone to call today."

"What?"

"He asked if he could call on me… on us, I suppose, and I said yes."

"Good heavens," Morvoren spluttered. "You'd best go and inform your mama and Kit of your social plans. They may not be too pleased. Good luck with that."

Chapter Ten

CAPTAIN OLIVER FEATHERSTONE called at Ormonde Abbey at precisely three o'clock in the afternoon, having ridden down from Marlborough on his flashy bay in the continued good weather. Ysella, who had been standing sentry at the window overlooking the front drive, spotted his figure in the distance. With a squeal of delight, she rushed first to inform Morvoren that her beau was on his way, and secondly down the stairs into the drawing room to join Mama, who was engaged in stitching a bonnet for young Master George.

Neither Mama nor Kit had been at all pleased that she'd invited a gentleman caller, although this time, forewarned by Morvoren's reaction, Ysella omitted to mention his friendship with Cousin Fitz. That would not have endeared him to Kit in any way, and she dearly wanted Oliver to make a good impression on her brother. After all, he'd said he had to have her, and that must mean only one thing. That he intended to offer for her hand. Perhaps he would do it today. How exciting that would be.

But Kit had taken umbrage and gone out onto the estate with Sam Beauchamp visiting their tenants and was not yet returned. Why he had to do that on a day when a very important question might need posing escaped Ysella. But gone he had. Brothers. They were a law unto themselves and most irritating.

Sam, who'd been there when Ysella had announced to Kit the

imminent arrival of a beau from London, had bestowed a look of misery on Ysella that must surely have been on account of his not wanting to visit all those tenants. Ysella could only agree with that sentiment. Very boring that would be, even if most of them happened to be nice people. Ysella was glad, yet again, for having been born a girl without the responsibilities her brother had inherited.

Snatching up her own sewing—a nightgown to match the bonnet but without so much embroidery required, which was lucky as Ysella was very bad at embroidery—she sat down beside Mama with the intention of pretending she'd been industriously occupied since luncheon. Mama, who had also expressed annoyance in no uncertain terms at Ysella issuing invitations to a house of sickness, gave Ysella a reproving frown. Both she and Kit had been forced to agree that sending a messenger to Marlborough to avert the visit was unthinkable, but that didn't mean they'd given it the seal of their approval.

A five-minute wait brought Bannerman to the door, opening it to allow Oliver to enter. "Captain Featherstone, Milady," he said to Mama.

Oliver swaggered into the airy room, his presence filling it, or so it appeared to Ysella. His resemblance to one of her idealized romantic heroes seemed even greater in this setting. Her bosom physically heaved at the sight of him, more handsome than ever with his gently curling hair arranged in an upsweep of curls that added to his already impressive height. This time, he wore an impeccable blue tailcoat over buff breeches, with the points of his collar even higher than they'd been in London, making it hard for him to turn his head. His top boots still shone, but were lightly flecked with mud from his ride over from Marlborough.

He swept a flamboyant bow to Mama. "Lady Ormonde, charmed to make your acquaintance once again. I swear you get younger every time I see you."

Ysella suppressed an unladylike snort. What a lie. No one could get younger, so he was just being flattering, and it was a mistake, because Mama was not susceptible to that kind of flattery. She should have warned him.

Mama held out her hand, which he took and kissed. "How perfectly lovely to see you again, Captain. And so soon…" Both her tone and her arched eyebrows insinuated the inappropriateness of his visit, and Ysella's forehead furrowed. This might be more difficult than she'd been anticipating.

"Won't you take a seat for a few minutes," Mama said, her clipped words suggesting a few minutes was all the time he would be allowed to stay for.

Oliver flicked the tails of his coat out of the way, and perched on one of the stiffly upholstered chairs, his eyes resting on Mama still. A wise move. Although, the thought of Mama catching a glimpse of the hot gaze meant for her made Ysella stiff with fear. The niceties of social etiquette needed to be adhered to for Mama's sake, even if in private. But Ysella was aching for Oliver to take her in his arms and bestow another kiss like yesterday's upon her. Inside her satin slippers, her toes curled in delight at the thought and a warm glow suffused her. The memory of that kiss and how it had felt had grown in her imagination out of all proportion.

"Are you passing through on your way somewhere?" Mama asked, managing to stitch and regard Oliver at the same time.

He shook his head. "Not quite. I've taken a room in Marlborough—at the Castle Inn. It came well recommended by a friend, and I'm finding it most comfortable."

"Do you have acquaintances in the locality that you intend to visit?" To Ysella's oversensitive ears, Mama's voice sounded stiff with reproach. Or was that her imagination? Enough to put off the most ardent of beaux. Would she be this forbidding if Oliver were to have a title to his name, or, like Meliora's boring husband, a lucrative career? Although, of course, he *might* be heir to a title she didn't know about. Just because his father was a bishop, it didn't mean he had no claim to an aristocratic lineage. An interesting thought.

Oliver nodded. "In a way, although I doubt very much my particular friend is in residence. Captain Fitzwilliam Carlyon of Denby Castle. I believe he is your nephew."

Oh no. Now Mama would tell Kit that Oliver was a friend of Fitz's. If only she could have warned him not to mention it.

A small smile twitched at the corner of Mama's mouth. She had a soft spot for Fitz, as did Ysella. She'd once told her daughter that a man who was a rake, as Fitz was, commanded an undeniable attraction for the ladies, perhaps leading them to hope they might reform him. "Dear Fitz," Mama said, with a slightly wistful smile. "I believe he is on leave from his regiment and in London at the moment, for the season. I'm sure I saw him at the Denby House ball looking handsome in his regimentals."

Oliver nodded. "You did indeed, Lady Ormonde. And it is due to him that I'm down here in Wiltshire. I told him I fancied some time in the country, and he was kind enough to describe to me how beautiful Wiltshire is. I might ride over to Denby Castle in a day or two, if it takes my fancy. Just to see if it's as lovely as Fitz informed me."

A tiny nub of worry formed in Ysella's heart, as Oliver demonstrated his adeptness at telling lies, something Mama, and Papa when he was alive, had always drummed into her was to be abhorred, whatever the cause. Not that she always adhered to that rule herself. But this must be the sort of expedient lie that didn't matter so much, taking the place of a truth Mama could not hear. She must never find out that Ysella had invited Oliver down here herself. She'd think it far too forward.

Mama managed another rather forced smile. "You have chosen the loveliest of seasons, although at the moment the weather is a little inclement for my liking."

An idea seized Ysella. "Might I ride out with Captain Featherstone a few times—to show him the country?" She looked from Mama back to him. "My brother, Lord Ormonde, has set up some obstacles in our woods. They make a ride so much more fun. I love to jump and my horse is agile as a cat."

Mama frowned. "I don't think Captain Featherstone will have the time to ride out with you, Ysella. Will you, Captain?" To Ysella's deep annoyance, everything about her tone implied the answer she expected should be a "no."

He met Mama's challenging gaze. "I could make time, if it would amuse Miss Carlyon."

Mama's eyes flashed a warning. She did *not* like to be crossed.

This was not going the way Ysella had planned. Why was Mama so hostile to Oliver? She needed to do something. A glance at the long windows gave her an idea. "Would you care to see our gardens and hothouses, Captain Featherstone? We're very proud of our pineapple plants."

Mama frowned.

Oliver, however, smiled and nodded. "If Lady Ormonde doesn't object. I have a particular fascination for hothouse growing."

Did he? That was news to Ysella, but as it provided a good excuse to escape from the drawing room, she wasn't about to complain.

Mama inclined her head. "Perhaps just for a short while as Ysella has a gown to finish sewing for her new little nephew. My son has been lucky enough to have gained an heir, Captain. A little early in his arrival, which has taken us by surprise, and we are behind in our sewing."

Before Mama could change her mind, Ysella leapt to her feet with such haste that the unfinished baby gown fell to the floor. Oliver bent and retrieved it, placing it with elaborate care on the table in front of Mama. He held out his arm. "Lead on, Miss Carlyon." And she tucked her hand into its crook.

Having sent for Martha to bring her a spencer, as despite the brightness of the day it was chilly for wandering slowly around the garden, Ysella and Oliver left by one of the numerous side doors that led into the formal gardens.

SAM AND KIT rode up the hill from the ornamental lake, the rooftops and random arrangement of chimneys belonging to the Abbey coming slowly into view over the brow. Sam glanced across at his employer and friend. While they'd been out visiting the tenants, he'd seemed perfectly happy, recounting to farmer's wife after farmer's wife, and some of the farmers as well, how his own wife and new son were doing.

It seemed news of Morvoren's illness had spread across the estate like wildfire, and at many of the homes they'd called at, small gifts had been pressed upon them. Sam's saddlebags bulged with crumbling pastries and paper-wrapped sweetmeats, and Kit's contained little bonnets and bootees, sachets of lavender festooned with lovingly handmade lace, and a selection of gaudy spring flowers picked from cottage gardens, their stalks wrapped in damp rags. These last must have been drooping by now, with their close proximity to the horses' warm bodies.

"I never cease to be amazed by the generosity of my tenants," Kit said, narrowing his eyes against the lowering sun. "It seems a cliché to call them the salt of the Earth, but I can find no other words to describe them. They have so little, and yet they all wanted to give something to Morvoren and my son. It humbles me."

Sam nodded. "Even the Widow Brooks, with her arthritis, had been out in her garden to pick flowers for Lady Ormonde."

Kit grinned. "She's made herself popular amongst the poor, with her constant concern for their welfare. If I'm not careful, I'm going to find I have no income at all from rents, for she'll have told them all they don't need to pay while they're struggling." He chuckled. "And *then* you'll have trouble balancing your books, old friend, and *I'll* be the one in need of handouts."

Sam let his reins slip through his fingers and his horse stretched its neck in appreciation. "All the same, I did wonder why you were so keen to get out of the house. I rather fancied you'd remain at your wife's side, with her so recently ill." He forbore from saying "at death's door" but that had been the gossip in the servants' hall. No doubt this thought had crossed Kit's mind as well, but it was best left unsaid, especially with her recovery so fresh.

"I had my reasons," Kit said, a frown marring his brow. "And Morvoren needs to sleep. I'm not needed now to sit beside her bed. Mama and Loveday have been competing with me for that honor."

Sam raised his eyebrows and waited for Kit to continue.

"Oh, very well," Kit snapped, as though driven to enlarging on his reasons. "It seems the beau my silly little sister has ensnared is not someone I would like her to associate with. Not someone any young lady's guardian would like her to even pass the time of day with, in fact. You heard her say he was coming to call today? Well, when she let slip his name, I recognized it. I know for a fact he's a friend of my cousin Fitz's, and while that in itself would render him unsuitable, I've heard rumors about him from acquaintances at White's who've had dealings with him that outweigh any association with Fitz."

He ran a hand through his unruly hair. "I can only hope the sentiments involved are entirely on his part, although Ysella is such a fool, I wouldn't be surprised if she hasn't hatched a fancy for him. She never did have any more sense than a…" He paused, as though lost for words to describe his sister. "Than a goldfish. And from what I've heard, the man's a cad, through and through."

A hollow formed in Sam's stomach as he remembered Ysella's face as she informed Kit of Captain Featherstone's imminent arrival. His heart twisted and sank into the toes of his boots. His hands tightened on the reins and his horse tossed his head. His whole body had stiffened, and a cold shiver ran down his spine.

Oblivious to Sam's reaction, Kit went on. "I've heard he's a man in need of a wealthy wife, although I've also heard he's the type of blackguard who would swindle you out of your money on some hairbrained get-rich-quick scheme. A bogus silver mine in Argentina is what was quoted to me. But I also heard that he's fought at least three duels in the past few years. A man died, I believe, but his father is high up in the church with a brother in government who hushed it up."

Everything coming out of Kit's mouth sounded like a death knell to Sam. His poor Ysella, duped and taken in by a scoundrel. This had to be stopped.

They had nearly reached the side of the house. Kit shook his head. "I'll put a stop to it, of course. After today's little fait accompli, I shall make sure she never sees him again, even if I have to keep her immured down here at Ormonde until Christmas. Let him set his sights on someone else's sister or daughter. Not mine." He grinned. "We'll take the horses around the back to the stables. I have a fancy to stand grooming them for a while."

They rode under the clock-towered archway into the stableyard and slid to the cobbles. Two grooms came hurrying out, but Kit waved them away. "We don't need you, thank you. We'll tend to our horses ourselves."

When they'd gone, he turned back to Sam. "He *should* be gone by now, unless he has fewer manners than I thought. I asked Mama not to let him stay too long. He's a mere captain in the militia, and I don't doubt but that he already knows Ysella has a small fortune in dowry coming to her, or he wouldn't have put himself out to come all the way down here after her. I don't want to see him if I don't have to. Not at the moment. I'm not in the mood for fending off my sister's suitors. I can trust Mama to have made it clear he's not welcome here again."

That sounded good to Sam's ears. He could trust Kit and the dowager to keep Ysella safe. Couldn't he?

Once in the looseboxes, sorting out the horses didn't take that long. Sam rushed the brush over his horse's flanks, picked out his hooves and then slung an armful of hay into his manger. Kit was deep in a conversation with his own horse, so Sam tossed an armful of hay in for him as well and walked out into the stable courtyard.

No one was around, and not having the same confidence as Kit that the captain would have recognized his dismissal by the dowager, he didn't fancy going inside the house in case he ran into him. Instead, he left by the archway and turned left, heading towards the gardens. He might just go and sit in the summerhouse, his favored spot for contemplation since his childhood. He had a lot he needed to contemplate today.

An archway sheltered an ornate ironwork gate set in the high brick wall surrounding the formal gardens. He pushed this gate open and headed away from the terrace and the house. He had to pass the Orangery, which was what the dowager called the hothouses, and as he did, he happened to glance through the windows.

They were arched, but not large, the heat inside being furnished by stoves rather than exclusively from sunlight. Greenery hung in abundance, and could produce all manner of fruits unavailable to those without benefit of a hothouse: grapes, oranges and lemons, cherries, peaches and figs, as well, of course, as the pineapples which Ormonde prided itself on. In addition to the fruits, a fine selection of exotic flowers grew within the capacious walls of the Orangery—among them oleander, hibiscus, and camellias that could be used even in winter to decorate the house.

But right at that moment, the exotic produce of the hothouse was not what caught his attention. Instead, his eyes riveted on the two people inside. One of them was Ysella, wearing a navy-blue spencer over a paler blue gown, but the other was a man. He was tall, made taller still by hair fluffed up in the artful curls that were the height of London fashion. Combined with those ridiculously high collar points, he resembled nothing more than a complete nincompoop. There was no denying, however, that he possessed a perfect Grecian profile: a long straight nose, a determined chin, and a high, pale brow. And the cut of his coat clung to his broad shoulders like a second skin.

It *had* to be the captain. Sam stared, unable to drag his gaze away. Neither Ysella nor this paragon seemed to have noticed him, so intent were they on staring into each other's eyes. They stood face to face, their bodies only inches apart, and the captain—that *dandy*—had her hands clasped in his as he leered down at her. Yes, that was a leer for certain.

Sam's fists clenched at his sides. How he would love to wipe that dreadful smug smile off that nincompoop's face. He'd done a lot of boxing growing up with Kit, who, being an only son, had required a partner to spar with. Kit had attended Eton, where boxing was part of the curriculum, unlike at the local grammar school in Marlborough, where Sam had boarded. He could surely land a facer on that immaculate nose and set it out of kilter. Hopefully for good.

As he watched, held fascinated by the sight, the captain, who was nothing more than the cad Kit had called him, inclined his head to Ysella's and their lips met. Sam's fury rose like the lava in a volcano, and it was all he could do not to charge for the doors and rush inside to break them apart. But it was not his position to do this, and besides which, it was only a kiss. Wasn't it? Was he not going to have to live with the idea that Ysella would kiss another man? But not this cad, this nincompoop, this *dandy*. How could she bring herself to kiss someone like that?

However, Ysella seemed to be returning the kiss with untoward enthusiasm. If it made her happy…

Something inside Sam cracked. Was it his heart?

He watched as she lifted her arms and, it had to be admitted with diffidence, put them around the captain's neck. The captain's hands on her waist drew her closer…

"Sam? Where are you?" Kit's voice rang out across the gardens.

Inside the Orangery, the two lovers sprang apart. Were they laughing? Sam turned and hurried towards the summerhouse.

They must never guess he'd been spying on them.

Kit came stomping through the gate, perhaps a little put out that Sam had deserted him in the stables. And at the same time, Ysella and her captain emerged from the Orangery looking as demure and innocent as babes. A quick glance over Sam's shoulder showed him her hair slightly disarranged, and her cheeks becomingly flushed, but that was all.

"Kitto," she called out in delight. "There you are. I have someone I'd like you to meet."

Sam couldn't stay to watch this. He hurried his footsteps past the summerhouse and out of the bottom gate. He did *not* want to see Ysella with a man, any man, that she'd just *kissed*.

Chapter Eleven

YSELLA SLAMMED HER bedroom door and stamped over to her bed. What a horrible pig Kit was being. She flung herself onto the bed and buried her face in her pillows. How could he be so mean? Who did he think he was? Papa?

Her mind went back to the afternoon, and Kit's face when she'd introduced Oliver. His first words had been, as they shook hands, "Ah, I see you are about to leave us. Nice meeting you."

Oliver, ever the gentleman, had been forced to nod his agreement. "I was just admiring your pineapple plants in the Orangery. But you're right, I need to be on my way, or I won't be back in Marlborough before dark."

Kit glanced up at the sky. "I'll wish you on your way then." And he held his arm out for Ysella to take.

She glared at him in frustration, but short of starting an argument, she could think of nothing to do.

"Miss Carlyon," Oliver said, bowing. "It's been a pleasure to renew our acquaintance." And he winked, just for her, as he rose.

Ysella started and glanced at Kit, but as Oliver had his back to her brother, he must have missed the conspiratorial gesture. What did it mean?

"Perhaps," Oliver said, with smooth finesse, as he turned to Kit, "I might call upon your sister again?"

And this was where Kit had turned into Papa. His so far bland expression had creased into a frown that didn't look all that apologetic. "I'm afraid that would be difficult, as the house is not open to receiving guests at this very moment, due to the illness of my wife. Ysella made a mistake in inviting you here today. We are not receiving callers and will not be again for some time to come. My wife needs complete peace and quiet."

Ysella had to interrupt. "But he won't be coming to see Morvoren or you. He'll be coming to see me!"

Kit's jaw hardened, just as Papa's had been wont to do. "That is of no matter, Ysella. It was rash of you to invite a London acquaintance to call on you at this time. Rash and selfish. Mama will be taking you back to London when Morvoren is recovered. You may invite your gentleman callers to Ormonde House, but not here to the Abbey while my wife remains ill. I'm sorry, but my mind is quite made up."

He made a bow to Oliver. "I apologize for having had to put it so bluntly, but my sister is nothing if not impetuous and doesn't give pause to think of others. It is most upsetting to have to receive visitors at this time, when my wife has been so ill. The house is all upside down." He paused and fixed Oliver with his hard gaze, and Ysella's heart sank into her boots. "I am sure you understand, Captain Featherstone." Said in a tone that Oliver could do nothing but agree to.

Kit's gaze returned to Ysella. "And rest assured that when Ysella returns to Town for the remainder of the season, *I* shall be accompanying her." Had that been a veiled threat? Ysella might not have been of the most astute at reading body language, but even she could read disapproval in every bone of Kit's body, and every word he spoke. *The pig.*

Oliver bowed a second time, somewhat stiffly, as though he knew he'd been put in his place and it wasn't a place he wished to occupy. "As you wish, my lord. No need to trouble your staff. I'll walk around to the stables myself and fetch my horse. Good afternoon."

He bowed to Ysella as well, his eyes smoldering delightfully.

"Good afternoon, Miss Carlyon."

And with that, he departed. Ysella watched him go. At the wrought-iron gate, he turned and looked back at her, touching his fingers to his forehead in a salute. Then he was gone.

Ysella swung around on Kit, her hard-controlled anger rising to the surface. "How could you do that?" she burst out. "He came to see *me*, not you. And you were so rude to him!"

Kit's brows met in a heavy frown. "Ysella, you should not have invited anyone to pay morning calls while Morvoren is so ill, as you well know. That was unforgiveable of you and showed great selfishness. Am I to assume you issued this invitation whilst still in Town, when you could have had no idea whether my wife would overcome her illness?" He took a breath. "For all you knew, you were inviting some jumped-up little fortune-hunting militia officer to call on a house in mourning." His eyes flashed at her in quite a different way to Oliver's.

Ysella's hackles rose. "I admit I suggested that he might call on me down here," she spat. "But I never for a moment though Morvoren might die. I'm sure if he'd heard Morvoren had died, he wouldn't have come. He's not a thoughtless oaf, you know." She very nearly added "like you" and just managed to stop herself in time. "And besides, it was only yesterday that I invited him to call today. When I knew Morvoren was getting better."

That last bit slipped from between her lips without her thinking. She clapped a hand to her mouth as though to hold her words in. Now she'd let the proverbial cat out of the bag. *Bugger it.* She nearly said it out loud but managed to stop herself in time. That would *not* have helped matters.

"You what?" Kit's voice was icy calm. "When, precisely, did you do that?"

In desperation, Ysella sought for some plausible excuse and failed to come up with one. She opened and closed her mouth once or twice, finally pressing her lips together in a thin line of opposition.

"Well?" Kit asked, shifting his position a little and looking more imposing and threatening than ever. "I'm waiting for an explanation." His words hung leaden in the air between them, and Ysella glanced over her shoulder, briefly considering whether flight in tears might be an idea. But he was between her and the house, and how ignominious would it be to be chased after and caught?

Perhaps the truth might be best. Small lies weren't too bad, she reasoned, as Oliver had told one himself, but if she told a big lie now, Kit would know, and it would be far too big for him to forgive. She had to bear in mind that as her legal guardian, he could prevent her from returning to Town when Morvoren was better, and even confine her in her room—behind a locked door—if he had a mind to.

"I, er, I went for a ride yesterday morning. But only after I heard Morvoren's fever had broken." The words tumbled over one another in her haste to get them out before he could interrupt her. "I was so pleased for her and you that I felt a gallop in the fresh air was what I needed. And I've not ridden all the while I've been in London. I didn't intend to meet up with Oliver, I promise you. It was such a surprise when I found him riding through the village."

Kit heaved an angry sigh. "No doubt already on his way here to see you."

Had he been? It hadn't occurred to Ysella to wonder what he was doing out there on their estate so far from his accommodation in Marlborough. Had he been hoping to either call upon them that day, or to see Ysella out riding? Well, if it had been the latter, he'd had his wish. "I'm sure it was just by chance," she said, holding Kit's gaze.

He laughed. Not at all a nice laugh. "Well, you needn't think you're seeing him here again, because you're not. And there are a lot of reasons for that. Firstly, and most importantly, I don't want any visitations at all from eager young beaux while my wife is ill. As I explained to that young man, she needs total peace, and she doesn't need you unburdening yourself to her about your woes.

So don't bother to tell her about this conversation." He paused, his hand reaching out to take hers. "And secondly, I happen to know Featherstone is a friend of Fitz's. Well, for me if not for you, that's no recommendation at all. If he's a friend of Fitz's, then he's no friend of mine."

"Is there a thirdly in your ridiculous list?" Ysella snapped, tugging to free herself from his hold.

Kit nodded. "Thirdly, the man is in the militia, not even the regular army off fighting Boney on the continent. He has no money of his own and he's a fortune hunter, Ysella, and he must be well aware you have a very attractive fortune ready for the picking."

She tugged her hand harder. "Oliver is not like that!"

"*Oliver?*" Kit's eyes narrowed and his voice lowered. "You're on first name terms with him already?"

"So what?" Ysella retorted. "You called Morvoren by her first name before you were married—before you were even engaged."

"And we are married now."

"So?" She couldn't think of a better retort, conscious of the fact that she sounded increasingly like a thwarted, angry child. Possibly even a *spoilt* angry child.

"You seem to have rapidly developed an uncalled-for familiarity with this fortune hunter."

"He's *not* a fortune hunter. And if we're familiar with one another, it's because we *love* each other. And we want to be married." She nearly added "so there" but just managed to stop herself in time. And anyway, that last bit wasn't entirely true as he certainly hadn't asked her yet, nor even mentioned the idea. But he would, of that she was sure.

"You *what?*" Kit's voice, that had been sinking lower and lower, perhaps because he feared some of the servants might be around, suddenly rose. "And when was I, your guardian, to be informed of this?" Still with her hand gripped in his, he gave her whole arm a shake. "Good heavens, Ysella, you've been out scarcely two months and are one of the most eligible girls of the season, with your fortune. And you've set your heart on a nobody in a fancy uniform?"

"You're hurting me."

He released her hand. "Tell me it's not true."

"I won't," Ysella returned. "Because it is. And you can't stop me."

Kit balled his fists. "I think you'll find that I can, until you reach twenty-one, which is not for another two years. And even then, I can make it very difficult for you to marry some nobody."

"Oliver is *not* a nobody, and you are such a snob!" Ysella shouted, forgetful of decorum now. "I hate you, Kit. I hate you. You married someone who was a nobody and so did Papa. So why can't I?"

Kit seemed to lose the last vestiges of his own self-control. Good. "Because neither of us married a cad! Featherstone is a friend of Fitz's and that means he's a rake and a cad, as are all Fitz's friends. He doesn't love you, Ysella; he loves your income."

"Oh, you're such a *pig!*" Resorting to calling him names might not have been such a good idea.

"And you are such a child!"

Ysella stamped her foot. Damn and blast it. Now she was showing him he was right. "Oh, go away!" She spun on her heel and bolted for one of the doors into the house, half expecting him to come running after her. However, no running footsteps sounded on the gravel apart from her own. She flung the door open wide, and galloped for the stairs up to her bedroom.

Which was why she was now lying on her bed crying into her pillow. Kit was so unbearably mean. He didn't want her ever to be happy. He only didn't like Oliver because Oliver knew Fitz. And why didn't he like Fitz? They were cousins, after all. And Fitz was always charm personified. Although, it *had* been one of the revenue men Fitz had been in charge of down in Cornwall who had shot Kit. Maybe that was it. Maybe Kit couldn't forgive Fitz for having been shot.

Only that wasn't true, was it? Because Kit had *never* liked Fitz.

Oh, why were men so unfathomable? Thank goodness Oliver wasn't like that at all. He wore his heart on his sleeve. He'd said he loved her in the Orangery, taken her in his arms, pulled her close and kissed her again just like he'd done yesterday. Only this time it had been better, because they hadn't been on fidgety horses. He'd drawn her close enough that she could feel his heart beating against hers, he'd put his hands in her hair, pressed her face closer to his as his tongue explored her mouth. And she'd touched her tongue to his, too, felt them entwine, wrestle, unite. It had been glorious. And her body had reacted in ways she'd never expected, with shivers of delight running up and down it the more he kissed her.

She stopped crying. That was better. She needed to think only of the nice things in her life. And Oliver was one of them. Kit was not going to keep them apart. What did she care if Oliver needed her inheritance for them to live on? That didn't matter. What mattered was that they should be together. She rolled onto her back, put her hands behind her head, and descended into deep thought.

FROM THE SUMMERHOUSE, Sam had watched the altercation between Ysella and her brother with interest, and deep sympathy for Ysella. His heart was torn. A part of him wanted her to be happy, but another part of him wanted things to stay the same. For her to continue living here at Ormonde so he could continue admiring and loving her from afar. After all, he was just a lowly land agent, son of a land agent and grandson of a tenant farmer. *He* could never have her.

When Ysella flounced off into the house, leaving Kit staring after her, Sam deemed it time to emerge from the summerhouse. Time was getting on, and it might be wise to go home to Mrs. Higgins and leave Ormonde and all its troubles until tomorrow.

He was not to get away so easily. Kit hailed him, and the two young men met in the center of the garden where a small fountain played and goldfish darted between the lilies.

"Can you dine with us tonight?" Kit asked.

Sam bit his lip, his escape to peace and quiet gone, and not at all sure he wanted to be witness to another show of Ysella's temper and Kit's ire. "I'll have to send a message to Mrs. Higgins if I do."

"That's done then," Kit said. "I'll have Bannerman send the kitchen boy down there. I need your company tonight. The company of a sensible man. I've had enough of women, and in particular, flighty girls."

He set off inside, but by a different door to the one Ysella had taken, and Sam followed him in, uneasy and a little unhappy at having to stay and see Ysella again. If only he could take her in his arms and soothe her troubles away for her, but that was never going to happen.

He needn't have worried. Ysella did not appear for dinner, but sent a message down with Martha to say she had a megrim and would stay in her room. The dowager was eating with Morvoren upstairs, so in the end, only Kit and Sam sat down in the dining room at the long table. Sam's place had been set to the right of the head of the table, where Kit sat, so they could converse without having to raise their voices.

After the first course of soup, a side of beef was served, and it was only while they were eating it that Kit broached the subject of Ysella. "If you were in charge of a chit like her," he said, pushing his beef around his plate in a desultory fashion, "would you allow her to marry whom she chose?"

Sam's face flamed as it always did when Ysella was mentioned. As the table was lit only by candles down the center, hopefully Kit wouldn't notice. "I don't know," he said, with diffidence. "I've never been in that position." Nor was he likely to be.

Should he be honest and say no, he would fight Ysella every

step of the way to prevent her from throwing herself away on a cad like Featherstone? Maybe not. Kit had to make his own mind up.

Kit sighed. "I could be wrong, I suppose, and he might truly love her. But he's a friend of Fitz's and all those rumors are attached to him, so what am I to think? I suppose even a cad can fall in love in the end. One thing I do know, though, is that Fitz won't have been able to resist telling Featherstone she has a sizeable dowry just to spite me. Everything he's ever done has been to cause me trouble."

Sam kept silent, not quite so sure that Fitz cared that much about Kit to try to do him harm. Apart, of course, from the time Kit had ended up shot. But that hadn't been by Fitz's own hand, and indeed, Fitz didn't know what had happened to this day.

"She was always a trouble even to Papa, and he died when she was only thirteen," Kit said, setting down his fork. "And ever since I've been her guardian, things have gone from bad to worse. Look at her schooling. She was *expelled*, Sam. A thing I only ever thought happened to the worst of boys. And her escapades in my old clothes, dressed up as a boy. Her forcing Morvoren to teach her to ride astride—in boys' clothes. The time she took a rowing boat out on the lake and it sank and she had to wade neck deep to the side. She would have drowned had it been any deeper. When she fell out of that tree and broke her arm." He sighed again. "I sometimes think she'd have been better off born as a boy."

Sam smiled at the thought, very glad she was a girl. "I don't think that would have made her happy. I think she's happy as a girl but wants the freedom of being able to do the things we boys—men—can do."

Kit laughed, with a hint of bitterness. "I've a baby upstairs in the nursery, and yet I have a child of nineteen I'm also responsible for. Not something I asked for. I suppose I should be glad some numskull has been unwise enough to want to take her on and should let her go. But I can't help but think she won't be happy, and he's only after her for her money. His reputation goes before him."

Sam set down his own fork, his appetite, which had not been large, gone. "For what it's worth, Kit, I think you're right and doing the right thing. She needs a dependable earl or even a baronet, perhaps an upright member of the clergy, to tame her wild ways."

But did she? In his dreams he knew that if he were lucky enough to have her, he would allow her to keep her wild, and undeniably attractive, ways. They were part of her charm, and he loved her for them. But did Oliver? Did Oliver love her at all or was he just after her money as Kit suspected?

Chapter Twelve

SITTING IN HER room, Ysella tumbled thoughts through her mind, searching for a solution to her predicament. For that was how she saw it. She had been thwarted by her brother, and her stubborn streak had no intention of letting him win. She was meant to be with Oliver, and no argument Kit could propound would make her change her mind. What a mean, selfish pig Kit was to treat her in this way.

She had to meet up with Oliver again, but now Kit knew she'd gone riding without a groom in attendance, she was unlikely to get away with that again. He'd be watching her. And he'd have the grooms watching her as well, knowing him. With no one to see, she gave in to the impulse to stamp her foot. Several times. Not even if she were to ride at six in the morning, which in any case would probably still be dark, would she be able to sneak out to meet Oliver. And on top of that, she couldn't hope that Oliver would spend his entire day riding back and forth through the more remote corners of the estate in the hopes she might escape surveillance and join him.

No. She had to get a message to him.

But who could she send? Not Martha, who had already made her disapproval of Oliver obvious and had probably informed Mama about her rendezvous with him in the park in London. The dreadful tattletale would go straight to Mama, or even worse, to Kit, should Ysella entrust her with a missive for her beloved. She had to find some other way of getting in touch with him. At least she knew where he was staying.

Try as she might, however hard she racked her brain, she couldn't come up with any solution. Well, she might as well write him the letter she intended to send, and keep it on her person in case an opportunity arose to send it. That would be an excellent idea.

She sat down at the bureau in her room and opened it. In one of the neat little alcoves resided the rose scented notepaper her dear friend Caroline Fairfield had given her at Christmas. "For writing notes to friends you will make in London, and perhaps to gentlemen admirers," Caroline had said. That would be perfect. She took a sheet and picked up her pen. What to write?

'Deere Oliver, I must apologize for my brothers behavior ~~today~~ yesterday. He is ~~very~~ extremely worrid for his wife, my deerest friend Morvoren, who has been ~~very~~ ill. Or he would not I know have asked you to leeve so presipitusly. He still refuses any callers at all ~~while~~ at the moment, but I am certun he will come around. I have an ideer that I will visit my dressmaker in Marl-bro with my maid and think he will not be so desprut that he will want to acompny me. They are the Missis Segewick in the High Streat. I will come on Wensday at noon. Your Ysella.'

There, that was a good letter. He wouldn't mind the crossings out. Ysella was not the best of communicators by letter, as Morvoren could verify, but she didn't care. She'd said what she wanted to say and arranged a meeting that no one could eavesdrop on. Now to find someone to take the letter to the Castle Inn, and make sure it wasn't that flapjaw Martha who would accompany her on Wednesday. She folded the letter, dripped some sealing wax onto it and when that was dry, carefully wrote Oliver's name and address on the front. *Captin Oliver Feathuston, The Cassle Inn, Marlbro*. Done.

As it happened, luck favored Ysella, and on descending the

stairs the next morning for breakfast, her blighted love not having diminished the hunger caused by having missed dinner the night before, she found a messenger boy waiting at the foot of the stairs.

A quick glance around showed no one else about. "You, boy," she called softly.

The boy, who looked to be a farm boy of about fourteen, turned his head. "Me, Miss?"

Ysella laughed, partly at her good fortune in coming downstairs at the very moment when a useful boy had presented himself and partly at the look of amazement on his face at being accosted by the daughter of the house. That she presented a very pretty countenance, she well knew, and it seemed the boy had noticed.

"Yes, you. I don't see any other boys about, do you?"

The boy fidgeted his feet and, as though his hands had suddenly grown enormous, quickly put them behind his back.

Ysella reached the foot of the stairs, and approached him, fixing her most charming smile on her face and batting her eyelashes at him. "What are you doing here?"

The boy fidgeted still more under her gaze, his cheeks taking on an alarming ruddy hue. "I-I had a message for his lordship. I'm waitin' for a reply... Miss."

Ysella wasn't in the least interested in what the message had been about. Instead, she batted her eyelashes a bit more at the boy, who reddened even further and took a step back as though afraid she might be dangerous.

She followed him, until his back came up against the wainscotting and stopped him from retreating further. "Do you think you could carry a message for me?" she purred, slathering on the charm.

He nodded, eyes big in his rosy-cheeked face.

She stepped back, satisfied. "Perfect. Do you think you can carry a message for me as far as Marlborough? To the Castle Inn?"

The boy hesitated. Marlborough was a long way away for a

boy on foot, and he'd probably be in trouble with whoever had sent him to the Abbey if he was away all day with no explanation for his absence.

Ysella pounced. "I can pay you." She held up her reticule in which she kept her pin money and gave it an encouraging shake. "But… you have to tell no one you've delivered my message. No one at all."

The boy's muddy brown eyes had grown wider at the mention of money. No doubt he was unused to having any of his own if he worked for his father on the estate. Any money he earned would go straight to his family, bypassing his own pockets.

"I c'n do that, Miss," he whispered, as though awareness of the secret nature of his mission had been immediately borne in upon him. He held out a grubby hand, the nails broken and blackened.

Ysella took the note out of her reticule and handed it over to her unlikely Cupid. Rummaging a little deeper, she came out with a handful of coins. Picking through them, she found a threepenny bit and held it up.

The boy's avaricious eyes narrowed a little and he didn't take it. His gaze fixed instead on the pile of coins in Ysella's hand.

Ysella sighed. "Very well, sixpence for you, young man, and you will need to hurry." She chose a second threepenny bit and the boy took the two coins with evident delight.

"Who do I give it to, Miss?"

"It's written on the letter."

His brow furrowed. "I don't read, Miss."

Footsteps sounded in the grand hall. Pressed for time, she leaned forward. Her nose wrinkled at the smell of not-so-clean boy. "Captain Oliver Featherstone, at the Castle Inn. Can you remember that?"

"Cap'n Featherstone. I got it. Mum's the word, Miss." He slipped coins and letter into a pocket in his faded jacket.

Ysella turned away from him to head for the breakfast room and nearly bumped into Kit coming out of the hall. Still angry with him, she flashed him a dark look and swirled past. Food was what she needed next.

Mama was in the breakfast room sipping a cup of coffee.

Flushed with success, Ysella bounced over to her and kissed her on the cheek. "Good morning, Mama."

"You seem in a good mood," Mama remarked, pouring herself more coffee from the silver coffee pot. "Would you like coffee?"

Ysella helped herself to a plate of kedgeree and sat down beside her mother, who poured her a cup of coffee. The kedgeree was mildly spiced just as Ysella liked it. She ate in silence for a short while, thinking.

"Mama?"

"Yes?"

Ysella frowned a little. "When Morvoren was ill, I went to the library and found the family Bible. Derwa once told me about…" Here she hesitated, uncharacteristically wondering if she was being intrusive, but she'd committed herself now and had to continue. "That between Kit and me you'd had… other children. Ones I don't know."

Mama set down her coffee cup and turned to face Ysella. At least she didn't look angry. "So you went to look for them in the family Bible?"

Ysella nodded.

"And did you find them?"

Ysella nodded again.

"And I suppose you want to know what happened to them?"

Ysella bit her lip. "Well… if you don't want to talk about them, don't. But when I found their names in there, with Morvoren being so ill, I promised myself that I'd try to bring them back to life by asking you about them if she got better. And she did. I've been waiting for a moment when I could ask you." She hesitated. "But not if you don't want to talk about them."

Mama frowned for a moment as though considering Ysella's request. "No. You're right. I've not spoken of any of them since they died. Not even with your father. Saying their names out loud and acknowledging their existence won't make them live again, but it will make them live in my memories. Your sisters remember them, I imagine, but I doubt Kit does. He was such a boy, things like that went over his head."

"What happened to them?" Ysella asked, forgetting her plate of food. All she wanted now was to hear the story of the brothers and sisters she'd never had the chance to meet. They were a family of four children, but they should have been nine.

Mama inhaled deeply. "My boy Corentyn was born in 1786, when Kit was only two. Your Papa was over the moon to have a second son, but Corentyn didn't thrive. We never found out what ailed him. Not even Doctor Busick knew. He died in his sleep at three months old."

"You must have been very sad."

Mama nodded. "The pain of losing a child never really leaves you." She pressed her hands to her heart. "It still hurts, right here, but don't worry. I want to tell you about them." She smiled. "Two years after we lost Corentyn another son came along—Gryffyn, we called him. Like Corentyn, he failed to thrive. At least that was what Doctor Busick put as cause of death. He died within ten days of his birth. As did Elowen, the girl born the following year. Your Papa and I began to think we'd been cursed. There seemed no reason that after three healthy children the next three could be so sickly. I began to worry for the children I already had, to think any of them might die at any moment."

Mama's eyes had taken on a faraway look as perhaps she pictured in her mind's eye those children she'd known so briefly. She shook her head. "After Elowen came Melyonen, a girl every bit as pretty as you and your sisters. She lived a little longer, but when Kit and the girls caught scarlet fever, she was too little to fight it off." She smiled, her eyes full of sadness. "She'd be two years older than you, had she survived."

What would it have been like to have had a sister that close to her in age?

"And Peran?"

"Ah yes, little Peran. My tiny, dark-haired Peran. That's what his name means, in the Cornish of my youth. Little dark one. He was born six weeks too early and lived only a day, but he still lives in my heart."

Ysella swallowed down the lump in her throat. "Where are they buried?"

"In the churchyard near your dear Papa's grave. A sad little row. When you came along, so healthy and robust, we didn't dare believe you might live. But you were always a fighter, Ysella, with a strong grip on life. Not like my five lost ones."

Ysella covered her mother's hand with her own. "Thank you for telling me, Mama. I'm glad I know now. I can remember them as well, even if I only know their names."

Mama smiled. "You can be such a sweet, thoughtful girl when you try, my dear. I'm lucky to have you."

A wave of guilt swept over Ysella. Mama wouldn't be saying that if she knew how she planned to go behind Kit's back.

WITH IT BEING only Monday, and two days to go before Wednesday, Ysella left suggesting to Kit that she should visit her dressmakers until Tuesday. In the meantime, she also had the brainwave of telling him she was sorry to lull his suspicious nature.

Congratulating herself on being so clever, she told him later on Monday that he was forgiven, she'd been a silly girl, and he was quite right about Oliver. She even went so far as to tell the same story to Morvoren, although she wasn't sure she'd been believed. As a fellow woman, Morvoren was much harder to gull than Kit. Having to do all this lying stuck in her throat somewhat, but it had to be done. She didn't want Kit suspecting anything when she announced her intention of visiting Marlborough on

Wednesday.

They were taking afternoon tea in the drawing room when she broached the subject. She'd been in to visit her little nephew in the nursery and had spent a happy hour chattering to Morvoren that afternoon, but had steered well clear of the subject of Oliver Featherstone. Let them all think she'd dismissed him from her heart.

"I was thinking, Mama," Ysella said, setting her half-drunk dish of tea down on the table. "I was thinking I might go and see the Misses Sedgewick and ask them to make some new gowns for little George. He can't go on wearing mine and Kit's hand-me-downs forever, and I'm being very slow with the gown I've been stitching."

Mama, who seemed not to have been party to Kit's diatribe about Oliver, thank goodness, smiled. "That sounds a nice idea, my darling. I'd come with you, only I want to stay with Morvoren. I feel she needs me still. Doctor Busick has said she can have George with her for a while each day now, and someone needs to be with her for that as she's still so weak."

"That's quite all right," Ysella said with a mix of magnanimity and relief. "I can take Martha with me. She likes a visit to the dressmakers." She dimpled, at her sweetest and most obliging, or so she wanted Mama and Kit to think. "I promised to buy her a new mob cap with lace finishings as she's so very good at styling my hair. As a present, that is. A treat for her. She's very keen to have it." Not quite true, but she could buy her one anyway, if necessary. In fact, she made a mental note to do just that to give credence to her story.

Kit, who'd been eating a slice of Cook's best Madeira cake, set down his crumb covered plate. He raised his eyebrows. "Just gowns for George?"

Ysella turned her innocent gaze on him. "Well, I *would* very much like a new gown of my own for when I return to Town, if that's agreeable to you, Kit. I have a picture of the one I fancy, and I'm sure the Misses Sedgewick could produce it for me. I've had invitations to so many balls and soirées, some of which of course I'll miss while I'm down here, that I need more gowns. One can't be seen out in the same gown twice. And when I get back, I fully intend to make the most of all my invitations. And I'd like to go to Almack's." She folded her hands in her lap, as demure as anyone could wish for in a sister. "Perhaps you'd like to come with me and give me some advice on what is á la mode at the moment?"

Mama snorted with laughter. "Whatever makes you think Kit will be able to advise you on that? Anyone less interested in fashion would be hard to find. Martha will serve you better, as I'm sure I've seen her reading your fashion pamphlets. If she can style your hair as well as she does, she'll be well able to help you choose the fabric for a new dress."

"And you don't mind the expense?" Ysella continued, determined to flesh out her excuse for a visit to Marlborough. "My pin money won't stretch that far."

Kit smiled. Was he fooled? He should be, as she was always after new gowns. "Of course, you can have a new gown. And thank you for thinking of little George. I've been too busy myself to think of ordering him anything."

"He's doing very well in your own old nightgowns," Mama said, with a hint of reprimand. "He can wait a bit longer for things to call his own."

"Nonsense," Ysella said, hammering home her advantage. "I spoke to Morvoren earlier, and she told me she wants all new things for George. She's happy for now that there are our old baby clothes, but she wants new ones. She told me she wants George to be the best dressed baby in Wiltshire." She smiled sweetly at Kit again so he wouldn't guess she'd just made this all up. "She just wishes she could choose them herself."

He smiled back. Yes. Fooled. Men were so easy to dupe. "Well, in that case don't buy too many, so when she's on her feet again she can choose some herself."

Ysella dimpled, satisfied with her ruse. "I shan't. Don't worry."

Chapter Thirteen

WITH PART OF her plan already in motion, all Ysella had to do now was get rid of that tattletale Martha, who, if they met up with Oliver in Marlborough, would undoubtedly report back to Mama and Kit.

"Tell me, Martha, how is your sister?" Ysella asked on Wednesday morning, when Martha brought in her breakfast tray, knowing full well that Martha's sister was in the same condition Morvoren had so recently been in, but in nowhere near such favorable circumstances.

Martha set the tray, containing toast and hot chocolate, Ysella's favorites, on her mistress's knee. "Finding it hard, Miss Ysella. What with the twins under her feet all the time and Joe out all day in the fields." Martha's sister, who'd once worked in the Abbey as a maid, was married to a tenant farmer and lived out beyond the village at the far end of the estate.

"Do you think she might like a basket of food from our kitchens?" Ysella asked, pretending an interest in her toast. "Something to make her feel a little pampered. A few special delicacies. And perhaps we could make a parcel of some of Kit's old clothes for the twins. They're out of petticoats now, aren't they?"

Martha nodded. "She would be that pleased, Miss Ysella. And the clothes'd come in right handy, seeing as how hard it is to keep those boys neat and tidy."

Ysella smiled inwardly while outwardly keeping an expression of earnest commiseration. "Then let's go along to the schoolroom after breakfast and have a look in those chests of old clothes. I'm certain there will be plenty to choose from. Some of my brother's childhood boots as well. And then, if you like, you can walk over there today with the clothes and food, and visit your sister. I'm sure she'd be very pleased to see you." She paused, pleased with her subterfuge. "Some flowers from the Orangery as well, I think, and we can ask one of the gardeners what fruit is ripe for the picking. No need for you to hurry back. Spend some time with her while you can. Don't worry about me. I can get Ellen to come and serve as my maid today."

Martha beamed at her. "Ooh, thank you kindly, Miss Ysella. I'll be sure and tell my sister 'twas you that sent everything over for her. She'll be that happy to have shoes for the twins. She says they wear them out something rotten now they're running about outside all the time."

Sorted. Ysella congratulated herself on her own perspicacity.

She and Martha spent the next half hour, after Ysella had dressed, rummaging through the contents of the chests in the schoolroom and finding the smallest of Kit's old clothes. There were indeed several useful pairs of his old boots and shoes, still with quite a lot of wear in them. Some boot blacking would soon have them looking as good as new. A grateful Martha, who was fond of her sister, parceled these up, along with the tiny breeches, shirts, stockings and jackets, in brown paper tied with string.

Once this was dealt with, Ysella accompanied Martha to the kitchens and organized the filling of a wicker basket with fruit, a large ham, jars of jams and jellies, a tub of thick cream and anything else she could think of until the basket was so full Martha was going to have a job carrying it all that way. The kitchen boy returned from the Orangery with a suitably colorful and flamboyant bouquet, and Ysella waved Martha on her way with a feeling of deep satisfaction and no guilt whatsoever. Then, with Ellen, one of the younger housemaids, in tow, she returned to her bedroom.

Once inside, she closed the door. "Now, Ellen," she said to the overawed girl whom she'd specially picked for her mousey countenance and matching biddable nature. "I am going into Marlborough to the dressmakers today, and I want you to come with me as I've given Martha the day off. But…" she fixed the timid Ellen, who was only about fifteen, with a hard stare. "I need you to be the soul of discretion. Can you be?"

Ellen's pale brow furrowed in confusion. "You want me to be what, Miss?"

Ysella sighed. "I mean I don't want you to tell anyone about today." She leaned closer. "Not even if they *interrogate* you."

"Interrogate me?"

"Demand you answer their questions. Shout at you. That sort of thing."

Ellen's brown eyes opened wide as saucers and she nodded, but with a definite hint of fear on her face. Hopefully, she was more afraid of Ysella's displeasure than she was of the threat of being interrogated, which probably wouldn't happen anyway. What a good idea it had been to dispose of Martha and replace her with a more biddable servant. Much as Ysella was fond of Martha, who'd been with her for a number of years now, she did have an annoying habit of behaving like Mama.

"The first thing we have to do," Ysella announced, going to the wardrobe, "is find me a much more suitable gown. Which one do you think will be most becoming?" She flicked a white gown embroidered with small yellow daisies out of the wardrobe and held it up to her body, glancing from her reflection in the cheval mirror to Ellen's nervous face. "This one or the one with roses on it?" She raised her eyebrows at Ellen. "Well?"

"They're both lovely, Miss Ysella," Ellen muttered.

Ysella flung the daisy dress down on her bed and whipped out the one with roses on it. Both gowns were not quite suitable for a morning trip to town, being practically sleeveless and very low cut. But as she was going to be disguising what she wore under a spencer, that wouldn't matter. And she wanted to be wearing a pretty gown to meet Oliver. "I'll wear the one with the roses," she declared. "With the red spencer. Put the daisy one away again and help me out of this boring old dress."

Ellen, whom Ysella had recruited twice in the past to stand in for Martha when she'd been ill, at least knew what to do for a lady. Unlike the first time when she'd had to be taught every little thing. She soon had Ysella out of her plain day dress and was helping her into the much prettier rose embroidered dress, a little hampered by Ysella repeatedly wanting to admire herself in the cheval glass. But it was done at last, and Ysella stood regarding her reflection with satisfaction. Let Oliver see her in this, and he would be hers. He'd want to make an offer for her straightaway. Surely Kit couldn't turn him away if he came cap in hand and humble? He was an officer, after all, and being the son of a bishop made him quite acceptable in society. Better than Meliora's stuffy old solicitor husband, for certain.

Martha had done Ysella's hair for her that morning, so all that now remained was to don her spencer and bonnet, pull on her gloves and descend the stairs to the front hall. And hopefully not encounter the prying eyes of either Mama or Oliver, who might notice the skirts of her dress below her spencer and comment on her choice being an odd one for a visit to Marlborough.

For once, Ysella was in luck. With Ellen trailing behind her, she negotiated the stairs and hallway without incident, and Albert the footman opened the front door to let them out. The barouche was waiting in the drive, with James on the driver's seat and another groom waiting to fold up the steps after she got in. Resisting the urge to hurry, she stepped with dainty decorum into the carriage and settled her skirts around her under the raised hood.

Ellen, who must never have ridden in the barouche before, got in with a lot more diffidence and perched her bottom on the seat opposite Ysella. Her eyes, if it were possible, went wider than before, reminding Ysella of Dash and Duster when they were begging for tidbits. If it rained, which Ysella hoped it would not, she'd have to let Ellen come and sit beside her under the hood.

The groom jumped up on the back step, James flicked his whip and clicked his tongue, and the barouche moved off.

For the first ten minutes, until they reached the gatehouse onto the road that marked the edge of the Ormonde estate, Ysella contented herself with sitting in silence, considering how she was to effect time on her own with Oliver.

Ellen, on the other hand, stared about herself in such amazement Ysella began to wonder if the poor girl had ever been outside the estate boundary. But Ellen's education in the wider world was not important. Ysella had other things to consider.

Part of Ysella's hastily hatched plan involved Ellen's complicity, so as they left Ormonde behind and headed for the Old Bath Road, she patted the seat beside her, inviting Ellen to sit in the capacious shelter of the hood.

Ellen settled beside her with some diffidence, and as soon as she'd done so, Ysella reached out and took her thin hand in hers. "Now, Ellen," she said, plastering on her most winning smile. "I am going to need your help."

THE MISSES SEDGEWICK, Honoria and Lucinda, two ladies who might have been cut from the same forbiddingly austere cloth, beamed with toothy delight when Ysella entered their shop. Like a couple of crows, all their plumage was black, a sharp contrast to the shelves of brightly colored silks and satins that adorned their shop.

At the very back, in the gloom furthest from the shop window, sat the row of little apprenticed seamstresses who did most of the work. Morvoren had once persuaded Kit to help the families of these girls, all of them younger than Ysella, with a gift of food when they'd produced her very first ball gown. Perhaps

Ysella, too, might send them some food if they produced the gown she wanted. Not that her main purpose was to purchase a new gown, but there was no harm in getting one anyway, as that would add color to her story. Kit would be most surprised, and probably suspicious, if she came back without having ordered one.

"I'm afraid I don't have much time today," she said, her gaze sliding to the door. Would Oliver dare to come right into the shop to find her? Not many men liked to dally in a women's dressmakers. Although Kit had never been bothered about doing so. If Oliver did, though, she didn't want to be still taken up with choosing her gown. "Perhaps you could show me the latest fabrics you have in stock?" She had a picture of the gown she wanted folded in her reticule. "I have the design here."

Oliver had made no appearance by the time Ysella had selected a peacock blue satin. She held up the picture she'd brought. "Like this, with embroidery around the hem and on the bodice in a slightly paler shade of blue. That will be perfect."

Miss Honoria made a show of measuring Ysella again, although they well knew her measurements as they'd made all her gowns for her first season.

"A fan to match, and slippers?" Miss Lucinda asked, holding up the suggested fan.

Ysella nodded, throwing yet another anxious glance towards the door. What if he wasn't coming? What if that dreadful boy had just gone off with his sixpence and thrown her letter away? It would be just like a boy to have done that. Oliver might have given up on her and returned to London to look for some other young lady to pay his attentions to. She might never see him again.

"And you said a layette for the new little heir?" Miss Honoria said. "How many gowns do you require?"

"Um, four," Ysella said, plucking a number out of the air. "Bonnets too. Slips, bootees, several shawls." What else did babies need? She should have paid more attention during her trips to the nursery. "Napkins?" So long as she didn't have to sew any of it, she'd be happy.

Wait. Was that Oliver strolling across the wide street in the direction of the shop. "I think that will do," Ysella gabbled in her haste to be finished. "Please add all this to my brother's account. I must go now." And with that, she swept out of the shop with the timorous Ellen trailing in her wake.

Oliver met her on the wide pavement outside. "Why, Miss Carlyon," he said with a bow. "How unexpected it is to meet you here."

Ysella beamed at him. "It's quite all right, Oliver. Ellen knows everything. She won't say a thing. I sent Martha to visit her sister, as she couldn't be relied upon not to report back to my mother and brother."

His smile became a grin, his eyes hot with a passion that set Ysella's impressionable heart a-pounding. "Well, in that case, perhaps you'd like to take my arm and we'll stroll along the street with your maid in attendance. All very respectable."

Ysella took his arm with relish, and, with Ellen trailing the ten paces behind Ysella had instructed, they made their way down the wide main street towards the western end of town.

"I didn't think you'd be able to come," Oliver said, after a few moments, keeping his voice low despite the distance between them and Ellen.

"I wasn't sure I'd be able to either. But everything fell into place just when I needed it to. Kit thinks I came to order a new gown and baby clothes for his new heir."

"And did you?"

She chuckled. "Of course I did. I'm not stupid. He'd be bound to notice if the gown and baby things don't turn up in a few days."

Oliver covered her hand with his. "I'm sure your new gown will be most becoming." He paused. "Although, of course, you need nothing like that to make your appearance attractive to me."

A little wriggle of excitement shivered through Ysella's stomach and descended. What was this feeling she was having in a part of her that was so private she didn't even have a name for it? How was being with Oliver making her feel like that? Whatever it was, she was very much enjoying it.

"You will have the opportunity to see my new gown when I return to Town," she said, trying to avoid thinking about that disturbing sensation. "I'm sure we'll be able to go back there soon. Every day, Morvoren seems improved. And little George is thriving."

Oliver sighed. "But if you go back to Town, you're going to meet some rich earl or duke and he's going to sweep you off your feet, and you'll forget all about your poor captain." His expression changed from one of longing to one that resembled Kit's spaniel, all big sad eyes. Rather disturbingly, it reminded Ysella sharply of the way Ellen had looked at her earlier.

"Of course, I won't," she retorted. "It's you I love." She stopped. Should she have said that? Was it not ill-mannered to declare yourself like that to a gentleman? Although he had already said it to her, after he'd kissed her so passionately in the Orangery before Kit came along and interrupted them. But she hadn't been sure he'd meant it, back then, or she might have said it herself to him in return. And Kit's angry words had lodged a greater doubt in her head.

Oliver stopped dead and turned to face her. "Can I believe my ears? You love me? I could scarcely dare hope that you might reciprocate my feelings." He took both her hands in his, clasping them to his chest. His dark eyes brimmed with a hot passion that made Ysella's toes curl with excitement in her elegant slippers.

However, her eyes flicked sideways, conscious they were making a spectacle of themselves and all the world could be watching. Or at the very least, someone who might report back to Kit. Was Oliver going to say he loved her again? Kit's declaration that Oliver didn't love her and only wanted her for her considerable dowry rang in her head. If only he would say the words again. That would dispel the doubt Kit's scorn for him had roused in her head.

Her wish was granted. "Ysella, I love you too. I could want nothing better than for you to be my wife. As soon as possible."

There it was. He'd asked her. He wanted her to be his wife. If she hadn't been standing in the street she might have jumped up and down with excitement and maybe squealed as well.

Instead, she gazed up into his eyes and found herself lost in their dark, passionate depths. Of course he loved her. No doubt could exist about that. Kit was quite mistaken and very mean. A mean pig of a brother who didn't want her to be happy, and who wanted to boss her about for the rest of her life. Oliver loved her, and she loved Oliver. Of course she wanted to marry him. "And I want to be your wife too." The words came out as a hushed whisper, for fear Ellen, still ten paces away and staring into a shop window, might overhear.

He glanced from side to side. They were outside a hat shop opposite the town hall. "Ysella Carlyon. Will you marry me? I'd go down on one knee if that wouldn't attract the attention of all and sundry."

"Oh, yes, yes, yes." This time she couldn't stop herself from bouncing up and down with excitement. "I will, I will, I will." Then her face fell. "But you'll have to ask Kit's permission, and I fear very much that he will say no." She frowned. "He seems to have taken against you due to your association with my cousin Fitz." She certainly wasn't about to share with Oliver all that Kit had accused him of. "He's never liked Fitz, although I don't know why. He's always been perfectly charming to me."

Oliver's eyes narrowed, as though he might be assessing her and the situation. "If you're right," he said, a hint of wariness in his tone, "and your brother is so against our marrying, then, perhaps..." He hesitated. "Perhaps we could... elope."

"Elope?" In one of Ysella's favorite romantic novels, the young heroine had eloped with her suitor to Gretna Green, so she knew all about eloping, and how romantic it was. But to do it herself? Should she? Was it quite the done thing for him to ask her to do it? On the other hand, the idea did sound terribly exciting and romantic. That someone should love her so much to want to do that.

She frowned. "But isn't Gretna Green in *Scotland*? And isn't that a terribly long way away? Further even than London or Cornwall?" She had very little idea of the geography of Great Britain.

Oliver nodded, starting to walk again. They were nearing where his inn was located at the far end of the street from the dressmakers'. "If we can make it to Scotland, we won't need your brother's permission to marry, and we won't need the banns to be called or a special license. The law is different in Scotland, and Gretna Green is the first place we'll come to when we cross the border. I believe the blacksmith there performs the ceremony."

"The blacksmith?" That didn't sound quite so romantic. But... eloping with a handsome suitor just like a heroine out of one of her romantic novels. The thought that it would teach Kit a lesson surfaced. *Haha.* She'd have outwitted him. They both would have, and it would be too late to change things then. She'd be married and have control of her fortune. And Kit would never be able to tell her what to do again.

Of course, Kit *might* follow her, but he had Morvoren, who was still so delicate, to care for, so he might not. She peeped up at Oliver from behind her lashes. "Very well. We shall elope, if that is what you think is best. But I think we had better do this as soon as we can, before Kit feels he can leave his wife safely to chase after us. We should leave as soon as possible."

What an adventure this would be, and Kit would be unable to stop them. The more she thought about it, the more enamored of the idea she became. Yes. She would elope with handsome Oliver and marry him at Gretna Green. And they would live happily ever after.

Chapter Fourteen

OLIVER RETURNED TO the Castle Inn, and Ysella, barely able to conceal her excitement, and Ellen rejoined James and the barouche when he brought it round to the dressmakers' shop. Ysella had called in at the haberdasher's near the Castle and bought the mob cap she'd told Kit she was going to buy for Martha. That had been a last-minute purchase, as she'd nearly forgotten about it. She also bought a length of wide blue ribbon to give to Ellen as a reward for her silence. A bribe, perhaps. Overjoyed at her luck, Ellen promised absolute silence about Ysella's clandestine meeting with Oliver. After all, Ysella told herself, there was practically nothing to tell, anyway, as Ellen couldn't possibly have heard their whispered plans.

Back at Ormonde, Ysella went to great pains to describe to Mama all her purchases, although Kit, whom she'd really wanted to tell, was conspicuous by his absence at luncheon. "He's eating upstairs with Morvoren," Mama said. "I had a tray sent up for them. She's a little stronger today, but Doctor Busick wants her to stay in bed another week."

"I ordered some beautiful baby gowns for George," Ysella expanded as they nibbled dainty sandwiches together in the drawing room. Luncheon was never a large meal.

Mama seemed delighted at Ysella's interest in the baby, and the conversation drifted to her reminiscences of when her own children had been that little, which, now the floodgates had been opened, brought more confidences about the lost children. Somehow, today, Ysella didn't want to hear about them for fear their tale made Mama too sad. And her, as well. She managed to turn the conversation towards lighter tales of when she herself had been a small child.

A tiny pang of guilt assaulted her, though, as she listened to fond reminiscences of her naughtinesses, which seemed to be all Mama could remember, as though she'd never been well behaved. Of course, she'd always known how much Mama loved her, but these little stories brought it home with a jolt. Tomorrow morning, when Ysella's absence was discovered, Mama was going to be distraught. Might it bring back to her the loss of her other children? Ysella surprised herself with her own insight.

Could she do that to Mama? The sandwich she'd been nibbling turned to dry sawdust in her mouth. Was she not doing a very selfish thing, running off like this?

"Ysella," Mama said, calling her back to the moment. "Is something wrong? You're not eating and are looking quite pale."

Ysella hastily popped the remains of her sandwich into her mouth, chewed a moment and swallowed. It went down like a lump of lead. "Nothing's wrong." Why was that lump lodged in her throat? It couldn't be the sandwich as she'd swallowed that. She forced a smile. "I'm perfectly fine."

Mama's expression said she didn't believe her.

Ysella took a small cake. "I think I'll go up and see little George in the nursery after luncheon." Anything to distract Mama's gimlet gaze, because if she wasn't careful, she was going to cry, and that was silly. Why would her decision to elope with the man she loved be bringing tears to her eyes and that lump to her throat? Ridiculous.

It worked. Mama smiled. "Every time I go to see him, he's changed a little. Jessie's little girl is thriving as well, which is good to see. What good fortune it was that she should have been born on the same day as George. Morvoren told me it's very important for a baby to have the first milk a mother produces." She frowned. "Something about something she called 'antibodies.' She does have such a lot of surprising scientific knowledge for a young lady."

Ysella smiled and nodded, catastrophe averted.

WHEN SHE WENT upstairs after luncheon was finished, she found George was not in the nursery. Nanny told her she'd find him in Morvoren's room, so she walked along the corridor, knocked, and went inside.

Loveday was bustling about tidying, while Morvoren sat up in bed, supported by many pillows, with George sleeping in her arms.

Ysella paused in the doorway taking in this delightful scene, the realization washing over her that she would be abandoning both Morvoren and George this very night, and possibly not seeing them again for some time. If Kit were very vexed, possibly not for years. A nub of indecision formed in Ysella's heart. Could she really give all this up? Was she ready for the changes being married to Oliver would necessitate? Had she made the right decision in agreeing to elope with him? Was she not being a tad impetuous? Perhaps, even now, she could persuade Kit to favor the match and accept Oliver's suit for her, and then she would have no need to abandon her family until the wedding, and afterwards would be able to visit whenever she wanted.

"Ysella," Morvoren called. "Come, sit beside the bed and tell me about your morning."

Ysella closed the door and did as she was told, perching on the edge of the chair by the bed. "Nothing much to report," she said, forcing a cheery smile. "I went into Marlborough to order a new dress. And I ordered some delightful baby gowns for George." She'd been going to say that when Morvoren was better, they could go in together and choose some more, but had to stop herself. When Morvoren was better, she would be married to Oliver and living who knew where. A sobering thought.

Morvoren sighed. "How lucky you are. I can't wait to be up and about again. Doctor Busick insists that I stay in bed, but I'm not sure that's such a good idea." She sighed. "I can't wait to be back on my feet again and able to look after George myself."

"And ride with me," Ysella said, before she thought. Another thing she was going to miss. Why was she only now thinking of all this? When she'd agreed to elope, none of this had crossed her mind, but now Oliver wasn't with her, she wasn't even sure she still wanted to run off with him. Not if it meant leaving all this behind.

Morvoren nodded. "I have missed my rides with you. Particularly the ones when we were wearing our breeches." She put out a hand and patted Ysella's hand. "Those were the most fun."

Ysella bit her lip. Would she ever be able to ride out again in breeches? Was Oliver the sort of man who would disapprove of his wife doing something like that? And where would they be living? The notion that neither of them had discussed this seared through her brain like a hot knife. As far as she knew, Oliver had not looked further ahead than a marriage ceremony conducted by a smelly blacksmith on the Scottish borders. She certainly hadn't up until this point. A hollow formed in her stomach.

"Are you all right?" Morvoren asked. "You look like you're miles away."

Ysella started. "Yes, yes. I'm quite fine. Just dreaming about riding astride again one day soon." She managed a smile. "I'm sure you'll be well enough for that before long." There, none of her reply had been a lie. She didn't want to have to lie to Morvoren.

Morvoren sighed. "I hope so. I'm so fed up with being confined to my bed." She looked down at George's sleeping face. "Although I'm very glad to have George in my arms at last."

Ysella stroked the baby's soft downy cheek. "I have to say, he does seem to be a particularly beautiful baby."

Morvoren nodded. "Although we are perhaps a little biased." She looked up. "But aren't you looking forward to your return to London to finish the season? I feel so guilty that you're missing so many balls because of me." She smiled. "I'm sure you'll find yourself another handsome gentleman. You're so pretty and vivacious. How can any man not be smitten by you?" She patted Ysella's hand. "I'm so glad you saw sense about that young man who was here the other day. If he's a friend of Fitz's, he can't be a true gentleman. Although, Loveday did tell me that she peeked at him over the bannisters and he looked very handsome and quite the dandy."

Heat rose to Ysella's cheeks. "He is indeed very handsome," she said, fidgeting a little. "But Kit doesn't like him and I have seen him for what he is, as you know."

Morvoren nodded. "Very sensible of you."

Ysella, who'd been gazing down at the baby, raised her eyes. "I just hope Kit won't take against any other suitor who pays me attention. Fitz has a wide circle of friends, so there's a risk any young gentleman might be a friend of his. I do feel it's a little unfair to take against a person just because they happen to know someone you don't like." She paused, conscious of the fact that she was somewhat contradicting what she'd said to Morvoren after Oliver's visit.

Morvoren pursed her lips. "Well, you know Kit doesn't like Fitz. So he's bound to think that any friend of his would be similar."

"But that's unfair too. I like Fitz. Mama likes Fitz. Why can't Kit?"

Morvoren shrugged. "He *is* a terrible rake, which you told me yourself. And you know he was in charge of the raids on the smugglers down in Cornwall which led to Kit being shot. He's not at all popular in Cornwall, which I've heard is why he's back in London."

Ysella managed a giggle that sounded false even to her, choosing to ignore the bit about leading the revenue men. "But being a rake is part of what makes him so charming. He's a dreadful flirt, but you know he doesn't mean it because he's so candid about having to find an heiress with a fortune. So you just don't take him seriously."

Morvoren shifted the baby's position slightly, as though her arm might be aching, her brow furrowing. "Does it not occur to you that perhaps Captain Featherstone has a similar need? And that is why he has been pursuing you. You said you've decided Kit was right. Have you changed your mind again?"

She said it so gently, unlike Kit with his blustering and shouting, Ysella was almost lulled into betraying herself. "I-I don't know. Perhaps. No. I don't know. I'm all confused." She shook her head, aware that if she wasn't careful, she was going to put her foot well and truly in it. She had to think clearly. "But I don't care anymore. It's of no interest to me. I shall never see Ol— Captain Featherstone again, I expect. Kit was right about him." Better make sure Morvoren wouldn't start to suspect she hadn't been honest the other day and wasn't being entirely honest now.

"Although he is—was—very handsome, and I did fancy myself a little in love with him." She tilted her head to one side. "I know now that I need to listen to those who know better, like you and Kit and Mama."

Morvoren's skeptical expression worried her. Had she laid the contrition on too thickly?

"Are you sure you're not still a little bit in love with him?" Morvoren probed.

Ysella groped for a response that wouldn't give her away, and that might match what she'd just said. How hard it was to fence words with a friend who knew her so well. "He told me he loved me," she tried. "And I believed him. I thought it wouldn't matter if he had no money of his own, as I have my dowry coming to me." Had she said too much? "But of course, none of that counts now, as I've told Kit I shan't see him again. Just as Kit wants." She bestowed a small frown on Morvoren. "But you must promise not to tell any of this to Kit. I don't want him to know Oliver said he loved me."

Morvoren returned the frown. "Do you expect me to keep secrets from my husband?"

"Well… I suppose not. I don't want you to *lie* to him. Perhaps just don't tell him unless he expressly asks? That wouldn't be keeping secrets, would it?"

"That's as may be. I'm not at all sure I approve of that young man. Captain Featherstone. I think Kit may well be right about him."

Not Morvoren as well. Ysella's heart sank. "Kit forbade him from coming here while you're convalescing. So I shan't be seeing him." Now she *was* lying. "But when I return to Town, when you're recovered, Kit won't be able to stop me from seeing him occasionally at balls." Her lower lip jutted. "He won't be able to stop him from dancing with me. And dancing with a gentleman doesn't mean I'm in love with him."

Morvoren patted her hand. "I thought you just said you'd never see him again. No, it doesn't matter. I understand how confused you must be feeling. You're young and you're impetuous, and it's only reasonable you should kick over the traces. And you're right. Kit won't be able to prevent you from dancing with the captain. But you must be sensible, Ysella, which I know you can be. Kit has told me some bad things about Captain Featherstone."

Ysella nodded, attempting to school her features into those of a wise and contrite young woman. It hurt to have to lie to Morvoren, but if she knew what she and Oliver had planned, she'd surely betray her to Kit.

SAM WAS IN his office going over the receipts for some of the new mechanized farm equipment Kit had ordered, when the door opened and his employer came in, a frown on his face. He'd clearly been out riding, as he still had his whip in his hand, which he was tapping with vigor against his leg.

"Good day," Sam said, laying down the papers and leaning back in his seat. "What can I do for you?"

Kit sat down with a thump in the chair on the other side of the desk. "I don't know." A scowl darkened his face. "I have a restlessness about me that I can't pin down." He looked up. "As though I'm waiting for something bad to happen."

Sam steepled his fingers. "If you're worried about Morvoren, I don't think you need be. And I gather little George is in rude health. Jessie Jenkins is proving to be a wonderful wetnurse. And having her live here is probably a wise move, although I daresay her husband isn't best pleased." He chuckled.

Kit shook his head. "I'm more than recompensing him for his troubles, and Jessie is being well-fed so she can produce as much milk as possible. It can't be easy feeding two babies." He crossed his legs and laid his whip across his lap. "I don't think it's Morvoren I'm so agitated about. I think it's Ysella."

"In what way?" Sam asked, cold tendrils creeping across his skin, yet warm blood rushing to his face, as it did every time Ysella was mentioned.

"Well, the trouble is, I just don't know," Kit replied, shaking his head. "She's being just too damned *good*, and it doesn't seem natural. Not like her at all. Mama suggested she might be sickening for something. I hope not. We've had enough sickness in this house and she'd have to be kept away from Morvoren and George in case she passed it on to them."

"I haven't heard of any outbreaks of sickness amongst your tenants."

"Neither have I. So it has to be something else. When that girl goes quiet, she's usually plotting something. I know her all too well."

Sam sucked in his lips. "She could just be missing London.

After the excitement of going to balls every week, Ormonde with no visitors must seem very tame to her."

"Or she's missing that cad. Even though she swore to me to have nothing more to do with him."

Sam's blood ran colder still. "That's true." Oh, how he wished it wasn't.

"But I sent him packing. Told him he couldn't visit while Morvoren is recovering, so, hopefully he's returned to London with his tail between his legs in search of a new heiress to dangle after. I hope he tries his hand with a tradesman's daughter—that's more in his line. A tradesman would be glad of an army officer and the son of a bishop for a son-in-law and probably overlook that he's a fortune-hunting cad. He's not good enough for the sister of a viscount." He laughed. "Call me a snob if you will, but I'd far rather see my sister wed to an honest Cornish tin miner than I would that man. There's something about him that rings false, officer or not. He's no gentleman."

Sam's heart did a small leap. If Kit was prepared to see Ysella married to a miner in place of Featherstone, might that mean his own suit would not be disdained? No. A faint hope. Whatever Kit said, he would want Ysella to marry well, preferably to a man with his own country house for her to run, and a title to his name. Surely? And besides this, Ysella would never love him. She'd bestowed her heart, if Kit's suspicions were correct and she'd been gulling them, on a ne'er-do-well rake. And he, Sam, had lost her forever.

Chapter Fifteen

FACED WITH THE problem of how to escape Martha's scrutiny yet again, Ysella racked her brain to find some way of getting rid of her that night. She needed the gullible and easily bribed Ellen, who would probably think everything Ysella wanted to do just an exciting adventure. Which it was, or so she kept telling herself. She pushed away the nagging whisper that it might be a hotheaded and irresponsible thing to do that would upset Mama far more than she wanted. No. She determined to see it only as an adventure.

As she changed for dinner that evening, Ysella peeked up at Martha who was arranging her hair with her usual precision into an artless and natural tumble of curls. The new lacy mob cap sat proudly on Martha's sandy hair. "You're looking a little tired, Martha, if you don't mind me saying so." Ysella patted her own hair and gazed into the mirror.

"Well, I suppose I am a bit, Miss," Martha, who'd had her customary half day off that day, agreed. "I walked over to my sister's again, and that's quite a long way. I found her house was all topsy turvy. *Again*. I spent most of my time over there cleaning for her while she was laid in bed like a princess telling me her ankles were all swollen so she couldn't get up. Those boys of hers were running wild."

Ysella groped for her limited knowledge of pregnancy, as

gleaned from Morvoren. "Is she very large and uncomfortable?"

Martha nodded, dusting powder over Ysella's pale cheeks. "She thinks as it might be another set of twins. And her husband's no help. If he's not out in the fields, then he's in The White Hart till all hours. So she told me, anyway. She's not best pleased with him, and I don't blame her. He could keep those boys in line a bit better than he does."

Perfect.

"You poor thing, having to spend your day off working." Ysella, who'd never done a day's work in her life, put up a hand to pat Martha's. "I tell you what. Why don't you take the rest of the evening off. You can send that silly girl Ellen up to do my evening toilette. She won't be as good as you, but I can tolerate her for just the one night, I suppose. And it's important to me that you get some rest."

Martha put down the hare's foot she'd been using for the face powder. "Well, if you're sure it won't inconvenience you. Thank you very much for that, Miss Ysella. I have to admit, it'll be a blessing to get off my feet after all that walking. You're sure Ellen won't be a nuisance?"

Ysella wrinkled her nose. Martha mustn't get the idea that she could be dispensed with and not missed, or she'd never get rid of her. No. What was she thinking? After tonight she wasn't going to need Martha ever again. Unless, of course, she took her with her to her new home with Oliver. She *would* be needing a lady's maid, after all, and better the one she already knew.

"Not at all. Ellen's not like a *proper* lady's maid, like you, of course, but I won't need much this evening. I'm sure I can take her in hand. You go off and get some rest. Soak your feet in a bowl of hot water." Papa had been wont to do that after a day's shooting, in front of the fire in the library, much to Mama's annoyance.

Martha made her a little, appreciative bob and stepped back. "All done, Miss. You look beautiful, if I might venture to say so."

Ysella stood up and smiled, nurturing her secret in her heart like the nub of a fire. "Thank you, Martha. Off you go now, and don't forget to remind Ellen she'll have to come up later."

AFTER DINNER, YSELLA had to accompany Mama and Kit into the drawing room for at least a modicum of time to keep them thinking everything was normal. Dashing off upstairs to her room would look most odd. She took a seat on one of the stiffly upholstered settees and picked up her sewing, just to have something in her hands. If she didn't, she'd be fidgeting so much one of them would be bound to notice. Kit poured some port and passed a glass to Mama, who was very fond of that particular drink.

The evening crawled. Mama asked her if she'd play the piano, but after a few tentative tunes which she muffed on almost every line, suggested, with a hard stare, that she should desist and come and sit quietly instead.

"I must ask you again, Ysella," she said, her anxious gaze resting on Ysella's face in a most disconcerting manner. "Are you ill?"

Ysella's heart thundered in a manner that might have made Mama think she was indeed sickening for something had she but tried to take Ysella's pulse. "I'm quite well, thank you, Mama." Was she giving herself away? She needed to surreptitiously take some steadying breaths and try to act normally or all would be lost. They'd be sending her up to bed and calling Doctor Busick, and then she'd never get away. "I'm really rather tired though," she ventured. "Perhaps I'll retire to bed now."

Mama gave her a hard look, but Kit, his head in a book, didn't appear to have noticed. That was good, as he was inclined to be more astute than Mama where Ysella was concerned. Although not as astute as Morvoren. Thank goodness she was still confined to bed.

Ysella kissed Mama on the cheek and went and did the same to Kit. He glanced up, his face distracted and returned to his book—some treatise on new farming methods that Sam had given him that must be terribly boring. Whatever did men want to read that sort of thing for when they could have a good novel instead? Preferably a romantic one. "Goodnight, Ysella."

Goodness, was she glad to be out of that room. She ran up the stairs to the first-floor corridor and sprinted to her bedroom. Closing the door behind her, she leaned against it, her chest rising and falling. This was really happening. She was fleeing with her lover. Put like that it sounded like an excerpt from one of her novels and fired her flagging confidence.

She rang the bell and scurried to the wardrobe where earlier she'd hidden a small valise. She'd already packed a clean nightdress, some underwear, and several gowns that afternoon, and now she added some of her toiletries. What else did you need if you were a girl eloping? She'd never had to do her own packing before. She could wear her spencer and a bonnet and gloves. If she wore her boots, she could put in the slippers she was now wearing. She took them off and added them to the bag.

A slight tap on the door indicated the arrival of Ellen. "Come in," Ysella called.

Ellen approached the open valise on Ysella's bed with wide eyes. "You sent for me, Miss?"

Ysella nodded. "I did. I need your help. I'm planning a…" She hesitated. "A nighttime jape. And I need your help." She moved closer to Ellen and put a hand on the girl's thin arm. "And just like when we went to Marlborough, you are *not* to tell anyone about it or it'll all be spoiled. Do you understand?"

Ellen nodded, wordlessly.

"Good. Then first of all, I need you to finish packing my bag. What else do you think I'm going to need?"

Ellen's mouth hung open. Whether at the surprise of having her opinion asked, or because her mistress was planning something clandestine at night was not obvious.

"Do close your mouth or you'll catch a fly," Ysella said. "Do I have enough drawers do you think? And slips?"

"F-for what, Miss?" Ellen stammered.

"Oh, for an adventure with my dear friend Caro. You know. Miss Fairfield. She and I are going to be having such fun." Poor Caro. If Ellen did blab about where Ysella had got to, Kit's first port of call would be Caro's house, several miles off, which would give Ysella and Oliver longer to get away.

"How many days for?" Ellen asked, making a supreme effort to be helpful but not bringing with her the air of experience for elopements that Ysella had hoped for.

"Never mind." Ysella dropped some more undergarments into the bag, which was now full. "That will have to do. I can always buy more." She paced to the window and looked out at the night sky. Clear and star strewn. A good night for her escape.

Ellen scuttled out of her way.

"Now," Ysella said. "You are meant to be here to help me undress and prepare for bed, and if anyone below stairs asks you if that's what you've been doing, then you will tell them yes. Is that clear?"

"Yes, Miss."

"So, we shall give it another twenty minutes, which is how long it takes for Martha to help me get ready for bed, and then you can go downstairs. And you are to tell no one that I've not undressed. Not even if they *torture* you."

This last melodramatic instruction left Ellen more goggle-eyed than ever. "Yes, Miss," she whispered.

Was that a tremble Ysella detected in the girl's hands? The poor thing must think torture a real threat. Possibly a good thing.

"Good. It's all settled then. Martha will be back at work to-morrow morning so you have no more to do for me tonight. Other than keep your mouth shut." Ysella picked up her discarded reticule from the bed. "And as a reward, here is a shilling. No, two shillings." She placed the coins in Ellen's hand, at the same time wondering if that was a wise action as her pin money was already much depleted. Might she need money for the journey? Or would Oliver have some? Surely he would. Even if Kit were right and he was a fortune hunter, a fortune hunter who *loved* her, then he must at least have his officer's pay for them to manage on until she came into her inheritance. And once they were married, Kit couldn't object to paying it over.

When Ellen had gone off clutching her two shillings, Ysella was left with nothing to do to while away the time which seemed to be passing very slowly. The hands on the clock on the mantelpiece barely seemed to move, although the loud ticking grated on her nerves. Every second lasted an eon.

She went to the window and looked out again, over the front drive, although that surely wouldn't be the way Oliver would come. The parkland lay dark and mysterious, the distant woodland just a smudge of shadow, the lake glimmering in the rising moonlight. A shiver ran through her body. She couldn't be certain if it was from excitement or trepidation. Probably both. She must banish all thoughts of Mama being upset. She had to shut out darling little George and ignore her regrets about leaving Morvoren. Even thoughts of Kit, whom she loved despite his autocratic ways.

Closing the curtains, she returned to her bed and lay down on it. She was going to have a long wait.

Eventually, Mama's light footsteps sounded in the corridor as she walked past Ysella's door to her room. Then, a short while after that, Kit came up and she heard his heavier footsteps as he went to bid Morvoren goodnight. A few minutes later the footsteps returned as he went to his old bedroom, where he'd been sleeping while Morvoren convalesced. Ysella waited. Probably he wouldn't go straight off to sleep, but she still had plenty of time. The clock on the mantel said eleven. She'd arranged to meet Oliver at midnight.

At ten minutes to twelve, she pulled on her spencer and bonnet, tucked her gloves into her reticule and picked up her valise. Goodness, did a few clothes weigh this much? She needed two hands for it.

Pushing open her door a crack, she peered into the corridor. All lay in darkness save for a couple of oil lamps still burning at the top of the stairs, left there in case anyone might miss the top step in the dark and take a possibly fatal tumble.

Unfortunately, boots did not make for silent movement, unlike slippers. On tiptoes, holding her valise in front of her, Ysella made it to the top of the stairs. The house lay silent and still, with not a sign of anyone being awake still. She glanced back. She might never see it again and she wanted it locked in her memory.

Then, taking a deep breath, she started down the stairs.

Why had she never before noticed how they creaked when you put weight on them? Every single one seemed determined to waken the devil, no matter how carefully she stood on them. Perhaps if she walked at the very edge. With one hand on the banister rail, and the other clutching that hefty valise, she found this made less noise.

At the foot of the stairs, she hesitated. She'd told Oliver to be waiting for her on the main drive where the road came out of the woodland, but that now seemed an awful long way to carry a bag this heavy. What to do? If she was late, how long would he wait for her? Or would he assume she'd changed her mind, or been caught escaping by her brother? He might leave without her if she didn't hurry. Or he might have changed his mind and not come at all, but that didn't bear thinking about.

Inspiration seized her, but for this she needed the door into the garden.

Struggling with her bag, she headed for the French doors that opened into the corner of the terrace. Unlocked. No one ever locked the doors into the garden. She pushed one side open and let herself out into the chilly darkness. No lights showed in the house, and the high garden walls cast deep shadows across the flowerbeds. She hurried towards the Orangery, which hid a second, far more useful building. The capacious gardener's shed.

By now, her hands and arms were aching and the idea of abandoning her bag entirely was beginning to seem desirable. But no, she would need at least a nightgown for tomorrow night and her hairbrush and wash things, or how could she remain respectable and clean? She set down her bag, pushed open the white painted door of the garden shed and peered inside, searching for the object she needed.

Aha. There it was. A wooden wheelbarrow. Perfect.

A few minutes later, anyone looking out of one of the Abbey's front facing windows might have made out a small figure walking down the drive pushing a laden wheelbarrow.

Despite the cold of the late winter's night, Ysella was sweating like a navvy by the time she and her wheelbarrow reached the edge of the woods. She stopped and set the wheelbarrow down. If Oliver wasn't here waiting for her as he'd sworn he would be, then she was going to abandon wheelbarrow and bag and go back to bed and give up on the idea of ever marrying anyone. She'd just have to become an old maid. It was all far more trouble than an adventure had a right to be.

A shadow moved.

Ysella caught her breath.

Oliver stepped out of the trees. "Ysella!" He ran towards her and gathered her into his arms. "I'd begun to think you'd changed your mind."

She put her arms around his neck and held on tight, deciding not to tell him about her own doubts. "Of course I didn't. It just took me longer than I thought it would to get here." She nodded to the wheelbarrow. "My bag was so heavy I had to improvise."

He laughed against her hair, his breath warm on her skin. "I shouldn't have doubted you, my love."

His mouth found hers, his tongue between her lips, hot and questing. She let her own tongue meet his, as glorious currents of excitement ran up and down her body. Pressed this close to him she could feel something long and hard within his breeches, jammed against her own stomach. An absolutely fascinating, and not quite believed, conversation with Morvoren before the London season began, had revealed to her how babies were really made. And it was *not* the way a girl at school had told her. So Ysella knew what she was feeling, and as well as the excitement coursing through her, so did a fear that Oliver possessed what felt like a very large male member. A cock, Morvoren had called it. Fear of where that was meant to go had Ysella drawing back from him in confusion.

He didn't let her, though. Instead, he kissed her all the harder, one hand moving up to touch her breast, his fingers sliding inside the top of her spencer.

She wriggled against his hold and her mouth came free. "D-don't."

He stopped, still holding her but less fiercely now. "Playing the innocent now, are we?" he said with a chuckle. "As you like, but you'll come to like it soon enough."

"I just…" Ysella managed, her voice taut. "I-I haven't ever done anything like this." She gulped. "No one's ever touched me like th-that before."

Oliver laughed. "If we're to be married, you'll have to get used to it, my dear. Come along. I have a hired carriage waiting. No expense spared—you didn't think I'd expect you to *ride* all the way to Scotland, did you?"

As it had never crossed Ysella's mind that he might, and if it had she'd probably have come in her boys' breeches to make the ride more comfortable, she remained silent. Mostly she was thinking about his hot hand sliding in over the tender skin of her breast and how it had made her feel. She wasn't *quite* sure she'd liked it, but it seemed to be what men did to girls they were in love with. She knew this because she'd seen one of the house maids in the back courtyard of the house with one of the grooms. He'd had his hand firmly inside her bodice and the maid had seemed to be enjoying it very much.

Oliver released his hold on her and instead took her hand in a strong grip. "Come along, and we'll be off. No time to waste. We have a long way to go before tomorrow night, and we need to get a head start on your brother who is bound to come chasing after you."

Would he though? Or would he decide to stay with Morvoren? A very small part of Ysella suddenly hoped that Kit would come after her and bring her back before Oliver decided to put his hands where she didn't want them again. But she was committed now, and anyhow, it was what people who were in love, or even married, did, so she couldn't object. No going back. She let Oliver lead her to where he had his carriage stationed in the shadows under the trees.

Chapter Sixteen

Sam walked up the lane to the Abbey the next morning through a gentle mizzle of rain that was really nothing more than low cloud. However, it was the sort of rain that could get you very wet without you noticing and had turned the air chilly. Hunching his shoulders and hurrying his steps, he turned his greatcoat collar up to his ears and pulled his wide-brimmed hat well down on his head. The rain might only be heavy mist, but it didn't do to linger in it.

The mud underfoot splattered over the boots young Jack had polished for him last night, and he wished he'd brought his gloves. It was odd how a bit of rain could make you this cold, but winter was intent on proving spring wasn't well established this year. Indeed, it felt as though summer would never come, what with all the unseasonable rain. He doubted there'd be much farm work going on in this claggy weather. The spring sowing had been delayed again and horses couldn't pull ploughs when their hooves were mired in mud.

Reaching the servants' courtyard, he pushed open the side door and let himself in. He had a perfect right to come in via the big front doors, but preferred to access his office from the back, as that was where it lay. His boots echoed along the empty corridor.

As he passed the kitchens, the door opened and Martha, pushing it with her bottom, shuffled out backwards carrying a tray of what must be Ysella's breakfast. He reached out and held the door for her, and she looked up and bestowed a grateful smile on him.

"Thank you, Mr. Beauchamp, sir."

Sam smiled back. He liked Martha. She was an honest, sensible servant who could be relied upon to do the right thing. A good choice of maid for the flighty Ysella, and one whom he knew would not hesitate to report back to Kit or the dowager if she thought any danger threatened her charge. Although why he should even be thinking of Ysella and danger at the moment, he couldn't quite fathom. Perhaps because of her nature. Even through spectacles he had to acknowledge were rosy tinted where Ysella was concerned, he couldn't avoid admitting she was flighty. But that was part of her charm.

He opened the door at the end of the corridor for Martha and she scuttled off up the backstairs to deliver her mistress's breakfast. Sam continued to his office and unlocked the door. Inside, he settled down to going over the rent books as quarter day wasn't far off and the tenants would be coming in to pay their dues.

He hadn't been there long before the door swung open and Kit came in, his face creased into a frown. "Did you, by any chance, see Ysella out walking on your way up here this morning?" he asked.

Sam shook his head. "I saw no one. It's not a day for man nor beast to be out enjoying the fresh air, surely? I can't imagine Ysella can have chosen to go for a walk. Can she?"

Kit clenched his jaw. "I've checked the stables, and Lochinvar is still there. As is Sweetlip. In fact, all the horses are accounted for. So, she can't be out riding, which might have been more likely. She's not a girl to let a bit of rain put her off riding her horse." His gaze darted around Sam's office as if thinking Ysella might have secreted herself in there somewhere. "And Martha, who found her missing when she took her breakfast up, says her riding habit is still in her wardrobe. Unlike some of her other clothes."

"Her clothes are missing?" Sam echoed. "You're sure?"

"Of course I am," Kit snapped. "And Martha thinks she might have taken a valise."

"Well, she can't have just gone for a walk then, can she?" Sam said, his heart beginning to pound. His stomach was already tying itself into a knot worthy of Gordius, king of Phrygia.

"No," Kit said. "She can't have. And yet she's not here." He paused. "I've had Martha go through her things to check what's missing." He sat down heavily in the chair opposite Sam's with a thump, as though his legs would no longer hold him up, and put his hand to his head. "I fear she's done something very stupid."

Sam's mouth had gone bone dry, but he managed a nod. This must have been why he couldn't rid himself of the idea that Ysella was putting herself in danger. Some sixth sense had warned him. "I very much fear you might be right. What are we to do?"

"Martha tells me Ysella gave her leave to go to bed early last night and had Ellen do duty as lady's maid. I think we'll have to start with interviewing the girl." He stared into Sam's eyes. "And Morvoren must know nothing of this in her condition. The shock might set her recovery right back. She's very fond of Ysella."

Sam got to his feet. "You take my seat, and I'll go and fetch Ellen."

His own legs felt somehow disjointed from his body as he hurried along the corridor to the servants' hall and pushed the door into the kitchens open. Ellen, who must have already performed her early morning duties such as fire lighting, was seated at the long table eating her breakfast porridge. As Sam came in, she sank her head down between her shoulders as though wanting to appear small and insignificant. Aha. She knew something.

"You," Sam snapped at her. "Come with me. Now."

Cook turned from the stove, a wooden spoon in her hand. "What's the girl done this time?"

Sam opened the door. "That remains to be seen. Excuse me."

Ellen, shrinking like a terrified mouse, scuttled out of the kitchen in front of him and hurried in the direction he pointed. At the office, he held the door open for her and she went inside, her face as pale as if she were on the tumbrils that had seen such recent use in France.

Kit had taken Sam's seat and was leaning back in it, his arms folded, his face dark with anger. Sam closed the door and pushed Ellen up to the table, then went to stand behind Kit, regarding the trembling maid with a scowl intended to subdue her into cooperation.

"Well?" Kit said. "Where has she gone?"

Ellen shifted from one foot to the other, wringing her thin, reddened hands, and remained silent. She might well be too terrified to speak. Understandable, as Kit had taken on the distinct look of his father, the old viscount, who some had said bore a striking resemblance to Old Nick himself and had possessed a temper to match.

"Answer when his lordship asks you a question," Sam said, a little more gently than Kit.

The girl's eyes shot from side to side like those of a hunted rabbit seeking escape. "W-where's *who* gone? M'lord."

"Do not attempt to fool with me," Kit snarled, leaning suddenly forward and making Ellen step back two paces, her eyes widening so much the whites showed all around her pupils. "Where is my sister? You attended her last night. Did you assist her to abscond?"

Ellen's mouth opened and closed a few times and her eyes shot to meet Sam's for a moment. Perhaps she thought he might be her savior.

"Go on," Sam said in encouragement, keeping his voice gentle even though inside he wanted to get hold of Ellen and shake the information out of her. "Tell us where she's gone, and you won't be in trouble."

An angry snort from Kit indicated his disapproval of this promise.

"Sh-she did make me promise not to tell no one," Ellen managed to stutter. "She's my mistress. I *had* to do as she did say. I couldn't say her nay." Her large brown eyes looked an appeal at Sam.

"That last is true," Sam said. "How could Ellen have denied Ysella what she asked? It's not the girl's fault."

"On the contrary," Kit snapped, ignoring Sam's appeal for clemency and glaring at Ellen. "*I* am your master and *my wife* is your mistress. It is to *us* that you answer. Tell me everything you know. Now."

"Sh-she've gone to M-miss F-fairfield's," Ellen managed to stutter.

Kit shook his head like a bull about to charge. "On foot? And did you see her pack her bag?"

Ellen, no doubt taking courage from Sam's words, nodded. "She did pack one. She told me not to tell no one. I wasn't to help her out of her gown, acos she were goin' out later to meet her friend for some… 'jape' she called it. If I done wrong, m'lord, I didn't mean to. I'm that sorry." She clasped her hands together in supplication, no doubt terrified of being dismissed from her position without a reference.

Kit put his head in his hands with a groan, so Sam nodded to Ellen. It wasn't her fault, no matter how much Kit might want to blame her. She'd been Ysella's easily swayed pawn. "You may go, but regard this as a lesson. If a young lady ever again asks you to keep a secret, you bring it to the man in charge of her straightaway, because she is *up to no good*."

Ellen bolted.

"Do you think she's really gone to Caroline Fairfield's?" Sam asked, afraid of the answer. Every part of him screamed out that she couldn't have. That she'd done something foolish and used Caroline as an excuse to inveigle Ellen to help her.

Kit shrugged. "I suppose it's possible, but on foot? In the middle of the night? Why? She hasn't seen Caro for several months. Not since before she left for London. What with

Morvoren being so ill, and us not accepting callers, Caro hasn't been over." His voice rose in hope. "I suppose it might be possible that Ysella has hatched a plan to go and see her—but in the middle of the night? Clandestinely? I don't think so. Caro wouldn't be party to that sort of thing. She's far too sensible."

Sam bit his lip. "What do you want to do?"

"We both know where she's gone. Get her back before it's too late," Kit said. "Before she compromises herself."

Sam stayed silent. Surely if Ysella had run off with Captain Featherstone, she was already compromised.

Kit shook his head. "I suppose I'll have to send James over on Lochinvar to see if she's at Caro's. Before we go off precipitously after her, I need to be sure she didn't tell Ellen the truth, unlikely as that is. We'd look a pair of chumps if she were truly at Caro's enjoying herself."

Sam nodded. But he doubted very much that James would find Ysella at the Fairfields' house.

HE WAS RIGHT. James was back within half an hour with the news that Miss Fairfield had not heard from Ysella for over two months bar a short and very badly spelled letter sent from London to tell her about her presentation at the royal court.

"We were right. She's gone off with Featherstone," Kit said, throwing down the note Caroline had sent him. "That's what she's done, the strumpet. She'll be ruined. After everything I said to her, which she pretended to agree with, she's defied me. She gulled me and, like an idiot, I fell for it."

He strode across to the fireplace in the library, which was where they'd repaired to in order to await James's return.

Sam's stomach twisted in pain. That cad had Ysella in his power to do with as he wished. The thought brought a cold sweat out on his forehead and down his back. He put a hand up to loosen his collar. "Are you going after them?"

Kit nodded. "I refuse to let him get away with this. All he's after is her money. I know it, else why would he have inveigled her into running away with him?" He looked up and grinned, looking more than ever like his departed father. "What he doesn't know is that unless I agree to her marriage, the money's tied up until she's thirty. *She* doesn't know it, either. Even when she gets to twenty-one and her majority, I have the final say. And I'm never releasing her money to that cad."

A tiny nub of hope rose in Sam's broken heart. Perhaps if Captain Featherstone could be apprised of this fact, he might decide marrying Ysella wasn't the cure-all he imagined for his prospects. But, the downside of this was that Ysella would still be ruined and find it impossible to return to London society and make a respectable match.

"I'll order our horses saddled," Sam said. "I'm coming with you."

BEFORE THEY COULD set out, the dowager had to be informed. Not something Sam relished doing. He and Kit encountered her in the breakfast room, nibbling some toast and drinking a cup of hot chocolate. Dash and Duster sat patiently by her feet, waiting for tidbits and eyeing her out of sorrowful spaniel eyes.

Lady Ormonde looked up as they entered, both dressed for the rainy day in their greatcoats and hats. Setting her coffee cup down, she dabbed her lips with a napkin. "Goodness, are you both off outside in this weather?"

Sam hung back. Let Kit break the news. He was having enough trouble keeping his own emotions under control and didn't want to have to cope with the dowager's inevitable reaction.

Kit didn't beat about the bush. "Ysella has eloped with Featherstone."

"She's *what?*" Lady Ormonde almost screamed, the toast falling to the ground where Dash and Duster fell on it with relish. Her hand went to her mouth and she looked at Sam where he stood near the door. "Tell me that's not true."

He nodded. "I'm afraid it is."

She seized the edge of the table. "My smelling salts. Quickly."

Kit grabbed her reticule and fished out the little jar, unstoppering it with practiced fingers. He waved it under her nose, and she revived.

"When?" she asked. "How did you find out?"

"We don't know exactly when," Kit said. "It must have been sometime during the night. But they'll have headed north to Gretna Green, as she's too young to marry without my permission. I'm assuming they have at least a ten-hour head start. Sam and I are going after her. We came to let you know, and to warn you not to worry Morvoren with the news. I don't want her upset."

The dowager nodded, her old astute self returning. "Very wise. But Gretna Green is a long way off—several days in the fastest of carriages." A thought must have struck her. "Oh, my poor child. My baby. She'll be alone with that man for several nights. What will he do to her when he has her in his power?"

Sam clenched his fists, this thought having already occurred to him.

"We're setting out after them now," Kit said. "They must be in a carriage of some sort, because she didn't take her riding habit. We'll ride, so we'll be faster than any carriage. Don't worry, Mama, we'll catch them. I'm taking pistols."

The dowager's face paled and she reached for her smelling salts again. "*Pistols?* Do you envisage having to fight to get her back? Oh, heavens above. You must be careful. The man will be desperate to succeed in his endeavor, I don't doubt." She rose to her feet and went to Kit. "Do not put yourself in danger, my darling boy. Remember, you have a wife and child who need you."

Kit bent and gave her a quick, fierce hug which she returned with fervor. "He is the one who is in danger, not me." He released her and turned to the door.

The dowager turned to Sam, her hand going out to catch his. She gazed up at him out of dark, troubled eyes. Eyes disturbingly like Ysella's. "Keep them both safe for me, Sam, I beg you. I shall rely upon your good sense to avert any danger to my children."

Chapter Seventeen

THE MIZZERLY RAIN was still falling when Sam and Kit arrived in the stableyard to find James holding the reins of Abelard and Hercules. Abelard, Kit's rangy black thoroughbred, swished his tail and stamped his feet in impatience, not having been out with his master since Morvoren fell ill. The bay, Hercules, Sam's no less handsome, but far less fiery beast, turned pricked ears towards his master.

A second groom was fastening Kit's and Sam's saddlebags to the saddles.

Sam took Hercules's reins and swung himself up into the saddle, and groped for the stirrup with his right foot. Kit leapt onto Abelard and turned towards the clocktower archway. Side-by-side, they rode out into the mist-shrouded park.

"We'll have to go into Marlborough first," Kit said as they cantered down the drive, their horses' hooves crunching on the gravel. "To check if Featherstone left yesterday as well." He wiped a hand across his face to get rid of the film of rain. "It's always possible that Ysella might be there with him, although I doubt it. I fear I'm right in my surmise. She's run off with him. Or rather, he's run off with her. If that's true, then she's more stupid than I thought her."

Sam held his tongue, despite hating to hear his beloved called stupid. Kit was right. Ysella, if not stupid herself, had done a very stupid thing. He itched to get straight off after her, rather than waste time chasing around Marlborough, but at least there they might be able to discover what sort of vehicle Featherstone had at his disposal.

However, the runaways must be miles away by now, and with every moment getting further away, so time was of the essence. And what was more, every minute he and Kit delayed brought Ysella closer to having to spend the night with the cad. Sam's stomach, which had been knotted since he'd heard the news, seemed intent on inducing him to throw up the remains of his breakfast, but he managed to hold it in.

Marlborough lay some eight miles distant along not so good roads that always made any journey by carriage take longer than it should. On horseback, able to canter along the muddy verges and avoid the worst of the winter's potholes, Sam and Kit made it to the town in under an hour.

They trotted down the wide, cobbled main street towards the Castle Inn at the far end. This hostelry did not resemble the average posting inn at all, having once belonged to, and been lived in, by the Earl of Hertford. Consequently, it possessed the façade of a minor stately home, with magnificent red-brick wings to either side of an imposing pillared portico.

Having left their horses with grooms in the stableyard, Sam and Kit strode through the inn's wide front doors in search of someone to interrogate. There they found the inn's proprietor, as stately as his hostelry, directing the polishing of glasses by a trio of young potboys.

"Good morning," Kit said, an edge of irritation in his voice. "Do you have a Captain Featherstone staying in your establishment?"

The proprietor, a tubby fellow sporting a pristine white apron, made a measured bow. "My Lord Ormonde. What a pleasure it is to see you grace the walls of my humble establishment." He spoke with a care that indicated he'd learned his pronunciation late in life.

Greasy fellow, fawning over Kit because he was one of the local gentry. Sam scowled, tapping his riding whip against his leg hard enough to hurt. Could the man not answer a straightforward question? He longed to take the fellow by the collar and shake the information out of him.

"Featherstone. Is he here?" Kit snapped, all niceties thrown to the wind.

The proprietor, a trifle crestfallen that this was all Lord Ormonde should want, shook his head. "I'm afraid your lordship has missed him. He left yesterday in rather a hurry." Behind him the three boys had taken advantage of his lack of attention, and were listening open mouthed and not doing any polishing.

"When?" Sam asked, unable to resist the temptation to interrupt.

"Yes. When?" Kit repeated, taking a threatening step closer to the proprietor, who backed up a hasty step.

The poor man almost cowered, his pomposity fled. Nothing overt had been said, but Kit's demeanor oozed anger. It seemed to at last dawn on the proprietor of The Castle that Kit and Sam weren't looking for the captain out of a desire for friendship. "Yesterday evening," he managed, his hands gripping the edge of the bar. "He was after trading his high-blooded galloper in for a gig and a roadster. A fine animal he had, that he'd ridden down from London, and why he'd want to swap it for something he couldn't ride, I don't know." He hesitated, then added, as if in an afterthought, "Milord." And a little, obsequious bow.

"And did he get what he wanted?"

The landlord nodded. "I believe so, Milord."

Sam's heart sank further into his boots, if that were possible. Featherstone had secured a vehicle he could carry Ysella away in and had what...? He glanced at his fob watch... a good twelve hour start on them.

Kit turned back towards the doors, the man forgotten, throwing his last comment over his shoulder as he reached for the door handle. "Thank you for your information."

He and Sam returned to the stables almost in a run. "Damn the man's eyes," Kit said as they retrieved their horses. "They could be as much as fifty miles ahead of us by now. If not more."

Sam set his foot in his stirrup and swung himself up into the saddle. "His one horse won't be able to keep up that sort of pace for twenty-four hours, and he'll have had to negotiate some bad patches of road after all this rain. He'll have had to stop to rest it, water it, feed it. And Ysella will have needed rest stops as well. It may not be that bad." Or it might be worse. Sam couldn't bring himself to say that.

"The only route they can have taken is north to Gretna Green," Kit said as they rode out of the stableyard. "We have to catch them before they get there. I won't stand by and see her married to a fortune hunter and a cad." He glanced at Sam. "For preference we have to catch them before she's forced to pass the night in his company."

Sam's gut tightened. "Surely, as a gentleman, he'll procure her a room on her own?" A faint hope. He didn't for a minute believe his own words.

"A gentleman?" Kit spat. "You think a gentleman would run off with a girl barely out of the schoolroom? To seize her inheritance?" He spurred Abelard on. "We have to hurry."

AT MUCH THE same time as Kit and Sam were setting out on their rescue mission, the object of their pursuit was sitting in the White Hart Inn on the road north nibbling at a luncheon snack of soup and bread with a distinct lack of enthusiasm. Unlike Captain Oliver Featherstone, who had tucked in with great gusto to a loaded plate of roast beef, potatoes and some indeterminate green vegetable.

Ysella pushed her spoon around the bowl of greasy soup, the lump in her throat preventing her from swallowing anything.

After Oliver had helped her into the gig he'd exchanged his flashy riding horse for, she'd settled back under the blanket he'd provided and determined she would enjoy their escapade and view it as an exciting adventure. But, in a gig, the potholes couldn't be avoided, and the drizzle that had begun at first light had invaded every part of her clothing, creeping under the blanket and chilling her hands and feet to blocks of ice. She'd suggested to Oliver that they should get out and walk in order to warm themselves up a little, but he'd pooh-poohed the idea with a dismissive laugh and she'd not dared suggest it again.

It had been a great relief when he'd turned the gig into the stableyard of a small inn, in a town she didn't recognize, and said they would take a break for food and to rest the horse. He'd asked the landlord for a private parlor with a fire, and Ysella had rushed to stand in front of it and warm herself up.

Oliver joined her after about ten minutes, a satisfied expression on his face. "I've traded our tired horse in for a fresher one," he declared. "So, once we've eaten, we don't need to wait around while our horse recovers. We can proceed posthaste."

Why he was looking so pleased about this, Ysella had no idea. The gig was bumpy and uncomfortable and twelve hours in it had left her feeling as though she'd been run over by a set of harrows. However, she had no opportunity to complain as their food arrived, brought by a buxom barmaid who seemed on far-too familiar terms with Oliver, thrusting her ample chest at him and batting her eyelashes suggestively.

Ysella contented herself with giving the hussy a hard stare and sat down at the table. Oliver not seeming to be in the mood for talking, they ate in silence. Probably he was as tired as she was. After all, he'd been the one doing the driving.

As Oliver wiped his last piece of bread around the plate to scoop up the remains of the gravy, Ysella pushed her barely touched bowl of soup away and lifted her eyes to meet his. "Do we have to go on today? I'm so tired and it's impossible to sleep in that gig, with all the bumps in the road."

His handsome face furrowed into a frown. "Of course we do, my love. We can't risk your brother catching us up, can we? Not before we're safely married, that is."

"I suppose not." Ysella fidgeted. "But it's raining and that gig is so cold."

Oliver brightened. "I'll get the landlord to provide you with some hot bricks to keep you warm. How does that sound?"

Better than nothing. Ysella bit her lip and stayed silent. This wasn't turning out to be nearly as much fun as she'd thought it would be. Not at all romantic to be driving through cold, wet countryside in the sort of rain that didn't feel like much but soaked you to the skin. Nothing like her romantic novels where the sun always shone, and an eloping couple reached Gretna Green in a matter of hours.

True to his word, though, Oliver procured three hot bricks wrapped in flannel for her, one to go each side on the seat, and one for her feet. So, a much warmer Ysella huddled under two blankets—Oliver had managed to get hold of a second for her—as they drove out of the inn's stableyard with their new horse, a bit of a step down on the first, between the gig's shafts.

The afternoon crawled past. Eventually, the bricks gave up all their heat and the cold began to seep into Ysella's bones again. The rain became heavier, and despite the gig's hood, Ysella's misery increased as night approached. At last, in a small town whose identity Ysella didn't care a jot about, Oliver drew the gig to a halt at another inn. Leaving horse and gig to be cared for by the ostlers, he led a half-frozen Ysella inside.

"A room for the night for my wife and myself," he called to the jovial, red-faced landlord. "And dinner to be served in our room, if you please. My wife is chilled from her journey, so make sure there's a good fire and the sheets are well aired."

What a relief it was to find herself in a bedroom with a blazing fire in the hearth. Ysella hurried to stand in front of it to warm herself, holding out her hands in confused delight. A little nub of fear had hatched in her stomach, and she had no idea how to deal with it. Had she been mistaken, or had Oliver called her his *wife* to the landlord?

Warmth began to creep back into her frozen fingers at last, making them tingle.

Oliver gave the boy who'd carried their bags up to the room a coin, and came to stand behind her. "Better get your wet spencer off. We can hang it up to dry for tomorrow. Perhaps you should have worn your pelisse instead. It might have kept you warmer." His arms went around her from behind, his fingers on the fastenings, brushing her breasts as he did so.

She couldn't argue. Her own hands were still too numb to manage fastenings.

He slid the spencer off her shoulders and hung it from a peg near the fire, but he didn't leave her. Instead, his arms went around her again, and this time they did cup her breasts.

Ysella stiffened. Was this the behavior of a husband to his wife? If so, wasn't Oliver taking the part he was playing a tad too seriously? She was not his wife yet, and she felt fairly sure betrothed couples didn't behave like this. "I'm cold," she whispered. "I need to warm up."

"I can do that for you," Oliver whispered into her ear, one hand sliding inside the low neckline of her gown, forcing its way downwards. A shiver of excitement ran through Ysella's body to be quickly followed by cold fear. Certainty that he was not meant to be doing this swept over her, followed by the sensation of being alone and unprotected and unable to prevent him doing so. She was alone with a man who was the next best thing to a stranger, no matter how he made her feel. Quite alone. They were not married yet, but he'd told the landlord they were, and he could do anything he liked to her, and she would be powerless to stop him. The most frightening thing was that she half wanted him to do something. Was she a wicked hoyden? Guilt, excitement, and fear mingled in her heart.

Oliver kissed her neck, his lips warm and firm on her cold skin.

Oh, but that was *nice*. Shivers ran down her treacherous body.

His hand slid a little further down inside the neckline of her gown, and a gasp escaped her lips as he reached her nipple. It hardened under his fingers. Was that something any man should do to a girl? Instinct told her probably not one he wasn't married to. No matter if the landlord thought them an old married couple. But, oh, it *was* nice. She arched her back against him, head back. She very much liked the sensations coursing through her body.

A knock sounded on the door. He whipped his hand out of her gown and went to open it, readjusting his breeches as he walked as though uncomfortable. A young girl came in, carrying a tray of plates. "Dinner, Sir."

Oliver, his face flushed, indicated the table. "Put it down and leave, please."

She did as she was told, scuttling from the room.

More beef and potatoes. Did inns serve nothing else? Ysella's experience of inns not being very extensive, she could only suppose that they did. There was also a large flagon of wine and two glasses.

"Come," Oliver said with a smile that sent more shivers down her body and made her want him to touch her again, which in its turn brought on a fresh wave of guilt at how wanton her behavior was. "Sit down and eat something. If you don't, you'll waste away. And food will warm you up faster than a fire will."

Ysella sat down and considered her plate of food. Perhaps she could eat just a little. She picked up her knife and fork. What would Mama be eating at Ormonde? And Morvoren? They must have missed her by now. Mama might be unable to eat for worry. She'd think she'd lost Ysella like her other children. Like little Peran. She tried to push these thoughts out of her head, but they would keep shouldering their way forward again.

Was Kit even now hot on her trail, or had he decided he couldn't leave his sick wife? If they'd discovered her missing some time this morning, they would still be a long way behind. If they'd set off at all. Maybe Kit had decided she was old enough to make her own decisions, although that seemed unlikely, given his apparent hatred and scorn for Oliver.

She nibbled some of the meat, which was over-cooked and dry with only a watery gravy. Oliver was right, though. She needed to keep her strength up.

"What are you thinking about?" Oliver asked.

"Home." The word popped out before she had chance to think.

He frowned. "No need to bother yourself with that. It's not your home any longer. Your home will be with me. We'll get ourselves a nice townhouse once we're married. That'll be your new home."

So it would. The reality of leaving home seemed to be descending on Ysella a layer at a time. Was she homesick? Was that what this nervous feeling in the pit of her stomach was? Did she miss Mama and Kit and Morvoren and baby George? Did she miss Ormonde and Lochinvar? Would she ever ride Lochinvar again? A host of questions tumbled through her head and she had to bite her lip to prevent the tears from falling. She really couldn't eat any of this food, feeling the way she did.

Oliver must have seen. "You'll get used to married life, have no fear. We'll get you some nice new gowns when we get back from Gretna Green. You'll soon forget your old life." He attacked his beef with gusto and poured himself another large glass of wine. He'd already drunk most of the flagon and his cheeks had taken on a ruddy flush.

She bent over her food. He could say that to her, but inside, Ysella knew she wouldn't get used to it at all. Not for a very long time.

$$\cdots \textbf{\textreferencemark} \cdots$$

Chapter Eighteen

"WHERE ARE YOU going to sleep?" Ysella asked, after the remains of their meal had been cleared away and Oliver had started on the brandy bottle the maid had brought.

Oliver raised his eyes at her. "In the bed, of course."

Ysella frowned. "Then where shall I sleep?"

He laughed, knocking back the glass of brandy in his hand and pouring another. "In the bed as well."

What? Ysella knew Kit and Morvoren shared a bed, but she also knew that most married couples had separate rooms. Mama and Papa had done, as far as she could remember. She'd never shared a bed with anyone before, unless she counted the time she'd had to share with Morvoren on their helter-skelter rush down to Cornwall to save Kit. And that had been only for one night, and Morvoren was another girl. Not a man claiming to be her husband, with all that might entail.

Oliver stepped up to the bed, which she was standing looking at. His arms went around her waist, and he pulled her round to face him. "We're as good as married, Ysella. I see no point in waiting on a brief service carried out by a Scottish laborer. No need to be shy with me. We can consummate our love tonight."

Ysella swallowed. What was he saying? Was he asking her to do the thing Morvoren had tried to tell her about even before they were married? Should she let him? Did she even possess the power to stop him if he wanted to do it? A small part of her very much wanted to let him, for various reasons. His touch around her waist was exciting her, and curiosity goaded her. Doing this would make her a woman in every sense of the word, and she'd find out what it was that Morvoren seemed to think was so nice about being married. And they *were* going to be married within the week, so did it really matter if they anticipated it by a few days? Gretna Green couldn't be that much further. Could it?

"You have no maid with you," Oliver said, his voice a throaty purr. "Would you like me to act as your maid and undo your gown and stays for you?"

She caught her breath as this enticing thought shimmered through her.

Without waiting for her permission, his hands were already fumbling with the fastenings down the back of her gown, his breath, redolent of the brandy, hot on the back of her neck. Should she let him? She had no one else to perform this service unless she called for one of the inn's female servants. And the sensation of a man doing her maid's job *was* exciting. Another shiver ran down her body. Of anticipation. Of fear of what lay ahead of her if she let him do this. But then again, she could hardly sleep fully dressed, could she?

She stood very still, her hearting beat so loud in her chest, no, in her *throat*, she was sure he'd be able to hear it. The fastenings came undone, and the front of her gown gaped. He put up his hands and slid her gown from her shoulders, fingers lingering on her bare skin, his touch electric, and let it pool on the floor at her feet. When she'd put this gown on last night for dinner, she'd not for a moment suspected Oliver would be the one who would be taking it off.

She stood before him in her petticoat and stays, head hanging and her face hot with embarrassment. No man had ever seen her in such a state before. He kissed the back of her neck, his mouth moving across her skin leaving a trail of fire. What would Mama say if she could see her now? No. She had to shove that thought away.

"Turn around," Oliver whispered, bending to kiss her neck. "Let me kiss you again."

Eyes closed, as though she might shut out the sin she was committing, Ysella turned around.

With one hand, he tilted her chin upwards and his lips found her throat. With the other he caught her by the waist and pulled her closer. A string of kisses roved down her neck to her breasts, warm and gentle, his tongue tickling her skin, making her want him never to stop. She closed her eyes as her stomach contracted with something she'd barely felt in her life. An ache formed itself below her stomach, in that nameless area she'd always deemed the most private.

"Take off your petticoat." He unhooked the back and pulled it off over her head, leaving her in just her stays and underslip.

Feeling very exposed, Ysella crossed her arms across her breasts as though doing so might delay the fate that awaited her.

He spun her around again, and, still kissing her neck, began to unlace her stays. He was adept and quick at it, his fingers as agile as Martha's. For a moment, Ysella wondered how he could have gained such skill before the thought drifted away as her stays came off.

She kept her back to him, her hands across her breasts, scarcely hidden now by the thin muslin of her shift. Her breath came in quick pants, and her heart thumped against her hands.

The sound of Oliver kicking his boots off broke into her trancelike state. This was going to happen, and although a part of her wanted it, a large part of her wasn't so sure. Shouldn't they wait until they were married? Wasn't it a sin to do this before being joined in wedlock by the church? But she wasn't going to be joined in wedlock by a priest. She was going to have a hairy-armed blacksmith declare her legally Oliver's wife. So perhaps this didn't count.

Out of the corner of her eye, she saw Oliver's coat fly through the air and hit one of the chairs by the table. She couldn't look. Then his breeches joined it. *Oh, oh, oh.* He must be nearly naked, just as she was. She hugged herself even tighter, tension keeping her body rigid.

He came up behind her, something hard and insistent jabbing into her back. His hands slipped around her and caught her arms, moving them away from her breasts. She let them fall to her sides, desperate for him not to think her a prude. He seemed so good at this, so experienced, so natural, that she wanted to give the impression she was as well.

His hands came back up and slid inside her slip, down to cup her naked breasts. Skillful fingers worked at her nipples, making them harden under his touch.

"Ha," he whispered, his breath heavy with the scent of the brandy. "You do want me, you little minx."

He spun her around. He still wore his long shirt so the thing that had been jabbing her in the back was hidden, although it tented his shirt alarmingly. Was a man's cock really this big? The only one she'd ever seen had been George's tiny one when the nursemaid had changed his napkin, and this thing beneath Oliver's shirt was nothing like it.

"Come to bed," Oliver said, pulling her towards it. She stumbled, still unsure she should be letting Oliver do this. "If you're worrying about getting with child, you can't the first time. And even if you did, we'll be married shortly so it won't matter. What's a few days?"

Beside the bed, she hesitated, but his hands were on her slip. In one movement he pulled it over her head, leaving her naked and vulnerable. He pushed her down onto the bed and climbed on top of her in one swift movement, his mouth descending to take a nipple between his lips.

Even through her fear of what was about to happen, the sensation of having her nipple sucked sent ripples of excitement through Ysella's body. She wanted this. Yes, she did. It was going to be frightening, but it was what married people did.

His knee forced her legs apart as though he were in a hurry.

When his mouth came up to kiss hers again, one hand descended to between her legs. She started so much when he touched her down there that his mouth came away from hers.

"Don't worry," he whispered, almost on a groan. "I know what I'm doing."

Did he? How? Had he done this before, and if so, who with? Some trollop? The terrible thought that *she* was no better than a trollop herself washed over Ysella.

Something nudged at where he had his probing fingers, pushing against her skin. Oliver grunted, his body stiffening over hers, and she felt his hips shove against her.

She didn't like it. Something far too large and thick pushed its way inside her, and a whimper escaped her throat. Was this the sex Morvoren had tried to explain to her—the sex married people enjoyed—the sex that gave women pleasure?

It was nothing like the fun she'd hoped for, not the fun she'd hoped for with those feelings she'd had when he'd touched her breasts. Not at *all* like that. He increased the speed of his thrusts and she grit her teeth. Why anyone might want to do this for fun, she had no idea. As she gripped the bed sheets, her body tensed under his. He thrust harder still, quivering, then emitted a long, satisfied groan and with one last shove, his body relaxed, his weight coming down on hers. It had taken all of one minute.

He lay unmoving on top of her for a while, panting, and Ysella bit her lip, tears running down her cheeks. Did married women do this for *pleasure*? Hard to believe.

At last, he shoved himself off her and rolled over, laughing. "That was good. It always hurts the first time for a girl. Now if your brother catches us before we get to Gretna, he'll have to let us marry. Or you'll be ruined."

Ysella lay very still, her head in a whirl. Had he only wanted to do this so he could force Kit's hand? Had he not wanted to do it because he loved her? Although as far as she was concerned, it hadn't seemed a loving act. More something he'd done entirely for his own pleasure, as he was the only one of them who'd seemed to like it. How could it be to do with love when it had produced such discomfort for her? Hopefully, Oliver wouldn't want to do it again. She pulled the bedcovers over her naked body and rolled over with her back to him, as tears of unhappiness continued to course down her cheeks. Such an odd thing for someone who loved her to want to inflict such discomfort. Kit had said that he couldn't live without Morvoren, and, when he'd said it, Ysella had been sure she felt like that about Oliver. Now, she wasn't quite so sure she felt the same. Because surely if he felt that way about her, he wouldn't have hurt her like this.

SAM AND KIT reached Oxford, where, all unknowing of that city's name, Ysella had taken her luncheon with Oliver, by six o'clock that night. With their mounts tired after a fifty-mile ride, Kit led the way to one of the many inns.

"The trouble is," Sam said as they handed their horses over to the care of the ostlers, "that we don't know what route they'll have taken."

Kit nodded. "I'm guessing he'll have gone for the fastest route and that's the one I intend to stick to. He won't want to waste any time taking silly detours. We should walk round every establishment in the town to find out if they're there, or if they've been seen by any of the landlords."

Sam nodded. "We can take half each. Try the places that only do food and drink as well, or stables where they might have procured a fresh horse."

"Good thinking. We can start with this one. Let's get inside and see what the landlord has to say."

The landlord of their establishment had rooms for them, but had not seen Featherstone or Ysella that day. He promised them a hearty meal and some good claret for when they returned, and they each set off to further their enquiries.

Sam worked his way along St Giles, going into every place he thought might possibly hold a clue, unsure of what he would do if he found they were staying there. No joy. He was just beginning to feel deflated and defeated, when the landlord of the last inn he came to proved to have seen Ysella.

"Very pretty young lady, freezin' cold, she were. With a gentleman who by the look of him had an army background. Very upright, he were. An officer, I'd say by the cut of him."

"That's right," Sam said, excitement fizzing through him. A clue, a veritable clue. "I don't suppose they're still here, are they?"

The innkeeper shook his head with a tinge of regret at not being able to please Sam, who had pressed five shillings on him as reward for the information. "I'm sorry, lad. It looks like findin' them's important to you. I wish I could've bin more help. Betsey, my barmaid, she might be able to tell you more. I saw her havin' quite a chat wi' the young gentleman. She's a bit of a flirt, mind, so you watch out for her." He gave a shout, and the same buxom barmaid who'd earlier brought Oliver and Ysella their luncheon, emerged, her eyes alight with interest when she spotted Sam.

"Yes surr?" she rolled the "r" of the word in an all too inviting manner and batted her long eyelashes at him. "What can I do for 'ee?"

The landlord quickly explained. "Did you get the names of the gentleman and the lady?"

She shook her head, never taking her saucy stare from Sam's face. "That I didn't, but the young lady, she didn't look too happy. When I took in their plates, she was all red-faced an' flustered, like. And he had a look in his eye as I'd know anywhere." She grimaced. "The look of a man what wants what a girl has to give. Or not give, as the case may be."

Good God. Sam's fists balled by his sides. An urge to punch something washed over him. Had Featherstone been importuning Ysella?

"What time was this?" he managed to ask. "And what time did they leave?"

The girl smiled, revealing uneven teeth. "When they got here, 'twere about midday weren't it?" She glanced at her employer. "He went off sharpish to the liv'ry yard to get them a fresh horse, and the lady, she went into the parlor to get warm by the fire." She rubbed her nose. "When he come back from the liv'ry yard, he did stop by me for a quick squeeze o' me dumplings. So I knowed he weren't no gentleman, not reely."

Her dumplings?

For a moment, Sam was lost for words, so, as if to illustrate her words, the girl put her hands under her ample breasts and bounced them up and down. "Many's the gentleman wants a squeeze o' them," she said with pride. "But not normally when they've got a beautiful young lady with 'em."

"And the time they left?" Sam repeated, his voice hoarse with disgust, all these facts seething through his brain.

"Didn't stay long," the landlord said. "Left about one, I'd say. We do hear the town clock strike here, and I'm sure I'd heard it strike the hour just before they was off."

Sam pressed another five shillings into the landlord's hand. "Thank you, thank you. You've been a great help. Good night."

Out in the street again, he ran back to the inn where he and Kit were staying.

Chapter Nineteen

OLIVER WAS SNORING. Ysella pulled the bedclothes over her head and tried to shut the sound out, but failed. Papa used to snore in the drawing room of an evening, or in his study, when he was in his cups, and after all that wine followed by the brandy, Oliver had definitely followed in Papa's footsteps. Which was a tiny bit disappointing in someone you thought loved you.

Unable to sleep, uncomfortable and sore in a place she hadn't realized could be so battered, and far too aware of the proximity of Oliver's naked body, Ysella cried quietly into her pillow. Was this how all girls felt on their wedding night? Not that this was her wedding night at all. She had the increasingly terrifying suspicion that she'd done a very silly thing in letting Oliver have his way with her before their wedding. And his words after he'd finished had added another layer of misgiving. Perhaps he was right though. Perhaps giving herself to him had been the thing to do to prevent Kit from undoing everything. It was certainly far too late to go back on this now. Anything other than marriage to Oliver would ruin her in the eyes of society, possibly in the eyes of her family as well.

From outside somewhere she heard a clock striking. Midnight. Was she never going to get any sleep? She wiped her eyes with one hand and tried closing them. But that only brought up images of Mama and home and little George. Would Morvoren be terribly upset that she'd left? She'd certainly be shocked at what she'd just done. Images of her own comfortable bedroom, of Lochinvar snug in his stable eating his hay, of Kit standing by the library fire, and rather absurdly, and for no reason she could put her finger on, of Sam in his office, flashed through her head. Images of safe normality. She gripped the pillow until her knuckles whitened. No, she did not feel either normal or safe here.

AT COCKCROW, KIT and Sam were in the stableyard mounting their horses, food for the journey provided by the innkeeper and packed in Sam's saddlebags. They clattered out onto the as yet quiet St Giles and set off heading north towards the Banbury road. At least the rain had stopped and, in the east, a watery sun was rising over the hills. Abelard and Hercules seemed none the worse for their fifty-mile ride yesterday, snatching excitedly at their bits and skittering across the cobbled road like a pair of two-year-old racehorses.

"They can't be far ahead of us," Kit said. They'd discussed riding on in the darkness last night, having decided that the runaways couldn't be more than thirty miles ahead of them. However, thirty miles on tired horses would have taken them until after midnight, and they had no way of knowing where Oliver would have decided to spend the night. As they couldn't have gone banging on every inn door they came to and rousing who knew how many innocent people from their beds in the early hours, with reluctance, they'd had to wait until first light.

Once out of the city, they pressed their horses hard, cantering wherever they could, but the road was not good. Spring should have been well established by now, but this year winter was hanging on by its icy, wet claws, and potholes caused by the weather wouldn't be filled until the weather looked up. But that would slow down the gig Oliver was driving more than it would two riders, and Sam had high hopes of gaining ground on Featherstone. However, he'd not allowed for the time it took to stop at every hostelry along their route and ask if Featherstone and Ysella were in residence. As Kit pointed out, slow as it made them, anything was better than overtaking them by negligence.

At just before ten o'clock in the morning, they rode up Banbury's high street, passing the famous Banbury Cross of nursery rhyme fame. With a heavy heart, Sam saw just how many hostelries they would have to approach before they could move on.

"Largest ones first," Kit said, with a long sigh. "I don't think even that cad will have taken my sister to a common inn."

Sam wasn't so sure. At the first inn they came to, they left their horses in the stables with instructions to the grooms to unsaddle and rub them down. Then they strode inside the inn and approached the landlord, a skinny fellow in a long apron who was supervising the cleaning of the taproom as the hour was still early to be expecting customers.

"Good day to you, my man," Kit said, laying his hat and gloves on the wooden bar. "We're in search of a man driving a gig. Tall, dark haired, a bit of a dandy, with the bearing of a soldier about him. He has a young woman with him. Slight, dark haired, and very pretty. Have you seen these two at all?"

The landlord's eyes shifted from Kit's face to Sam's, and he fidgeted with unease. "Aye," he mumbled. "I might have done. What's it to you, I have to ask, before I give out information on my customers? They seemed as nice a married couple as any I get here."

Sam shut his eyes for a moment. Had he just heard the man correctly?

"A married couple?" Kit exploded. "Tell me they didn't share a room?"

The landlord's hands gripped a corner of his apron. He must know already from their faces that whatever his guests had been up to, it wasn't anything good. "I'm sorry to say, they did." He eyed Kit up and down, assessing his status. "Milord."

"Are they still here?" Sam blurted out, his hand going to his hip, almost as though he expected to find a weapon there. But they'd left their pistols stowed in their saddlebags.

The landlord shook his head. "They left about an hour and a half ago. Heading north." The wariness in his eyes deepened. "I'd no way of telling they weren't what they said they were." He'd taken on an apologetic tone, no doubt fearing blame being apportioned in his direction.

Sam couldn't keep quiet. "How did she seem? This morning? Was she… happy?"

The landlord shrugged. "My wife saw her more than I did. She went in to help her dress as the young lady had no maid with her. I'll fetch her for you. Agnes!" A shout brought a stout matron at least twice her skinny husband's width into the taproom with such alacrity that surely she must have been listening at the door.

"Young Mrs. Wainwright, this morning, how did she seem to you when you helped her dress?"

Mrs. Wainwright? Sam bristled with fury, his fists balling by his sides. Oh, to give that despicable man a good hiding. He'd pull his cork, plant him a facer, rearrange his physiog, break every bone in his wicked, lust-filled body. He'd make it so the man could never seduce a girl again. He'd…

Agnes, a redoubtable woman with her gray hair scraped back into a tight bun and topped with a small lacy mob cap, set her hands on her hips and looked from Kit to Sam and then back again, interrupting Sam's increasingly violent thoughts. "Runaway, is she?"

Kit nodded.

"Under age and eloping?"

Sam's turn to nod.

"Well, you're too late."

"What d'you mean?" Kit asked.

The woman shook her head. "Quiet and kind of withdrawn,

she were this morning, when I went in to help her. Mr. Wain-wright, he'd gone down to take breakfast in the taproom. Got an eye for the ladies, that one. Caught him pressing my girl Meg up against the scullery door, his hand up her dress. Soon stopped him doin' that. Not that Meg minded any. She's a soft spot for a pretty face, and that Mr. Wainwright's got one for sure."

If Sam had his way, he wouldn't be keeping that pretty face for much longer.

"Get to the point, woman," her husband snapped.

"I got her dressed and her hair done, but she didn't want no breakfast. When she went downstairs to the taproom, I stripped the bed to wash the sheets. I know that mark of blood on the sheets when I see it. Your girl's not a girl anymore. He's had his way with her."

"The bastard!" Sam burst out, unable to control himself any longer, fisting and unfisting his hands.

"I'll kill him," Kit said, his voice icy cold. "I'll kill the black-guard."

"You'll have to be quick," Sam said. "Because if I get to him first, there'll be nothing left of him for you."

Kit banged his fist on the bar. "They have but an hour and a half on us. We'll catch them today. Innkeep, fetch us some porter and bread and cheese. We'll eat it while our horses are attended to and then we'll be on the road again. He'll not have another night with my sister nor another night on this Earth, if I have my way."

Sam swallowed. If, as seemed likely from the evidence of Agnes, Ysella had already lost her maidenhead to the fellow, what was to become of her after the death of her seducer? Was Kit even thinking straight? Despite his own boiling fury, Sam had to keep a clear head. Someone had to, because Kit clearly wasn't.

The innkeeper fetched them sustenance and he and his wife retreated. Sam managed to eat only a small portion of the food, but downed the porter and took a refill. After the second tankard, a modicum of common sense came over him. "We can't kill him," he said. "If we kill him, it's us who'll be in trouble for it. You especially."

Kit scowled. "He's defiled my sister. Snatched her from her family, run off with her and debauched her. What else should a man do? It's a matter of honor."

"If you hang for killing him, what's Morvoren supposed to do? And Ysella as well. She'll have lost her place in society and have no protector." Although in that dire situation, Sam would himself stand by her as protector if allowed.

Kit banged his tankard down on the bar. "Are you saying we can't exact punishment?"

"I am. We just have to get her back. If we do that, he can go rot." Much as it rankled to say this, common sense had to take precedence here over the longing for revenge. Easy to see Kit and Ysella were related—both of them hotheaded and impulsive.

Kit bit his lip. "I shall challenge him to a duel. It's the least I can do in defense of Ysella's honor."

"I don't think that's a good idea, either. They're illegal."

"Only a little. I know for a fact, most duels go unremarked."

"If you have to do something like that, then of course I'll be your second, but who will be his? If you go challenging him to a duel and hope to get away with it, you have to carry it out correctly. I don't see how you can do that. A duel is *not* a good idea. And didn't you say he's already killed a man in a duel? He must be a good shot. He *is* a soldier, after all. Suppose he kills you? Ysella and Morvoren would be alone in the world. And so would little George."

"He'll just have to find someone who'll stand for him. I don't care. My aim is to kill him, not let him kill me."

Sam sighed, sensing he was on a losing wicket here. "Wounding him would be better. Less likely to cause a storm afterwards. If he has any sense he'll flee with his tail between his legs."

"That's it." Kit threw down his half-eaten food. "I've had enough. I'm not waiting around here while the cad makes off with my sister. It's time he learned a few home truths about her

supposed fortune. I'll wager that'll make him change his tune."
He laughed, sounding and looking just like his late father again. "I
can't wait to see his face when I tell him he can't get his hands on
her money for another eleven years."

Sam bit his tongue. He wanted to exact revenge on Featherstone as much as Kit did, but he was nowhere near as hotheaded.
It would be up to him to make sure Kit didn't do anything stupid
that would jeopardize Morvoren's future happiness. Ysella would
not want her brother to be jailed, or worse, hanged, because of
something she'd done.

The horses were still being groomed in the inn yard when
they got there. "Saddle them up," Kit almost shouted. "We're
leaving."

A few minutes later they were trotting up the high street and
leaving Banbury behind them.

YSELLA SAT IN the gig beside Oliver with the blankets pulled up
over her knees and her hands tucked underneath them. Today, he
hadn't bothered to ask for hot bricks and she was already cold as
he'd put the hood down which he said would help the horse to
pull the gig faster. Today, he didn't seem nearly so loving as he
had yesterday. Was it something she'd done? Had she not
performed last night as he'd expected her to? At least he hadn't
wanted to repeat the experience. He'd got dressed in a hurry in
the morning and disappeared downstairs, leaving her to try and
get herself ready to leave alone.

When the landlord's wife arrived to help her dress, Ysella had
nearly thrown herself into her ample arms and hugged her. She'd
been racking her brains about how to get dressed without the
help of a maid, terrified lest she had to ask Oliver to help and he
decided a repeat of last night was required.

But it had been so embarrassing. She'd been sure the landlord's wife had known every detail of her story just from looking at her face. Surely the guilt at having behaved like a common strumpet was written in large letters across her forehead, along with the words "not married" or "fornicator" or even "loose-moraled woman." Once she was ready to leave the inn, she kept her head down to avoid meeting the accusing eyes of those who must be able to read what had happened last night in the way she looked and walked.

Their horse was lively this morning after a night's rest and some good fodder, its hooves beating a tattoo on the road where the surface was reasonably firm and level. However, much of the rest of the road was in a parlous condition, being rutted and muddy, and in some places other road users had beaten a way through hedgerows and driven through the fields on either side of what was little more than an uneven track. Oliver followed suit where it was expedient.

Ysella regarded his classical profile. He still seemed handsome to her, but now she saw a certain arrogance in his features, and a hardness that she'd missed before. The thought that he'd had what he wanted from her dawned, and that she was little better than the scullery maid at Ormonde who'd given herself to the gardener's boy and found herself with child. Which had led to the immediate dismissal of both unfortunates.

Her breath caught in her throat. Supposing she were to be with child? Could it happen the first time she'd done it? Oliver had said not, in his haste to persuade her to acquiesce to his attentions, but had he been right? Morvoren, with her superior knowledge, had given Ysella quite an informative lecture, with diagrams, on how a baby was made. And she'd definitely done the thing that caused that to happen. Did it happen every time you did it? Hot color suffused her face and she looked away from Oliver, out at the drab passing countryside.

They passed through a few villages where out in the fields the men had their teams out ploughing, despite the wetness of the ground. They'd be doing that at Ormonde. A flock of gulls peppered the gray sky, settling on newly ploughed ground to search for worms and leatherjackets. If she and Oliver went to live in London, she'd never see the march of the countryside's seasons and all that involved again. A sense of fatalism descended over Ysella. She'd made her bed, and now she'd have to sleep in it. A very accurate idiom for what she'd done last night, not that it had involved much sleeping.

The gig breasted a hill and began the gentle descent towards some woodland and a river valley. From behind, there came a shout.

Ysella peered over her shoulder. Two riders were galloping towards them. One of them was waving his arms.

Oliver twisted around, the grim smile on his handsome face rendering it quite unpleasant. "So, they've caught us up at last, have they?" he snarled. "Well, they're too bloody late. You're mine, and there's nothing they can do about it."

He heaved on the reins and brought the gig to a halt.

Chapter Twenty

S AM HAD BEEN the first to spot the tiny shape of the gig ahead
of them. "There!" he cried, his heart soaring. "Just approaching that woodland. Come on." He dug his heels into poor
Hercules's sides and urged him into a gallop, as Kit did the same
to Abelard. They thundered down the uneven road surface,
careless of the many ruts and potholes.

The driver of the gig was proceeding at a steady trot and they
were gaining on him fast, when Kit shouted. The head of one of
the gig's passengers peered over the folded down hood. A small
white face beneath a bonnet stared back at them.

The driver, who must have seen he had no chance of outrun-
ning them, made no attempt at flight but brought the gig to a
halt.

Sam and Kit hauled their sweating horses to a stop to either
side of the vehicle, Sam on Ysella's side, itching to snatch her
straight out of it and onto the pommel of his saddle. He con-
trolled this impulse with some difficulty.

Featherstone, holding the reins casually in one hand, sat close
beside Ysella, the smug smile on his face turning his good looks
sour, his other hand resting on her thigh in the ultimate of
possessive gestures.

Ysella, her brown eyes wide with what had to be a mixture of
terror and surprise, stared from Sam's face to Kit's and then back

again. A tear ran down her cheek. Her pale face, and the dark circles beneath her eyes, gave her the appearance of a frightened, half-starved child, not a young woman old enough to elope with her lover. If Sam's heart hadn't already been cracked in two, it would have broken for her now.

"Well met," Featherstone said, a jaunty tone to his voice, as though this were some social event and they were all good friends. "Very fortuitous. Now Ysella and I won't need to drive all the way to bloody Scotland. We can get married down here."

"There's nothing well met about this," Kit snarled. "Get down from there, Ysella. I've come to take you home."

Ysella's frightened gaze darted between her brother and her lover. Sam saw the indecision in it, and his heart ached for her, despite knowing what she'd already done. He still cherished the forlorn hope that the landlord's wife had been mistaken.

"She's going nowhere," Featherstone said, his lips curling into a grin as he tightened his hold on Ysella's thigh. All handsomeness vanished, leaving just cruelty and self-satisfaction on his face.

The man was an evil cad, and Ysella had to be rescued and he'd be the one to do it. Sam slid down from Hercules's saddle and stepped up to the side of the gig. "Come, Ysella. Get down and rejoin your brother. You don't want to do this."

"Oh yes, she does," Featherstone drawled. "In fact, she was very willing to do it last night. Very willing indeed. It's too late for you to try locking her away like Sleeping Beauty, Ormonde. She gave herself to me last night and, even now, she might have my child in her belly. How would you explain that away if she's not married to the father?"

It took immense self-control on Sam's part not to set his foot on the gig's step, lean over Ysella and lock his hands around Featherstone's neck. How he longed to throttle the life out of him. But even though he would like it to be, this was not his fight, but Kit's.

Kit brought Abelard closer to Featherstone's side of the gig. "You will find," he said, his voice hard enough to shatter rocks, "that you have been misinformed on the state of my sister's inheritance. Something I am certain is the thing you find most attractive about her."

Sam put out his hand to Ysella. "Come. Get down. This is going to get nasty and you need to be out of the way."

Her brown eyes, rimmed with pain, met his, and she put her small, icy-cold, gloved hand into his. She made to rise.

"Sit still, Ysella," Featherstone snarled, the hand on her thigh tightening still further. Sam didn't release her hand. If this became a tug-o-war, then so be it.

Featherstone hadn't taken his gaze from Kit's face. Was that a trace of worry that had elbowed out the smug self-satisfaction?

Kit smiled at him, a smile that didn't reach his cold eyes. "If my cousin Fitz told you she has a sizeable dowry, then he was right. But what he didn't know and couldn't tell you was that I have control of when she gets it, and how much she gets of it, if any, until she turns thirty. If I don't approve of the man she marries, then she'll not get a penny for the next eleven years. Think you can live like that? Is she worth waiting that long for? Do you love her enough to live on your captain's pay for eleven long years? Support a family, pay rent on a house in Town, provide for her all by yourself? And I can tell you, she has expensive tastes and is used to only the best of everything."

Featherstone's mouth fell open.

Kit's smile vanished, and his eyes narrowed. "Not the heiress you thought her, is she?"

Featherstone's grip on Ysella's leg slackened and Sam took advantage, pulling her towards him. She half climbed, half fell out of the gig into his arms. Holding her tight against him, he pulled her to where Hercules stood calmly observing the scene. He caught his horse's reins in one hand, the other arm remaining encircled around Ysella. His whole body thrilled with the feel of her pressed against him, warm and safe as though this were where she was meant to be. All he wanted to do was protect her from harm—from the harm this man had inflicted on her.

Featherstone shook his head. "You're lying." But the doubt showed in his eyes.

"Try me," Kit retorted. "Ask my estate manager. He does all the books. He knows."

Featherstone looked at Sam.

For a moment Sam held the man's anxious eyes, seeing what lay within his soul. His greedy, avaricious soul. "It's true. Ysella gets nothing until she's thirty if Lord Ormonde doesn't like her choice of husband. Not a single penny."

"And that means you," Kit said. "Because, Featherstone, I don't like *you*."

Featherstone's mouth worked. "You mean you'd see your sister in penury?"

Kit nodded, his mouth a set line.

"And her children?"

"If they were yours."

A long silence stretched out. Featherstone looked across at where Sam still held Ysella tight within his embrace, her small hands pressed against his chest. "Well," he said, with what looked like deliberate calm. "It's a good thing I no longer wish to marry your sister then."

"What?" Ysella's startled voice cut through the charged air. "But you said you loved me." For a moment she struggled in Sam's arms, before her body sagged against his.

"That was when you had a sizeable fortune to your name, my dear Ysella," Featherstone snapped. "You were a sight more attractive back then. A shame, but there you are, a man's got to do his best for himself and damn the consequences."

In one swift movement, Kit leaned forward from Abelard's saddle and grabbed Featherstone by his lapels, dragging him half out of the gig. "I knew you for a fortune hunter the moment I laid eyes on you. A fortune hunter and a cad." Abelard, deprived of a controlling hand on the reins, took a few steps forward and Featherstone came right out of the gig. Kit released his hold, letting him drop into the wet mud underfoot.

Ysella gasped in shock, but made no effort to go to him.

Featherstone lay in the mud for a long moment as though totally surprised by what had just happened to him. Then he pushed himself up, his face contorting in anger. His clothes were liberally covered in filth. A sly, malevolent expression replaced the anger. "How dare you insult me so, sir?" He brushed himself down, but that didn't improve matters, merely smearing the mud still further. "I take offense at your treatment of this honest suitor for your sister's hand." He glanced across at Sam and Ysella. "And I challenge you to a duel."

Oh no. Sam had thought he'd only needed to persuade *Kit* not to challenge the man, but he'd not taken into account that the bounder might challenge Kit.

Ysella gave a small scream of horror and buried her face in Sam's coat. He held her a little tighter.

"Accepted," Kit spat. "Although I don't know where you'll find yourself a second in the middle of nowhere. You can see *mine* is ready and waiting." He nodded at Sam. "Now, get back in your vehicle and go and find someone stupid enough to want to help you before I knock you down again."

"I don't need a second," Featherstone erupted, clearly boiling with a rage more to do with the indignity he'd just suffered than anything regarding Ysella. Sam knew a man whose pride had been dented when he saw one. "I'll fight you right now." A dangerous light glowed in Featherstone's eyes that Sam didn't like one bit.

Sam pushed Ysella behind himself. "We're not doing it without the proper seconds. You'll have to furnish one or back down." Hopefully, this would prevent the duel taking place and calm matters down. Sam would far rather have punched Featherstone on the nose a few times, well, a lot of times, than faced him in an illegal duel. The former would give him a lot more pleasure.

Abelard fidgeted under Kit's overtight hands on the reins. "And prove yourself the coward you are." His lip curled in a sneer worthy of his father.

Oh no. Trust Kit to add fuel to the flames. Sam swore under his breath. All he wanted to do was get Ysella away from this man as fast as he could.

"No one calls *me* a coward." Featherstone climbed back into the gig. "At the next village, I'll drag the blacksmith or the baker out to stand second for me. You see if I don't. Now, get out of my way." He lashed the horse across its back with the whip, and it leapt forward in its traces, jerking the gig along behind it, the wheels sending mud flying.

Sam watched it make its rattling way along the road, one hand still on Ysella's arm where she stood beside him now. She gave a little sob. He turned around, and without thinking, took her in his arms again. The most natural thing, to hold the crying girl tight against his chest, to put his hands on her back and pat her sorrows away. If that were at all possible. If only he could keep on doing this.

"Right," Kit said, wheeling Abelard around and spraying still more mud up. "To the next village it is."

"No!" Ysella cried, her voice muffled against Sam's greatcoat. "You mustn't fight him, Kit. You mustn't." Her voice shook. "I'm not worth it. I'm a terrible sister and I've done terrible things. It's all my fault. Don't fight him. Please don't. I don't want you getting hurt because of me."

Kit looked down at her from the great height Abelard gave him. "On the contrary, Ysella," he said, his voice just as cold as it had been with Featherstone. "I'm not fighting him for you but for my own honor. As you have none of your own worth fighting for."

Sam bristled at Kit's words and held Ysella tighter. Tears ran down her face, but she didn't argue with his description of her. Instead she wailed, "He's a soldier, Kit. Don't fight him. He'll be a deadly shot. I know he will be."

Sam nodded, determined to deter Kit from his course. "And he'll get first shot as he challenged you. He could kill you, and then what will become of Ysella? You'd not be there to control her fortune, and he'd marry her in a trice and get his hands on her money, which is what he wants. And it's plain he doesn't love her. Even she can see that now. That'll be why he's challenged you. He must think if he kills you, he'll get what he wants." He looked down at the girl in his arms. "And I'm sure she doesn't want to marry him now she's discovered all he was after was her fortune."

For answer Ysella burst into more sobs. They might have been because she thought she still loved Featherstone, or for his betrayal of her, or out of fear for Kit. Sam had no idea. All he wanted was to be able to stem her tears and tell her everything was going to be all right. But he couldn't.

He fished his handkerchief out of his coat pocket and handed it to her. She blew her nose on it with vigor.

"What are we waiting for?" Kit said. "He'll be at the next village already selecting some yokel to act as his second. Get back on your horse. Ysella can ride with you, as Hercules is more up to weight than Abelard."

Sam looked at Ysella. She didn't appear to be in any condition to ride, but he had to do as Kit said. He couldn't let his employer continue on without him to the village. Who knew but that Featherstone wouldn't be lying in wait around the next corner like a common ruffian, preparing to forestall the duel by picking Kit off in advance.

He held out his hand. "Here, put your foot in my hand and I'll give you a leg up. You can sit on the pommel of my saddle."

"If I had my boys' clothes," Ysella said with a sniff. "I could ride astride very easily."

"Well, you don't," Kit almost snarled, as though her boys' clothes had been the root cause of her predicament. "So get up quickly and we'll continue."

With uncharacteristic obedience, Ysella set her small, booted foot in Sam's hands and consented to being hoisted onto the front of his saddle. Sam mounted himself and settled her half on the pommel and half across his lap, her legs hanging down on the left of Hercules. This was going to prove an awkward ride. It had been all right to hold her close and comfort her on the ground, but now she was almost in his lap, with the pressure of her weight resting on his legs, a wave of embarrassment washed over him. She had her head down, her whole body leaning against his chest, perhaps in shame at what she'd done and how Featherstone had treated her, so hopefully she wouldn't notice his hot cheeks.

They set off down the road in the direction the gig had departed.

YSELLA NESTLED AGAINST Sam's strong chest, keeping her head bowed. She had no desire to look either him or Kit in the eye. How dare Oliver reveal what they'd done last night as though it were something to boast about? Her feelings for him had undergone a radical transformation the moment he'd declared he no longer wanted to marry her, his words still echoing through her mind in a most confusing manner. But her poor deceived heart still ached for what she'd thought she was going to have.

He'd said he didn't want to marry her if she had no fortune. His sneering laughter. His smug face when he'd told Kit and Sam how she'd wanted to do that *thing* last night. How he'd persuaded her into it by telling her they'd soon be married. How her body had betrayed her by wanting to do it. How it had hurt and he'd just rolled over afterwards and gone to sleep, when really, she'd wanted him to hold her in his arms and reassure her. How mortifying this whole affair was becoming. More tears ran down her cheeks to soak into Sam's coat front.

The fact that she was even now being held in Sam's strong arms added more layers to her humiliation. That he should see her like this and know what she'd done. It was bad enough that Kit should discover her stupidity, but for Sam to have been witness to it as well? Sam, her dear friend, a man who'd always been there for her whenever she needed him. Sam, who would now see her as soiled goods. She'd never marry now. And if she had a child after what Oliver had done to her, it would be a bastard, without rights of any kind. Perhaps she should run away, but this time by herself, instead of bringing shame on her family.

How quickly fancied love could change to hate. Yes, she hated Oliver for how he'd duped her. But he wasn't the only one to blame. She was too. She'd been everything she shouldn't have been—headstrong, selfish, thoughtless, and above all, foolish. And Oliver had taken full advantage of that.

And now he'd challenged Kit to a duel, all because Kit had, rightfully it now seemed, seen him for what he was and come to rescue her. She should have listened to Kit. It would be all her fault if anything happened to Kit. Oliver, as the challenger, would get first shot, and he would kill Kit. Then he'd come back for her and make her marry him to get his hands on her fortune, and she'd be stuck with a man she could no more love now than the lowest beggar in the street.

She began to feel warmer as Sam's body heat seeped into her. The smell of horses and some faint remembrance of men's perfume overlaid a hint of sweat. The smell of a real man, not a dandy like Oliver who reeked of heavy perfume. Ysella snuggled in closer to Sam's reassuring bulk, a suggestion of safety adhering to his presence. If Oliver did kill Kit, heaven forbid, then surely Sam would never let him take her.

$$\cdots\!\cdot\!\circ\!\!\infty\!\!\circ\!\cdot\!\cdots$$

Chapter Twenty-One

Y SELLA STOOD BESIDE the tiny inn's back door next to a row of barrels, watching the innkeeper checking over the two pistols Kit had provided for the duel. Oliver stood close by, his eyes fixed on the innkeeper. Did he think Kit would cheat and give him a dud pistol? She added that to the growing list of things she didn't like, no, hated, now, about Oliver. It only served to make her more conscious of her own terrible behavior and bring fresh heat to her cheeks.

"She's not to watch," Kit said to Sam, who was also closely observing the innkeeper's actions. He'd turned out to be a retired mail coach driver with a good working knowledge of pistols, and quite happy to be asked to stand as a second when an unknown gentleman had come hammering on his door.

Although Ysella was now of the firm opinion that the term "gentleman" no longer seemed to fit Oliver.

Kit slipped out of his coat to stand in his shirt sleeves and brocade waistcoat, and Sam laid it on one of the barrels. Oliver had already removed his.

The innkeeper, clearly enjoying this interlude to his landlordly duties, had eagerly offered up his orchard behind the inn as the prospective battleground. And he'd informed all parties present that no one was likely to disturb them, and that the local constable never came to the village.

Sam nodded, a hint of relief in his eyes.

Ysella felt none of that though. What was it about these men that made them think they could keep on telling her what to do? They were all at it. Kit and Oliver were both tarred with the same brush. They both only saw her as an object, not a person. And now this object was to be fought over. Ridiculous.

The innkeeper set the pistols side by side on the lid of another of the barrels, and Sam approached Ysella, an apologetic expression on his face.

"Ysella," he said, his voice gentle and persuasive. "Kit's right. It's best if you don't witness this. It could be bloody. You should wait in the inn."

She looked him up and down. Everything about him was so familiar to her, from the top of his sandy head to his mud-spattered boots. He knew her as well as Kit did, if not better, as for years Kit had hardly been at Ormonde. He must know that she couldn't wait inside like a normal girl would. That she wasn't a girl to have the vapors at the sight of blood. She shook her head. "No. This is all my fault. I have to watch. You can't stop me."

By the makeshift weapons' table, Kit shook his head in exasperation and turned away. "Very well. Let this be the start of her penance. To watch her lover's punishment." He picked up one of the pistols and strode into the orchard.

Ysella bit her lip. No use pleading with him any further. He'd made his mind up and she might only make matters worse. She was going to have to watch this farce, for that was what it was, to the bitter end. What if she bolted now and took Abelard and ran? Would they still pursue their duel?

"Stay by the gate then," Sam said. "Keep well away from the line of fire. We don't want you being hit by a stray shot."

Ysella stopped at the open gate, one hand on the rough wooden gatepost, her heart hammering against her ribs. Did she want Oliver to die? Her heart was torn. Until so recently she'd considered herself in love with him, despite what he'd done last night and how much she hadn't liked it. Could she change her mind this quickly, or was it only pique that he'd said he didn't want to marry her without her fortune? But one thing she didn't want was for him to kill Kit.

"Twenty paces apart," Sam said to the innkeeper. "Does that meet with your agreement?"

"Twelve," Oliver said. "All the better for me to kill Ormonde."

The innkeeper shook his head. "This is my orchard and if I say 'tis to be twenty paces, then that's what it'll be." Presumably he wasn't keen to be left with an unaccountable dead body to deal with if they stood closer together. The local constable would have something to say about that, for sure.

Ysella heaved a sigh of relief. She knew from experience, as Kit had taught her to shoot when she was a girl, that at twenty paces it would take a crack marksman to hit his target. If only Oliver were not a soldier with a soldier's experience with pistols. But Kit was a good shot too. She didn't want either of them to die. Kit because he was her brother, and Oliver because she didn't want Kit jailed for murder. But there was nothing she could do to stop this.

An urge rose in her to tell Sam to kill Oliver if he should manage to kill Kit, but they were too far away now, lining up ready to fire, and she didn't think Sam had a gun of his own, anyway. Sam and the innkeeper had marked out the twenty paces, and both young men now stood facing one another, slightly at an angle so as to give a narrower target.

Both of them raised their pistols.

Ysella held her breath.

A sharp report rang out and Kit staggered backwards, his hand up to the left side of his head. Smoke rose from Oliver's pistol.

Ysella had to hang onto the gatepost to keep herself upright. Blood was flowing between Kit's fingers, but he was still upright, and his face had contorted with rage.

Ysella didn't need telling. Oliver had been aiming for Kit's head. The intent had been to kill him. This wasn't just a case of wounding an opponent for the sake of one's honor, or discharging one's pistol into the air and saving face. This was all-out war.

"Are you all right to continue?" The innkeeper asked Sam and Kit.

Kit nodded. "I am." He dropped his hand revealing an ear covered in blood that was now running down into the collar of his shirt. He lifted his pistol again and pointed it at Oliver, who stood very still, his face deathly pale. He must realize Kit knew his intention had been to kill, and now feared Kit would do the same to him.

The barrel lowered, now directed at Oliver's lower limbs, lingering near where his legs met his body. Kit held it there for a long moment before the nose of the gun rose towards Oliver's head. Would he take a headshot as Oliver had? Did he want to kill him? Was he the better shot of the two? Or might he have the better pistol? Or luck on his side perhaps?

Ysella caught her breath again.

Kit's shot rang out, echoing around the orchard. Oliver staggered and a red flower of blood blossomed on his right sleeve. The pistol he was still holding dropped from his slack fingers and his left hand shot up to cover the wound, but he didn't fall. Winged only. Not a wound he should die from.

To her immense surprise, Ysella felt nothing but relief. Relief that Kit hadn't killed him and would have to be arrested or become a fugitive, relief that it was all over and honor, at least for the two men, had been satisfied.

The innkeeper dashed forward with the box of bandages he'd brought with him to attend to his man, and Kit walked over to the gate, a handkerchief held to his bleeding ear, while Sam went to join the innkeeper to check on Oliver's wound, as etiquette demanded.

For one dreadful moment, Ysella thought she was the only one who saw what happened next. Oliver, who'd had his back to them all, swung around, his hand going to the top of his boot. As it came up, a small pocket pistol caught the sunlight as he leveled it at Kit's back.

Ysella opened her mouth to scream.

But she hadn't been the only one to see his perfidy. Sam, who was closest to Oliver, threw himself at the gun, and he and Oliver crashed to the ground. The pistol went off with a sharp crack, and now Ysella did scream. All she could see was Sam on the ground on top of Oliver, pounding him with his fists, and Oliver trying to fight back but very much on the losing side.

Kit ran back, and he and the innkeeper pulled Sam off Featherstone, who lay in the dirt with his nose and mouth bleeding and his face mottled red from Sam's furious blows, his chest heaving for breath. Sam's own nose dripped blood onto the front of his coat. He gave himself a shake. "That's for what you did to Ysella," he spat, and gave Featherstone a kick. "And for cheating in a duel. You're no gentleman, and if you breathe a word anywhere of what you've done to her, I'll make damn sure everyone in London who matters knows you cheated in a duel and tried to shoot your opponent in the back."

Ysella ran to Sam's side and clutched his arm. "Oh, Sam, that was magnificent. You saved Kit's life." How could she have ever fancied herself to have feelings for the creature lying on the ground at her feet, abject in the mud for the second time today. He would have murdered her brother in cold blood. She'd seen it with her own eyes.

Sam put an arm around her and led her away from where Oliver still lay sprawled. She went willingly, the realization that she never had to see him again filling her with relief.

Leaving the innkeeper to put a bandage on Oliver's grazed arm, Ysella, still with Sam's supportive arm around her, followed Kit back inside the inn. The taproom was empty of all but the old man who'd been sitting in the corner by the fire when they'd arrived. The innkeeper's wife, who had probably been watching the goings on in the orchard from the kitchen, bustled in. With a comforting smile for Ysella, she took her place behind a makeshift bar constructed of rough planks on top of barrels. "What can I get for you, Milord?"

Kit shot Sam a quick smile. "Brandies all round. For the old man in the corner as well. And tell us the nearest place we can hire a carriage to take us back to Wiltshire."

THE JOURNEY HOME was a far slower affair than the madcap race north had been. In the end, they had to ride as far as Banbury to hire a carriage to take Ysella home, raising some eyebrows on their arrival with her sitting in front of Sam on Hercules.

They took a private parlor at the old Reindeer Inn, where a tolerable dinner was served to them by the landlord himself. While they ate, he enquired for them as to where they could hire a carriage and driver and came back as they were finishing the meal with the news that he'd procured one for them.

Sam, who'd not had much of an appetite, had been watching Ysella covertly as she pushed her own food around her plate and took only small sips of her claret. Try as he might, he couldn't put the unwelcome image of her being violated by that cad out of his head. Her whole demeanor had changed. Gone was the feisty girl he was used to. In her place, had appeared a downtrodden, unhappy young woman. And, perish the thought, what was she to do if Oliver was right and she really was with child? That awful scenario plagued his mind as he attempted to do justice to the good food.

Kit ate in a silence that matched the other two, but he at least managed to put away his food, as though his close brush with death had stimulated his appetite for living and all things associated with it.

At last, they were ready to leave. The carriage was not of the best, but it would do well to transport them to Oxford where Kit said they should spend the night. And tomorrow, they could hire a more respectable vehicle for the journey back to Ormonde. So, with Abelard and Hercules tied on behind the carriage, they set off back along the Oxford road, a somewhat subdued and silent party.

Once at Oxford, Ysella retired immediately to the room Kit had taken for her, leaving Kit and Sam to eat alone in their small private parlor. A fire blazed comfortingly in the hearth and the food again was good. Between them they finished off two jugs of claret and started on the brandy bottle the landlord brought them. At length, leaving the table, they took the two wing chairs to either side of the fire and settled down with their glasses.

After the cold of the day's journey, the heat of the flames came as a pleasant relief. Both Sam and Kit rested their muddy, booted feet on the fender and relaxed back in their seats. A warm sense of achievement settled on Sam. Ysella was safe from that cad, and the world was the right way up again.

"What am I supposed to do with her now?" Kit asked, swirling his brandy around in the glass and staring into the flames.

Unsure whether he was supposed to reply, Sam just shrugged. He'd imbibed enough of the brandy now to be feeling exceedingly mellow. He was going to sleep well tonight for the first time in days, secure in the knowledge that Ysella was safe again.

Kit crossed his legs at the ankle. "She can't go back to London, that's certain. Not now."

Beyond worrying if Ysella might indeed be with child, nothing else about her future had crossed Sam's mind, so glad was he to have her back safely "within the fold." He forbore from asking "Why not?" which would have been stupid but had been the first thing he'd thought of. No. Kit was right. She was what would be termed "spoiled goods" now, and no member of the ton would offer for her.

He heaved a deep sigh. If ever a girl needed a friendly advocate, it was Ysella, but arguing for her to continue with her old plans would take her away from him. Sam steeled himself to make a sacrifice. "Need anyone ever know?" He poured himself another brandy. "I doubt Featherstone is going to go shouting about it. Not after having tried to murder you, and what I threatened him with."

Kit nodded. "That's true, but it doesn't detract from the fact that she may be..." He hesitated, perhaps unwilling to put the thought into word.

"That she may be with child?" Sam said, the words sticking in his craw as well. How much it hurt to have to say them.

Kit nodded. "I can't let her go back to Town if we don't know she's... presentable. And she won't be, if she has a bastard growing in her belly." He sighed. "Morvoren would know what to do. I don't even know how long we have to wait before we can be sure she's not. We need to get home as quickly as possible so I can talk to Morvoren."

Sam took a long gulp of brandy, fiery heat burning a track down his throat. The thought of Ysella's belly growing to the proportions Morvoren's had taken on troubled him no end. With an alien, unwanted child. And her with her reputation in ruins. As it would be if anyone caught a whiff of the scandal she had caused.

Yes, calm and sensible Morvoren would know what to do.

Chapter Twenty-Two

MORVOREN DID KNOW what to do, as it turned out. Once they'd arrived back at Ormonde, and Kit had sent Ysella to her room in disgrace with orders not to come out of it again for a week, Sam went with him to see Morvoren in her room.

"You're back," she exclaimed, looking up from the book she was reading. "How was Bath?" Kit had taken her there to take the waters when she'd first been with child and had suffered from a lot of sickness, so this was where Kit had told his mother to say they'd gone. Sam knew, because Morvoren had confided in him, that she had only pretended to drink the sulfurous waters to please Kit.

She looked very becoming with her hair loose to her shoulders and a pretty, pale-blue shawl wrapped around her. Some color had returned to her thin cheeks and an air of health hung about her that had not been there when they'd left such a short time ago.

"Ah," Kit said, taking the chair beside her bed. "A small white lie. We haven't been to Bath."

Morvoren inclined her head to one side much as a dog will when being talked to. "I had a suspicion you hadn't been."

What? How had she known? Sam distinctly remembered Kit asking the dowager to tell Morvoren that they had gone to Bath on business to look at some agricultural machinery Kit was thinking of buying.

Morvoren, who seemed to be taking all this very calmly, smiled at their discomfiture. "I'm not stupid, and neither are the servants. Loveday has brought me every bit of gossip from the servants' hall while you've been away, so I know Ysella has been missing. And I can see, Kit, that you have been in some kind of fight by the state your ear is in." She indicated the stool beside her dressing table. "Do sit down, Sam, you look like a spare part standing there fiddling with your cuffs."

Sam pulled the upholstered stool nearer to her bed and sat down, trying hard to leave his cuffs alone.

"I didn't want you getting upset about Ysella," Kit said. "Not with you having been so ill."

Morvoren sighed. "Oh, Kit, darling, I'm well on the road to recovery now, have no fear. I should be up and about if it weren't for Doctor Busick. My legs will atrophy if I have to stay in bed much longer. And being upset over Ysella would not have set me back at all but given me something to think about. I'm so bored having to sit here all day and sew or read. And you know how much I hate to sew. Now, tell me what's been happening to her, because otherwise, all I have to go on is the gossip from the back stairs."

So, Kit, with Sam adding in his own bits here and there, recounted the tale of their rescuing of Ysella. When he at last ground to a halt, having informed his wife that Ysella was now confined to her room, a silence fell.

Sam watched Morvoren as she frowned down at her hands as though deep in thought. An intelligent and resourceful woman, as well as a sensible one, she must surely have an answer to their problems. Hopefully.

She reached out and took Kit's hand, but her eyes were fixed on Sam, a speculative gleam in them. "Let me sum up the problem," she said, her gaze brimming with a mixture of determination and compassion. "Ysella fancied herself in love with a man who has turned out to be a cad. Who has been proven by his *own* words to be nothing but a fortune hunter. A man who only wanted to marry her because he thought she had a sizeable inheritance coming to her. Thanks, in part, to Fitz. And, because it was revealed to him that you could delay her coming into her money until she's thirty, he promptly withdrew his offer. Whereupon this degenerated into a rather childish fight resulting in you and him taking part in a duel—which is quite illegal nowadays, and a very silly thing to have done."

She bestowed a frown on Kit, then glared at Sam. "I would have expected you, Sam, to have persuaded my husband of the foolishness of fighting a duel with not just the illegality of the thing, but also all the risks involved."

Sam opened his mouth to say that he'd tried, but she held up a hand. "No. Let me have my say. You wanted my advice in this, and that's what you're going to get."

Sam shut his mouth, feeling put in his place. In the light of what he now knew about Featherstone's attempted perfidy, perhaps he should have tried harder. Neither of them had told Morvoren how close Kit had come to being murdered.

"But the nub of the matter is that while Ysella was with the man she fancied she loved, he persuaded her to consummate their love and she is now no longer a virgin."

Heat rose up Sam's face. Morvoren could be a tad too blunt at times, but that was her upbringing. She didn't possess the gently bred reluctance to talk about all things personal that most women had. Not that he had much experience of women or their conversation himself.

"So," Morvoren went on. "You are now quite rightly worrying that she might be with child. I can tell you that the chances of that are probably minimal, but that depends on a number of things. To ascertain a more accurate idea of her risk, I would need to talk with her myself."

"I'll see to that," Kit said, a hint of annoyance in his voice. Having told Ysella he didn't want to see her again for a week, Sam could see how he didn't want to have to go back on his word so soon after saying it.

"I can fetch her here if you like," Sam offered.

Morvoren shook her head. "This is women's talk. You can fetch her when you two leave, but neither of you is staying while I talk to her. It will be too embarrassing for her and for you. We will be discussing intimate matters. I also intend to help her find an answer to her problem—the problem of not being able to return to her London season in view of what's happened to her."

"Do you have any ideas of what we should do?" Kit asked.

Morvoren shrugged. "A few. But I need to talk to her first. She needs to be in agreement with my suggestions before I share them with you. I think it best if I see her straightaway."

YSELLA TAPPED ON Morvoren's bedroom door, heard a sweet voice bid her enter, and did as she was told. She found Morvoren sitting propped up in bed with a book open in her lap. She looked almost back to her old self, although still a little thin.

Ysella inwardly cringed with hot embarrassment. The certainty that she'd never be herself again washed over her. Gone was the old Ysella and in its place was the unforgiveable strumpet who her beloved Kit hated so much he'd said he didn't want to see her again for a week.

Morvoren smiled and patted the bed. "Come and sit here, beside me. No, not on the chair. Here where I can hold both your hands and comfort you."

Faced with such obvious compassion, Ysella burst into tears and flung herself into Morvoren's open arms, the book squashed between them. Eventually, her sobs began to lessen and she pushed herself upright again. She must look a sight with her eyes all red-rimmed and her face blotchy. No one would ever love her again, now she was not just spoiled but ugly as well. What an idiot she'd been.

"Oh, Ysella," Morvoren said. "How shall we sort this all out?"

"I don't know," Ysella said, sniffing. Where was her handkerchief when she needed it? She never seemed to have one. "I'm so sorry I've caused all this trouble and nearly got Kit killed. I didn't mean that to happen. I didn't know Oliver was only after my money." Her woes poured out in an avalanche. "He was so handsome that all the girls wanted to dance and go in to supper with him. But he chose *me*, and he said he loved me." She frowned. "And I *thought* I loved him, but now I think about it, I don't love him at all!" She wrinkled her small nose. "In fact, the very thought of him makes my toes curl with horror and my blood boil in my veins."

Morvoren passed her a clean handkerchief and patted her hands. "First love can be very hard, especially when someone sets out to fool you."

"He was so sincere," Ysella whispered. "I didn't for a moment think he was out to gull me. How was I supposed to know?" If this was life, then she wasn't sure she wanted what it had offered her. "How am I supposed to know if a man loves me or not? Are they all like Oliver? Out just to get what they want, and when they've had it, they don't care anymore about you."

Morvoren shook her head. "You're still very young, Ysella, with no experience of men. It's little wonder you were taken in by him. Partly, it's my fault. If I hadn't been the way I was, then Kit and I could have taken you up to Town ourselves and overseen your coming out."

Ysella shook her head. "No, it was nobody's fault but my own, and I will take the consequences. I deserve them for being such a fool." More tears ran down her cheeks and she gave an unladylike snort to clear her nose. "I'm sorry. What does being polite matter now? I'm never going back to London to the balls and parties. I'm never going to be happily married. I'm disgraced, and, on top of that, I might be with child." There. She'd said it. The thing that had been eating away at her ever since Oliver had declared he no longer wanted to marry her.

Morvoren patted her hand again. "That may very well not be the case. You'd be extremely unlucky if it were. Now, think carefully and tell me when your last courses began. Then we can work out the risk you took."

"My courses?" Ysella's cheeks flamed. This wasn't something she'd ever talked to anyone about before. Well, only Morvoren when she'd been explaining how babies were made, and that had been too embarrassing for words. She didn't even mention it to Martha, who seemed to have a certain intuition about when Ysella would need the cotton pads she used.

"Um," Ysella said, hesitating. "I think about two weeks ago."

Morvoren's face fell. Something must be bad about what she'd said.

"Well," Morvoren said, after a pause. "There might be some small danger of being with child. You were at the start of the at-risk time, although strictly speaking, no time in your monthly cycle is without some level of risk. But the chances are you're not. Higher than the chance that you are. As I said, you'd be very unlucky to conceive the very first time you had sex."

Ysella blushed again. Even after a year she couldn't quite accept Morvoren's casual references to things young ladies were not supposed to know about. "But I might be?"

Morvoren nodded. "But most likely you're not."

"When will I know?"

"In just over two weeks, if your courses don't arrive. That could mean you were with child. Although you also could just be a little late starting them. That can happen. They're not always perfectly regular."

Ysella freed a hand from Morvoren's grip and covered her mouth. "I think I feel sick."

"Come here for a hug." Morvoren held out her arms.

Ysella collapsed into them again, burying her face in Morvoren's soft shawl. "What am I going to do?"

Morvoren stroked her hair. "Well, to decide what to do you have to answer some questions."

Ysella nodded. "Go on."

"Firstly, do you want to return to London for the rest of the season? That is, if in two weeks you find out you're not with child?"

Ysella shook her head. "No. I couldn't go back. I couldn't face it. I don't think I ever want to go to Town again. Someone is *bound* to know, and even if they don't, I'll *think* they do. And I don't think I could trust a man again. Not after Oliver. I don't want any man like Oliver paying court to me ever again. I want to stay here, where I feel safe."

"And do you want to remain here unmarried for the foreseeable future?"

Ysella bit her lip. "Unmarried with a child?"

"No. I mean if there's no child. If there's a child, which I'm sure there won't be, we'll have to deal with it differently. What I mean is, do you wish to remain unmarried here at Ormonde for the rest of your life, a maiden aunt to my and Kit's children?"

Ysella was silent. Did she? For the rest of her life? That was forever. She'd be as old as Mama, who must be about a hundred, and only ever be an aunt. Did she, Ysella, want to reach that age without a husband in her life and children of her own? Although, of course, she didn't want *this* one, if it even existed. She shook her head. "No. I don't. I think I *would* like one day to be married, but no one is likely to take me, and I couldn't go to a man with a lie in my heart. No one will want me if they know what I've done."

"Men marry widows all the time."

"But I won't be a widow, will I? I'll just be a… a strumpet. A fallen woman. No better than the women who perform in bawdy houses."

"Then perhaps I have a solution."

"You do?"

Morvoren nodded. "Ysella, you are a flighty flibbertigibbet with little common sense. No, I don't mean that as an insult. It's part of what makes you so loveable. But you have been attracted to a man who was a little bit too much like you. A rake, a fortune hunter, a man with no sense of how to behave. In him, it was not at all attractive."

"I suppose so." How was Morvoren so wise at such a young age? Ysella would give her right eye for a small part of Morvoren's clever common sense and calm demeanor.

"What you need is a husband who knows what you've done but doesn't mind. A husband who will cherish you for what you are and let you be yourself. A husband who already cares deeply for you."

"I do?" Maybe Morvoren was right. "But where am I to find such a man here in the wilds of Wiltshire? Do you want me to tell him the truth about what I've done? I don't think any of the young men around here would accept me knowing that."

Morvoren hugged her tighter, her breath warm on Ysella's hair. "All you need to do is look beyond the end of your nose. There's a man, right here where you see him every day, who cares very deeply for you. You should marry Sam."

Chapter Twenty-Three

S AM WAS GLAD of the desk between him and Kit. It gave him something to hold on to, which he was much in need of doing. He gripped its edge with both hands until his knuckles whitened. *What* had Kit just asked him? *What* did he want him to do?

"So you see," Kit said, shifting awkwardly in his seat, probably as discomfited by what he was asking as Sam was at being asked. "Morvoren thought this would be a solution that would be, er, agreeable to all parties. I've been thinking about it for a few days, and I've come to the conclusion that she's right. She usually is."

Sam swallowed, struggling to find his voice but aware that an answer was required. "And does Ysella agree to this?" he finally managed to croak.

Kit nodded. "She has learned her lesson and will do as she's told where choosing a suitable husband is concerned. She told Morvoren she has no desire to remain an old maid in my house and I'm certainly in agreement with that. She might one day lead any daughters Morvoren gives me astray."

Sam almost smiled at the thought of Ysella becoming the sort of maiden aunt who led her nieces into scrapes, only the gravity of the matter preventing him. "But does she want to marry... *me?*"

Kit nodded. "The far more important question, my friend, is do you want to marry her?" He rubbed the side of his nose. "You are aware of both her misfortune and her foolish mistake. You know what she has done. She cannot return to Town to continue the season for she might be with child and her reputation will be shot. I can only hope no whisper of what she's done reaches the arbiters of the ton, but I fear it might, despite your threats to Featherstone. She would risk being shunned. Her only hope is to be married forthwith to someone for whom her foolish behavior doesn't matter."

For a moment Sam bristled at Kit's casual assumption that Ysella's possible condition wouldn't matter to him. He was taking for granted that because Sam was just his land agent, his estate manager, marrying her and acting father to a possible bastard wouldn't be a problem. Well, would it?

He frowned down at his hands and deliberately loosened their grip on the desk. It seemed his secret dream might be about to come true. But did he want it to happen in this way? Ysella didn't love him as a husband wanted to be loved, as he wanted to be loved, of that he was certain. She saw him as a friend only, a dear and familiar friend, but a friend her brother had seized upon to do her the ultimate in favors. Was this fair for either of them? He wanted to love her as a wife. She needed the seal of marriage on her misdemeanors.

Should he seize this opportunity and see it as a way to get what he'd so long wanted? Ysella herself. Could he turn her down if no love came with the deal? Was he man enough to take what was offered, or was that being cowardly and venal?

"If you don't take her," Kit said, "and she is with child, I don't know what we'll do."

Unfair of Kit to put such pressure on. It wasn't him being asked to play father to another man's child. But then, she might not *be* with child at all. He had no idea of the likelihood of that, but he presumed it must be low. And she would be his, even if it were only to admire and love from afar. She'd still be his, and no man would be able to take her away from him. Ever. He came back again to the conundrum of whether he could live with knowing she didn't love him. Already, in his heart, he knew he couldn't do to her what Featherstone had done, not unless she loved him and wanted it. And surely that day would never come. He was just Sam, her old friend, not handsome like the dashing captain. He might love and worship her, but she would never love him.

He swallowed. The one thing he could do, though, was keep her safe far better than Featherstone would have been able to. He could give her the stability she needed, and if necessary, he could give her child a name.

"I'll do it," Sam said, the thought that he might be making the biggest and most costly mistake of his life surfacing as he said the words. "I'll marry her."

Kit got to his feet. "Good man." He held out his hand and Sam took it. "Congratulations. I'm away to send James with a letter to the bishop requesting a Common License. With that, you can be married as soon as next week. Oh, and Morvoren asked if you could go upstairs and see her if you agreed to her plan." And he departed.

Sam stayed seated, more than a little stunned by what had just happened to him. Had he dreamed it? Or had the one thing he'd thought unattainable actually happened? He pulled out the large bottom drawer of his desk and poured himself a large shot of whisky from the bottle he kept there. Its fiery strength burning a track down his throat convinced him he wasn't dreaming.

Kit hadn't actually said Ysella wanted to marry him, though. He'd said she'd do as she was told. The thought that she might be being forced into this surfaced and his stomach twisted. He couldn't bear to be the cause of more unhappiness. He needed to speak to her. But he'd speak to Morvoren first—she always had sensible ideas and opinions.

He found Morvoren reclining on the chaise longue in her bedroom, where she could look out of the window across the park. She wore a pretty pink peignoir and a warm plaid blanket covered her legs. When he came in, she laid the book she'd been reading in her lap and looked up at him with a commiseratory smile. "Sam, fetch that chair and come and sit beside me."

He did as he was bid. "I can see you've guessed why I'm here."

She nodded. "I've been expecting you."

"So you thought I'd agree to your plan?"

She nodded again. "I knew you would."

He fiddled with the edge of his waistcoat, rubbing it between his fingers. "Am I that transparent?"

This time she smiled, a compassionate glow in her eyes. "I'm afraid you are. At least to me."

He looked down at his hands. "How long have you known?"

"Since the first time I saw you with Ysella."

He digested this piece of information, his cheeks glowing like beacons. "And so you thought I'd be happy to get her by any means."

She shook her head. "No. That wasn't why I suggested this. I gave Kit the idea because I think you are the right man for Ysella. She has no need of a title, nor even to marry a rich man. And she doesn't possess the common sense to pick a man for herself, as she's proved."

"That doesn't mean she'll be happy with me."

Morvoren smiled again. "I think she will be, Sam, if you take everything gently. Marry her to give her respectability, but then woo her. She sees you as a friend, a man she's known since she was a child. Allow her to see you as a man who loves her, and she'll come to love you in return. I'm sure of it. When she realizes you love her in that way, which might take a while, so you'll have to be patient, love will grow between you. Mark my words."

Sam looked up. "I love her more than my own life. I'd do anything for her. Anything."

"Then don't be in a hurry. Let her come to you. And she will. All you have to do is be patient with her. She's very young in many ways." She took his hand in hers. "Now go and see her yourself."

YSELLA WAS SITTING on a chair she'd dragged over to her window, staring out at the depressing sight of another very gray day. Mist shrouded the tops of the trees on the far side of the lake, and it felt as if the whole sorry landscape had been drained of color to match her mood.

She put a hand to her belly. Might there be a child growing there, all unnoticed? If there was, could she ever love it after the way Oliver had treated her? How swiftly feelings of love could turn to hatred. Several days had passed now since he'd said those terrible words—that he no longer loved or wanted her. She knew, now, that he'd duped her into sleeping with him so he could use it as leverage to force Kit to allow her to marry him. No. It had been worse than that. He'd done it to her even though he'd never loved her, only her fortune. With that gone, he'd no longer wanted her.

Why couldn't she have been like Morvoren and found a man who loved her? Why was she so cursed with bad luck? Morvoren's words came back to her, loud enough for her to have been in the room with her. *"There's a man right here where you see him every day who cares very deeply for you."*

Ysella had met that declaration with a laugh. "Don't be silly. Sam doesn't feel like that about me. We're just friends." Yet, as she'd said the words, doubt had crept in.

Sitting now and staring out of the window, she saw his kind face before her eyes, the devotion in his eyes, the color flaring in his cheeks when he was near her. Did he care for her? Was Morvoren, wise in so many things, correct in this one? It could be... Might she be able to conjure feelings of her own about him if she married him as Morvoren wanted... eventually? After all, she knew him well, and he had kept no secrets from her, except perhaps this one.

A gentle tap on the door disturbed her thoughts. "Come in," she called, expecting it to be Martha.

The door opened. Sam stood on the threshold, his hands by his side contracted into fists as though he had no idea what to do with them.

Ysella stared. That the object of her thoughts should so suddenly appear, as though summoned, shocked her. He had never been to her room before. As the son of the last land agent, he'd been present all her life, but strictly in a ground floor capacity. A friend for her sisters and Kit, a second big brother for her. A dancing partner when all three sisters had been learning, someone to ride out around the park with.

"Ysella," he said, his voice hoarse. He knew. Kit had spoken to him already.

She rose to her feet, one hand resting on the back of her chair. "Sam."

"Would you mind if I came in?"

She shook her head. "No."

He stepped inside and closed the door behind him, but didn't move away from it as though he feared she might bolt if he came closer. He fidgeted his hands, then hid them behind his back, resembling nothing more than Kit when he'd been a boy and dragged before Papa for some crime.

Ysella managed a smile. He was her dear Sam still, and her heart went out to him in his discomfiture.

He didn't smile back. "I have an important question for you."

Good heavens. Had he come to ask for her hand in marriage formally? She gave a tiny nod of her head for him to go on, as the hand on the chairback gripped it ever more tightly.

He swallowed and his Adam's apple bobbed. "Ysella," he began. "I have come to ask you if what Kit and Morvoren have suggested is what you want."

She opened her mouth but he held up his hand to prevent her speaking. "No. Hear me out." He took half a step forward. "I do not wish to cause you unhappiness in any way. If there is any doubt in your mind about this, if there is anything you would prefer to do, given the circumstances, then please, tell me now." He paused. "I am your humble servant, Ysella. I only want to do what you wish. Not what Kit or Morvoren wishes, but what *you* yourself wish."

Such uncalled-for devotion after what she was guilty of. What could she say? She licked her lips and found them paper dry. "Morvoren and Kit have spoken to me. Kit has pointed out my choices very clearly. I am spoiled goods, Sam. No man would take me as his wife now, knowing that. Better that I ask you if it is what you want than you ask me."

"I am yours," Sam croaked. "You must know that I consider you one of my dearest friends, Ysella, and have done for a long time now. It would be an honor I do not consider myself worthy of to have you as my wife."

A little smile tickled the corners of Ysella's mouth. He'd called her his dearest friend. Was Morvoren wrong to say he loved her? Or were there different kinds of love—she certainly felt love in many different ways: for Mama and dear dead Papa, for Kit, Morvoren and her sisters, for baby George and for Lochinvar and the dogs. She'd fancied herself in love with Oliver, and how she felt about Sam was quite different to that. Did he feel about her as she'd once briefly felt for Oliver, or was all his love for her just the love of deep friendship? How was she supposed to tell? She'd misread Oliver with a vengeance.

"You are very kind," she said at last. "You know the reasons for my need of a husband. You should also know that I do not wish to remain an old maid all my life, which is my only alternative if no man can be found to take me on." Time to be honest. "I like you very much, Sam, but I have to tell you that I do not love you. Not in the way you might like in a wife, I fear. I would make you a very poor wife indeed."

He shook his head. "But we are good friends, Ysella." He smiled at her. "And friendship is a firm basis for any marriage. I already know you don't love me, but to have your daily companionship, your presence in my life, will be enough for me. I will make no demands upon you, have no fear. We shall live our marriage of convenience as the friends we are. You will find me ever constant in that vow."

Ysella regarded Sam for a long moment, digesting his words. Perhaps she would not have to do that terrible deed, that had hurt and made her sore, again. They could live as friends, seeing each other every day, and if she bore that bounder's child, she would have the seal of matrimony on its birth.

"Thank you, Sam," she said. "I should very much like to marry you as soon as possible. If that is all right with you."

He crossed the room to her then. For a moment his arms lifted as though he wanted to take her in his arms and hold her close as he'd done at her rescue, but then he let them drop. With her acceptance of his proposal, if it had even been that, a barrier seemed to have erected itself between them.

Ysella made no move either, except to hold out her hand to him in stiff formality.

He took it, and, bending over it, applied his lips to the back of it. "Thank you, Ysella. I shall endeavor to prove myself the man you wish me to be."

Chapter Twenty-Four

JAMES RETURNED LATE the following day from Salisbury where he'd obtained the Common License from the bishop for a cost of three pounds. They would have to wait another week, and then they could be married in the local church by the Reverend Whitaker. Kit and Sam rode over to the vicarage together and engaged his services. It was, Kit explained as Sam stood silently listening, to be a very quiet affair with only the family present. If the Reverend Whitaker was surprised by this request and the speed with which the marriage had been arranged, he kept his opinion to himself.

Ysella, to Sam's surprise, put her foot down about that. "A girl only gets married once in her life," she said with a defiant jut to her lower jaw. "And I would at least like my dear friend Caro to be present."

Sam frowned. "Are you sure? Might she not be a little surprised at the haste with which we are to be wed?"

Ysella shook her head. "She'll hear we've married in a hurry anyway, so she might as well come. Then if she wants to ask me why, I can tell her the truth."

Sam's all-too unsettled insides performed a leap of concern. "Is that wise? Should you not keep it to yourself?"

Ysella frowned at him. "She's my best friend apart from Morvoren, and I'd like her there. And she would never divulge my secret." For a moment Sam thought she might stamp her foot.

"I'll let Kit know," Sam said, his voice wary. Was it altogether a good idea to let her get her way even before they were married? Might she think she could go on like that after the wedding and force him into agreeing to things he didn't approve of? After all, Kit must be hoping Sam's influence would calm her down. But he couldn't find it in him to say no to her for one good reason— because he loved her. That she didn't love him didn't matter for the moment, and to make up for this, he wanted to give her everything else she could possibly want.

So, Miss Caroline Fairfield and her Mama and Papa were duly invited to the wedding.

It was a small affair indeed. Sam was pleased that Morvoren had been allowed out of bed shortly after the engagement was brokered, and had declared herself well enough to attend the service. Baby George, of course, remained at home in the nursery with Jessie Jenkins and his milk sister. The last thing they needed, Sam reflected with a rueful sigh, bearing in mind Ysella's possible condition, was the sound of a baby crying mid-service.

And so it was that Sam found himself standing at the altar at exactly eleven in the morning in his smartest coat and breeches, his heart hammering so loudly he was sure Kit and the Reverend Whitaker would hear it. In the front pews sat the Dowager Lady Ormonde, very regal in a puce satin gown, beside her friend Mrs. Fairfield and her husband. Caroline, always an astute young lady, wore a slightly puzzled frown on her face that Sam didn't like.

Neither of Ysella's sisters had been able to attend, for which Sam was grateful for small mercies. He'd grown up alongside Derwa and Meliora and a strong sense of embarrassment threatened him every time he thought of how they might disapprove of his having the temerity to marry their youngest sister. He couldn't rid himself of the thought that they had most likely always seen him as only the son of the land agent and a person of low rank and importance. Admittedly, he was the land agent himself now, and his father was dead. Which meant he had no family of his own on his side of the church.

To make up for this, he'd invited Mrs. Higgins, his house-keeper, so his side would not be quite empty, and she sat, stalwart in her best bonnet, back rigidly straight, but with an expression of the strongest disapproval on her face. Possibly she didn't like the idea of his marrying above his station, or it might be that she resented the idea of a woman, any woman, coming to usurp her place controlling his household. Not that he could imagine Ysella running a household herself. Not successfully, anyway. She was far too flighty for that.

The doors at the end of the church opened, and Kit led Ysella inside, her hand tucked demurely into the crook of his arm. Sam caught his breath. The Misses Sedgewick had produced the loveliest pale lemon gown at very short notice. A short, embroidered train swept the flagstoned floor behind her, and small puff sleeves emphasized the delicate roundness of Ysella's arms. She wore long gloves to above her elbows and carried a bouquet of flowers from the hothouse at Ormonde in a cascade of whites and yellows. A heavy veil hung to her waist obscuring her face, but Sam knew without any doubt that she would be beautiful beneath it. The most beautiful bride in the world.

Kit led her with stately, measured steps up the aisle towards Sam as the organist played, his face solemn with the portentousness of the occasion. With carefully studied precision, he handed Ysella to Sam, whose heart felt as though it might burst with happiness. This was it. This was his wedding to the woman he loved above all else. Sam gazed down at her, too awed by the occasion to smile. She looked so small and delicate beside him that he felt hulking and clumsy. Through the gauzy veil, she gave him a tremulous smile as her eyes met his.

Ysella stood on the path that led to Sam's front door, her veil removed now but still in her wedding gown. This was it. She was married now, for better or for worse. She was Sam's wife and could never be anyone else's. No matter that he'd said they could live as friends and he'd make no husbandly demands on her, she was still his wife and that made her his possession. He could change his mind any time he wanted, and she would be able to do nothing about it. A sobering thought.

She'd seen his house before, of course, countless times, and even been inside it with Kit, as a child, but only into the kitchens. But back then it had been Sam's father's house, and Sam merely a callow boy, like Kit. As for her, she'd been a very small girl, trailing in their wake, eager for their approval, and wanting to join in with everything they did, somewhat to Kit's annoyance. Now it lay before her, a blank she could remember nothing about.

Sam made as if to take her hand, then let his own hand drop. That barrier again, stopping them from touching one another. They were married, but they were also strangers, stranger to one another than they'd ever been. "Come inside," he said, his voice laden with the same awkwardness she felt.

She followed him up the path.

The front door opened into a long corridor off which several closed doors suggested rooms she'd never entered as a child. Mrs. Higgins, who must have gone home straight after the wedding service, was waiting just inside the door. She bobbed a curtsey, sour faced and dour. "Mrs. Beauchamp, ma'am. Welcome home."

How forbidding the housekeeper looked. How unapproachable and disapproving. Did she know what Ysella had done and why she was marrying Sam? All the servants must know she'd run away, and that Sam and Kit had brought her back. It didn't take the brains of a genius to work out why she was now being married off in a hurry. How mortifying to be the subject of intense disapproval from people who'd cared for and served her for most of her life. Worse, even, than having to brave out the London season again, because at least she didn't know the people in London. She felt as though she'd disappointed everyone connected with Ormonde.

Sam pushed open the door into what looked like a drawing room. An air of disuse clung to it, as though Mrs. Higgins had spent the last few days airing it ready for the new mistress of the house. Perhaps Sam never used it. Perhaps no one had used it since Sam's mother died, and that must be thirty years ago. A fire burned in the grate, but the room still felt chilly. And unwelcoming, much like Mrs. Higgins.

"We'll take tea in here, thank you, Mrs. Higgins," Sam said.

Was that a *snort* from the housekeeper? Ysella watched her leave, her step loud on the tiled floor, her back view rigid with disapproval.

"Do sit down, Ysella," Sam said, as if she were an honored guest. But she wasn't, was she? This was her house now as well as Sam's. Ormonde would never be her home again.

She perched on the edge of the rather faded chaise longue and folded her hands neatly in her lap, unable to rid herself of the sensation of being an unwanted interloper. What was she supposed to do now? Not that she wanted to be sewing, and most likely the piano in the corner would need tuning before she could play it, but she needed something in her hands to stop herself from fidgeting.

Sam went to stand beside the fire, one arm leaning on the mantelpiece. An ornate clock, twin candelabras and the statue of a horse's head occupied its run. She peeped sideways at him from behind her lashes, hoping he wouldn't see her doing so. But he was gazing out of the window at the distant, rather-gray view of the park and she was safe.

For the first time in her life, Ysella saw Sam as a man, and not just the friend of her childhood. Seeing someone every day, as familiar as the furniture around her, had made her blind to what he really looked like, immured to his attractions. As tall as Kit but broader, his wide shoulders pleasingly filled his well-cut coat. His hair, which more often than not was windblown and untidy from being outside on the estate, had been artfully arranged to resemble one of Ysella's fashion pamphlet pictures, but added nothing to his good looks. She preferred him windblown and natural, not stiff and formal like this.

She studied his face. A good shape, with a strong chin and a nose that was neither too large nor too small. A pleasing face. Maybe a handsome face, despite him not being at all like Oliver. She dismissed that thought forthwith. She did *not* want to start comparing Sam with Oliver. That would be to venture down a dangerous road. She must not think of Oliver ever again.

They waited in an uncomfortable silence until Mrs. Higgins returned with a tray of tea which she set on the low table near the chaise longue. "Would you like me to pour for you, Ma'am?"

Ysella jumped. She was "ma'am" now, of course. "No. No, thank you. I will do it myself." No need to let Mrs. Higgins think she could do nothing for herself. Sam had already explained that apart from the odd-job boy who did the gardening, polished his boots and brought in the wood, his only servant was the housekeeper.

Mrs. Higgins departed, taking her air of frosty disapproval with her, and Ysella poured tea for Sam and herself. She held Sam's out to him.

He took it, and sat down on one of the upholstered chairs. "Thank you."

Ysella bit her lip. This was worse than awful. How could two people who up until just over a week ago had been the best of friends now have nothing to say to one another? "I take it that you don't often use this room," she tried. As an icebreaker, it lacked a lot.

Sam nodded. "I'm told my mother used it, but of course I don't remember as she died shortly after I was born."

Ysella nodded. The room did have an air of having been trapped in time. Were the ornaments on the mantel his mother's?

Had she chosen the chaise longue and the other bits of furniture? Ysella had a disturbing sense of having intruded into his mother's domain, despite her death having been so long ago. "It's a lovely room."

Sam nodded. "I used to sneak in here as a child to see if I could capture her spirit."

This was better. "I do that in Papa's old study. Kit doesn't use it, so I thought no one but me ever went there. Until one day I found Mama there, sitting in Papa's old chair, sniffing his box of cheroots."

"I think we none of us want to abandon the past."

Ysella sipped her tea. It was a good China blend. "That's true." What to say now to keep this stilted conversation going?

Sam spoke into the awkward silence. "Your mother has sent Martha down to wait upon you, so we'll have two female servants in the house." He chuckled. "I think that might account for Mrs. Higgins' long face. She won't at all like having another woman about the place."

"Does that mean me, too?"

He pulled a wry expression by downturning his mouth. "I fear it might. She's been used to a bachelor establishment for a long time now. But you must be firm with her and take no nonsense. She may have begun as my housekeeper—well, as my father's housekeeper—but she is yours now, and she must listen to you. You are the lady of this house now."

Ysella wrinkled her nose. "I'm afraid I have to admit that I know very little about housekeeping. I fear Mama intended me not to have to concern myself with anything other than choosing what to order for dinner."

Sam smiled, the smile reaching his eyes and making them very tender. Ysella's susceptible heart, in need of succor, did a treacherous leap. Was she bad for wanting him to put his arms round her and hold her close? To make her feel safe and wanted? Because that was all she wanted right now. Nothing more.

He set his empty cup down. "In that case, do not concern

yourself with the daily running of the house above telling Mrs. Higgins what you would like to eat. You may spend your days as you wish, Ysella, and you will not find me asking you to do otherwise."

"That sounds perfect. What I would like to do, then, is to ride out every day. I will be able to do that, won't I? Lochinvar is still in the Abbey stables, so I can walk up there and ride him if I want to?"

Sam's smile widened as though she'd said something pleasing. "Nonsense. I'll send James down with him and another horse every morning when I go up to start work in my office. I'm sure Kit won't object. James can accompany you on your rides."

Ysella sucked in her lips, pressing them together. Wouldn't it be nicer if her husband wanted to ride out with her of a morning? Much better than taking one of the grooms, even if it was James who'd shared her and Morvoren's adventurous dash into Cornwall a year ago. She'd have to work on that.

Chapter Twenty-Five

"How is it going?" Kit asked, as he and Sam rode down the hill towards the ornamental lake.

Sam, riding slightly behind Kit, couldn't see his face. Which thankfully must mean that Kit couldn't see his, either. This was not a conversation Sam wanted to have face to face. "Tolerably well," he said, unable on the spur of the moment to think of any other way to describe his marriage.

It had been a month since the wedding, and although Sam and Kit had worked together on most days, both had steered clear of the subject until now, as if for some reason it was sacrosanct. Although once, early on, Kit had casually slipped in the awkward question of whether Ysella would be requiring baby George's castoffs in the near future. He'd heaved an audible sigh when Sam had assured him that she wouldn't. Neither of them had been looking at each other then, either. Far too embarrassing a subject with all its awful connotations.

Kit's shoulders stiffened. "I only ask as Ysella seems to be spending an inordinate amount of time at the Abbey." He paused, still not turning around. "More and more every day."

Hot color had flushed Sam's face, but there was nothing he could do to get rid of it. Willpower alone was not sufficient. "I'm sure it's because she likes to spend time with Morvoren and little George. Her mama as well." He could hardly say how much her unwillingness to remain in their own house had been upsetting him. And her apparent unwillingness to be in his company.

Kit shook his head. "Mama has hardly seen her. It's Morvoren who appears to be the center of her interest. And George, of course. They're together most of the day. Now Morvoren is back to full health, she and Ysella have been riding out in the mornings, and in the afternoons they walk in the gardens with little George and Nanny."

Sam fiddled with Hercules's neatly pulled mane. What could he say to that? Having told Ysella she could do as she wished, if she had taken him at his word and decided to spend all day at her old home, then who was he to argue with her? Spending it cooped up in his house, *their* house, with Mrs. Higgins seemed a poor alternative, even with Martha there, and he was always so busy with the estate. He couldn't be expected to take time away from work entertaining her. Even, that was, if she wanted him to entertain her, which he was fairly sure she didn't. "Um," was the only word that emerged from his mouth.

They'd reached the track that ran around the edge of the lake. Kit turned Abelard left towards the mill. "I've spoken to Morvoren about it."

"You have?"

"Shall we canter?" Without waiting for an answer, Kit applied his legs to his horse's sides and set off along the smooth green sward. Instead of stopping at the mill, he kept on past it, heading slightly downhill and following the bends of the little river towards the village.

Sam urged Hercules after him, pulling up when Kit did at the start of the woodland. Kit brought Abelard in beside Hercules and gave him a long rein so he could stretch his neck and relax. Sam did the same, letting the reins slip through his fingers to the buckle end, carefully not looking at his brother-in-law.

Kit took up the conversation exactly where he'd left off, as if they hadn't had a good gallop in-between whiles. "Morvoren thinks it's being here at Ormonde that's giving Ysella the opportunity not to behave like a wife." He gazed into the distance, perhaps as keen as Sam not to have eye contact. "She thinks that if you and my sister were elsewhere, somewhere new, that Ysella would come round to behaving in a more wifely fashion. She wouldn't have the distractions she has here. She would cease to be a daughter and a sister and become a wife, instead."

Sam bit his lip. Never having had a wife before, nor even a mother, he wasn't at all sure what behaving in a wifely fashion entailed. However, he had surmised that Ysella might not be conforming to it. "Do you want me to leave? Are you giving me my marching orders?"

"Good heavens, no." Kit shook his head with vehemence. "I would never do that. But I do want my sister to make a go of her marriage and have the chance to be as happy as Morvoren and I am. And so far, this doesn't seem to be happening."

Sam sat up a little straighter in the saddle. "Is she so unhappy? That must be my fault."

Kit shook his head. "No, Sam, I don't think it is. Unless you're guilty of giving her too free a rein. You have to remember that this is Ysella we're talking about. Give her as much as half an inch and she'll take a mile. Which is what she's doing at the moment. She's so often at the Abbey that she might as well still be living there, unmarried and still a girl."

"But I want her to be happy."

They'd reached the ford, their horses splashing through it. Ahead lay the village, which ostensibly they were visiting to inspect the tenants' roofs in case they might need rethatching this year. "All very laudable," Kit said, shortening his reins as Abelard snatched at the hedgerow on his left. "But happiness isn't necessarily arrived at through laxity."

"You think I'm being lax with her?"

Kit shrugged. "Possibly." He grinned. "She's very hard to be strict with. Isn't any woman? Although Morvoren would disagree with me on that, in no uncertain terms. But as for Ysella...

Many's the time I've set out to be angry with her and had her completely set me about face. She's so contrite and persuasive, it's nigh on impossible to remain angry with her for long."

Sam chewed at his bottom lip. Might Kit be right? Might Ysella be exploiting his good nature and doing exactly what she wanted all the time, to the detriment of their relationship? Carrying on as if she were still just Miss Ysella Carlyon, not Mrs. Beauchamp. "So what *is* your solution? I'm presuming you have a suggestion to make that doesn't involve me leaving my position here at Ormonde?"

Kit drew rein and finally turned to face Sam, his cheeks a little flushed, perhaps at the personal nature of this conversation. "Well, it doesn't involve you leaving my employ. But it does involve you and Ysella leaving Ormonde. For a while, at least."

"What? Where do you want us to go?"

Kit grinned, as though he were a magician about to perform an impressive theatrical feat. "I would like to send you both down to Carlyon Court in Cornwall. Ysella's only been there a handful of times in her life, as have you. And it's a part of her heritage, as it is mine. She's three-quarters Cornish, don't forget, and the sea is in her blood. I'd like you to take on Carlyon Court and run it and the associated land and farms around it as you see fit. You can have free rein to treat it as your own. I trust you not to make a hash of it, and I think Ysella would find a new start beneficial. You both would. I think the Cornish air and the simple Cornish way of life will suit you both well."

Sam stared. He had indeed only been down to Carlyon Court a few times, but the last visit was still fresh in his mind. He'd chased down to Cornwall as an escort for Morvoren and Ysella as they'd raced to save Kit from the ambush of the revenue men. They'd been only just in time to prevent Kit's death on the beach. Sam had escorted Ysella back to Ormonde almost straightaway, once they'd been certain Kit's arm wound was not too serious, but Morvoren had remained down there until Kit was well enough to travel.

From what he'd seen of Carlyon Court on his infrequent trips with Kit, he remembered a rambling old house with as many new additions tacked onto it as Ormonde, only in a different style. Whereas Ormonde climbed here and there towards the sky, the Court spread out long and low, its gabled roof sunken down over its windows like a thick fringe much in need of a trim.

But he'd liked it, and Kit might well be right. A new start for Ysella and him might be just what was needed. "When do you wish us to leave?"

Kit reached out and patted his arm. "Good man. As soon as possible, I think. Best to get it over with, as I doubt Ysella will be well pleased to leave Morvoren and George. But you can tell her you'll take your horses down with you, if you want. Or buy new ones down there. I don't mind. As I said, I'll leave the purse strings in your capable hands."

Sam grimaced. "I doubt Ysella will go anywhere without Lochinvar."

"Very true. Would you like me to tell her about my decision? I can couch it as a need for your skills down on the surrounding estate. I don't want her feeling as though she's been banished. Not that she doesn't deserve it, of course, after all the trouble she's caused us." He put his hand up to his ear, which still retained the scab from the wound that had taken off a portion of the lobe.

Sam grimaced yet again. "No, I'd best be the one to tell her. I am her husband, after all. I'll follow your lead though and tell her I have no choice… I think. She'll have to accept it then."

"You want me to leave Ormonde?" Ysella almost snarled. "You want me to leave Morvoren, who is my dearest friend? And baby George, who changes every day? You want me to leave Mama and Lochinvar and the dogs?"

They'd just had dinner and retired to the drawing room to take tea, and Ysella had been sitting on the chaise longue. As soon as she'd heard what Sam had to say she'd leapt up and was now standing with her skirts dangerously close to the fire, her hands on her hips and her dander up. How dare he take her away from everything she loved. How dare he suggest this.

"It's not my choice," Sam said, eyeing her warily.

She flounced. "You could have said no. Oh, how I hate Kit now." She couldn't bring herself to put it into words, but what lay behind her anger was the fact that after her adventure with Oliver, she'd thought herself home at Ormonde, the only place she felt safe, for good. Marrying Sam had reinforced that feeling, and now horrible Kit had undone all her feelings of safety. "I shan't go."

She eyed Sam to gauge his reaction. He'd been a pushover when she'd started spending more and more time at the Abbey, and she expected him to be now. Gradually, she'd come to take more and more from him, and had been considering suggesting that at least two nights a week could be spent in her old bedroom—alone, of course. That was very much her private territory.

"Well, I'm afraid you're going to have to," Sam said, his calm voice only serving to annoy her more. "Because I have to go where Kit sends me. He's my employer as well as my friend and brother-in-law, and he wants me to work down at Carlyon Court for a while. But he suggested you might want to take Lochinvar with you. I shall be taking Hercules."

Ysella stuck out her lower lip in rebellion, her foot tapping as though she were fighting the impulse to stamp it. "How long for?"

Inspiration seemed to strike Sam and his face brightened. "I don't know, but if we're there in winter I've heard there's good hunting. And beaches to ride along."

Ysella let out a squeal of shock. "Winter? Do you mean we might be down there for months? George will be running about and talking before I see him again."

"Well, perhaps not that long. It's up to Kit, Ysella. I have no say in the matter and nor do you. We are married now and you certainly can't stay here while I go down to Cornwall. That would not be the done thing at all."

Ysella compressed her lips. What was she to do? For once, Sam was standing firmer than he'd ever done in their short month of marriage. How far did she dare push him? "Well, I think I might stay here anyway," she tried. "And pah to whether it's done or not. I'm sure Morvoren will want me to, so I can help with George."

He regarded her out of his gentle gray eyes. "No, Ysella, you won't. You will accompany me down to Cornwall, and run the house. That is what a wife does."

Good heavens. Nonplussed, Ysella was speechless for a moment. Not for long though. "Kit will let me stay here."

Sam shook his head. "He most certainly will not. He particularly asked me to take you with me. He wants the house opening up properly, as no one has lived there full time since he was a child. Your father used to go down every summer, but Kit says he lived in only one or two rooms. He wants you to hire some extra servants and bring the house back to life."

Ysella scowled. "But I know nothing whatsoever about housekeeping." She was scraping the bottom of the proverbial barrel here, as she did know quite a bit, just chose not to admit to it. And Mrs. Higgins had seemed very glad she hadn't tried to interfere with the daily running of Sam's house. If she didn't let anyone know she could do it, they were less likely to ask her to try.

"I'm sure you can learn about it," Sam said, far too kindly, his gray eyes set with annoying firmness and implacability. "It's probably just common sense."

Ysella bridled. "Well, you know for a fact that I have none of that."

"Then it'll be a good opportunity for you to learn some of

that at the same time."

She stamped her foot. It had been twitching for a while, and she'd been trying hard to control it, but now she properly stamped it. "What if I refuse to go?" How daring she felt. But he was being rude to her telling her she had to learn about housekeeping and common sense. She had the right to be rude and challenge him. He was only Sam, after all.

"If you should be so unwise as to do that," Sam said, a look in his eyes Ysella had never seen before, "then I'm afraid I should have to put you over my shoulder and carry you down there myself." He paused. "Even if I have to tie you up to do so."

For just a moment, Ysella's stomach twisted at the rather delicious thought of being slung over Sam's shoulder and manhandled all the way down to Cornwall. Then the thought flew away. This was Sam she was talking to, not Oliver, not that she would ever feel like that about that dreadful cad ever again. And yet she'd had that stirring in her most private spot, just as she'd had when Oliver had kissed her and slid his hand inside her bodice. And she'd felt it about Sam. What was the world coming to?

"You would not dare treat me so disrespectfully," she managed, chin tilted upward in defiance.

Sam smiled, and again Ysella experienced that fleeting sensation of excitement as she caught the look in his eyes. "Just you watch me," he said. "Sometimes, Ysella, you behave like a spoiled child. And part of that is my fault. I'll not let it go on. You will do as you're told in this, and prepare to leave tomorrow."

Chapter Twenty-Six

THE CARRIAGE RUMBLED through the gates and onto the weed-strewn gravel drive of Carlyon Court. Behind it, Ysella, clad in her dark green riding habit, sat Lochinvar. Beside her rode Sam on the steady bay Hercules. Unlike the mailcoach, nor their last madcap dash west, they hadn't hurried on the road, but had broken the journey three times at wayside inns. And a lot of the time, as the weather had at last taken a turn for the better, they'd ridden, leaving the coach, driven by James, to carry just their luggage and Martha.

Ysella wrinkled her nose at the weeds and long grass and glanced at Sam. "Do they not have a gardener or two down here? I'm sure it didn't look this bad when we were here last year."

He shrugged. "That will be one of the things I shall have to look into. Kit said Carlyon Court has fallen into a parlous state much in need of my organizational skills." He chuckled. "Not that *I* recall much from our last visit down here. But if I were you, I'd be more concerned with what it's like inside than out."

Ysella, whose mood had gradually improved with each day spent in the saddle, smiled back at him. Poor Sam, having to take all this in hand. However, her feelings of pity didn't run deep—she'd already decided to let him cope with the housekeeping he'd threatened her with. Far too boring now the weather actually felt like spring. Instead of tedious things like organizing staff, she would be off to find a way down to that glorious beach she'd glimpsed last time she was here. There must be a way down there on horseback, surely.

The carriage ground to a halt in front of the main doors.

Sam halted Hercules and slid down from the saddle, then held out his arms for Ysella. She unhooked her right leg and slid into his waiting grasp. But he only held her for a moment, releasing her as she found her balance. A small part of her rather wished he'd kept on holding her, but she dismissed that thought as ridiculous. Why on earth would she want Sam holding her?

Martha climbed out of the carriage to stand on the gravel behind them, her critical gaze taking in the state of the drive and the neglected air of the house. James remained seated on the box. He, too, had seen the Court only last year.

By the front door, a couple of iron rings had been embedded in the stonework. Sam looped their horses' reins through them and turned to the door itself, which appeared to be locked.

A frayed rope hung beside it, to which he gave a hearty tug. The sound of a distant bell ringing carried to them through the thick oak of the door.

Ysella tapped her foot. From what she remembered of the few servants here, they were not going to be in a hurry to answer any peremptory ringing of the front doorbell.

At last, just as Sam was stretching out his hand to ring the bell again, the sounds of bolts being shot back heralded the door creaking open just a crack. The wrinkled old face of the woman who'd opened it for them last time they'd been here peeked out, just as grumpy, just as unwelcoming.

This was too much. This was their house, and the servants needed some straight talking about prompt responses. Ysella pushed the door hard and it swung wide, revealing the stooped figure of a woman so old and wrinkled she could have been a witch from one of Ysella's childhood storybooks. Last time they'd been here in the dark, but this time Ysella got a better look at her.

"About time too," Sam said, striding into the wide, and very gloomy, front hall. "Things are going to have to change here. Who is in charge?"

Ysella followed him. The light now streaming through the open doorway showed a hallway made darker than was natural by an abundance of oak paneling, an oak staircase and dark oak doors. The only thing that wasn't constructed of ancient oak appeared to be the floor, and that was large slabs of gray slate. Not a very welcoming sight. Last time she'd scarcely noticed anything about the house, so anxious had she and Morvoren been to get to Kit.

Sam stopped in the center of the hall and looked around at the white sheet draped furniture. Was that a suit of armor under the sheet by the bottom of the stairs? He fixed the old lady with a firm stare. "Go and fetch the other servants. Mrs. Beauchamp and I have brought a carriage load of our belongings down from Ormonde and our driver needs help unloading."

The old lady scuttled away as fast as her ancient legs could carry her.

Martha, who had followed Ysella and Sam inside, gazed around herself with a wrinkled nose and finally gave a huff of disapproval. "Don't look like they were expecting us," she remarked.

Impressed by Sam's firm instructions and the speed with which they'd been obeyed, but determined not to say so, Ysella turned away and flung open the lefthand door. The long dusty table and many chairs declared this to be the dining room. Sunlight shafted in between the cracks in closed shutters, dust motes dancing in the beams. Leaving the door open, she tried the righthand door. The drawing room, clearly, but in here every-thing had been draped with sheets as the hall had been. She turned towards the stairs.

"I have a nasty feeling the bedrooms are *not* going to be aired," Sam said with a sigh. "But by all means go and look, and perhaps you could report back to me. We may well have to put up with some discomfort before we get the house back the right way up."

Ysella dimpled at him, excited by the sense of adventure the state of the house was instilling in her, and skipped up the stairs followed by Martha, not quite so light of foot, and probably far less enthusiastic. At the half landing, the stairs divided, going right and left into a gallery that ran all the way around the upper floor and gave onto the hallway. As with downstairs, the shutters had all been closed and darkness held sway up here, except for the bright shafts of light that had sneaked their way between the slats. At the large landing window, Ysella reached up and unhooked the shutters to fling them back and let in the light. More dust motes danced in the sunlight in profusion, but the once well-polished oak floors shone in the brightness. This had been a lovely house in the past, and it could be again.

Martha, running a finger over the dusty windowsill, gave a huff of disgust that Ysella ignored.

Instead, with a curious hand, Ysella wiped a patch of window clean and peered out. Unkempt gardens stretched to a tree-lined boundary, and beyond that the land seemed to drop away. Was that the sea? She rubbed a bit more of the window clean and leaned in closer for a better look. It was. The day was fine, and the sea stretched away into a hazy blue distance. Ysella's romantic heart, that had already been bursting with the newness of everything she'd seen, soared. Kit had said the sea was in her blood, and now it was calling to her. She would definitely have to find a way down to the beach as soon as possible, but preferably not via that same cliff path she'd had to negotiate a year ago. She had a feeling it would be even more frightening in daylight than it had been at night, when she couldn't see the drop and had only heard the crash of breakers on the cliff's feet.

But Sam had sent her to explore upstairs, and that was what she'd do. Curious about the house's secrets, she proceeded along the gallery, Martha following behind. The doors up here must surely lead into bedrooms. She pushed open the first one. In the center of the room, on a faded silk rug, stood a large four poster bed, the cover in disarray as though someone had been sleeping in it only that morning. The room smelled musty and sharp, as though whoever had slept here might not have been very clean.

Martha huffed again and tutted several times.

She tried the next room, finding it in the same state. Had the *servants* been sleeping up here? Despite her avowal of not being capable of housekeeping, Ysella's instinct had her heading back down the stairs in a hurry. She arrived at the bottom to find four people had just assembled themselves in the hall in front of Sam. The same four people she remembered seeing here before. Two men, one considerably older than the other, a woman of blowsy middle-age, and a lanky boy with a shock of sandy hair.

The boy spotted her first. "Miss Ysella," he cried out in excitement, having been a willing party to the flouting of the revenue men the last time she'd been in Cornwall. "Miss Ysella, I dint rightly know it was you what was here. Doryty dint say."

The old woman, who must have been Doryty, gave a cuff to his ear which he dodged with agility as though he were used to doing so.

"Miss Ysella?" The older man, white haired and portly, stepped forward with a quick bow. "The boy's right. We dint know it were you come."

Ysella stopped three steps up, giving herself the superiority of height over the assembled company. "I have just been upstairs," she said with cold deliberation, one eye taking in Sam's impressed expression. "And seen the mess in the bedrooms. I think you have some explaining to do." She paused and looked from one face to the next. "Have you perhaps taken to sleeping in the best bedrooms?"

The middle-aged woman stepped forward, smoothing her grubby apron. "I'm Rosie Enyon, Miss, Jem's ma. It were right cold up in them attics this winter and right into spring. We only come down to keep a bit warmer."

Ysella frowned. "No matter the reason, you should not have presumed to occupy the best bedrooms, thinking your master far away and ignorant of your actions. He has asked Mr. Beauchamp and me to come down and set the house and estate to rights." She paused. "Mr. Beauchamp is my husband, so I am no longer Miss Ysella. You may address me as ma'am."

To say this was met with a stunned silence would have been a gross underestimation. Her gathered servants looked from her to Sam and then back again. All of them knew who and what Sam was, and every one of them looked not just surprised but shocked.

Ysella didn't give them time to think. "Rosie. Upstairs now and sort out two of the bedrooms for us, and make sure the sheets are spotlessly clean. Martha will help you."

Martha huffed again at the prospect of having to do a housemaid's work.

Ysella ignored her. "I shall take my mother's old room." She met Sam's eyes. "You men, outside and help James with our belongings. You as well, Jem." She glanced at the old woman. "And you can go to the kitchen and prepare something for us to eat. It's been a long journey." She looked back at Sam, whose eyes held admiration. "My husband and I will wait in the drawing room."

SAM PULLED THE dust covers from the furniture, setting a cloud of dust fluttering through the stuffy air of the drawing room. The furniture revealed was old-fashioned but serviceable—probably the furniture that had belonged to the old viscount, or perhaps even to his father, who Sam knew had only inherited the title from a childless older brother late in life.

Moving on from the seating, Sam went to the three long windows and, unfastening the catches, swung the wooden shutters back to reveal the small leaded panes of yesteryear, the glass marked by the bullseyes that indicated its extreme age. The late afternoon sunlight streamed into a room, which, like the hall, had long ago been decorated with oak paneling. Everything about this house was dark. After Ormonde, with its high stuccoed ceilings and munificence of windows, Carlyon Court seemed a gloomy rabbit warren.

Ysella was busy removing the rest of the dust sheets, adding them to a pile on the floor by the main doorway. "This place reeks of the last century," she said, wrinkling her nose and sneezing. "And not the end of it. I wouldn't be at all surprised if it's not changed at all since my grandfather was a boy. And *he* would be a hundred were he alive now."

Sam had moved to the hearth, where the ashes of the last fire, possibly from years ago, had never been removed. Bending, he gave it a prod with a brass poker. Was that the skeleton and desiccated wings of a bird that had fallen down the chimney? All the chimneys were going to need a good sweeping before they risked lighting any fires. He straightened up. "A good thing it's no longer cold, although these shut up rooms hold the chill well."

He ran a finger along the mantelpiece, his fingertip coming away thick with dust. "If we're to get this house back to its former glory, I suspect we're going to need more servants than that motley group. One of whom is too old to still be working, I'd say."

Ysella walked over to one of the long windows, and Sam followed her. Just unkempt gardens with nothing to indicate how close they were to the sea. She sighed. "You're right. This place feels awful, but I think that we can improve it."

At least she seemed to be looking at this in a more positive frame of mind than he'd expected. Perhaps the challenge was spurring her on. After all, this was going to take a lot of work to put to rights. He looked down at her. How beautiful she was in the golden light of the late afternoon, the sun's rays gilding her hair and face so she resembled a bronze statue. How small and delicate, yet how resilient. If only she could find it in her to love him, then his life would be complete.

His fingers twitched, and he glanced down. How close her hand was to his. How much he wanted to reach out and touch it. To take it in his own, to thread his fingers between hers. He resisted the impulse. He mustn't frighten her off. If he could have nothing else, he'd have her as his friend again, even if that took a long time to happen. He could be content with her friendship.

She looked up at him out of her wide dark eyes, her face besmirched with dust. She had the longest and thickest lashes he'd ever seen. Her lips curved in a smile. Oh, how he longed to kiss them. "The views from upstairs are much better than the ones from down here."

Lost for words and in his own longing, Sam nodded. "You can see the sea from up there. Kit showed me when he brought me down here. I had a bedroom with a view of the sea."

She nodded. "I opened the shutters on the landing window. The windows were dirty but I cleaned a spot to peer through." Her smile widened. "D'you know, Sam? I think I might be going to like it down here. After seeing the sea when we were down here before, even if it were ever so briefly, I rather have a hankering to see it again, up close this time." She dimpled, naughty as a schoolgirl. "And perhaps if it's warm enough, I'll be able to paddle my feet in it."

"Then you shall do it, Ysella," Sam said. "I promise you that."

Her hand slipped into his and squeezed. "Thank you, Sam."

His heart felt as though it would burst, her touch sending shivers through his body. He'd held her hand before, particularly on the occasion when they'd taught Morvoren to dance, but somehow, this sudden warm contact she'd initiated felt quite different. More intimate. For a start, he was alone with her in the drawing room. Before, she'd just been Miss Ysella. Now, she was his wedded wife, even if only in name. He could only dream that one day she might want to do more than hold hands so chastely. Like a pair of old friends.

$$\cdots\!\oplus\!\cdots$$

Chapter Twenty-Seven

THEY RODE DOWN to the sea the very next day. Cubert, who was the younger of the two men, and had turned out to be the old woman Doryty's youngest son, gave them directions. Carlyon Court being set a short way inland and above tall cliffs, this involved riding north for a mile or two, until the shoreline dipped, at last, to sand hills and a wide stretch of beach. Perfect for a gallop, Cubert promised.

Sam refused to let Ysella go alone, which had been her first idea. Then she'd offered to ride with James as escort, but, as Sam pointed out, James was to take the carriage back to Ormonde that day and shouldn't be delayed.

So, after a substantial and very tolerable breakfast of eggs, bacon and coffee taken in the freshly cleaned dining room, they set out together on a bright, late-spring morning. Overhead, the harsh cry of the gulls wheeling in a pristine blue sky heralded their journey.

Ysella had only ever seen tiny Nanpean Cove before, where her Uncle Jago lived, the scene of the abortive raid by the revenue men only a year ago. According to Cubert's effusive description, this new beach was going to be far superior from the point of view of riding. Jaunty in her green riding habit and a matching hat, she sat up straight on Lochinvar, who seemed well-rested after his five days of constant travel, gazing about herself with interest.

Their way led down narrow, high-hedged and stony-banked lanes, with no view at all of the sea to begin with. It climbed across the broad headland that Cubert swore was all that divided the Court from Branok Bay. "It do mean 'Bay o' the Ravens'," he'd told Ysella, with some small pride. "And they do say as there were them old priests there once. Them druidicals. Ravens was holy to them, so they chose the bay as a spot for their temple." He blushed. "If'n you don't mind me tellin' you this. Miss Ys-Mrs. Beauchamp."

Ysella had laughed out loud. "Oh, Cubert. Please keep calling me Miss Ysella. Mrs. Beauchamp makes me sound like an old married woman, and I don't feel like one at all." Her turn to blush as the import of her words soaked in, hopefully only to her and not him. Shouldn't she be feeling like an old married woman by now, and not a girl anymore? In truth, she didn't feel married at all, what with sleeping in separate rooms, and only coming together for the occasional meal, and conversing awkwardly like distant strangers. With a shrug she shook off the feeling.

Sam, smart in a well-cut dark blue coat, trotted by her side on Hercules, his sandy hair, unencumbered by any hat, blowing in the breeze. She studied him out of the corner of her eye. He *looked* happy, but was he? Might *she* be responsible for making him unhappy? Morvoren had said Sam cared for her, which she'd known to be true. They'd been friends for years, since she, Ysella, had been a child and he a gangly youth. And she cared for him. A lot. Did he secretly want more from this marriage than the clumsy attempt at continued friendship they were making? Was she cheating him of something?

She shook herself. No. She would not think about that. Sam had known what he was agreeing to when he'd said he would marry her. He'd offered it up himself. Said they could live as friends, and friends had nothing more between them than she'd been prepared to give this past month. However, the paucity of what she'd offered him gave her a sharp twinge of guilt, which she shoved aside. No. She wouldn't think about it. He was happy. Look at him. He was smiling. He *must* be happy.

The lane curved to the left, and the road began to drop away steeply. Slowing Lochinvar to a walk, Ysella caught her breath. Before them stretched an expanse of sandy beach that made Nanpean's small cove look like a garden compared to parkland. A border of rolling sandhills separated it from the moorland scattered with isolated forms that backed onto it, and, far out, white topped waves made a pretty fringing to the sand. "Oh, my goodness," she gasped. "I never thought a beach could be so *huge.*"

She met Sam's gaze. "Have you ever seen anything like this before?"

Sam laughed and nodded. "You forget that I've been down here with Kit on my own. We traveled on the mailcoach which stops at Penzance. I saw the beach there—which I have to say is bigger even than this. And there's a little island part way along it, with a sort of castle perched on top of it. Very picturesque. I believe people go to Penzance just to see it."

That sounded most unusual. "I should like to see that. But for now, Branok Bay will do me. I'm itching for a gallop and I should imagine poor Lochinvar is too, after all the dreadful roads he had to put up with on our journey down here." She urged Lochinvar into a faster walk. "Let's hurry."

The lane wound down the side of the headland, with cliffs to their left and small, stone-banked fields to their right. Beyond the fields lay open moorland, dotted with the small white shapes of sheep. Overhead, the swooping gulls kept up their constant screeching cries.

As they reached level ground, Ysella urged Lochinvar into a trot. "These are the same kind of sandhills they have at Nanpean," she called over her shoulder to Sam. "Difficult to walk over on foot, and it seems much the same to ride over."

"They're called dunes," Sam rejoined. "Sand dunes. I believe the word has a similar origin to the word 'downs' for the chalk hills of Wiltshire."

Trust Sam to know that.

She was forced to slow Lochinvar to a walk over the shifting dry sand. Hummocks rose before her, surmounted by clumps of long, spiky grass, the dips between them harder packed and easier to negotiate. The distant rumble of the sea drew her on beguilingly, as she led the way along what seemed to be a well-used track. As the sandhills parted, the wide expanse of the beach opened up in front of her.

"We're in luck we've found the tide right out," Sam said. "See the high-water mark, where all the seaweed and driftwood's been cast up? That's all the beach we'd have if the tide had been fully in."

"The tide?"

Sam nodded. "Twice a day the sea comes right in, but it takes a long time to do so. It's not a sudden thing, so we're quite safe. It carries with it all the bits you see before you and deposits them at its furthest reach."

How handy that Sam knew everything. A trait to be valued in a friend.

Ysella surveyed the evidence of the sea having come up to within thirty yards of the sandhills. "So, with it this far in, we wouldn't be able to get out beyond those rocky headlands to left and right?"

Sam nodded. "The water will come in and swamp them at high tide, but today we'll be able to ride out beyond them onto the furthest beaches. Those that are unusable for most of the day. They're backed by cliffs, so there's no access to them when the tide is even halfway in or out. Most likely there are strong currents, so it wouldn't be a good idea to swim for safety if one were caught along there with the tide coming in."

Ysella swallowed. "I can't swim, so that would do me no good. I couldn't swim to safety even if I wanted to." Kit had learned to swim in the lake at Ormonde as a child, which had seemed manifestly unfair to her when she found out. She'd kicked up a rumpus at not being allowed to do the same, and even hitched up her skirts and gone wading in the shallows until Papa had sent Kit in to drag her out. Girls, it seemed, were not allowed to learn to swim. After that she'd watched, bitter with jealousy, when Kit had friends home from school and in old breeches they'd cavorted in the lake.

"That big old pike'll bite your feet off," she'd threatened, but they'd laughed in her face. Mean things.

"Swimming is a useful skill if you live beside the sea," Sam said. "However, I've heard it said that sailors never learn to swim, so if their ship is wrecked, they drown the quicker."

Ysella shivered. "I should not like to drown at all, so even if I *were* a sailor, I'd be sure I knew how to swim." She waved a hand to the left, in the general direction of Nanpean Cove. "Can we canter on the sand? It looks most tempting, and Lochinvar is itching to stretch his legs. I can feel it."

Keeping the horses in a gentle canter, which Sam said was advisable as sand could vary in consistency, they rode south along the beach towards the first jutting cliffs, a small headland that separated Branok from the next small inlet. A series of such rocky arrangements poked their noses across the sand, each one sheltering the equivalent of a little cove. At last, they reached where the cliffs towered out across the water, and there was no more sand to be found.

Ysella slowed Lochinvar to a trot and then a walk, his sides heaving. "Can we walk the horses in the sea? I've heard tell the salt water is good for their legs."

Lochinvar didn't seem to have heard the same saying. At first, he shied away from entering the edge of the sea, seemingly very nervous about the small waves rolling in to meet him, and then bothered by the splash his back legs were making behind him. But as Hercules had no such qualms, being of a calmer temperament all round, he consented at last to walk on the landward side of Sam's horse, where he couldn't see the waves coming towards him.

Thus, Ysella was forced to ride on Sam's righthand side, up close to keep Lochinvar from shying every time a fresh wave rolled in. As her leg rubbed against Sam's, a pleasant tingle ran through her body, and an overwhelming sensation of being safe with him, and perhaps not just safe from the waves. She smiled, content for now with what life had offered her. "The waves are very pretty with their foamy white caps."

He didn't look at her, instead staring out into the hazy blue distance where sea met sky. "Today they are, but Kit told me they can be treacherous in bad weather. Your Uncle Jago once told me there've been a lot of ships wrecked along this coast. You see all the rocks just sticking up above the waves?"

She nodded.

"Well, there are as many and more hidden beneath the water, waiting to trap any ship that comes too close."

Ysella stared out beyond the rolling waves at the expanse of blue-gray water. How innocuous it looked, stretching away towards a distant horizon. "But don't the ships' captains know not to come too close inshore? To keep away from the hidden rocks? Or are there some further out as well?" Her brow furrowed. "How deep *is* the sea?" She gave a shrug. "Today, it doesn't look dangerous at all."

Sam kept his gaze on the sea. "Jago told me it's storms that drive the ships onto the rocks. With an onshore wind they can't fight against, they are doomed if they come too close to land."

"Storms?" She wrinkled her brow. "What happens to the sea in a storm?" The only storms she'd ever known had been in Wiltshire when she'd been tucked up safely inside Ormonde's stout walls. Unlike poor Martha, she'd loved the roar of thunder and the crack of lightning, leaping out of bed to stand at her window and watch the tumultuous sky.

He turned to look at her at last. "Just wait until the first high wind. I'll show you what it's like then, but we won't go near the sea when there's a proper storm raging. Apparently, there can be freak waves bigger than the rest that can wash a man out to sea.

And a horse. So your Uncle Jago told me."

Ysella shivered again. That something so beautiful could transform into a thing that could snatch and drown a man seemed unbelievable. But Jago had told Sam there'd been shipwrecks, so surely the sea must become more violent even than the sky in a storm. Whatever Sam said about keeping away from the sea when it was dangerous, she'd very much like to see it for herself. Up close. Best not to tell Sam, lest he assume he could be as controlling of her as Kit.

"Come," she said, tossing her head. "Shall we canter again while the tide is out? Would you like to race?"

THAT AFTERNOON, SAM was taken up with estate matters in the newly cleaned office, so Ysella found herself left to her own devices, which suited her well. She should, perhaps, have been overseeing the rest of the cleaning Sam had directed the servants to get on with, of which there remained a great deal, there being a lot of rooms. But the fine day lured her out into the gardens, escaping Martha and leaving the boring tasks of housekeeping behind. Overgrown lawns and leggy bushes and trees, fresh with the green of spring, stretched away in every direction around the house, even to her inexperienced eye much in need of some care and attention. Like the house.

Maybe she should have swallowed her own dislike and asked Sam to bring Mrs. Higgins, who kept a spotlessly clean house, to accompany them. Then she could have let her shoulder all the responsibilities Sam seemed to think were hers. But no. That would not have done. Mrs. Higgins liked her even less than she liked Mrs. Higgins. Best to start afresh without her.

She found the boy, Jem, on his hands and knees weeding the drive.

"Hello, Jem, you look busy."

He looked up at her out of a face liberally covered in freckles, his hazel eyes twinkling in a friendly fashion. "Mr. Beauchamp wanted me to make a start on the weeds. Said the drive were a disgrace."

He sounded a tad resentful at being consigned to this most boring of duties. Did she detect an undercurrent of unrest amongst the servants at finally having to do some work?

Ignoring that thought, she smiled back at him. Perhaps he considered he'd forged a partnership with her when he'd led them all to Nanpean to save Kit. Perhaps he had indeed. It would be good to have a friend here, amongst the servants she didn't know. She had Martha, of course, but *she* knew nothing of the house or gardens, and definitely not a thing about further afield.

An idea seized her. "A good thing too as it is very over-grown." She waved an airy hand at the small section he'd cleared. "It looks much nicer now. But I think you can leave it for a while. I'd like you to show me the way down to Nanpean, as I feel a need to call on my mother's brother and make my presence here at the Court known to him." She dimpled and was rewarded by the hot flush that rose up Jem's cheeks. "And not by the clifftop route you took us on before. I never want to have to take *that* particular path ever again."

He scrambled up off his knees with an appreciative grin, a scrawny specimen in homespun shirt and tatty brown breeches. His stockings had wrinkled around his ankles, above boots as scuffed as if he'd been scraping them down a gravel road for hours. Wiping his muddy hands on his trousers, he made a sketchy bow. "'Course I'll show you, Miss Ysella." He eyed her pretty morning gown and lacy shawl, his gaze lowering to her daintily shod feet. "The path's a bit rough. Will you mind that?"

Ysella shook her head. "Lead on, Jem. I have a hankering to get to know my uncle a little better than I do at present." Which was not at all. She'd probably seen him once or twice as a child, but those memories eluded her. And last year, when Kit had been shot and she and Morvoren had taken care of him, Jago's presence had been that of a shadowy background character she'd taken little notice of. Then, once Kit was on the mend, she'd had to return to Ormonde with Sam.

Jem's alternative route down to Nanpean's narrow valley might not have been along the top of the precipitous cliffs that had blocked her way on the beach that morning, but it nevertheless was not an easy walk. The path led between high stone and earth walls capped by straggly hawthorn bushes, with no view of the sea or anything much at all apart from the path itself. From time-to-time, muddy patches almost blocked the way, which Jem, in his scruffy boots, strode through without a care, but she, in her ordinary shoes, had to teeter around the edge of.

On top of that, it seemed a long way, much further than the clifftop path. Going mostly downhill, it twisted and turned around small fields and patches of scrubby moorland. Might it have been better to have taken Lochinvar and gone by road? But then Jem could not have shown her the way, and Sam was far too busy. If only she'd put on her boys' clothes this morning, with her pair of Kit's old boots. She'd stowed them away amongst her things when Martha hadn't been looking, and they'd have been useful for this long walk. How unfair that boys and men got to wear the sort of clothes where they could do what they liked, and she had to suffer in a gown and stays, and these silly shoes that were looking worse by the moment. She might have to throw them away after today.

At last, though, the valley opened up before them and Jem pointed with a grubby finger. "There's Nanpean, Miss." A twist of woodsmoke rose into the blue sky from one of the squat old farmhouse's several chimneys.

Uncle Jago was Mama's older brother. The story of how Mama had met Papa was one Ysella loved to hear. So romantic that Papa, who'd been living at Carlyon Court, had one day ridden out and met the most beautiful girl in Cornwall. Those had been his exact words when he'd told Ysella the story, his face suffused with the love he still felt for Mama. The same sort of expression Ysella had seen on Kit's face when he looked at Morvoren. She'd thought Oliver had looked the same when he'd gazed at her. How wrong she had been. He'd been seeing piles of money, not her. Never would she look to find the light of love in a man's face again, because if she saw it there, she would know it couldn't be trusted.

The path leveled out, leading between a field with a solid cob grazing in it and an orchard of small, stunted trees, bent by the wind from the sea to look as though they were stretching out their long, beseeching arms inland.

Jem led the way into the farmyard by a small side gate, and Ysella approached the front door of a long, low, stone-built farmhouse. A porch had been constructed to give some shelter from the elements that no doubt ravaged the farm in winter, built from bits of sea-bleached driftwood.

She knocked on the door.

After a moment, it swung open to reveal a small woman of early middle-age and rotund figure. Jenifry, Uncle Jago's… housekeeper. She wore an apron and mob cap, the strands of her light brown hair escaping around a face flushed pink with heat. For a long few seconds, the woman stood there staring, before her expression changed from one of surprise to one of delight. "Miss Ysella! Well, I live an' breathe. 'Tis you, m'dear. Come back to Nanpean. Come in, come in. I've a pot of tea on the stove keeping hot and cakes in the oven."

Her gaze slid past Ysella to Jem. "Him an' all. Can't be sendin' a boy back up that long path to the Court without a bite to eat and a dish o' tea. I takes it you've come from up yonder?"

"Goodness, Jenifry," Ysella managed, when her hostess paused to take a breath. "I didn't expect you to remember me, what with all the things going on last time we met." She and Jem followed Jenifry into the house. Everything was just as Ysella remembered it. The long oak table where Kit had pretended to be drunk at cards, the stove on one side of the room, and the wingback chairs to either side of it. A cat sat in a basket in front of the stove licking a batch of kittens, and a black and white sheepdog lay on the floor beside the window, ears cocked to keep an eye on the newcomers.

"Sit you down," Jenifry said, "and tell me all the news. Your uncle's away into Penzance this morning, so we've an hour or two to gossip without interruption."

This was better than Ysella had planned, Jenifry was a far more welcome person to talk to than an old man would have been. In truth, she'd been nervous at the thought of meeting the gruff and ferocious looking Jago again, so his absence was a boon. Ysella settled down to tell her all about Morvoren and baby George, carefully skirting around her own problems.

Chapter Twenty-Eight

SAM ROSE FROM the desk in his new office with a feeling of accomplishment. More than two weeks had passed since their arrival. He'd managed to hire three new girls from the nearby village to help with the cleaning, and two young men to work in the wilderness that was the gardens. Rosie had already proved she could manage to provide edible, if not spectacular, food, and Cubert had taken to waiting on table and the duties of a footman with gruff resignation. That none of them possessed any kind of livery to wear could be addressed later.

He closed the ledger book in which he'd inscribed the names of his five new servants, recruited from the somewhat unpromising and poorly trained workforce from the local village. All of whom had now been accommodated in the attic servants' quarters, which were next on the list for deep cleaning.

He glanced at his fob watch. He'd worked too late. Again. Dinner would be served very shortly. As old Gerren, Rosie's white-haired father, had been sent into Penzance today in the trap for more kitchen supplies, it was to be hoped tonight it would be something a little less simple than the stew they'd had last night. Unless, of course, that was all Rosie could manage, which was entirely possible. It had been tasty and filling, but not quite what Ysella was used to. For himself, he was quite happy to exist on homely stews, but he wanted Ysella to feel at home, so he wanted the food, and everything else here, to more closely resemble Ormonde. Rosie permitting. Hopefully...

He glanced down at his clothes. Really, he should change for dinner, but did he have time? Probably not. He doubted if Ysella would notice. She didn't seem to notice much about what he did, as though he didn't matter to her any more than the servants did. A depressing thought. He put away his books, tidied his desk and headed for the hall.

Ysella was already there, dazzlingly beautiful in a white gown with tiny puff sleeves and the smallest of lemon flowers embroidered across the bodice. Her hair had been piled up in rich chestnut curls, a few of which had escaped to lay across the alabaster skin of her shoulders. The sight of her took Sam's breath away, leaving him fumbling in the darkness of his confusion.

She bestowed a radiant smile on him. "Shall we go in? I've been down to the beach at Nanpean again today with Jem, and I'm quite famished."

A pang of jealousy stabbed at Sam's heart. She'd been spending a lot of time with Jem, but of course, he couldn't be seen as any kind of rival for Ysella's heart. The boy was only fourteen and looked no more than twelve. But theirs was a budding friendship that nagged at Sam incessantly. He longed to be the one to walk down to Nanpean with her, to stroll along the sand hand-in-hand and to point out what the tide had deposited, but something held him back from asking her every time he steeled himself to do so. The sensation that she preferred the simple, uncomplicated company of a child wouldn't go away.

Rosie had risen to the occasion. Sort of. They had some kind of indeterminate soup to begin with, followed by a very tolerable joint of mutton in a sauce whose ingredients Sam didn't want to enquire after. But it all tasted good, and he would have tucked away a good proportion of it had he not been, as usual, rendered without appetite by Ysella's presence.

She seemed to have a good appetite though, after her afternoon of exercise and fresh air, clearing both her soup bowl and her dinner plate. Rosie had cooked something called a spotted dick for dessert, which turned out to be a boiled pudding with dried fruit peppered through it. This reminded Sam too much of his schooldays, and he declined to try it. Ysella, on the other hand, ate hers with gusto and returned for seconds.

"You seem to have worked up quite a hunger, Ysella," Sam said, leaning back in his seat and sipping on the claret he'd had brought up from the well-supplied cellars. At least the resident servants hadn't found that, or if they had, they'd left enough to keep him and Ysella in wine for some time to come.

She nodded. "I went down to see Jenifry again, and this time I finally met Uncle Jago." A smile flitted across her face. "I must say, he's an intimidating fellow. I'm not sure he approves of me, and I can't understand what Kit sees in him, to be honest. He's nothing at all like Mama. You wouldn't think they had the same parents." She chuckled. "But Jenifry is lovely."

"It's a long walk," Sam said, who'd been down to visit Jago himself several times over the past two weeks. Ysella probably didn't know he'd done so, though.

"And such a climb back up. But the walking is doing me good. I'm sure it makes me less puffed now, thanks to all the exercise I'm getting."

Sam got to his feet. "Shall we take tea in the drawing room. Or would you prefer coffee?"

She stood up with a giggle. "Do you think the tea might be contraband? That would be funny if it were. I assume the smuggling didn't stop with the raids carried out last year. Jenifry told me they'd just have moved where the stuff comes ashore and kept on going. I'd wager all our servants, too, know exactly what's going on."

Sam laughed himself, glad to be able to exchange banter with her. Dinner seemed the only time of day he was with her at the moment, there was so much work to do. He'd managed to persuade her to spend at least her mornings supervising the house, something she'd taken to quite well, although she continually professed herself bored with it.

Now they had more maids, though, the work was progressing more quickly. She'd also undertaken to supervise the gardens, or rather young Jem, so not a lot of gardening was being done yet, at least, not by Jem. She always seemed to be taking him off, asking him to show her new paths to walk on, and where to pick the wildflowers that were popping up everywhere. She came home every day with armfuls of bluebells and the pretty white three-cornered leeks, or posies of cowslips, primroses, pink campion, stitchwort, and tiny violets. The house now had vases of wildflowers decorating many a windowsill.

They went into the drawing room and over to the hearth. The fire blazed, courtesy of the local chimneysweep, but nevertheless was fighting a losing battle at keeping at bay the chill of spring the house never seemed to lose. It must be those thick walls.

"I think there's a storm brewing out to sea," Sam said as he took one of the tapestry-upholstered wing back chairs that had belonged to Ysella's grandmother. "So tomorrow I wouldn't venture too far from the house, if I were you."

She raised her eyebrows at him. "How can you tell?"

"The clouds. They've been building up on the horizon all day, and, this evening, shafts of sunlight were spearing through them. They're only that noticeable when a storm is brewing." He shrugged. "If we're lucky, though, the storm will pass us by out to sea and head off south into the Bay of Biscay."

"Where's that?"

Cubert, considerably spruced up since his appointment as first, and only, footman, came in with the tea tray and set it down on the low table.

"You can go," Sam said. "I'll pour." He turned back to Ysella. "The Bay of Biscay is hundreds of miles to the south, near Spain and Portugal. Did you never have a lesson in the geography of the world?"

She pulled a face. "Far too boring. I never had a governess

who could keep me applied to the work she wanted me to do. We spent a lot of our time walking in the gardens. When she could find me."

Sam shook his head. "It amazes me that you ever gleaned any education at all. Our children won't…" He stopped, blazing heat racing up his throat to his face.

Ysella blushed a matching scarlet.

"I'm sorry," Sam spluttered. "I didn't think."

She fluttered her hand at him. "That's all right."

But he could see it wasn't.

To fill the now gaping silence, he poured their tea and passed Ysella hers. As she took it, their fingers brushed, a current of electricity surging up Sam's arm. She started. Had she felt it as well? Was it to do with what he'd let slip? Thoughtless fool that he was. Their eyes met.

Ysella's lips parted and her bosom rose and fell as though she were finding it hard to catch her breath. Was this still just embarrassment? Or did she want to say something?

Sam couldn't tear his eyes away from her.

The moment seemed to stretch on forever, then she took the cup, her gaze dropped, and she leaned back in her seat, studious disinterest on her face as the color faded.

Sam hesitated before picking up his own tea, afraid that with his hand shaking so badly he would spill it, or give himself away by letting it rattle.

"I think I'd like to have my bedroom decorated," Ysella said, a little awkwardly. Was her voice strained and tense, and if so, why?

Sam struggled to regain his composure, convinced he hadn't been mistaken in her reaction. "What color do you fancy?"

The moment of tension between them dissipated, melting away into the cold air of the drawing room. Lost but not forgotten.

For a while, then, they talked of their plans for the house and gardens, and Sam told her about the tenant farms he'd visited and the plans he had for innovation on them to help with production levels. All things he'd learned from books and shared with Kit at Ormonde. He expounded for a while on how more modern machinery, and specially bred stock, could make a farmer and his farm more efficient, which in itself could produce more revenue for the farmer, and perhaps higher rent for the landlord. He forbore from mentioning the veiled hostility with which he'd been met at nearly every farm, the suspicious glances, the resentment of his presence.

She listened to him with a rapt attention that seemed quite out of character for her. Surely, she wasn't interested in harrows and seed drills and broadcasting and different breeds of sheep? But it filled what could have been an awkwardness between them, and he was glad of her pretended interest.

They drank their tea, called for more, and eventually, with night drawing in, it was time to retire to bed.

Ysella rose, her hand to her mouth to stifle a yawn. She must be tired with all the time she was spending out of doors in the fresh sea air, walking with Jem. A further pang of jealousy assaulted Sam. She should be walking with *him* down the quiet, wildflower-strewn lanes. *He* should be picking flowers for her to add to her bouquets. Not a simple farm boy, who, regardless of his extreme youth, was undoubtedly smitten by his young mistress. Sam shook himself, angry that he could feel jealous of a child.

He held out his arm, and Ysella took it, the touch of her fingers gossamer light through the broadcloth of his workaday coat. Out of the drawing room, across the hall, up the stairs, turn right at the half-landing and into the gallery. Ysella's room lay at the far end, his, two doors down. No interconnecting doors for them, as Ysella's parents had had.

He walked to her door with her.

She stopped and turned towards him, a questioning look in her eyes, her face serious. What did she want? Might she be about to say something? Was that an invitation in her eyes or was he imagining it?

"Thank you, Sam," she said, slipping her hand off his arm. "Thank you for making Carlyon more of a home for me."

Sam gazed down at her, captivated by everything about her. "It's been a pleasure for me to do so." He reached out and caught her hand. Even through the thin silk of her glove he could feel the warmth of her skin. A shiver of excitement ran down his back. Might she be softening towards him? Might this be the night she invited him into her bedroom? And if she did, would he go? No. She didn't love him. If she invited him, it would be from pity, or some other such emotion. Would he let her give herself to him knowing it wasn't out of love?

"That makes me very happy," she whispered, her voice low and clear in the quiet of the upper gallery.

"My only wish is to see you happy."

She bowed her head, looking down at their joined hands. "I know." She paused. "And for that I feel… a little guilty."

He squeezed her hand. "Never feel like that."

She shook her head, still not looking up. "I feel you have received the bad end of the bargain. You have a wife, but you do not have a lover."

If he hadn't known her so well, he would have been shocked. "Ysella," he whispered, his whole body stiff with tension. "I did not marry you to take you as my lover. I married you because… because of how much I care for you. I know you don't love me. I know you never can. I would never make a demand of you that you did not truly wish to fulfill. You have not in any way discomposed me. I assure you."

Only that wasn't true. He wanted nothing more right now than to take her in his embrace and kiss her lips, her eyes, her cheeks, her throat. He wanted to scoop her up in his arms and carry her into her bedroom, banging the door shut behind them and shutting out the world that held Oliver Featherstone. He wanted to love her so much that she'd never think of Featherstone again.

"A pretty speech," Ysella said, and slid her hand out of his with gentle firmness. "I bid you goodnight, dear husband." She raised her head, stared into his eyes for a long moment, then, on tiptoe, kissed him on the cheek. "Good night." A chaste and friendly kiss only. A sister's kiss for a beloved brother.

She pushed open the door and went inside her bedroom.

Sam stood outside the closed door, one hand to his cheek, touching the spot she'd kissed. She'd never done that before. Was that an indication of her changing feelings? Did he really mean what he'd said to her?

Chapter Twenty-Nine

A LOUD CRACK of thunder woke Ysella. The house trembled around her and rain hammered on the windowpanes like bullets. Lightning shot across the sky, illuminating the night, and its fiery fingers lanced between the heavy curtains. Thunder rolled again. Where had this come from so suddenly? Had she slept through some of it?

Throwing back the covers in total disregard for the chill of the room, Ysella jumped out of bed and ran on bare feet to the window. Throwing the curtains wide, she pressed her nose to the glass to peer into the night. And what a night to be out in. The wind screamed through the eaves of the old house as though a coven of banshees were racing around the rooftops on their brooms, and draughts scuttered across the floor from every corner of the room, chilling her bare feet.

Somewhere inside the house a door banged, and the night sky rent in two as jagged lightning forked towards the Earth. For an instant, it illuminated the silhouettes of the trees around the garden, their branches bent and twisted by the force of the wind. She counted in her head. One, two, three, four, five, six... crash. Thunder rolled, reverberating around the old house and shaking it to its foundations. The storm must be only a mile away, maybe out to sea where Sam had seen the clouds gathering.

More lightning blasted its jagged way across the sky and

another crash sounded, far too close at hand for comfort. Had the house been struck? More thunder. Mama had once told her thunder was just God moving his furniture about. Well, if it was, then he was not at all good at it. He must keep dropping it.

The bedroom door flew open, and Martha bolted in, a flannel robe clutched about her nightgown and her feet bare. "Ooh, Miss Ysella, I came to see if you were all right on your own."

This was so patently not true that Ysella laughed out loud. Martha had a morbid fear of storms and had played this trick before at Ormonde.

"Get in my bed then, Martha. You'll be all right if you stay here with me."

Martha needed no further encouragement. She jumped into the large bed and snuggled down, drawing the covers up to her chin. "Aren't you getting back in, Miss?"

Ysella shook her head. "No, I'm not. I love to watch a storm, as you well know, and this one feels different. Wilder, more out of control." She turned back to Martha as excitement bubbled up within her. "I should very much like to go down to the beach and see what the sea looks like in this storm."

"Ooh, Miss Ysella, come away from the window in case a bolt of lightning sees you and strikes you dead."

Another crash of thunder and Martha's head vanished under the bedclothes. "I don't like thunder," she squeaked, her voice muffled.

"Rubbish. Lightning can't see you any more than… than a tree can." Ysella turned back to the window and the almost terrifying display going on in the sky, as more bolts of lightning seared down towards the Earth. Might they be striking the sea, and if they did, what did that mean for a ship out on the water?

"Is anyone else awake?" Ysella asked, although how anyone could sleep through this racket was beyond her. Maybe deaf old Doryty might, but surely not any of the others. Not up there in the servants' quarters nearer the storm than she was down here.

Martha's head didn't reappear. "Everyone, I think," she replied from under the covers. "Those three girls what the master hired are down in the kitchens making hot drinks for themselves and anyone as wants one. No one wanted to stay upstairs. Lest the house gets hit."

So Sam might be up too. Was the house safe with the wind tugging at it in vicious snatches? Might the roof blow off? Another crash from outside. Could that be roof tiles loosening and falling? Would Sam be outside looking at the house, or upstairs checking from inside for leaks? Suppose he went outside and a roof tile hit him on the head? Her heart did a little lurch of fear as she realized she wouldn't like that at all.

More thunder rumbled directly overhead now, and the skeleton of the old house creaked as though in pain. But it had stood here for centuries and not been blown into the sea yet, so surely even in this howling storm it wouldn't suffer damage. Or not too much, at any rate.

The gale howled around the house, rattling the windows, pulling at the heavy curtains, whistling a wild, exciting tune. What would the sea, so calm and glassy flat the other day, look like now? How high would the waves have risen? Ysella longed to see it for herself.

She turned away from the window to fetch her peignoir from the end of her bed. "I'm going to see if my husband is up." No need to say that she wanted Sam to take her to where she could see the storm better. Martha would be horrified and might even try to stop her.

The floor was cold under her feet, but it was too dark to find her slippers. She pulled the peignoir on over her nightgown and did up the ties. Taking the candle from beside her bed, she tried to light it with a spill stuck into the embers of her bedroom fire. After a moment, the spill caught and she set it to the candle's wick, sheltering it from the draught with her hand. It caught, and the candle flared, throwing great shadows around the room. "You stay here, Martha, where you're safe. You'll be fine in my bed."

She let herself out into the corridor. The sound of someone

sobbing hysterically carried to her from downstairs. One of those silly new girls, no doubt. Best to try Sam's room first, and see if he was still in bed.

She knocked on his door.

No answer. She knocked again.

Still no answer. Taking her courage in both hands, an action very much needed as she'd never been inside his bedroom before, not even when it had been being cleaned in preparation for his occupation of it, she turned the handle.

The room before her was a smaller version of her own, but a lot less feminine in its decoration. The bed against the far wall lay empty, the covers thrown back as though he'd jumped out of it in a hurry. Ysella took a moment to study her husband's room in curiosity. There was the broadcloth coat he'd worn to dinner, there his discarded white shirt. On an impulse, she picked up the shirt and held it to her face. The faint smell of the soap he used and a hint of sweat clung to it. She breathed it in, savoring the moment.

But this wasn't getting her anywhere, and if she wanted him to take her where she could see the sea, then she would need to find him.

She went back to the corridor and headed down the stairs. Perhaps he was in the kitchen having one of the maids prepare him a hot drink. A good idea. She'd look there.

Since she'd arrived at Carlyon Court she'd only once ventured into the kitchens, only to have Rosie, who now saw herself as cook and housekeeper combined, send her packing with a hard stare. The domain of the cook, the mistress of the house was rarely welcome there. But at least she knew where it was.

At the foot of the stairs, she heard footsteps hurrying from where the kitchens lay, and Sam appeared, carrying an oil lamp, still in his nightshirt and a thick woolen dressing gown. Two men she didn't recognize, in common, homespun clothing, were with him.

He stopped the moment he saw her. "Ysella. What are you

doing up? Aren't you frightened? Go back to bed. You'll catch your death. This house is as full of holes as a Swiss cheese."

Ysella shook her head. "It's only a storm. I'm not scared." She peered at the newcomers. Was one of them Uncle Jago's man Jowan? A disreputable rogue at the best of times, now, by the light of the lamp, he resembled a denizen of hell's deepest depths. His long, wet hair hung down his face revealing a sizeable bald spot, and his eyes appeared to be starting from his face. A face twisted into the most remarkable grimace. "What are these two men doing here?"

Sam glanced sideways at them. "There's a ship being washed onshore down in Nanpean Cove. Jowan and Kenal came to tell me. I've sent Jem to the village to fetch some men with ropes. I'm going down there to see what I can do."

Suddenly, the idea of seeing the sea in stormy weather no longer seemed anywhere near so attractive. The thought of a shipload of people in trouble on it banished all feelings of excitement. "*You're* going? Can you not send our men?" He mustn't go into danger. He mustn't.

Sam shook his head in impatience. "What sort of a gentleman would send his workers but not go himself when lives are at stake?"

"A sensible one. This ship's not your responsibility and nor are the men onboard it."

He scowled at her. "*It* may not be, but the people in the local villages *are*, and they are going down there to try to save the souls of the people on the ship. I owe it to them to go too."

Why was she so frightened for him? Was it more than the fear for a dear friend? She descended the last few steps and caught his arm. "You don't need to go, Sam. I need you here. Stay with me."

Just for a moment she thought he would. His gray eyes, glowing a little in the light of the oil lamp, held her gaze for a long moment, indecision writ large in them. Then he shook her off. "No, Ysella. Kit sent me down here to act as master of his estate, and as such I have a duty to do so in his place. He would go if he were here. I'm going to find some clothes. Get out of my way." And he pushed past her and ran up the stairs two at a time.

Ysella looked back at Jowan and Kenal, caps in hand, hair plastered to their pale faces. "Keep him safe for me."

Outside the thunder rumbled again, and the wind rattled at the heavy front door as though eager to get in. Jowan tugged his sparse forelock. "I will that, Missus."

SAM TUGGED ON the trousers he kept for working outside with the men, tucking an old shirt into the waistband and slipping his braces over his shoulders. He pulled on his top boots and snatched up the simple fisherman's gansey he'd taken to wearing for work. Pushing thoughts out of his head of Ysella's stricken face when he'd told her he was going out to help, he picked up the lantern.

It swung in his hand as he strode back along the gallery, casting leaping shadows up the walls. At the top of the stairs, he nearly collided with Ysella who'd come racing along the gallery from her room. She was dressed much as he was, in the boys' clothes she and Morvoren had a disturbing penchant for wanting to ride out in.

He held the lantern up to illuminate her face, the golden light making her eyes glow like coals. "What the hell are you doing?"

She glared back at him, pulling her coat on. Kit's old coat, that was. "If you're going, then I'm coming too."

He shook his head. "No, you're not. Get back to your room. I'll send Martha to keep you company if you're frightened."

"No need," she snapped back at him. "Martha's already there, and I'm *not* scared. If you're going out in it, then so am I. It's only a storm, and you said you'd show me what the sea looked like in bad weather. And besides which, I want to help."

"Not in a hurricane." Sam had to raise his voice to almost a shout above the increasing howl of the wind and the accompanying creaks and groans of the old house. His only hope, much as Ysella had concluded, was that it had stood the rigors of previous storms and remained intact, so this one would leave it standing.

"What d'you think I'm going to do?" Ysella shouted back. "Blow away?"

He shook his head again. "You might. It's no place for a girl."

She reached out and took hold of his hand, hers small and chilly in his. "I'm not just any woman, Sam. I'm your wife."

Words deserted him. All he could feel or think of was her hand in his, somehow persuasive and comforting, and the electric current fizzing through his body.

"I won't do anything silly," Ysella shouted into his face. "You have my word."

What on earth did she want to come with him for? Being his wife wasn't a good reason for her to put herself in danger. Unless… He stared into her pleading eyes. Was that worry he saw in them? Not for the first time he wished with fervor that he understood women a bit better. Their ways remained a mystery to him, particularly Ysella's. "Very well. If you insist, and you swear you're not going to turn vaporish on me, then you can come. But you stand where I put you, and you don't move. You don't get in anyone's way. If I see danger, you go back. Do I have your word on that?"

She nodded, eyes shining in the lamplight, a decidedly unholy expression of glee on her face as though she thought this some big adventure and not an expedition setting out to try to save lives that might well already be lost. "You have my word."

"Then let's find you a gansey and a better coat," Sam said. "Something that'll keep the rain off you a bit better than that one. Hurry up."

Chapter Thirty

WRAPPED IN SOMEONE'S rather smelly old gansey and a well-worn but oversized peacoat, a piece of rope cinching it around her narrow middle, Ysella followed Sam out into the stableyard. In their looseboxes, the horses neighed in anxiety, their hooves clattering on the cobbles. One of them was kicking at his door. Probably the highly strung Lochinvar. Ysella would have liked to go in to reassure him, but Sam had her firmly by the hand.

With buildings surrounding them on all four sides, they were sheltered from the worst of the wind, but the rain lashed down without mercy, plastering Ysella's hair to her head and running into her eyes and mouth. It was like being drowned while not immersed in a body of water, as though the air had become the sea. Or at least how she imagined that would be.

Other men appeared: Jowan and Kenal accompanied by the two young men from the village who now worked for Sam. Gray-haired old Gerren emerged from the servants' door followed by someone whose long skirts were already sticking to her legs. Rosie the cook, Jem's mother. How Sam could have argued it was no place for a woman yet hadn't batted an eyelid about allowing Rosie to come irked Ysella, but she was heartily glad of her breeches, still partly dry under her heavy peacoat. Cubert came out of the stables with a coil of thick rope over each shoulder. Nine of them assembled altogether, counting Jowan and Kenal.

It seemed all the household had turned out for this rescue apart from Martha and the three new maidservants. Ysella's heart soared with pride at being a part of this, at belonging to something intangible but worthy. How glad she was not to be inside hiding under the covers with Martha.

The cobbled yard swam with water, rivulets pouring off the roof to splatter into the puddles, and from beyond the archway came a crash that might have been a tree falling. Was that the very ground shaking? What if it had hit the house? Might the rain even now be pouring down inside? She'd think about that later.

"Which way?" Sam shouted at Jowan, his grip on Ysella's hand tightening, the lantern swinging wildly from side to side.

"The back track," the old man shouted back. "Best keep off the cliff path in this wind."

Thank goodness. It hadn't occurred to Ysella that they might go that way, but the fact that they weren't was a great relief.

As Jowan seized the yard gates, the wind snatched them out of his grip and flung them open. They crashed against the stonework, just missing sandwiching him against the wall.

"Leave them open," Sam shouted. "Might keep them from being damaged."

"What if the horses break out of the stables?" Ysella cried, fear for Lochinvar foremost in her mind for a moment.

"They won't," Sam shouted back as thunder rolled overhead again, the wind stealing his words. "They'll be safe. Don't worry."

Stepping out of the shelter of the stableyard tore Ysella's breath away. Lightning lit the sky just as she did so, showing her the devastation wrought in the gardens. Two enormous trees lay sprawled across the lawns, their branches reaching almost as far as the side of the house, and those still standing looked as though at any moment they'd join their recumbent friends. Their branches screamed, bending in supplication, and broken pieces of them littered the grass.

"No time to stand gawking," Sam said, his face close to her ear, and he pulled her after him.

Thunder rolled overhead again and again, as though the sky might rend itself in two. Was that what lightning was? The sky splitting wide open and showing a glimpse of heaven? If that was heaven, it couldn't be offering eternal rest as vicars promised. Ysella peered upwards into the driving rain, in time to see a jagged bolt of lightning lance down towards the ground. It lit the countryside up like daylight for a second, and she saw that Jowan was leading them down the narrow path that led by the inland route to Nanpean farmhouse.

Underfoot, the ground was slick with running water, turning everything to mud. She slipped and slid on the rocky track, gripping Sam's hand for much needed support. Once or twice, he had to put a supporting arm around her waist and, despite the desperate situation, Ysella felt that same electric current run between them.

She leaned her weight on him, conscious of how safe he made her feel with his strong arms and sturdy body. Why had she insisted on coming with him? The need to acknowledge to herself why she was here rose and had to be answered. The thought of Sam going into danger had terrified her. She'd wanted to be there, beside him, keeping him safe, just as he did for her.

The high earth and stone walls to either side of the path gave a little shelter from the gusts of wind, but nothing from the rain. Water found its way in at the neck of Ysella's coat, running down her neck and soaking into her shirt under her thick gansey, but the struggle of walking kept her warm. Sweat joined the rain in running down her back.

In daylight, with the ground dry, the walk down to Nanpean was not an easy one, being steep and unforgiving and pocked with hidden rocks. Now, in the black of night, with only the light of a few oil lanterns and the intermittent flashes of furious lightning, it had become a nightmare.

Ysella slipped on a wet rock and sat down hard on her bottom, almost pulling Sam down with her. He hauled her back up again and, without even checking she was all right, kept going. She didn't complain. This new masterful Sam was somehow far more attractive than the one who kept giving in to her every little whim. He'd gradually been asserting himself over her these last weeks, and she had to admit she liked the dynamic making itself known between them. Enough for her to push him into arguing with her whenever she could.

The journey down into the little valley seemed to take forever. Ysella had no idea how long a ship could survive if it was being wrecked on this rocky coast. Presumably its crew would fight to save it all the way. The wind direction must have an influence on their chances of success though—and the wind was blowing hard inland tonight.

At last, the path leveled out and, within a few minutes, they were in Nanpean's yard. Instead of turning towards the house though, Jowan led them straightaway down the steep path to the beach. The stunted hawthorn trees to either side rattled in the wind, their twisted, thorny branches snatching at the would-be rescuers as they passed. Ysella shrank as close to Sam as she could, and his strong arm went around her shoulders, pulling her closer still. She put out her own arm out to encircle his waist and help her stay upright. To be nearer to his solid, dependable presence.

The rain, which had nearly stopped, had made no difference to the dunes at the end of the path. Instead, the wind had whipped up the loose sand to send it in swirls across the cove, stinging Ysella's face and getting in her eyes and up her nose.

Peering at a night made starless and moonless by the storm clouds, she halted, open-mouthed at the sight before her. The tide was well in, massive, white-topped breakers pounding up the steep incline of the beach and snatching back the sand into the sea with a deep sucking noise. Out beyond the sea's foamy edge, rows of even more enormous waves seemed to be racing inland as though they intended to swamp the tiny cove or pound it to submission. The primal force of the storm buzzed through her body, banishing her fears for an instant.

At first, she couldn't see the ship.

Sam stopped beside her, holding tight to her hand.

Wiping her wet hair off her face, she turned to him. "Where is it? Has it got away? Is it safe?" The hope that it was, and that they weren't needed to save it, lay foremost in her mind.

He shook his head. "No. It's there by the headland, coming in fast. The sailors won't be able to keep her off much longer with this wind and the incoming tide driving them onto the rocks."

She peered through the darkness, straining her eyes to search for anything that might resemble a ship. Lightning forked across the sky to strike somewhere out to sea, silhouetting the shape of a three-masted merchantman, her tattered sails flapping loose amongst her rigging.

"She tried to put an anchor down," someone nearby shouted at Sam. "But the wind and tide're too strong and it didn't hold. She's comin' in."

Other people were crowded onto the small amount of beach the angry sea had left them. Ysella looked around at the shadowy shapes huddling together in small groups. Men, women too, wrapped in big coats and tightly clutched shawls, staring in impotence as the ship drew ever nearer to the rocks.

"She won't be the first this cove's taken," another voice said. A woman's this time. "Nor the last, I don't doubt."

A third voice chipped in. "D'you remember the storm o' ninety-three, when three ships ran aground here in one night?"

A chorus of "ayes" rumbled across the beach amongst those near enough to hear.

"That were rich pickin's," the same woman remarked. "Shouldn't wonder if we don't get some good stuff ashore tonight."

Rich pickings? Was she talking about the goods the ship might be carrying? Ysella turned to stare at the assembled people, villagers from Nanpean, no doubt. Soon they'd be joined by the neighboring villagers as well, all of them, perhaps, intent on profiting from the misfortune of others. Like carrion crows on the carcass of a dead deer. Here to pick over the corpse of this unlucky ship. Did Sam know what they were here for?

She turned to Sam, pulling him closer so she didn't need to shout for all to hear and could speak into his ear. "Are they all only here to loot the goods that come ashore?"

Sam shook his head. "Not all of them. And I intend to make sure some of us at least make an effort to save the crew." He looked down at her, his face close to hers. "But if the poor of these parishes can use what comes ashore, who am I to prevent them?" He gestured around at the crowded beach. "These people are not like you or me, Ysella. They're poor. Dirt poor. Many of them have nothing and live hand to mouth all the year around. Anything that comes ashore on this beach tonight is theirs as far as I'm concerned. As long as we try to save the lives of the crew."

He held her gaze. She stared into his gray eyes, shadowed and hidden now by the darkness of the night. The wind whipped at his hair making a wildman of him. The moment stretched into forever.

"She's comin' ashore," someone shouted, and the moment shattered.

Another flash of lightning dazzled the sky, showing the ship lumbering towards them as though she might race up the beach and lodge herself in the dunes. But the wind caught her and she broached. The sea tossed her onto the jagged, wave-lashed rocks of the headland with a splintering crash of her timbers that rose above the howling of the wind.

She settled onto the rocks with a kind of sigh, and her bowsprit shattered. A tangled mess of spars and ropes hung from her broken masts, her hull tilting drunkenly to one side.

"We'll never get to her," shouted a voice Ysella knew. Jago.

Already objects were floating away from her, washed from a jagged gap in her sides, and being carried towards the beach on the foam-topped waves. A few people ran into the surf to seize the prized treasure, careless of what it might be or the danger to themselves.

"We have to try to save the crew," Sam shouted. "It's our duty." He let go of Ysella's hand. "Bring the ropes."

SAM TURNED TO Ysella, taking her by the shoulders. "Stay here with Jenifry."

"What are you doing? Don't leave me."

Bloody girl. She promised she'd do as she was told. He might have guessed she'd change her mind. "Do as I say, Ysella, or I'll have to send someone back with you to the house. And we need all the men we can get down here."

Her voice rose in fear. "Not until you tell me what you're going to do."

He ignored her words and turned away. "I can swim, and none of the others can. I need to do it." He met Jago's eyes. "And as master of Carlyon Court, it's my duty."

Jago didn't argue. He must see the logicality of this. Thank goodness. Sam couldn't ask any of the men here to do what he wouldn't do. What he was afraid to do. And even though he could swim, he was afraid.

Before he could change his mind, he undid his coat and kicked off his boots, which would have only served to drag him down.

"What're you doing?" Ysella shouted, seizing him by the arm, her fingers digging into his flesh.

He'd almost forgotten she was there. "Go with Jenifry."

Jago caught hold of Ysella, pulling her hand away from Sam's arm. "Do as you're bid, girl." The words came out as an angry snarl, and Jenifry stepped forward to take her.

"Tie the rope around my waist, and make the knot a good one," Sam said to Jago.

On the beach, more containers and bundles were being

thrown ashore by the waves, and the water's edge was crowded with people fighting over them. No one seemed to be looking at the ship anymore. He couldn't blame them. A wrecked ship was unexpected booty for poor villagers. They could see where it had ended up and must have given up the sailors as lost.

Jago wrapped the thick rope around Sam's waist and tied a knot. Sam pulled on it to make sure it would hold. He wasn't feeling suicidal.

With a desperate wail, Ysella yanked herself free of Jenifry's hold and flung herself into Sam's arms with such force she nearly knocked him over. "Don't go!" Her voice was almost a scream. "Let someone else do this. It doesn't have to be you."

Out of instinct, he wrapped his arms around her, holding her against his chest. "I have to do it, Ysella. No one else can swim. They're all sailors and fishermen themselves, and you *know* sailors can't swim. If I don't go, those men out there have no chance." He nodded at the ship. "It's breaking up. I have to get to them."

"Don't go. Please, don't go."

He shook his head. "I'm their lord of the manor now, Ysella. But they haven't accepted me yet. If I can show them what I'm prepared to do, then maybe they'll accept me." He tightened his hold on her. "It's all right for you. You're their Miss Ysella, Elestren Tremaine's daughter, Jago's niece. They don't need to accept you, because you're one of them already. I have to prove myself."

Her ferocious gaze met his, her lips parted as though she were about to speak. Instead, she suddenly leaned forward and pressed her lips to his. A jolt shot through him worthy of the lightning overhead. Her lips were cold with rain, and the kiss hard and determined. His mouth parted under hers and he kissed her back with all the pent-up desire of the last six weeks and beyond.

Her mouth opened in return, her tongue met his, as though she, too, were intent on making up the ground they'd left untrod. If only this kiss would never end.

She broke the kiss. He never would have. "Be careful," she said, breathless and flushed, and stepped out of his embrace, her anguished eyes fixed on his.

"Hurry up," Jago shouted. "She's breaking up fast under the pounding of those waves."

Sam dragged himself away from Ysella's gaze. He had to concentrate. He mustn't think about her and that kiss. Or maybe he should. Maybe he should think about it when he stepped into the water. Maybe it would keep him alive and help him save those lost souls.

Jago had gathered a covey of the strongest men on the beach, many of whom had left their wives to stake their claims on the loot now being washed ashore through the ever-growing hole in the ship's side. The men took hold of the rope that was around Sam's middle, to a man giving him a thumb's up.

Swallowing hard, Sam walked into the sea.

Chapter Thirty-One

YSELLA WATCHED SAM walk into the water in just his breeches and shirt, the rope, suddenly looking thin and flimsy, secured around his slim waist. The waves crashed around him, taller than he was, and he disappeared under one. Her heart leapt into her mouth and her hand shot up to cover it.

"He's on a rope, girl, don't fret," Jenifry said from her right, a comforting arm around Ysella's shoulders. "They can pull him back if they think he's in trouble and they need to."

Ysella turned and grabbed her free hand. "I'm frightened for him."

"I know you are, maid. I know you are. He's a brave lad, doin' that fer fellers he don't know. 'Tis hard to be in love with a hero."

In love? Ysella opened her mouth to tell Jenifry she'd got it wrong and Sam was just her friend, but shut it without speaking. Right now, she had to admit he felt like more than a friend, but not quite her husband. Or did he? She didn't understand her jumbled feelings at all.

She swiped her wet hair out of her eyes, straining to see Sam's head, bobbing now beyond the breakers but still being cast up on the sea's strong swell. The men on the beach were letting out the rope a bit at a time, half a dozen of them helping Jago keep a tight hold on it. If he got into trouble, she had to keep reminding herself, they'd haul him back in. And the rope was strong. It wouldn't break. Would it?

On the beach, fights were breaking out over the salvaged goods. Someone had broached a barrel of brandy and half the men were heading towards reeling drunk. Some of the women too. Shouting, even laughing, as though the tragedy of the ship and her sailors didn't matter to them.

It seemed an age before Sam drew anywhere near the ship. Overhead, the sky had already lightened a little as if dawn were approaching, and the thunder sounded further away. The storm must be heading east. Ysella didn't have to strain her eyes so hard to make out Sam's head, still above the waves.

Just as he was reaching out to take a hold of the side of the ship, a huge wave swept him away from her and up against the rocks, shaking him like a rag doll. Ysella had to clamp her hand across her mouth to stop herself from screaming. He disappeared into the raging, foamy water for what felt like an age. Then, just as she was giving up all hope and her tears were mingling with the scudding rain that had started up again, there was his head. He was striking out towards the ship, and, on it, hands were reaching down to grab hold of him.

The strong arms of sailors heaved him aboard, and he disappeared from sight.

How many crew might need rescuing and what was he going to do? She put her knuckles to her mouth and gnawed them, biting the loose skin. Jenifry's arm around her shoulders tightened. "I knowed he could do it."

Were the waves rolling up the beach less furious now? More flotsam was coming ashore—broken bits of wood, the bright colors of a bale of silk, unraveled by the tide. Was that a body, floating on the swell like a broken doll? People, ignoring the body, gathered up the wood into piles. No doubt it would be used for something.

Not being able to see Sam now was worse even than when all she could see of him was his head among the waves. Those desperate men on board the ship could at this moment be knocking him out and stealing his rope. She might never see him again. That thought was like a mortal stab in the heart. Was this *love* she was feeling or just friendship? Did your heart feel as though it might break over a mere friend's danger? She had no idea.

An eternity passed before Sam appeared above the ship's rail again, more visible now the early morning light was growing. Others were with him. But *they* had the rope, not him. It no longer encircled Sam's waist but had been stretched taut, as though they'd secured it to something on board ship. Instead, Sam was tying loops of rope onto sailor after sailor, and as he finished, each man was leaping into the sea, attached to the safety of the rope.

Jago must have seen what Sam was doing and realized something more was needed. Even Ysella could see that to attach thirty or forty men to a rope only anchored by six men on the beach was not going to be safe.

"More men!" shouted Jago, his head twisting to where the beach still thronged with eager magpies intent on bettering their fortunes. "We need more men here to hold the rope! To me!"

Struggling from Jenifry's embrace, Ysella ran to take a hold of the rope. All around her people ran to help, even the drunks, lining up behind her, gnarled hands gripping the wet hemp. Her own hands were soft and small, but she hung on tight, careless of how much the rough wet rope rubbed them raw.

More men on the ship were leaping into the water, each of them attached by a loop of rope to the lifeline, their heads bobbing in the swell and surf. Ysella strained to spot Sam, still on the deck of the ship, directing the escape. Why wasn't he coming himself? Why was he putting himself in such terrible danger when she needed him here?

But the men in the water weren't safe yet. The ship's goods, some of it in heavy barrels, bobbed around them, the waves threatening to send them crashing into the men. And if one man stopped, the others couldn't get past him.

In the surf, the villagers dragged the first of the men out of the water, the rescued staggering as though their legs were too weak to hold them up. Men, women too, supported their sagging bodies, sharp knives wielded to slice through the wet loops keeping them attached to the rescue rope. The line of burly men holding the lifeline dug their heels into the wet sand, and Ysella did the same, leaning back as the heavy, soaking rope threatened to pull them into the sea.

The rain, that had almost stopped once before returning as drizzle, fell more heavily, hammering at her in blinding gusts, her wet hair in her eyes. She couldn't see the man in front of her, never mind the wreck with Sam still on it. "Heave!" Someone shouted close at hand. "Hold her steady."

"She's goin' over!" Someone else shouted.

A crash reverberated around the high cliffs, louder even than the roar of the sea. The ship teetered sideways where she already lay aslant on the rocks, as a huge wave crashed into her underbelly, and she was gone.

"Sam!" Ysella screamed, letting go of the rope and running into the edge of the sea. "Sam! Where is he? Where is he?"

Half-drowned sailors struggled ashore, the rope slack now in the water as though the far end had been severed, or whatever it had been fixed to had broken. Ysella scanned their haggard faces in desperation. They all looked the same—red-eyed from the salt, faces ghostly pale in the dim pre-dawn light, sodden clothes clinging to their battered bodies. In amongst them bobbed the goods their ship had been carrying. A couple of limp bodies, like bundles of rags, bobbed face down between the goods.

No, oh no. Not Sam. Let it not be Sam.

She ran to the first body and heaved it over onto its back in the water. A young face stared back sightlessly at her, dark haired and pallid. Not Sam. She ran to the next. "Sam!" This was not him either.

Jenifry ran to her, splashing through the water. "'Tisn't him,

Miss Ysella. Not him."

"He was still on the ship!" Ysella almost shrieked, desperation forcing her on. "I have to find him. I have to. He can't be dead."

"Ysella!" A voice rang out above the roar of the sea, biting into Ysella's consciousness. Jago. Uncle Jago. "I see him."

She turned. Jago was running into the waves towards something bobbing further out. She made to run after him, but Jenifry grabbed the back of her coat, pulling her back. "Let Jago get him. Tide's too strong out there for the likes of you."

Impotent, her body stiff with terror, she watched Jago reach Sam. Saw him grab him under the chin and begin to tow him back. That it was Sam, Ysella had no doubt at all.

Jago struggled through the waves and pulled Sam's limp body into the shallows. Gasping for breath, he let him fall to the sand, where he lay sprawled on his back as the water lapped around him, eyes closed, hair plastered to his head, skin waxy pale.

Ysella dropped to her knees on the sand, reaching out and grabbing hold of his sodden shirt. It had ripped and a long cut stretched across his naked and unmoving chest. "No! He can't be dead. Do something, Jago! Do something!"

Jago pushed her aside. With strong hands, he rolled Sam onto his side and started thumping him on his back. Water ran out of Sam's mouth, but, for a long moment, nothing else happened.

On her knees, Ysella's lips moved in silent prayer. *Don't let him be dead. Please, God, don't let him be dead. I love him. I haven't told him I love him. I can't lose him. I can't. Don't let him be dead. I'll never do anything bad ever again. Please don't let him be dead.*

Sam coughed, his chest heaved, and more water spluttered out of his mouth. He lay retching in front of Ysella, eyes open now, body convulsed. With life.

Jago helped him sit up, almost cradling him in his arms. "All right now, my ansum. You're safe now, brave lad. You did it. They're all safe on shore."

Ysella hurled herself into Sam's arms, clinging on as tightly as she could, her fingers snagging in his ripped shirt. She was never,

ever going to let him do anything like this again. How cold the naked skin of his chest was against her cheek. She wrapped her arms around him as though she might pass him some of her own warmth.

"Back to the house," Jago said. "I've a warm fire in the hearth and brandy in a jar. Can you get up?"

Ysella felt Sam's head nod. "If Ysella will let me," he managed, his voice raspy. "I think I can stand."

Jenifry's strong hands took hold of Ysella's shoulders and pulled her away. She went unwillingly, arms outstretched towards Sam.

Using Jago as support, Sam struggled to his feet, bending double as he coughed again and spat up more water, a hand to his ribs as though they pained him.

"Let's get all the survivors up to my farm," Jago called out.

THE WALK UP the hill to Nanpean farmhouse seemed to take forever. Sam had to concentrate hard on putting one foot in front of the other, leaning heavily on the two people supporting him, wary of his painful ribs. On the one side, Jago walked, Sam's arm pulled over his shoulder. On the other side, to his surprise, the small figure of Ysella labored, her arm tight around his waist. Her grip hurt his battered ribs, but he wasn't about to tell her that. The feel of her supporting grip sent waves of warm comfort through his body that far outweighed the pain.

That this might be a dream, or he'd died and gone to heaven occurred to him as he felt her hand go to his chest as he stumbled. The feel of her skin on his sparked his exhausted body into life, provoking a response he'd never have thought it capable of after being pummeled on the rocks and half drowning in the sea.

But if it had been a dream, it would surely have been located in some more pleasant spot than at dawn in the aftermath of a violent storm. And if he were dead, surely Ysella wouldn't have been present. Unless, of course, they'd all died down there on the beach and he'd not noticed. His head whirled, thanks to the blow he'd taken from a spar as the ship's deck had reared up under him, throwing him backwards away from the rail. He'd shot a hand out as the last remnants of the crew went sliding down the rope bridge he'd made and managed to catch hold of a dangling rope. Just before the ship fell backwards off the rocks into the deep water, he'd had time to fling himself into the sea, but unattached to the lifeline and at the mercy of the waves.

The suction of the ship going down had tugged him under, but he was a strong swimmer, unlike the men he'd been trying to rescue. However, with no rope to hang onto he'd had to rely on the tide and waves to carry him back inshore, and the undertow was horrendous. The last thing he recalled was an iron-bound seachest rushing towards him, then nothing.

Voices echoed around him, snatched at by the wind, but he couldn't pay them any attention. All that mattered was Ysella's arm around his waist. The path in front of him, where his feet, shoved back into his boots by Jago, stumbled, was growing easier to see as behind the clouds the sun must finally have crept above the horizon.

He was alive. He'd managed to survive the loss of the ship and he was alive. And what's more, Ysella had kissed him before he'd gone into the water, and now here she was, toiling by his side, her small figure something for him to lean on. An urge to stop walking and fold her to his body almost overwhelmed him, but if he did that, he'd probably never be able to start walking again.

How far was the farmhouse? It seemed to take forever before Jago supported him through an open door into a room blazing with heat and lowered him into a chair by a glowing range. He put his aching head back and closed his eyes, repeating to himself again and again his litany of things to be grateful for. He was alive. Ysella had kissed him. He was growing warm at last.

Someone pushed a beaker into his hand. "Drink this," Ysella's voice said. "It's hot."

With a supreme effort, Sam lifted his head and opened his eyes. The room, which he'd previously thought of as large for a farmhouse, now seemed small and crowded.

Ysella knelt on the floor by his side, her hands on the arm of his chair, her eyes fixed on his face. "You idiot," she said, but he had the feeling she didn't mean it.

One of the many other people in the room approached. He was of late middle age and wore the semblance of a uniform. Someone had wrapped a bandage around his close-shaven head. The random thought that this man must have lost his old-fashioned wig in the sea, and that one of the villagers might find it and decide to wear it, floated into Sam's head and he had to suppress a low laugh.

"Mr. Beauchamp," the man said, making a smart bow, despite his bedraggled condition. "I'm Captain Danvers of the *Constance,* and I believe it's you I have to thank for the rescue of my men. And myself, of course. All was such chaos onboard as we tried to attach the men to the rope you'd brought, I didn't recognize you until just now, when your wife's uncle told me it was to you I owe my life. A truly brave act." He held out his hand to Sam.

Sam's arm was too heavy to lift. Someone had fixed weights to it. He tried twice and gave up. "I'm sorry, Captain, but my limbs seem to have turned leaden of a sudden."

The captain's lined face creased into a smile. "No matter. I just wanted to say you are the bravest young man I've ever had the honor to meet. A true hero."

Ysella's hands moved from the arm of his chair to rest on his right arm. She squeezed. "He certainly is."

Was that pride in her voice? Had he done something she was proud of? That hadn't been what he intended when he'd volunteered to stage this rescue. His eyelids drooped. How very tired all this being heroic had made him. The last thing he was aware of was Ysella's cheek pressed against his hand.

Chapter Thirty-Two

THE RESCUED SAILORS remained at Nanpean until the morning was well on, Captain Danvers having insisted on sending for the authorities to try to recuperate some of the goods the locals had salvaged. This was despite Sam pointing out that he was seeking to deprive the same men who had helped haul his crew ashore and saved their lives. And of course, there were the bodies of the three who had drowned to deal with before the crabs and gulls got to them.

Behind Captain Danvers's back, Jago dispatched young Jem off to warn the people of both the villages which had benefited from the unexpected largesse on the beach about the imminent arrival of the revenue men. No doubt, by the time the authorities arrived in the form of one of the volunteer constables from Penzance and a few revenue men, all would have been safely stashed away.

A warm feeling pervaded Ysella at the thought of foxing the authorities, and she felt a deep understanding of why Kit had taken to smuggling. It must surely not have been so much for the financial gain, which he didn't need, but the joy of outwitting those in charge, much as she herself had felt at Ormonde when she'd escaped the nursery, or, later on, the schoolroom. The fear she'd felt last night vanished with the coming of the bright rain-washed day, and only the excitement of the night's activities, and in particular the stormy sea and how it had looked, remained. Perhaps she could take up smuggling herself while she was down here at Carlyon Court. So long as it didn't involve going in a boat of any sort—she'd seen enough of what the sea could do to ships.

The sailors and their officers from the merchantman returned to the slim pickings remaining on the beach with the constable, and the arrival of Sir Joshua Penveen, the local magistrate, absolved Sam of any further responsibility for their welfare. As Jago said, "Let someone else take on the ungrateful sods, and you and I shall look after our own." After last night, her feelings for Jago had changed and he was no longer the rather frightening ogre she'd thought him.

Sam sent all the tired servants back to the Court, and Jago and Jenifry provided a plate of thick, meaty stew for a midday meal only Sam and Ysella ate with them. Ysella, who hadn't slept a wink, unlike Sam, discovered herself famished and finished off two platefuls of the food, washing it down with several horn beakers of what had to be contraband brandy. With that washing about in her veins, she felt ready for anything as she and Sam set off back up the track towards home.

Home. They'd only been here a little over two weeks and yet already it felt like home. More so than ever after last night, as though those frightening events had put the seal on their tenancy of the Court.

In the mellow warmth of the late afternoon, so surprising after the ferocity of the storm, Ysella and Sam walked back up the still muddy track towards Carlyon Court. The tranquil sky rose in an arc overhead, devoid of all but the normal sea breeze, and only a few fluffy white clouds scudded across a cerulean backdrop. The storm of last night might never have happened.

As he'd done the night before, Sam had a firm hold on Ysella's hand, as though he were determined not to let go of her. Ysella, for her part, had no objection to this and was happy to walk between the high, rain-washed banks, leaving Jago's farm well behind them.

The sun beat down on her back as she strode along beside Sam, still, of course, dressed in her boys' clothes. How much easier it was to move about in them than in the confines of a long gown. The unfairness of it all swept over her. "I wish I could always wear breeches," she said, on a sigh.

Sam, who'd been gazing into the distance with a faraway expression on his face—was he suffering from shock?—turned to look at her, a smile flickering. A large bruise marred one side of his face, which he'd insisted didn't pain him too much. "I must admit that you do look very becoming in your breeches, Ysella, but I fear that the sight of you in them shocked old Sir Joshua Penveen to the core." As her hair was hanging in loose curls to her shoulders, it had been impossible to hide her gender from the ruddy-faced magistrate. Not that she'd cared. And he'd been more shocked than ever when he'd discovered her identity.

"Pah," Ysella snapped. "As if he counts. And he's a man, anyway, and has always had the pleasure of the freedom of movement breeches give one. Unlike us females. I have to say that the more I wear my breeches, the more I don't want to have to take them off." She bestowed a smug smile on Sam. "How would I have helped to haul the sailors ashore last night had my legs been tangled in the wet skirts of a *dress*?"

He laughed. "I think Kit would have something to say about you wanting to gad about dressed as a boy the whole time."

Ysella laughed back. "Kit's not here." This repartee with Sam reminded her of the way it had used to be between them, of how it had been with her and Kit as well. Relaxed and carefree. She hadn't felt like this in a long while, but now adrenaline coursed through her veins, along with Jago's brandy, and she felt strong enough to meet the world.

But perhaps she wasn't quite ready to meet Sam. Not in the way she half-sensed he would have liked. A way she didn't want to think about. Not now. Not yet. Not after the offhand way she'd treated him for the last six weeks. The memory of how she'd kissed him, and he'd kissed her back, before he'd gone into the water, brought hot color to her cheeks, and she looked away from him, suddenly tongue-tied and shy. Had she shown herself up? Did he despise her for having done that? Did he think her a tease?

She let go of his hand and skipped on ahead. "I don't intend to take my breeches off today, that's for certain." How daring she was being, and how deliciously naughty it made her feel. How alive. The thought that down on that beach last night Sam might have died crept back into her head only to be pushed aside. She wouldn't think of that, even though his survival might be the reason for her high spirits.

Sam stopped, hands on his hips and legs apart. "You don't?"

She turned around, walking backwards with small steps. "No, I don't. And you can't make me."

That she was baiting him, and it was fun, she was dimly aware of. The urge to tease had risen like a tide, and all she wanted to do was exchange daring remarks with him. To push him to what, she had no idea, but the excitement of it tingled through her body. Did she, perish the thought, want him to take her in his arms right now and kiss her again? A funny feeling developed in her stomach as she remembered yet again the way he'd kissed her on the beach.

She watched him from beneath her lashes, all girl, despite her boys' clothes.

Sam took the bait and sprang towards her. "Well, in that case I might have to make you."

With a squeal, she turned and fled, booted feet pounding up the narrow, stony lane, more suitable for the Gentlemen's pack ponies than for a laughing, running girl.

She'd gone fifty yards with him gaining on her fast when beneath her boot, a stone turned and she missed her footing. Her arms stretched out to break her fall as she crashed to the ground, the air shooting out of her lungs. She lay winded on her face for a moment.

Hands seized her shoulders. "Ysella, are you all right?" How strong he was as he rolled her over. She kept her eyes closed, feigning unconsciousness, her heart hammering so loudly she was sure he'd hear. She felt his fingers on the side of her neck as he searched for her pulse. "Ysella?"

She could sense him kneeling beside her, looming over her, see his worried face inside her head. She couldn't help it. A giggle escaped, and she flicked her eyes open. "Fooled you."

He didn't move. One hand rested on either side of her shoulders, his face hovered over hers, his eyes fixed on hers. He wasn't smiling. Instead, his face had gone suddenly serious. "Last night," he said, still not moving. "Why did you kiss me?"

She sobered. "I thought you might be going to die."

He compressed his lips. "I know. I thought so myself. But why did it make you kiss me?"

His gray eyes bored down into hers, the color of the sea on a misty day. The color of storm clouds. The color of a gull's feather. "I don't know," she whispered, as though their proximity had reduced the requirement to talk normally. She wetted her lips with the tip of her tongue. "I-I didn't want you to die and me not having ever kissed you. I wanted to know what it would be like if… if you kissed me."

She could hear his breathing, coming fast now to match her own. Did she want him to kiss her right now? The thought intoxicated. Of course she did. Every cell in her body vibrated with the desire to have him take her in his arms and… What if he leaned forward now and pressed his lips to hers? And after that, what next? She would like very much to be kissed, here, lying on her back on the grass and mud, in her boys' clothes and with the sun shining down on them both, as though nothing else in the whole world mattered.

He removed his arms and sat back on his heels. "Come along, we'd best get back to the house before you shock any more local dignitaries with your appearance." As though he was talking to a child.

She sat up, bristling. Was that how he saw her still? As the child who'd trailed round Ormonde behind him and Kit? She was *not* a child. She was a woman, and he needed to be made to see her as that.

He rose to his feet and held his hand out to help her up, but she ignored it and stood up on her own, one hand out to the wall for support. A woman who didn't need help from a man.

No longer holding hands, their short-lived intimacy fled, they continued back up the path to the Court in silence.

SAM COULD HAVE kicked himself. Why the hell hadn't he kissed her when he had the chance? She'd been lying there on her back in the path, humor dancing in her eyes, and with it an invitation, and he hadn't kissed her. She'd said she hadn't wanted him to die without her having kissed him, without knowing what it was to be kissed by him. Was that not enough of an invitation for any man?

He glanced furtively sideways at her but she was walking with her head down, her chestnut curls bouncing on her slim shoulders. How pretty she looked, even dressed in those dreadful breeches. How beguiling. And he'd let the opportunity slip through his fingers because he was a coward. Because he feared she hadn't done it because she loved him, but merely to try to make up for the fact that in six weeks they'd never so much as kissed. So that he wouldn't die without ever having kissed his wife.

At the house they parted, and Ysella disappeared upstairs, presumably to find the cowardly Martha and change into something more befitting the mistress of the house. He watched her slender figure as she ran up the wide wooden staircase, then stood for a long minute in silence, cursing himself afresh. He could still have caught her in his arms right here and snatched that offered kiss, but he felt it would have been a cheat's kiss, and he couldn't do it.

Rosie emerged from the door to the servants' hall, carrying a vase of flowers. Seeing Sam standing, staring up the stairs, she stopped beside him. "Penny for your thoughts, surr?"

Sam sighed and shook his head. "Just feeling rather tired, Rosie."

"Me an' all. 'Twas a good thing what you done. A brave thing. There's many masters round here wouldn't ha' done such a thing for folks they didn't know."

He shrugged. "Someone had to do it. I couldn't just stand there and watch them all drown."

She nodded. "Gone upstairs, has she? To her smart lady's maid?"

Sam glanced sideways at her. How did she know he was staring after Ysella? "Gone to change her clothes."

"She do make a good boy. A right pretty one."

He nodded. "But she can't stay like that, no matter how much she'd like to."

Rosie grinned. "Fair lovestruck, aren't you, my ansum?"

For a moment, Sam considered reprimanding her for her affrontery in commenting on his feelings, but he was too tired for an argument, and he felt sure there'd be one. And besides which, she was quite right. Instead, he just shrugged.

"She do like you too. Only she won't say."

Sam turned to face her. "She does? I mean, I know she likes me as a friend. But I fear not in the way I'd like her to like me." What was he doing saying this to his housekeeper? But she had about her the comforting air of someone he could confide in. Someone with an innate wisdom he could draw on. "What do you think I should do then?"

Rosie's face broke into a wide grin. "Why, woo her, thass what, lad. A girl, any girl that is, she do like bein' wooed. You can't just expect a girl to give of herself if you don't put no effort into it. Love don't just happen overnight, no matter what you've heared. Thass a girl what needs wooin', mark my words." She patted his arm. "She's got feelin's for you, thass for sure. But she won't be showin' them to you lessen you puts some effort into it."

Sam straightened up and managed a smile back at her, even though it made the side of his face hurt afresh. "Thank you for your wise words, Rosie. I had no idea you dispensed wisdom as well as pies and stews."

Rosie set the vase of flowers down on the small table at the foot of the stairs. "Been married three times m'self, so there don't be a lot I don't know about wooin'. You put yourself out to spend time with Miss Ysella, 'stead o' workin' all day in your office or visitin' the farms. She needs to be with you if you want her to love you, which I can see you do, plain as the nose on my face. You mark my words. That girl loves you already, but she just don't know it herself yet." She wiped her hands on her apron. "And now I'm off back to the kitchen to get dinner on, or you'll be givin' me my marchin' orders. Wise words don't fill bellies."

With no more ado, she abandoned the vase, whether it was where she'd intended it to be or not, and bustled back through the servants' door. After she'd gone, Sam stood for a while longer, contemplating what she'd said and the way Ysella had behaved on the beach. Perhaps Rosie was right. Perhaps Ysella needed some gentle wooing.

Chapter Thirty-Three

"I THINK I might come riding with you this morning," Sam said, as he and Ysella sat at breakfast in the dining room on the day following the aftermath of the shipwreck.

Ysella, who had been eating a slice of toast, set it back on her plate and fixed him with a surprised stare. "You will?"

Sam nodded. "I was wondering if you'd like to dip your toes in a more manageable bit of the ocean? If we ride along to Branok Bay. The weather is set fine for the day, there's very little wind blowing and the waves should be small enough not to present any danger to us."

"Paddle? With my bare feet?"

"Yes. Barefooted. I thought if we were to take Jem with us on the pony he uses for the lawns, he could take care of our horses while we walk along the beach."

A smile lit Ysella's face that was reward enough for Sam. "I should *love* that." She sprang out of her chair. "I shall go and put my riding habit on."

Sam held up a hand. "Why don't you wear your breeches?"

She froze, her head coming round slowly to stare him in the eye. "My *breeches?*"

"Yes. Your breeches. Can you imagine how awkward it would be to walk along in the sea with all the extra fabric that's in a riding habit trailing behind you? And if it were to get wet, which it most likely would, think how uncomfortable that would be for you on your ride back."

"Oh, Sam!" Before he could stop her, she bounced up to him and bending over, kissed him on the cheek. "Thank you, thank you, thank you." As she retreated, she glanced back over her shoulder and he saw the light of mischief in her eyes. "Martha will be so cross!" Then she was gone.

Sam sat in his chair for a minute longer, all appetite for his breakfast flown out the window with Ysella's chaste kiss still tingling on his cheek. At least he'd made her happy this morning. That was a start.

ASTRIDE LOCHINVAR AND Hercules, both of whom were skittish and lively as they hadn't been out for a few days because of the storm, Sam and Ysella took the lane towards Branok Bay. Martha had confined Ysella's glorious hair with a black ribbon, and no one who saw her could have mistaken her for a real boy, despite the breeches and gansey she'd donned. She seemed to have taken more than a passing fancy to the gansey, and it did suit her well. However, despite the puritanical dress, she looked what she was, a beautiful young woman dressed in the clothes of her brother.

Sam kept Hercules close enough to Lochinvar that his leg kept rubbing against Ysella's knee, and as she made no effort to move away, he assumed she probably didn't mind. Or liked it. He certainly did. The simple touch of knee against knee sent tendrils of electricity coursing through him, making riding an uncomfortable business. He chided himself for nurturing feelings of lust. He mustn't think of her in that way, lest he frighten her. He must remember what she'd suffered with that cad.

Jem, delighted to be removed from his gardening duties yet again, jogged along behind them on the fat gray garden pony. As he was far younger than the two new outdoor servants Sam had employed, this necessitated him receiving all the worst and most boring jobs, so his elation at escaping their control and being treated with a trip to the beach was not surprising.

His long skinny legs dangled down on either side of the pony, which was very small and did not possess a saddle, but nothing could deter Jem from enjoying himself and, every so often, he broke into a tuneless whistling.

"Have you ever paddled in the sea?" Ysella asked Sam, pushing a tendril of hair out of her eyes. They were riding through the dunes now, halfway along the beach, a fresh wind off the sea picking up the dry sand and twirling it in the air in little dust devils.

He shook his head. "This'll be the first time for me as well."

Emerging from the dunes, they found the tide halfway in, or it could have been halfway out. Sam had no idea and Jem, when asked, was no help. Leaving Jem sitting on the pony near the path through the dunes, they took their horses for a canter along the beach before returning to Jem and dismounting.

"Now for a paddle," Sam said with a grin at Ysella, handing Hercules's reins to Jem and giving him his sternest glare. "Wait here and don't let them wander. No going to sleep."

He turned to Ysella. "Give Lochinvar to Jem and take off your shoes and stockings."

YSELLA ROLLED HER stockings up and slipped them inside her boots, then, with a quick wave to Jem, who was already looking bored and fed up, she headed towards the high-water line. A thick matting of dried seaweed, bits of rope and old cork floats from fishing boats, mixed with shells and dead crabs blocked her way.

Sam bent over to pick something up from the mess of dark seaweed. "I believe this little thing is called a mermaid's purse."

He was holding out a piece that looked much the same color

as the seaweed, but had four pointed corners to it and might have been some sort of container. Sam smiled. "Some kind of egg case no doubt. I only know because Jem showed me the one he has in his collection of things he's picked up off the beach."

Ysella picked up a long, flat, lozenge-shaped white object. "I wonder what this is. Do you think Jem will know?"

Sam shrugged. "It looks almost like some sea creature's bone, although it's a strange shape to be useful as a bone. We really need to get someone who knows about sea life to come down here with us. I'm not sure Jem is the right one to ask. He couldn't tell me what the mermaid's purse might be for—other than that he believes it to truly be what its name implies." He chuckled.

Ysella beamed. "Who's to say it isn't what it purports to be? Don't forget, Kit thought Morvoren might have been a mermaid and sometimes…" Here she giggled. "Sometimes I wonder if she might have been." She handed him the piece of bone. "Can you put it in your pocket so we can ask Jem later? But I think Uncle Jago might be better. Perhaps if I walk down to Nanpean Cove, I can persuade him to give me a natural history lesson. I'm not so much in awe of him as I was. Not now. After the other night."

"That would be nice. I'd like that. Tomorrow, maybe?"

What was this? Was he saying he'd come with her and they could go somewhere together *again*, only tomorrow? She fiddled with the hem of her gansey, a garment she suspected had at some point been worn by Jem. "Won't you be busy in your office?"

He shook his head, stepping over the line of seaweed. "No. Not tomorrow. In fact, I'd rather spend some time with you, Ysella, than lock myself in my office all day."

She hopped over the seaweed as well, peering up at him, her heart doing a little involuntary leap. How nice it would be to walk down the track to Nanpean with him, perhaps holding his hand, his skin warm against her own, the birds singing, a soft sea wind blowing. She had the entire picture conjured in her head inside a short few seconds.

However, her inner defense mode, that had been active ever

since the Oliver affair, kicked in with a vengeance, protecting her from committing to anything. "Race you to the water," she cried, instead, and set off across the wet sand.

She arrived at the water's edge first, but whether that was because she could run fast in her breeches or because he'd let her win, she couldn't be sure. Panting, she halted, the water cold on her bare toes.

Sam pulled up next to her, also panting. "Good heavens. I didn't notice the other night how cold the sea is." He did a little dance, hopping from one foot to the other.

Ysella giggled. "You do look funny. Once you've been in it for a while it starts to feel warmer."

Sam grinned. "How anyone could swim in this voluntarily, I don't know. I swear it's colder than the lake at Ormonde."

She dimpled, swiping that stray curl out of her eyes again. "Well, *you* did."

He waded out to ankle deep, the tail ends of the gentle waves rippling in towards them at an angle. "That was different."

"Was it? You didn't have to do it."

"Oh, but I did. No one else there could swim. There was only me could take the rope out to the ship."

Ysella, who'd waded out a little deeper, squealed as a bigger wave splashed in and soaked the knees of her breeches. "Come out a bit further. It's really not that cold anymore. I wonder if it would be safe to swim in it on a calm day like today?"

He joined her, and she fixed him with her most solemn stare. "Sam. I have a question to ask you."

"Go on."

At least he sounded open to it. "Would you teach me to swim?" She held his gaze, waiting for the answer, awareness of everything this request implied. Of him having to hold her wet body, of what she might wear to learn. Of how it might feel to have him touching her like that.

She saw him swallow. "I-I'm not sure Kit would approve of his sister learning to swim."

She took a step closer, the waves lapping around her calves, and lowered her voice. "It has nothing to do with Kit anymore. He's my brother, and always will be, but *you're* my husband. And besides, if I were ever in a shipwreck, wouldn't it be better if I could swim and save myself? I don't want to be like a sailor and drown the quicker because I can't swim. That's so silly if you're near the shore and could swim to safety." She peeped at him through her lashes, well aware of her own charms.

She was very close to him now. Oh, how she wanted him to take her in his arms and kiss her. Never had she wanted something so much. This was different to how she'd felt with Oliver. That had been the foolish infatuation of a girl. This was surely something a woman might feel. Perhaps she needed to take the initiative. He was her husband, after all, and she *was* a woman now.

Another half step had her so close he must have been able to hear her pounding heart. He was so tall, she had to put her head back to keep looking up at him, holding his eyes as he gazed back down at her. Now or never. She'd done it before on the night of the storm, so why not now? But that had been on the spur of the moment, not planned like this was. No. She had to be brave and bold, and just a tad shameless. Perhaps the knowledge of what she'd done with Oliver, which was quite definitely shameless, encouraged her to take the next step.

Standing on tiptoes, she caught hold of Sam's waistcoat and pulled him towards her. She found his mouth, closing her eyes as her lips touched and tasted his, slightly open in surprise. She kissed him as she'd done on the night of the storm when she'd thought she might never see him again—quick and urgent. Then she pulled away from him, lowering herself back down onto her bare heels in the wet, draggy sand, and released her hold on his waistcoat. There, she'd done it. Her cheeks flushed with heat.

He was looking at her with a question in his eyes. She resisted the inclination to step back away from him and stood her ground. Someone needed to.

"Did you mean that kiss?" Sam asked. Not the question she'd been anticipating.

She heaved in a tremulous breath. "I did."

He stared down into her eyes as though he were fighting some kind of inner battle. What about, she didn't understand. She only knew that it must now be his turn to kiss her.

He heaved a sigh much like hers, as though he'd been holding his breath. Perhaps he had. "Would you like me to kiss you?"

So polite, not like Oliver who'd stolen her kisses. She nodded. "I would." Idiot, of course she would.

He bent his head and their mouths met again, tentative and searching. His was still a little chill from the wind, the tang of salt on his lips. How gentle he was. A small part of Ysella wanted him not to be gentle but to be demanding, but the rest of her tingled at the delicacy of the contact.

After a moment, she let herself kiss him back, her mouth opening under his, and felt his arms go around her, holding her against his body. How strong he felt, how solid, how safe. She lifted her own arms and locked them around his neck as shivers of electricity ran down her body and her legs trembled beneath her. If he were to release his hold, she might collapse into the water at their feet.

His tongue came questing, oh so gently, invading her mouth, and for a moment she froze. No. This was not Oliver. This was her lawfully wedded husband, a gentleman who would stop if she wanted him to, who would never force her into anything. He'd proved that already in their marriage. She let her tongue meet his. How exciting this felt, how gloriously wanton. Her fingers ran through his hair, so soft and silken, and down to cup his rough, stubbly cheeks, holding his face to hers. His hands, tight around her waist, pressed her body to his.

She felt his arousal hard against her belly and jumped back, the kiss abandoned.

He must know why she'd jumped. "I'm sorry," he floundered. "I can't help it. I didn't mean to frighten you. You're so beautiful, and that kiss was so…" He gulped. "No man could be unmoved by such a kiss."

Why must all men, although this was making an assumption as she didn't know any in this way apart from Oliver, be slaves to that thing in their trousers? That thing she'd not enjoyed at all. And now Sam was the same, Sam whom she'd hoped would be different.

"I-I'm sorry," she muttered, gazing at the water swirling about her feet. "Can't you stop it from doing that?"

His voice shook a little but she didn't raise her head to see his face. "I'm afraid men have little control over their reactions in this way. Can you blame me if holding you in my arms and kissing you like that has had this effect on me?" He rubbed a hand across his eyes. "Being like this." He gestured downwards but she refused to let herself look. "Being like this doesn't mean I have to act on it. I know what happened to you, Ysella. I understand you might be afraid. I won't touch you again unless you want it. I promise."

She blinked up at him out of eyes that had suddenly filled with tears. "You promise?"

He nodded. "Come, let's walk further along the beach, and have no more kissing." He held out his hand.

After a moment's pause, she took it, and they started along the water's edge, walking in the shallows and kicking up a spray like two errant schoolboys.

Chapter Thirty-Four

WALKING AT THE water's edge, Sam and Ysella reached the first minor headland where it buttressed out towards the sea. Here, low cliffs surrounded by jagged rocks and rockpools separated the main beach from the series of small coves running along the coast. Abandoning Sam's hand, Ysella ran to explore the rockpools, bending over them in delight as she studied their contents.

Indulgent as a parent, Sam watched her as she exclaimed over what they held, coming back to him with a small crab held delicately by its shell to wave under his nose.

"Is this a baby crab?"

He shrugged. "I suppose it might be. I think we'd better store that one up to ask Jago tomorrow." He held out his hand and she set the tiny crab on his palm, its small feet tickling his skin. "I think we'd better put him back."

She ran to replace the tiny crab in its rockpool home, and moved on to the next, scrambling over the barnacle-covered rocks in her bare feet.

Sam strolled on, gazing out to sea where a few fishing boats made tiny dots on the horizon. Might the next land they'd come to if they set sail from this beach be the distant Americas? He needed to look at a map of the world.

Ysella ran back to him as they entered the next small cove, to walk by his side in the sea's edge, feet kicking up a shower of water. The next small headland was much closer. He peered at it, the brightness of the sun making him squint. Surely that dark patch there might be a cave.

Ysella had seen it as well and ran on ahead.

Sam threw a glance back over his shoulder at the advancing tide, which was definitely coming in rather than going out, and the small amount of dry sand still between the first headland and the sea. It might not be moving all that fast, and he had to get her back safely before they became trapped, unlikely as that seemed. Throwing caution to the wind, he ran after Ysella.

The dark mouth of the cave yawned before him, Ysella's small figure just inside the entrance. Sand ran into the cave and dark rock loomed overhead. Sam blinked in the poor light, straining to see better. Water ran down the walls and, where it ran, bright colors had streaked the rock in a rainbow of vivid hues.

Ysella gasped. "This is magical."

He stepped up behind her. "Like some kind of underwater magic grotto."

She nodded. "I expect it probably is underwater when the tide comes in. Just look at those colors." She glanced back over her shoulder at him. "Can we go in a bit further?"

The temptation to step closer and put his arms around her in this secretive, magical place rose, but he'd already frightened her away once this morning. He mustn't rush things and do it again, no matter how much he longed to. "It'll be even darker if we do that."

She shook her head in scornful dismissal. "Pah. I don't care. We can go in as far as there's a bit of light, surely? I want to see if there are more of these beautiful colors. See how they've formed only where the water runs."

"It'll be the minerals in the water," Sam said. "I went to Bath once, long ago, where they have the therapeutic baths for the sick. The water there is stained with minerals and the skin of the attendants who help people turns a bright orange all over from long exposure to the water."

"I don't want to believe it's only minerals," Ysella said, pulling a face at him as though she maybe didn't believe his tale of the Bath attendants. "I want to believe it's magic, so don't spoil it for me with your science."

"Best hold hands in the dark," Sam said, holding his out.

She flashed a sideways look at him, but took his hand, hers warm in his.

The sandy floor was level, leading back at an angle to the wide cave entrance and turning to the left as they went in deeper. The walls in here glimmered with the radiance of the mineral deposits, catching what little light there was. The roof stayed high, and not even Sam needed to duck. It was indeed a magical discovery.

"What's this?" Ysella had halted by what seemed to be the face of a young woman carved into the rock, her visage as streaked with color as the walls. She was beautiful.

Sam stepped up beside her and stared. Someone, who knew when, had come into the depths of this cave and for some unknown reason carved out the face of a woman in the rock. "Might she be the object of someone's love?" he suggested, reaching out to rest a finger on the woman's cold cheek. How much she resembled Ysella, with her delicate features set in a heart-shaped face. The craftsman had captured the tumble of curls to slender shoulders. She seemed to have grown out of the rock.

"If so, he must have loved her very much," Ysella whispered, her voice echoing around the high cave walls and vanishing off in endless repetition down into the darkness within.

Sam swallowed, his hand tightening on Ysella's.

She returned the pressure.

For a few moments they stood in silence, regarding the lonely image of the woman.

"Wait a minute," Ysella cried. "Look. What's this?" She ran

her fingers over the rock beneath the carving, tracing something out.

Sam moved to give her more light and bent forward to examine what she'd found. Lettering, carved into the rock. Crude but nevertheless lettering.

Ysella's head bumped into his as she also struggled to read what some long-ago hand had carved beside the stony image of the woman he loved.

"*Mar not my face but let me be,*" Ysella read aloud, peering more closely at the rock, her hand still gripping his. "*Secure in this lone cavern by the sea.* He's dedicated this poem to her." She clasped her hands in excitement. "How romantic."

Sam wiped a hand over the last two lines in the hope of making them clearer. "*Let the wild waves around me roar, kissing my lips for evermore.*"

He straightened up, sobered by the simple sadness of the four lines. "I'd wager she drowned here on this beach and he erected this as his own private memorial to her. I doubt many people venture this far into the cave, and if they do, this carving's hard to spot, the writing even less easy."

She straightened as well. Without looking at him, she spoke, her voice loud in the silence of the cave, only the distant roar of the surf disturbing it. "If I were to drown, would you make a memorial to me?"

Sam froze.

She turned to face him, her eyes glittering like the glassy mineral deposits, not brown any longer but sparkling with fire. "Would you?"

"You know I would, Ysella."

She shook her head, and a stray curl dropped over her eyes. "No, I don't know it, Sam. Morvoren said you care for me. We've always been friends. But since we've married, I haven't been sure." She hesitated. "It's as though I feel you drawing back from me all the time. As though you're afraid of something. Afraid of me, perhaps."

Sam put up his other hand and brushed the curl back for her. "If I were to lose you," he said, groping for the words he needed, "I shouldn't be able to live. I more than care for you, Ysella. I love you."

She opened her mouth to speak, but he hushed her with a finger to her lips. "No, don't speak yet. Hear me out." It was as though the darkness of the cave had freed his heart. In here, hidden from the world, surrounded by the trappings of magic and lost love, he felt he could finally say what needed to be said.

"I have loved you for a long time, Ysella, but I never dreamed you could be mine. I thought you always destined for some lord's hand, not mine. When… what happened to you… happened, I hurt inside for you. I felt your pain. I hated what he did to you. But… I've always wanted you to be happy, and if Featherstone could have made you that, I would have been content. I would have lost you, but I would have known you were happy. And that would have been enough for me."

He hesitated. "But that wasn't to be. Things… happened that could not be undone. Morvoren suggested that I would make you a steadfast husband. She was right. I will, with all my heart's devotion." How hard it was to put into words what he'd felt when they'd married. How he'd felt he could hope for nothing more than friendship, and how now, here in this magic place, he dared to hope for more. He tightened his hold on her hand.

"But I knew what you'd suffered. You, an innocent, had been defiled, duped, conned into thinking you were loved by a man who was only after your money. You were in his power and unable to protest. He did with you as he wanted and you had no escape."

He watched her face working, as though she wanted to intercede but couldn't, her eyes large and dark and glistening with tears. He mustn't stop.

"I made a pact with myself when we married, and a promise to you, that I would not expect you to carry out your marital duties, such as they are supposed to be. Only if you ever wanted that, would I relent. But I knew you didn't love me. And although there's a part of me that would accept even a tenth of your regard, I would not force you into anything you didn't want to do." How awkward he felt having to skirt around the notion of conjugal rights, of the marriage bed and all it entailed, without putting it into direct words. "But if you could ever love me back, I would be a contented man." Hot color rose to his cheeks at this last sentence, but she wouldn't have been able to see. How inept he sounded. How badly he'd explained himself. He went to turn away from her. Best to get back to the beach.

YSELLA'S HEART HAMMERED in her throat. If she opened her mouth it was going to come leaping right out and land in the sand at her feet. Then she'd be dead and he'd have to carve her image on the rock wall, here, beside this long-lost woman's face.

And now he was going to turn away from her and leave it at that. He already had one of her hands so she reached out with the other and caught him by his other sleeve. "No. Stop. I have something to say, too."

He turned back to her but his face was against the light, hidden from view. Impossible to see his expression. She slid her hand down until she was holding his other hand as well. "I love you." There. She'd said it. Now it was out in the open. He loved her and she loved him. Surely, they could make it work.

He stood very still. Damn it, if only she could see his face. More was needed. "You're right in saying I've been hurt." The darkness around her made this easier. The blank canvas that was his face gave her confidence for honesty. "Oliver lied to me throughout, and his behavior, which was of the most dishonest, has made me… hesitant to commit myself."

She sucked her lips in for a moment, considering how to put this. "He told me we should be married within a few days and there was no point in waiting." This was so embarrassing even in the dark. "I believed him. I believed he loved me. I thought I loved him, but it turned out to be nothing but a sham, and all I really felt was an infatuation. He was a shallow, greedy man, out only to better himself at my expense. I know now that he persuaded me to… do *that*, just so he could force Kit into allowing him to marry me. He had no intention of taking me to Scotland. He'd planned all along for Kit to catch us up, but for it to be too late. He thought Kit would rather see me married than ruined."

She was into her stride now, putting the events of those few days into words was helping her to see them for what they were. She saw clearly now, whereas before, her sight had been blurred by too close a proximity to the events.

"I am very glad Kit refused to let him marry me, for I should have been most unhappy. I know that now." Her bare toes curled into the sand. "I did not find the act he persuaded me to participate in to my taste." How red her face must be. "It was… painful. I was not comfortable doing it. But he said he loved me, so I did. I thought that was what you did when you loved someone."

A long pause ensued. He said nothing. He didn't move. Had she shocked him? She drew a breath. "My feelings for you have changed since we were married. I think… Perhaps all that's come to me is realization."

She hesitated. Using these impersonal words made this easier. She felt almost as though she were talking about someone else. "Perhaps I've always loved you, Sam, and just didn't know it." She swallowed. "But I've been avoiding you and pushing you away, because the idea of marriage and all it entails frightens me." Silence hung between them. "I want to be a properly married woman, but I'm afraid of what that entails."

She waited. She had nothing more to say. It was for him to respond now.

He shifted his grip on her hands, his thumbs rubbing the back of them in gentle circles. It felt reassuring. How warm his skin was even in this cold cave.

Suddenly, he dropped onto one knee in front of her. "Ysella Carlyon, will you do me the honor of being my wife, in every meaning of the word?"

A little gasp escaped her lips. The thought that this was like a proposal by a hero in one of her novels flashed through her head for a moment, but was gone in a trice. No, she'd thought Oliver a fictional hero and that was what he had been, fictional. Sam was a true hero, and everything about him was real. "Yes, Sam," she whispered, confidence surging through her. "Yes, I will."

The sand about her feet ran with water. They both looked down.

"Christ," Sam almost shouted, leaping to his feet. "The tide's coming in."

Chapter Thirty-Five

SAM RAN OUT of the cave dragging Ysella by the hand. Their feet splashed through the shallow water that before had looked inviting and gentle but now seemed to have morphed into a threatening, unstoppable upsurge. The small headland between this little cove and the main beach was already lapped by waves breaking against the jagged rocks. The one they needed to get back around to Jem and the horses.

"Quick. Run," Sam shouted, barely hesitating, but setting off across the sand as fast as he could. If it got any deeper, they'd have to swim for it, and Ysella couldn't swim. As he ran, he glanced sideways at the cliffs, rising sheer and steep to the headland above, in case they might present a way out if they were trapped. Nothing, and by the look of the wet sand, the tide would reach right to their feet when fully in.

They reached the rocky outcropping. The waves breaking on the rocks were increasing in size and ferocity as the water deepened. They had no other way out, and the longer they left it, the worse it was going to get. No time to waste.

Ysella tugged on his hand. "If I drown, will you carve my face on the rock in that cave beside that other girl's face? Promise me?"

He swung round. "If we have to swim for it, I won't let you drown. That's what I promise." He tightened his hold on her hand as her pale, terrified face looked up at him. "This way."

He led her into the surf. He should have realized going into that cove, and then that cave, was a dangerous and foolish thing to do. He should have found out about how fast a tide could come in. The boy would have known. He could have asked Jem if it was safe to walk that far along the beach. What would he say to Kit if he let Ysella drown? It didn't bear thinking about. If she drowned, then he would go with her. He couldn't go on without her, not now they'd found one another at last.

At least the waves were smaller than the other night. But when they came, they soaked both of them up to the neck and threatened to lift them off their feet. Even Sam, who was over six feet tall and solidly built. Putting himself between Ysella and the waves, he transferred his hold on her to an arm around her waist lest she be washed away from him. Her own arm wrapped around his waist, seizing a handful of his soggy gansey in a tight fist.

The tide was coming in much faster than he'd thought it would. Why had they lingered in that cave? Was that what the drowned girl had done? And now Sam had done it to Ysella—brought her into danger. They were almost halfway around the headland now, the waves getting stronger every time one rolled in. Branok Bay lay ahead of them, much reduced by the incoming tide. There was Jem with the three horses, standing not where they'd left him but at the water's edge, staring in their direction.

Sam fought the undertow that was threatening to drag them both out to sea. Ysella's head went underwater and he snatched her back up. She came up gasping and spitting water, her hair plastered to her head. What a fool he'd been to trust the deceptive calmness of the treacherous sea. This wasn't like the night of the storm. Then he'd had a rope around his waist on his swim out to the ship. Now he had nothing at all except the weight of Ysella in his arms.

A large wave swept him off his feet and he nearly lost his hold on Ysella. She clung to him, pulling him down, her dark eyes full of fear. "Help me," she spluttered. He had to fight her to turn her in his arms so she was lying on her back, his hand hooked under her chin and holding her face barely above the water. She struggled against him, arms and legs thrashing.

But he had her firm at last and kicked out for the beach, towing her with him. She stopped struggling. Another wave came in and carried them towards the shore. As the wave swept past him, Sam felt sand beneath his feet, the sand being pulled back into the sea by the strong undertow. Clutching Ysella, he threw himself forward and the next wave went over both their heads. But they were on the beach, with solid sand under them.

Jem came splashing through the waves, the horses abandoned. He reached for Ysella but Sam had her tight. "Get back to the horses," he managed, in between spitting out salty water. Dripping wet, he struggled to his feet and pulled Ysella to hers. Arms wrapped around her to hold her up, he staggered onto the sand.

Jem had retrieved the horses. "I did think you was goners then," he announced, the light of glee in his eyes, presumably at having witnessed the drama of a near drowning. "I was a-wondrin' what I was goin' to say to Ma when I come home wi'out you both."

"I trust you're pleased that we're *not* drowned," Sam said, his tone dry, unlike his clothes and hair. This boy seemed to be a bit of a ghoul.

Jem shrugged, possibly annoyed at losing his role as bearer of bad tidings. "You gotta know the tides round here, or you're in trouble."

"We worked that out for ourselves," Ysella retorted, wiping her wet hair out of her eyes. "You might have warned us."

Jem shrugged again. "I dint know you was goin' to walk round into Merrin Cove wi' the tide comin' in, an' then dawdle about there an' not see as the tide was near right in. I don't have the Sight, like old Doryty do."

Ysella nestled against Sam with a shiver, whether at the cold or the thought of having nearly drowned, he didn't know, but he tightened his arms around her. She might well catch a chill in these wet clothes. How awful would it be to have rescued her from drowning to see her fall ill and die from something as simple as that. She had to be kept safe. Lochinvar pawed the sand with an impatient hoof. Sam reached for his reins. "We'd best get my wife back home as quickly as possible before she takes ill from her soaking."

"Why is it called Merrin Cove?" Ysella asked, her voice muffled against Sam's gansey. "It anything to do with the carving in the cave? The carving of the woman with the poem beneath it? I want to know."

Jem wrinkled his freckled nose. "I don't know nothin' about any writin'." He shook his head. "If there were any, I couldn't read it, anyways. But they do say, or old Doryty did say, that is, as the woman's face in the rock was Merrin Tremaine, a girl what was drownded in that cove a long time ago." He shrugged his skinny shoulders. "P'raps she did the same as you did—stayed too long and let the tide come in." He regarded Ysella. "Wi'out Mr. Beauchamp to pull you out, I don't think as you'd'ave made it on your own. Same as her."

"Tremaine?" Ysella repeated, shifting in Sam's arms. "That was her surname?"

The boy nodded. "Same as old Jago."

Ysella twisted in Sam's arms so she could look into his face. "But my mother was a Tremaine. That must surely make Merrin Tremaine a distant relation of mine."

Of course. No wonder Sam had thought the carving looked like Ysella. "Jago will know the story," he said. "But we can't go and ask him that now. We need to get you home and out of those wet clothes. Let's find our boots, and then I'll give you a leg up onto Lochinvar."

BY THE TIME they reached home, Ysella was beginning to dry out in the warm breeze and see what had happened to them as a big adventure. Nearly having drowned was nothing like having really drowned, and all she could see was that Sam, her hero, had saved her life. Thinking about this caused a glow that went some way to warming her up. He was certainly clocking up a nice tally of brave deeds of heroism. Quite the dashing gentleman. Quite the romantic hero from a book, only she didn't really want to see him in that way in case it made her think of Oliver. She never wanted to think of that young man again.

They dismounted in the front drive of the Court and left Jem to lead the two horses and his pony round to the stables. For a moment after the horses had departed, Ysella stood irresolute on the gravel, peeking sideways at Sam.

She caught him watching her and held out her hand.

He took it, threading his fingers between hers in a curiously intimate gesture. "Shall we go in?"

No one was in the wide hallway, which was probably a good thing considering the state they were both in, clothes still damp and hair akimbo.

"Shall we go upstairs to change?" Sam asked, his gray eyes meeting hers. Was that hot passion she read in them?

Ysella's insides turned to liquid. Did he mean what she wanted him to mean? That this might be *the moment*. Could she do it as she'd said she would? Be his wife, his true wife in every way. He wasn't Oliver. He'd stop if she didn't like it. He'd said she didn't have to do *anything* she didn't like. *She* was in control of this. She nodded.

Hand in hand, they climbed the stairs and turned right on the half landing. Hand in hand, they walked along the gallery. At Sam's bedroom door, he halted and reached for the handle, but she gave his hand a tug. It was for her to invite him in.

Their eyes met, his questioning and hopeful. She tugged again and took a step towards her own bedroom.

He followed her.

At her door they halted again, eyes locked for a long moment. Then Ysella opened the door and stepped inside, pulling Sam after her. She closed the door with a well-aimed foot.

The four-poster bed stood in the middle of the room, a stark reminder of what they were here for. Ysella's breath came fast and her skin blossomed with heat. She could put up with anything, even this, for Sam. All she wanted to do was make him happy, but at her own pace.

Still beside the door, they faced one another, unmoving, eyes still locked.

Ysella pulled her damp gansey off over her head and let it drop to the floor. After a moment, Sam did the same with his.

The silence between them stretched out, fizzing with electricity. Then Sam reached up and undid the top button of her shirt. His fingers strayed to the pale skin at her throat, oh so gently.

Ysella drew a shuddering breath and, with shaking fingers, began to unbutton his waistcoat, a hot sensation forming in the base of her stomach, and crawling lower. Was this how she should feel with the man she loved slowly undressing her?

With unsteady fingers Sam undid the next button on her shirt, and then the next. Her shirt gaped, revealing her stays and the swell of her small breasts. Would he touch them, like Oliver had. She knew now that had been an invasion. Would Sam do the same?

He didn't. Instead, he shrugged off his waistcoat and tossed it to the floor. How hot his eyes were. Hot with passion. The sight of them frightened her a little. Only the fact that she knew he was a gentleman and she could stop whenever she wanted kept her going.

He pushed her braces from her shoulders and his hands went to her shirt, pulling it out of the top of her breeches to hang almost to her knees. It was much too large for her.

She should do the same for him. Dark hair, much darker than the hair on his head, curled across his chest, where purple bruises from the shipwreck blossomed, and down his belly to the top of his breeches. With a tentative hand, she touched his well-muscled chest, letting her fingers skim the bruises and run over his taut stomach. His body tensed beneath her touch. How warm his skin was, how his muscles rippled under it. She caught her breath as he did the same, and for a moment his eyes closed. The thought that her touch was giving him pleasure coursed through her. She let her fingers stray across his chest, wondering at the hair on it.

He caught his breath again, and his hand cupped her cheek, his thumb caressing her skin. "I love you, Ysella, and I will never hurt you. You don't have to do this if you don't want to. I don't want you to feel you have to do it for me. If you do it, it must be for you."

She shook her head. "I want to." Her other hand joined the first, exploring his torso, running up and gliding over a nipple. She felt him jerk in response to her touch and knew her power. And in that moment, she knew that power was what she needed. Oliver had deprived her of all power, taking choice away from her, but here, now, she held the power because Sam had given it to her, willingly. She let her hand return to his nipple and was rewarded by his sharp gasp of pleasure.

She could do this. He was letting her.

In one swift movement she pulled her shirt off over her head to stand there in just her stays and breeches. Let him look. It was her allowing this, not him taking it.

Sam let out a quick gasp, his hand lifting towards her, then falling back to his side. "I think we need to take our boots off." His voice was husky with passion. "Sit down and I'll pull yours off, then you can do mine."

He yanked her boots off with no trouble, but she found his harder to do, collapsing backwards onto the floor as the last one finally came free. He helped her up off the rug and for another pregnant moment they stood face to face, drinking one another in.

Ysella broke the silence by putting her hand on the top of his breeches, feeling his stomach contract as she did so. "I believe these will need to come off."

"And yours."

She undid one of the buttons on his fall, her fingers skimming the definite bulge, still a little afraid. But she was in control. She had nothing to fear. She undid another button, and another. His breeches fell to the floor, but the long tails of his shirt covered his arousal. She let her hand skim against it beneath the linen, more curious now than afraid, and felt it jerk as though it had a life of its own.

He suppressed a groan, badly. Men clearly found it very pleasurable if a girl touched their cock. She congratulated herself for having named it. That too, imbued her with confidence and diminished her anxiety.

"Shall I undo your stays?" he asked.

She compressed her lips. Once he'd done that, she'd be practically naked, and, for some reason, the act of him undoing her undergarment seemed to poach her sense of control. However, she nodded. She could allow him that.

He moved behind her and she felt his fingers fumbling with the laces. The realization that he was too nervous to do it properly gave her back her feeling of power. Here was a man who was perhaps as afraid as she was. She allowed for different reasons.

Her stays loosened and her hands came up out of instinct to cover her breasts, but he didn't turn her around. That was for her to do. Still with her back to him, she undid the fall on her own breeches and let them fall to the ground. She was naked now, with not enough hands to cover her modesty.

Behind her, she heard him remove his own shirt.

Still with her back to him, she gave a nervous giggle. "This is the middle of the day."

"I know."

"What will the servants say?"

"Do I care? Do you?"

"They'll know."

"They'll be saying 'about time too'."

She giggled again. "Is that what you think?"

His hands came up and rested on her shoulders. Was he going to turn her around? "I don't think anything. All that's in my head right now is how much I love you, and how much I want to please you."

"Please me?"

"Yes. Please you." His voice dropped. "You know this act you're fearing doesn't need to be feared. A man derives pleasure from it, and a woman can too, if it's done correctly."

"Oh." She digested his words. "Have you done it before?"

He was silent a moment before he spoke. "Yes, but not for quite a while. I know how to give a woman pleasure. I learned from an expert, when I was hardly more than a boy."

But he wasn't married. So who had he done it with? Who had the expert who'd taught him been? On second thought, she didn't want to know.

She waited, but he said nothing more, just stood there with his warm hands on her shoulders, waiting.

She was in control. "Close your eyes." Taking a deep breath, she dropped her hands from her breasts and turned around.

His eyes were closed. "Keep them like that," she said.

He did as he was told, his dark lashes splayed on his cheeks. She surveyed him with slow precision from head to foot. His sandy hair was still tangled from the sea and wind, his cheeks had a healthy flush to them that might either have been from being outside all morning or from how he felt right then. Possibly a mix of both.

She studied his wide shoulders and the muscles of his arms, the little hairs along his forearms, the curling, much darker hair on his chest. Her eyes dropped further to where his cock stood out from amongst more dark hair, long and thick.

"You can open your eyes."

They flicked open and met hers. For a long moment he held her gaze before his eyes fell, and he took in her body.

When his gaze returned to meet her eyes again, she took his hand and led him to the bed. With a little, inviting smile, she lay down on her back, her head on the pillow. This would be all right now. She was in control.

SOME CONSIDERABLE TIME later, Ysella lay awake on the bed, listening to the sound of birdsong carrying in through the open window, more content than she'd ever been. Beside her, Sam had dozed off on his back, one arm thrown back above his head, his fingers, those clever, loving fingers, slack and relaxed.

She gazed at his sleeping face, so handsome, but above all so kind, and so gentle. He'd been more than gentle with her. He'd done things to her she'd never dreamed of doing, asking every time if she minded, and touched her in places she didn't know could react in the way they had done. He'd brought her to the point of desperation before he'd finally consummated their love, and it had not been as it was with Oliver. It hadn't hurt because she'd been ready for it, and because he'd ensured she was on the point of the ultimate in physical pleasure.

And my goodness, what an experience that had been. How could a girl *not* like what had happened when he'd finally slipped inside her. She gave a little shiver of pleasure, her own hand running across her skin. Skin that he'd called beautiful as he'd peppered it with kisses, starting on her lips, then descending to her throat, her breasts, and lower still. Another shiver trembled through her, and a longing for more of the same.

She propped herself up on one elbow and looked down at Sam. How peaceful he looked. It would be a shame to wake him, but... She bent and kissed him lightly on the mouth and felt him stir under her touch. Emboldened by their new familiarity, she set her hand on his belly, and slid her hand southwards.

His lips moved under hers, his mouth opened as hers did, their tongues met. Under her questing hand she felt a stirring. What fun it would be to do this all again.

THE END

About the Author

After a varied life that's included working with horses where Downton Abbey is filmed, riding racehorses, running her own riding school, owning a sheep farm and running a holiday business in France, Fil now lives on a widebeam canal boat on the Kennet and Avon Canal in Southern England.

She has a long-suffering husband, a rescue dog from Romania called Bella, a cat she found as a kitten abandoned in a gorse bush, five children and six grandchildren.

She once saw a ghost in a churchyard, and when she lived in Wales there was a panther living near her farm that ate some of her sheep. In England there are no indigenous big cats.

She has Asperger's Syndrome and her obsessions include horses and King Arthur. Her historical romantic fiction and children's fantasy adventures centre around Arthurian legends, and her pony stories about her other love. She speaks fluent French after living there for ten years, and in her spare time looks after her allotment, makes clothes and dolls for her granddaughters, embroiders and knits. In between visiting the settings for her books.

Social Media links:
Website – filreid.com
Facebook – facebook.com/Fil-Reid-Author-101905545548054
Twitter – @FJReidauthor

* 9 7 8 1 9 6 3 5 8 5 8 2 7 *